The Sins of Their Fathers

Make Us Traitors

Gilda O'Neil

arrow books

This edition published by Arrow Books in 2005

Copyright © Gilda O'Neil 2005

The right of Gilda O'Neil to be identified as the author of this
work has been asserted by her in accordance with the Copyright,
Designs and Patents Act, 1998

The Sins of their Fathers Copyright © Gilda O'Neil 2002
Make Us Traitors Copyright © Gilda O'Neil 2004

Arrow Books Limited
The Random House Group Limited
20 Vauxhall Bridge Road, London, SW1V 2SA

Random House Australia (Pty) Limited
20 Alfred Street, Milsons Point, Sydney,
New South Wales 2061, Australia

Random House New Zealand Limited
18 Poland Road, Glenfield
Auckland 10, New Zealand

Random House (Pty) Limited
Endulini, 5a Jubilee Road, Parktown 2193, South Africa

The Random House Group Limited Reg. No. 954009

www.randomhouse.co.uk

A CIP catalogue record for this book
is available from the British Library

Papers used by Random House are natural, recyclable products made
from wood grown in sustainable forests. The manufacturing processes
conform to the environmental regulations of the country of origin

ISBN 0 09 190735 7

Printed and bound in Great Britain by
Bookmarque Ltd, Croydon, Surrey

The Sins of Their Fathers

For Ali Gunn

Acknowledgements

And with my special thanks to Kate Parkin
and Kirsty Fowkes

Acknowledgements

She knew Gabriel O'Donnell was no angel, but this time it was different. No matter what lies he tried to tell her, or how he tried to twist it, Eileen was sure that it was Luke who was telling the truth. That was *how it all started: with Pete Mac making the biggest mistake of his whole stupid life, because Gabriel had asked – no, he had* insisted – *that the boys take the gun.*

November 1960

Chapter 1

Commercial Street, the broad thoroughfare linking Whitechapel to Shoreditch, had been built in a grand moment of
Victorian moralising, optimism and innovation. Designed
to slice its way through one of the East End's most
notorious rookeries, the idealistic intention behind its
creation was the sweeping away of overcrowding, disease
and corruption, in the foul and crime-ridden slums that
were so uncomfortably close to the City of London – the
fabulously wealthy hub of the greatest Empire ever seen.
The road would literally open up the area to the light,
making it available for inspection by authorities and
worthies alike, allowing them to check on the feckless
underclasses, who lived on their very doorstep.

Just thirty years after its completion the world's gaze
would again be focused on the area. Not to admire the
social and environmental improvements, but to be
appalled and stunned by the brutal acts of the proto-serial
killer known as Jack the Ripper, and consequently on the
shameful, persistent presence of such grotesque poverty
and depravity.

The bold new road had proved itself embarrassingly
worthy of its name, as a shocked public realised that
commerce of many different kinds took place in its
shadowy environs, and, despite the best intentions and
interventions of the Establishment, they would long
continue to do so.

*

3

The racing green Jaguar inched along Commercial Street in the dense fog, passing between the elegantly looming hulk of Hawksmoor's Christ Church and the squat, practical form of the Spitalfields wholesale fruit and vegetable market, at little more than a brisk walking pace.

'Still nothing?' The driver was hunched over the wheel, squinting through the windscreen, the swishing wipers doing little to aid his view.

The man in the passenger seat rubbed the heels of his thumbs into his eyes, feeling the strain of staring out into the silvery blanket of heavy, wet air.

'Not a thing.' He dropped his hands and sat up, suddenly alert. 'Hang on. Over there. Corner of Fleur-de-Lis Street.'

Brendan O'Donnell eased the motor to a halt.

A tall, plump teenager – acid yellow blouse, tight crimson skirt, and bare, corned beef legs – said something to the two girls she was standing with, then wiggled her way over to the car. She didn't seem bothered by the cold.

She rested one hand on the roof of the Jag and, with the other, released one of her breasts from her top and pressed it against the passenger window. Puckering up her fuchsia painted lips, she blew them a kiss.

'Hello, boys,' she mouthed, rubbing her breast from side to side across the window, flattening the dark brown nipple, and leaving greasy smears on the glass. 'Fancy doing business?'

Brendan signalled, with swift, angry hand movements, for his brother to wind down the window.

'Who the fuck are you?' he demanded, leaning across Luke, and ducking his head to get a better look at her.

'Any one you want me to be, darling. But it'll have to

4

be double if you want me to take on the two of you.'

Brendan looked about him as if someone had just released a bad smell. 'If you don't stick that tit away, and get off this motor – *now* – even *you* won't know who you are. So, just do up that blouse, and go and tell your mates you're all pissing off back where you came from. Got it?'

'Charming,' she said, flipping them tipsy and tottering back to her post.

Brendan watched the girls in disbelief. They obviously had no intention of moving. He looked at his watch. Half eleven. Nearly bloody dinner time. 'Where the fuck's that idiot Pete Mac?'

The whereabouts of Peter MacRiordan, Luke and Brendan's brother-in-law, were, as they so often were, a mystery.

Luke glanced at his brother. 'I wouldn't put it past the daft bastard sending them home cos of the fog.'

Brendan flung open his door. 'Wait here.' Basic rule: never leave a smart motor unattended in an unknown situation.

Luke sank down in his seat. Content to get no more involved in this than he had to.

Fists clenched in anger and ready to attack, Brendan looked about him, his actions sharp and agitated, trying to figure out what was going on. For birds to have such bottle, there had to be someone looking after them. Someone who really scared them.

And there he was. Over there, on the corner of Wheler Street.

A bull-necked, muscled up, black man in a heavy navy overcoat and suede porkpie hat, standing under the streetlight on the junction with Commercial Street. Like he had every right. Across from him stood another huddle of ropey looking toms – cheap, bottom of the market brasses, just like the one who had propositioned him and Luke. Toms that Brendan had never seen before.

Was this bloke taking the piss or what?

Brendan weighed up the situation. He wasn't scared. He'd been involved in plenty of physical stuff in his time. Bad stuff. A few years ago, when he was still in his teens, he had beaten a man to death, single-handed, on a bombsite in Stepney, and walked away without so much as a backward glance. But he wasn't stupid either. This was one *very* big bloke. He had to get it right. Or lose.

He took a deep breath and started to move. Fast.

'Here, you,' he hollered, jabbing his finger, steaming in. 'What the fuck do you think you're doing?'

The man frowned, and lifted his chin to one side as if in thought, then pushed his ear really close to Brendan's mouth, the shock making Brendan back off. 'Would you say that again?' His voice had the singsong lilt of the Caribbean. 'I don't think I heard you right the first time.'

Brendan recovered quickly. His finger was in the man's face. 'What, don't understand English, moosh?'

The man took off his hat, ran his hand over his head, flattening his cap of shiny, oiled curls even closer to his skull. 'Are you being impolite to me, man? Unneighbourly?'

'*Me* being impolite? You're having a grin, right?' Brendan took a moment to look him up and down. 'This, pal, is our patch. Ours. The O'Donnells. We run things round here. All of it.'

The man replaced his hat, turned down the corners of his mouth and shook his head. 'Sorry, I ain't never heard of no O'Donnells.'

Brendan didn't like this. The bloke was too confident.

6

Maybe he wasn't alone. Time to put on a show. Let the bloke know they were team handed.

'Luke!' he shouted across the road to his brother, who was now standing by the car, smoking, watching the giggling girls. 'Luke!' he hollered again, putting on the hard man bit for the stranger and the toms. 'What's MacRiordan got to say about this *gentleman* being here?'

'Dunno.' Then, as an afterthought, 'Still no sign of him.'

Brendan could feel the situation slipping away from him. How could Luke show such weakness in front of this big, flash slag? Always have your team look tough, in control. That was the only way to play this game. He wondered about Luke sometimes, he really did.

He flashed a menacing look at the now smirking black man, and turned on his heel, determined to collar Pete Mac and find out what the hell he thought he was up to. Brendan had specifically told him to collect the first of the takings before noon. Before they got busy with the dinner time trade. You never knew who might be on the creep in this fog.

And the pub on the corner of Hanbury Street seemed a reasonable place to start looking for him.

As he strode off, Brendan could feel the man's eyes watching him every step of the way.

The Heart was packed, just as it always was late on a Friday morning. The Spitalfields wholesale fruit and vegetable market on the other side of Commercial Street had shut up shop for the day, and, after grafting since the early hours, the porters and wholesalers were enjoying the beginning of their weekend by downing rows of pints and eating massive fry ups. And, after stoking up, many of

7

them would be keen and ready to share some of their hard-earned wages with the toms across the street. But the O'Donnells' toms were nowhere to be seen. And neither was Pete Mac. Not in the pub, anyway. His lardy bulk and ginger hair would show up even in a boozer as crowded as this one.

But then again, there was no sign of anybody who looked like he might have anything to do with the big black bloke either. These were market people to a man, not the sort to earn a living doing anything more dodgy than letting the odd box of carrots or tomatoes fall off the back of their barrows.

Brendan allowed himself a brief smile. Nobody in here? Nobody out there in the street with him? It was beginning to look like the stranger might be all on his Jack after all. Now why waste an opportunity like that?

Leaving the fug and bustle of the pub, Brendan stepped back out into the cold, damp air. He whistled and showed out for Luke to follow him. Then, with Luke on his heels, he sprinted back to where the man was standing on the corner, and yelled 'Oi! You!' from right behind him.

As the man turned, Brendan landed him one – *smack!* – an uppercut right on the chin.

'Jesus Christ!' Brendan waved his hand up and down. The bloke's jaw was like iron.

One of the girls, who was standing on the corner of Fleur-de-Lis Street started squealing. 'Millie, here quick, look. They're only thumping Joshua.'

In case one of the girls decided to run off to a phone box and call for reinforcements, Brendan acted fast. 'Grab him, Luke.'

Before Joshua could work out what direction he was coming from, Luke had grabbed Joshua's arms, and

8

dragged them behind his back. Brendan got stuck in, punching with all his force, one fist after the other, straight into the man's guts.

Tough and impressive as he was, the surprise had given Brendan and Luke the advantage, and the succession of blows to Joshua's solar plexus soon winded him. He flopped forward from his waist, gasping, trying to catch his breath. 'All right,' he wheezed. 'That's enough.'

Brendan, panting from the effort of pummelling the man's massive bulk, stepped away from him as though giving him a chance. But before Joshua could straighten up again, Brendan drew back his arm, and then threw his whole body weight forward, whipping his upper body round in a tight quarter circle. He landed a sickening, crunch of a blow to Joshua's nose, spraying blood in a high, scatter-gun arc. Joshua's brain hadn't even had a chance to register the pain, when Brendan pivoted round, and landed a direct kick to the man's balls.

A bellow came roaring from somewhere deep in Joshua's chest.

It was over. For now.

'Let that be a lesson about what happens when you mess with the O'Donnells.' Brendan snatched up Joshua's hat from the pavement and stuffed it in the man's hand. 'You keep off our patch. Right?'

Joshua crumpled his hat in one single, pan-sized palm, raised his bloodied head and looked at Brendan through rapidly swelling eyes that could still show their anger. 'You'll wish you hadn't done that,' he said flatly, then limped off along Wheler Street towards the fog-shrouded railway arches.

Before he disappeared from view, he turned and pointed at Brendan and Luke in turn.

'I'm telling you. And you. Mr Kessler's not going to like this.'

Kessler. Brendan registered the name with no more than a flicker of a frown.

Joshua paused to spit a bloody gob of phlegm into the gutter then, suddenly, he started staggering back towards them.

Brendan and Luke stood ready – hearts thumping, fists alert – but he lurched straight past as if they didn't exist, and shouted at the now gawping girls. 'And you lot had better still be here when I get back. You got that?'

He didn't wait for a reply. He was gone.

Brendan and Luke started to cross Commercial Street, ready to explain to the girls that, if they knew what was good for them, they'd sling their hook and take their chance at upsetting the big black bloke rather than get on the wrong side of the O'Donnells, when a familiar voice stopped them in their tracks.

'All right, lads. What's the story here then?'

They turned round.

Peter MacRiordan.

'Hurt your hand, have you, mate?' he asked Brendan. 'Them knuckles of your'n look right sore. You don't wanna get an infection. They can be nasty. Get yourself down the London for a bandage and a dab of iodine.'

Brendan sucked at his fist, clearing the blood, then shoved Pete Mac hard in the chest, rocking him back on his heels. 'Where the fuck have you been, you lazy arsehole? And where's our fucking toms got to?'

'They not here, Brendan?'

Across the street, the girls were watching the three men.

'Looks like another ruck's starting,' bawled one of them, to the group on the opposite corner. 'But don't

10

reckon this one's gonna be very exciting. The ginger bloke's not exactly got Joshua's muscles on him, has he?'

'But you should see the size of me willy, darling,' Pete Mac shouted back, treating the girls to a grin and a friendly wave.

Brendan slapped Pete Mac's arm down to his side. 'This ain't a joke, Pete. There's you standing there like Billy fucking Big Bollocks, while we've had to clean up your mess. Again.'

'What you on about now?'

'Give me fucking strength.' Brendan lifted his fist, only just stopping himself from smashing it into Pete Mac's face. 'Who do you think they are?' He jerked a thumb over his shoulder at the girls. 'They're Kessler's. And if we don't stop him, he's gonna think he can put them wherever he feels like it. That's what I'm talking about you stupid, brainless prick.'

'Who d'you think you're talking to?' Pete Mac considered grabbing hold of his brother-in-law's lapels, show he wasn't scared, but thought better of it when he saw the look on Brendan's face. He stepped back, shooting his cuffs and adjusting his tie instead. 'Keep your hair on, eh, mate?' he said. 'And how about you and Luke getting yourselves out of that road? Don't want you getting knocked over, now do we? How would I explain that to Gabe? *Sorry, and all that, but your boys went under a bus*. That don't sound very nice, now does it?'

Brendan stepped up on to the pavement. His face now so close to Pete Mac's he could feel his breath on his face. 'Buses?' he said, his voice low, more threatening than a shout. 'You wanna worry about more than fucking buses. I give you one simple job and what do you do, you useless, streak of piss? Now, *where are our girls*?'

On the other side of the street, the toms, with the instinct for self-protection of women who had been on the wrong end of too many men's fists, began to melt away into the fog.

'Don't waste your time on him, Brendan.' Luke placed a hand on his brother's shoulder. 'Let's get back to the yard. Dad'll be expecting us.'

'Yeah,' snarled Brendan. 'With the fucking takings. The takings we ain't got cos of this idiot.'

'Well, I ain't coming back to the yard,' said Pete Mac, his face and neck flushing red. 'I need a drink to calm me down. Brendan's showed me right up. Going on at me like I was a little kid in front of all them tarts.'

'I showed you up?' Brendan was poking Pete Mac again, backing him towards the road. 'If you'd been doing what you were told, there wouldn't be no strange tarts, now would there? And we'd have some takings, wouldn't we? Eh?'

'I overslept,' said Pete Mac, staring down at his feet. 'I was out late last night.'

'What, round your bit of stray's again?' Brendan spat the words through his teeth, slapping Pete Mac around the side of the head. 'You piece of shit.'

Luke grabbed his brother's sleeve. 'Brendan, leave it.'

Brendan shook off his hand. 'Don't you start.'

'Come on. This ain't the place. And we've all got some figuring out to do about what happens next.'

Brendan made as if to swipe the back of his hand round Pete Mac's face. 'You don't know how lucky you are Luke's here, MacRiordan. Now get in that motor. I ain't letting you out of my sight.'

*

As he bent forward to put the key in the driver's door, Brendan caught Pete Mac's reflection in the window. He was standing behind him with his mouth all scrunched up like a cat's arsehole, acting like he was the one who'd been wronged. The bloke was a complete moron.

Brendan turned to say something to him, when a small, skinny boy, who'd been collecting spoiled fruit and vegetables from the gutters round the market, slunk past them at just the wrong moment. Without warning, Pete Mac's hand flicked out and caught the shabbily dressed child with a whack right across the narrow of his back.

The boy gasped with shock and pain. 'Oi! I never done nothing.'

'Bugger off or you'll get another one,' he growled.

Luke and Brendan looked at him in disgust. If he wasn't their brother-in-law . . . But he was, although neither of them had ever been able to understand how a useless, lazy, bullying toe rag like Pete Mac had ever managed to get a girl like their sister Pat to even look at him, let alone let him get near enough to knock her up.

It was one of life's fucking mysteries.

'This is a really gorgeous colour, Pat.' Catherine, who was stretched out on the sofa, flat on her back, held her hand high above her head, admiring her freshly painted nails. 'Coral Moon. Really dreamy.'

'If you can manage to keep still for five minutes instead of fannying around, I can finish your other hand for you. But if you'd rather do it yourself then that's fine by me. You can just see what sort of a mess you can make of it.'

Eileen O'Donnell stopped knitting and frowned at her elder daughter, who was kneeling on the rug beside the

13

sofa, with the nail varnish brush poised in midair. She had a face on her like she was having her arse grated.

'Patricia,' Eileen said, in her soft Irish brogue. 'Please, don't snap at your sister like that. There's no need for it.'

Catherine, keeping her wet nails well away from the upholstery, dug her elbows into the cushions and hoisted her shoulders off the sofa and smiled broadly. Her whole face lit up as her cheeks folded into childlike dimples. 'She didn't mean anything, did you, Pat?'

'No. Course I didn't.' She closed her eyes and sighed wearily. 'But Mum's right. I'm sorry, Cath. I'm feeling a bit tired, that's all. Come on, let's get this finished or they won't be dry before you go out.'

Eileen's frown deepened as she looked at her girls. From behind, you could barely tell them apart. They had the same slim but curvy build, and their glossy black hair styled in the latest urchin cut, and both of them dressed in all the latest up-to-the-minute gear. Although, it had to be admitted, Pat had stopped showing much interest in buying her own things, and seemed content just to benefit from Catherine's many castoffs. Today, she was wearing bronze, clam-digger slacks and a black gypsy blouse that had hardly been on her sister's back, while Catherine, despite it being gone noon, was still in her pink baby dolls. Eileen could only wonder how she didn't catch her death in this weather, and thanked goodness for the four bar fire they'd had installed when they ripped out the old cast-iron fireplace.

She nibbled at her lip. Looking at them, anyone else would simply see two young women who knew what was what, and, what's more, what they liked. It's certainly what the salesmen saw after the pair of them had finally persuaded her to get rid of nearly all of the perfectly good furniture from the front room, and to replace it with the 'contemporary' things that the girls had been raving on and on about. At first, Eileen hadn't been at all sure about the bright, swirly-patterned hearth rug, the shiny blue laminate wall units, the grey and red three-piece suite with its splayed, spindly legs that looked as though they were about to break; and as for the matching poodle lamps they'd made her buy to go on the strange, triangular shaped occasional tables . . . Poodle lamps! It was like living in some smart shop window in the West End instead of in a terrace on the Mile End Road. And it had certainly cost enough. More than most families in Stepney could even dream of. But the girls had been right. It all looked, as Catherine would say, 'gorgeous'. And they could afford it. Even Gabriel had said he liked it. After she'd asked him.

As she always did, Eileen hurriedly pushed aside any thoughts about her husband's lack of interest in anything more domestic than the food on his plate and the whiskey in his glass, and allowed herself a smile as she remembered the bustle and excitement of those shopping expeditions. And the pleas and promises from the pair of them that she'd *just love it all* when she got it home.

Her smile faded. It was a pity Patricia's excitement wasn't so much in evidence these days. When the girls turned round and she saw their faces, they told their mother very different stories.

Catherine, a dead spit for the young Audrey Hepburn, was, as Patricia had once been, a real live wire, always jigging about and singing along to the latest rock and roll records and making them all laugh with her daft antics. While Patricia looked as if she had the worries of the world on her shoulders.

It was so hard being a mother. Wondering what was best for your children. Getting the balance right. With

15

Catherine, Eileen worried that she might have a bit too much of the free spirit about her, and she couldn't stand the thought of her youngest child getting caught out as Patricia had been.

The girls nowadays seemed to think they could get themselves done up in whatever clothes and make-up they felt like, and act as if they had the same freedom as the boys – to Eileen that was all wrong. But, then again, if she had a choice, she would have loved to see the old sparky Patricia again, acting up and gadding about the way she used to. It was as if a light had gone out and no one had bothered to replace the bulb.

It was no mystery what had happened. Eileen, like the rest of the family, knew what was wrong with her. It was being married to Pete Mac. If only she hadn't let the great oaf get anywhere near her. But it was too late for regrets. She might have lost the baby, but, before the eyes of God, she had made her vows. Till death her do part.

She could only hope that Catherine had learned from her big sister's mistakes and that she would carry on having plenty of fun going out and about with her friends before she tied herself down to some man.

Gabriel O'Donnell ran his fingers through his hair, and then tugged distractedly at his tie, staring unseeingly at the electric fan as it vibrated and edged its way across the scratched and battered surface of the desk. Being winter, it wasn't intended to cool the air, rather to clear it. But it made little impact on the heaviness of the smoke-thickened atmosphere in the harshly lit lean-to, barely disturbing the stacks of scruffy papers that supposedly legitimised the business dealings of the chaotic scrap yard outside.

'No, Jimmy,' he said – again – his jaw aching from the

effort of keeping his temper under control. 'Just listen will you? There are definitely no changes to the arrangements. You pay the boys as usual and –'

He stopped, shocked, in mid-sentence.

Jimmy had interrupted him.

Gabriel stared at the telephone as if it were smeared with something he'd just scraped off the bottom of his shoe.

It was a long moment before he took charge again. 'I said, *Jimmy*, there're no changes to the arrangements. Brendan'll be round later.' He raised his eyes and looked at his two sons and his son-in-law as they came in through the scuffed metal door. '*And you fucking remember it, right?*'

He slammed down the phone. 'That,' he said to the three young men, 'was Jimmy the Stump. He's not a happy man.'

'What's up with him this time?' It was Pete Mac talking. 'Miserable bastard's always bleating on about something or other.'

Brendan O'Donnell exchanged a look with his father, and then glared at his brother-in-law. 'Do us all a favour and shut up for once, will you, Pete?'

Gabriel continued. 'What's up with him is, he's paying *us* good money, and now two of Kessler's goons have gone in his boozer and threatened to smash it up. In front of all the customers. One of Jimmy's barmen said something, and, do you know what happened? They glassed him. In a boozer we're meant to be looking after. How does that look? Eh? I'll tell you, it looks like a right show up. And I'm not having it.' He turned to his eldest son. 'I want this sorted out, Brendan. Today. I want you to get yourself round that yard of theirs and –'

'But Dad –' It was Luke.

'Jimmy the Stump, Pete Mac, and now you getting mouthy with me, Luke?' Gabriel rubbed his hand over his chin, clearly bewildered by this new turn of events. 'Can I ask who you think you are, interrupting me?'

'I was only going to say, Dad; shouldn't we calm down, figure out if the Kesslers can really do us any harm?'

Brendan shoved his brother in the side. 'Luke!' he hissed at him under his breath.

Gabriel rose slowly to his feet. The only sound in the room apart from the furious snorting of his breath, the whirring of the fan on his desk in front of him.

He spoke slowly, his voice deceptively quiet, the words' sharp edges softened by traces of an Irish burr beneath his rough cockney. 'Any harm? Have you gone raving mad?'

Luke shifted around uncomfortably. He knew it wasn't done, questioning his dad, but he had to do something. Play for a bit of time. 'No, it's just –'

Gabriel thumped his fist on the table, silencing his son. 'I'll explain to you, shall I, Luke? If he didn't want to do *any harm* he wouldn't have fucking come back here, would he? He'd have moved out to Essex. Like other people.'

'Or Kent,' suggested Pete Mac.

They ignored him.

'But, no, he came right back here to shit on my fucking doorstep. Moving in on businesses in *my* toby. Don't you think that's harm enough? The bastard moves out of here twenty years ago, talking some old shit about saving his family from the blitz, when everyone knows it was him what swallowed, the fucking coward. And now he's giving everyone some old toffee about coming back here

18

to get his family away from the riots. Riots that were over *two years ago*. Turning up here like he's never been away. Like he's just nipped out for a packet of fags, and found himself a bit waylaid on the way home.'

'Maybe you'd have done the same, Dad.'

'You *what*?'

Luke's mouth was so dry, he could hardly speak. 'Moved us out if you thought there were gonna be riots.'

'Luke. Son. The O'Donnells don't run away from anything.'

'Well, his haulage firm's not treading on our toes.'

Gabriel looked at Luke with genuine puzzlement. What the hell had got into the boy? 'But going round Jimmy the Stump's fucking is. That *is* pissing on my patch.' He smacked his hand on the table again. 'For fuck's sake, Luke, this is a business we're running here, not some two bob bit of spivvery. A business I've worked my nuts off to build. A business I've had to fight every step of the way to put together. And if this business is gonna thrive, we don't need them fuckers moving in mob-handed from West London. What do they think? We're gonna just hold up our hands and surrender? Let 'em take whatever they fancy. I'm not having it. Understand?'

Gabriel's head ached and his heart was sore. He hadn't slogged his guts out dragging himself out of the Galway mire to be rolled over and shat on by a fucking Russian or Pole or whatever the cunt was.

He dropped down heavily on to his chair, leaned back, and loosened his tie.

'Barry and Kevin were just here.' The words came out as a weary sigh. 'Someone's offering better odds opposite every single one of our street pitches. And Anthony phoned in earlier.' Gabriel directed a look at Pete Mac.

'Reckons one of the girls told him they all went out as usual this morning, but one of Kessler's heavies turned up and they were too scared to stay. So scared they'd rather face a big fucker like Anthony. And now Jimmy the Stump's bending my ear'ole about protection. What is this – a Sisters of Charity set up I'm running here? I supply the gambling, protection and whoring pitches for them cunts to work?'

Pete Mac silently cursed Anthony. Fuck him. Now Gabe knew the girls hadn't worked today. He'd have to smooth things over. 'Look, Gabe,' he said, all cajoling smiles and tipped-to-one-side head. 'Before we get carried away here, Luke might be right. Maybe we shouldn't be worrying ourselves.'

'What?' Gabriel mouthed at his idiot son-in-law.

'I mean, little bits of protection? Street betting? Everyone knows that's gonna disappear when the new shops are up and running. And as for the toms . . . Who needs all that agg? Let the Kesslers have it. We've got better things to think about. Proper business.'

'Brendan, will you get this stupid cowson out of my sight?'

Pete Mac didn't speak until he'd backed away, well out of Brendan's reach. 'Stupid cowson am I? You didn't say that when I got that demolition contract last week. And all that lovely copper piping laying about on the building site next door.'

'How do you think you got that contract, Pete? And how do you think we – you – have such a good life? Shifting a few second-hand bricks? Choring a few lengths of copper pipe when the night watchman's not looking?'

Out of his depth, Pete Mac's face contorted into a *moue* of confusion.

20

'No, Pete, it's because I'm not a mug, that's how. And don't you *ever* think you can treat me like one. I know every move you make, you bollock-brained moron. You're only tolerated here because of our Patricia. You remember that. And you remember *no one* mugs me off. No one. And that's why I'm not having the Kesslers coming around here, thinking they can do what they fucking well like.'

Hard as he tried, Pete Mac couldn't keep quiet. 'But you haven't seen the big black feller he's fetched with him, Gabe. Built like a brick shithouse.'

Brendan flashed him a look of pure contempt. That was the reason he hadn't been around to mind the girls: he'd seen the bloke minding Kessler's girls and bottled out.

Gabriel snatched a cigarette from the packet of Players on the desk, lit one, and took a long draw, pulling the smoke deep into his lungs. 'I'm sick of all this. There's Poles running the protection up in Leeds. Scotsmen making a move on the firms in Liverpool. Maltese and Italians all over the poxy West End. Well, I'm telling you, I'm not having Kessler thinking he can move the League of fucking Nations in round here. Got any problems with that, any of you?'

No one answered him.

'Good. So, perhaps now you'll do as you're told and get yourselves round that haulage yard and put the fear of fucking Christ up the bastards.' He studied the red glow of the tobacco. 'Burn their fucking lorries out. Frighten the shit out of 'em. Do whatever you have to do, but just fucking do it.'

Brendan and Pete Mac walked towards the door, but Luke hesitated. 'Dad, I –'

Gabriel shook his head. 'Forget it, son, just do as you're told.'

As Luke reluctantly joined the others, Gabriel spoke again. 'Hang on. Not you, Pete.'

The three of them turned to face him, Brendan with his hand on the door.

'In case there's any trouble. Go round yours and get Patricia. Drop her round home.'

'She's already there. Went earlier.'

'Good. So you can go with Brendan and Luke. I'll call Eileen. Tell her to make sure Patricia stays indoors with her and Catherine.'

If Pete Mac wasn't in such a bad mood he'd have laughed out loud. The old fool thought he was so clever, but he had no idea that whenever she had the chance, his precious little Catherine was off out, here, there and everywhere with her mates. And all with Eileen's blessing.

Gabriel stubbed out the barely smoked cigarette, pushed back his chair, and reached down by his feet. He pulled out a heavy canvas bag, and heaved it up onto the desk. 'And you'd better take these with you. You'll be needing something a bit more serious than blades and brass knuckles.'

'Dad, shouldn't we think about this?' Luke was looking really concerned. 'Pete Mac's right. There's all sorts of rumours about the lunatics they've got on that firm.'

'Are there now?' Gabriel got up and went over to a dull-grey metal stationery cupboard stuck in the corner behind a wonky-legged coat stand. He unlocked it, and took something wrapped in oily sacking off the top shelf. It was the size of a table leg, but obviously a lot heavier. He carried it back to his desk, set it down carefully, and opened it up. 'Then you'd better take this with you, hadn't you?' He picked up the sawn-off shotgun and held it out to them. 'Silence them rumours once and for all.'

Gabriel stood at the single, grimy window, watching the three young men slope off across the scrap yard.

Brendan: a mirror image of his own dark Irish looks, but with twenty-two years less wear on his face. Then, Luke: a year younger, but just as tall and as immaculately turned out his brother – sharp, three-button, navy blue suit, pure white shirt, well-polished shoes – but somehow less of a presence than Brendan. Maybe that's what being the younger brother did to you. But they were two handsome men all right: dark-haired and powerfully built, just like him, but with eyes of deep, violet blue – like Eileen's – instead of green like his.

And then there was Peter-bloody-Mac-fucking-Riordan.

His son-in-law, with his pale freckled face, his wiry, carrot red hair, and his wide, countryman's body that was already threatening to run to fat just as his father's had done. His suit had, no doubt, cost as much as his sons' had done, but it certainly didn't look it, not on him.

He was a stupid fuck, but, apparently, he made Patricia a happy woman. And even if he didn't, it was too late now. The good Lord forgive him, it was only a pity she hadn't had the miscarriage before the idiot had got her walking up the aisle.

Gabriel turned from the window and closed his eyes as if in pain.

Before he knew it, Catherine would be bringing home some useless, spotty Herbert, who they'd all have to make welcome, and smile at, and shake his hand like he was God's bloody gift. But Gabriel wouldn't make the same

23

mistake again. Catherine would stay safely at home with her mother. At nearly eighteen years old, she was his and Eileen's baby, the surprise who'd completed the family he'd always dreamed of having, and no man was going to get his dirty hands on her for a good few years yet.

He walked back to the desk and flopped down in his chair, ripped his tie from his neck, and lit another cigarette. He'd had plenty of dreams over the years and a whole lot of them had come true, but he never forgot what his mother had said to him when he was still a raggedy-arsed kid back in Ireland. He'd sworn to her that one day his dream of having a good life would come true, that he'd have money in his pocket, food in his belly and be beholden to no one. He would be someone. He'd be Mr Gabriel O'Donnell.

Now you just remember, she'd said to him, pointing a work-calloused finger at him across the rough deal table in their dirt-floored hovel, *when dreams do come true, boy, they have a nasty habit of turning into nightmares*.

And this was a nightmare all right. Having the Kesslers turning up on his fucking doorstep, and then having to argue not only with Pete Mac, but with his own bloody son into the bargain. Christ alone knew what had got into Luke.

Gabriel put his hands over his eyes, feeling the headache tightening like a steel band round his forehead. Eileen had always been too soft on the kids; ever since they were babies she'd spoiled the lot of them.

One of the phones on his desk began ringing, the phone that no one but Gabriel was allowed to touch.

He dropped his hand from his eyes, picked up the receiver, and breathed softly, lovingly into the mouth-piece, 'Rosie, my own darling angel . . .'

24

Chapter 2

'Is it going to be a big wedding, Sammy?' the girl asked, her voice at once shy but with a discernibly wheedling edge to it.

'Big?' Sammy paused, concentrating on shifting down to third. He was driving as cautiously as if he were taking his test, extra careful not to crunch the gears of the car he had borrowed from his older brother Daniel – the brother who was out on business with their father, and who would kill him stone dead if he knew he'd even touched his motor.

'Are you kidding?' he went on. 'If my mother thought Daniel wanted the Chief Rabbi to be there, Dad'd make sure he turned up. They wouldn't deny our Danny anything.'

'And I bet Rachel's dress is gonna be really pretty.'

As she spoke, the girl stared out of the car window into the fog. Why was it that when you were born that's what you were for the rest of your life? It didn't matter if you were a dog in a kennel or a princess in a palace, that's what you'd always be. It wasn't fair.

Take Rachel, she'd been born into a nice, Jewish family, and what did that make her? A nice Jewish girl, just right to marry Sammy's big brother, Daniel.

Jewish. Exactly what she wasn't.

Her attention was snatched back by Sammy's laughter. 'Don't know whether it's pretty or not,' he said, slowing the car to a halt by the offside kerb. 'But I know her

25

mother's as bad as mine. I'm telling you, whatever it comes to, Rachel'll have exactly what she wants. And I guarantee it won't be no schmutter. And the knees up afterwards? That's going to make that Princess Margaret's do look like a shotgun job at Gretna Green.'

The girl stared down into her lap as visions of virginal white net, sparkling crystals, and creamy, teardrop pearls, danced around in her head like will o' the wisps – there, but just out of her grasp.

'Sammy . . .'

'Yeah?'

'Do you think I'd look nice in white?'

He didn't hesitate. 'No.'

His bluntness stunned her. She pulled the fur collar of her astrakhan coat tightly up about her face. 'I'm cold. I want to go home.'

He rolled his eyes. 'Will you let me finish? What I meant was: I think you look best . . .' He turned off the engine, leaned over, and whispered something in her ear.

'Sammy Kessler!' she squealed, all shoves and mock offence. 'You are *so* rude.'

'Course I am. That's why you love me. Now come here.'

'Don't, everyone'll see.'

'In this fog?' He slipped a hand inside her coat, cupping her breast, and nuzzling into her ear. 'They'd need flipping good eyesight.'

She lifted her chin, luxuriating in the damp warmth of his breath on her neck. 'Where are we anyway?' The words came out as a soft moan.

'Sclater Street.'

She pulled away from him, ducking her head and squinting up at the high brick wall, trying to make out the lettering on the street sign. 'What the hell are you up to, Sammy? We're practically outside your dad's yard.'

'So?' He ran his fingers through his springy fair hair. 'You are such a panicker.'

'Say someone recognises me?'

'You can hardly see a hand in front of your face out there. And even if you could, who'd recognise you in that new coat? Makes you look just like a film star.'

'It is lovely,' she said, stroking the high fur collar that she knew framed her pretty, heart shaped face perfectly.

'Nothing but the best for my girl.'

My girl . . . She smiled up at him.

'Is it nice and cosy?'

She wrinkled her nose with pleasure. 'Really lovely.'

'Good, it'll keep you warm while I'm gone. I'll be two minutes. Tops.'

'Sammy!'

He took hold of the door handle. 'I've just gotta nip in the yard and make sure the lazy so-and-so's have got all the lorries back.'

But he didn't get out right away; he sat there looking at her, as she returned her gaze to her lap, resigned to waiting for him.

She knew Sammy's father insisted that his transport business was all shut up before sunset on Fridays. His mother liked the family to do things properly, religiously. Her own mother was the same. And it seemed it wasn't only their mothers who had things in common. His dad sounded a lot like hers as well. Both men didn't actually care much about their 'official' means of making a living – a haulage business in Sammy's dad's case, a scrap metal yard in hers – other than the fact that they acted as useful fronts for their other activities. Activities the women were kept well away from. But both men kept their wives happy by paying lip service to their religions. And in turn, their wives ran well-kept, comfortable homes, and turned a wifely blind eye to the reality of what was going on right under their noses: the businesses which kept their families in such style. She and Sammy wouldn't be like their parents. They'd tell each other everything.

Sammy pushed her fringe of heavy dark hair away from her face, physically moved by her almost childlike beauty. 'Just think,' he whispered, 'if we hadn't moved back to the East End, I'd never have met you.' He could hardly believe it was just two short months since he'd gone with his brother Daniel to that club in Ilford.

Danny had promised him a good night: a few drinks, the chance to pick up a couple of shiksas, and the guarantee of having some right laughs. They'd both had the drinks, all right, plenty of them, and they'd both met the shiksas, but only Daniel had had the laughs.

Sammy had gone and fallen in love.

He had known from their very first meeting that he'd make his life with her. The fact that she wasn't the good Jewish girl his mother had always presumed he would marry, didn't matter. He would set up something of his own, get away from the family, make himself independent. He loved her. No discussion. He just needed to work out how he was going to do it. How hard could it be?

Sammy touched her cheek, and felt himself harden as the soft, peachy skin of her cheeks folded into the dimples he couldn't resist.

'You gonna be okay?' he asked, his voice low, full of desire.

She nodded again, her violet-blue eyes wide and round.

'Remember what I told you? You're my bashert. The

one meant for me. What are you?'

'Your bashert.' She paused, dropping her chin shyly. 'Can I have a kiss before you go?'

'Do you really have to ask?'

Eileen stuck the end of her knitting needles in the ball of wool, got up from her chair and went to answer the telephone. She still moved with the quiet grace and dignity that had first attracted Gabriel O'Donnell when they had been little more than children back in Galway.

'2314,' she said, her accent retaining far more of the Irish than her husband's.

'Is that you, Eileen?'

'Yes, Gabe.'

'Where are the girls?'

She hesitated for a split second. 'They're here. With me. Listening to the wireless.'

'Let me talk to them.'

Again, Eileen paused for the briefest of moments, looking across at Patricia, signalling with a raised finger to her lips for her to be quiet. 'You can't, love, not really. Pat's painting Catherine's nails. Primping and preening as usual. You know what the pair of them are like.'

Patricia made a big show of widening her eyes and dropping her jaw, but Eileen rejected the admonishment with a flap of her hand. 'I'll give them a message, if that's all right with you.'

'Fair enough. Tell them I don't want them going out in this fog, and I'll send someone to drive Pat home later.'

'Don't worry yourself, Gabriel, they'll be grand. We're sitting here snug as bugs.'

'Mum,' gawped Patricia, as soon as the receiver was safely back in its cradle. 'If I'd have done that . . .'

29

'Done what?'

'Pretended Catherine was still here.'

Eileen bent forward and patted Scrap, a now Labrador-sized bundle of tan fur that she'd rescued from an abandoned litter of tiny, trembling puppies dumped outside her husband's yard in an old cardboard box. 'A little white lie never hurt anybody.'

Patricia picked up her almost cold cup of tea from the occasional table, went to take a sip, but then put it down again. 'D'you reckon?'

Brendan O'Donnell steered the dark grey car through the fog-bound back doubles of Bethnal Green. He'd forgone the pleasures of driving his Jaguar, opting instead for the staid anonymity of a Standard saloon borrowed from one the men who worked in the scrap yard.

Pete Mac, still furious as a hornet about the way he'd been treated, sat in the back next to Luke, the front passenger seat being occupied by a heavy canvas bag. The bag that contained several lengths of tape-wrapped lead piping, four pickaxe handles, four lump hammers, and the cloth-wrapped sawn-off shotgun.

He rapped his knuckles agitatedly against his top teeth. 'I'm not kidding, Brendan. I mean it,' he snarled in his flat, Romford growl. 'What does your old man expect us to do? Blow their brains out for 'em? I can see the headlines now: *The O'Donnell Gang Goes Barmy. Ten Fucking Dead*. Including two O'Donnells and one sodding MacRiordan. No, better, we get fucking hung for murder. I mean, striping a bloke's face or arse is one thing, or using knuckle-dusters, that's all right with me. I've got no problem with any of that. But guns? We're not fucking cowboys and Indians.'

Brendan flashed a look at his brother in the rear-view mirror. 'Will you shut him up, Luke?'

Luke said nothing; he just stared down at his feet, and gnawed distractedly at his cuticles.

'I'd like to see him try,' sneered Pete Mac. 'I'd knock his block right off his shoulders.'

Brendan snorted scornfully 'You sure, Pete? You couldn't knock the skin off a rice pudden.'

He sniffed angrily. 'All I'm saying is, I don't like the idea of going over there tooled up. Not when we ain't got a clue how many geezers they're gonna have on parade. And if the size of that one on Commercial Street's anything to go by then we're gonna be right in the shit. Right up to our fucking necks.'

Brendan shook his head. 'So you did turn up then? And saw the size of him –'

Pete Mac shifted in his seat. 'Not properly, like.'

'I knew it.'

'And you thought you'd just leave us to it,' chipped in Luke.

'That's why you went amongst the missing when you should have been keeping an eye on the girls.'

'I was just being careful. It was all right for you, there was two of you.'

Brendan's lip curled in disgust. 'You should be ashamed of yourself. If –'

Brendan never finished the sentence. He braked so suddenly that the mini-armoury on the front seat shot onto the floor and rolled under the seat, and Pete Mac bashed his head, with a dull thud, on the side window.

'Oi, Brendan. That bloody hurt.'

'Serves you right for staring out of the window like a fucking spaniel,' muttered Brendan. 'Now give your eyes a chance. There's a brand new Jag parked over by the Kesslers's yard.'

'Anyone in it?' asked Luke, suddenly interested.

'Yeah. And it's got to be one of the Kesslers,' replied Brendan. 'Can't see it belonging to one of their drivers, or anyone else round here.'

'Is he alone?'

'What is this, Luke?' snapped Brendan. '*Take Your Pick*? How the fuck do I know if he's alone? I don't even know what the Kesslers bloody look like, let alone whether they've got sodding company or not.'

'I know what Sammy Kessler looks like.' Luke rested his elbows on the front seat and stared hard through the windscreen. Praying silently that what he'd dreaded wasn't about to come true.

Brendan twisted round. 'How?'

Flustered, Luke sat back in his seat. 'Some bloke pointed him out to me. In a pub.'

'What pub?' asked Pete Mac, gormless as a sack of spuds.

Brendan and Luke both stared at him.

'*What pub*?' Brendan screwed up his face in wonder at his brother-in-law, threw open the door and got out.

'Pete,' he said, sticking his head back in the car, 'just get out here and give us them tools. We're gonna surprise him, whatever boozer he uses and whoever he's with. Right? Luke, you jump in the driving seat. Get the engine running, in case we need to shoot off a bit sharpish.'

As he took the bag, Brendan grinned. 'Here, let's see what you're made of, Pete. Cop hold of this.'

Brendan held out the sawn-off to his now grim-faced brother-in-law, who had shoved his hands deep into his pockets.

32

'Aw, sorry, I forgot. There might be a nasty big man to scare you.'

'Scare me?' Pete Mac's lips twisted with anger. 'Give it here.'

'All right, but mind you don't aim it at your bollocks, eh, Pete. We don't want no accidents, now do we?'

Reluctantly, Sammy pulled away from her, running his finger gently down her cheek. God, she was a good-looking girl. He was going to work out a way to be with her if it was the last thing he did.

'I'll be two minutes, okay?' he said, getting out of the car.

He had one foot on the pavement, with his body half twisted away from the steering wheel, and his gaze angled down at the ground, when he realised something was wrong. A hand – a big hand – had clamped over his shoulder. But he didn't look up to see who was standing over him, he was too busy concentrating on the truncated barrels of the sawn-off shotgun that someone was pointing in his face.

'Hello,' said Brendan, talking to the top of Sammy's head over Pete Mac's shoulder. 'It's Kessler innit? And who's your little friend? Bit shy is she?'

The girl had pulled her coat right up to her ears and was trying to crawl out of the passenger door onto the road.

Brendan groaned as if he were disappointed by such a pathetic escape attempt. 'Pete, get round there and stop that bitch getting away, will you?'

Pete Mac, sawn-off in hand, his determination to prove himself to Brendan making him act flash, did as he was told with a lip-curling smirk. 'My pleasure, Brendan, old son.'

33

Sammy Kessler had no chance to think things through. He just knew it couldn't get out that he was seeing a shiksa. He flung himself sideways to cover her with his body.

The violence of his sudden movement, combined with his weight, threw her right out of the car, and she went sprawling, face down onto the roadway.

Making a wild grab for the sawn-off, Sammy tumbled out of the car on top of her, muffling her screams in an arm-waving, leg-flailing confusion of body parts.

He scrambled to his feet, planting them firmly on the ground, and tried to wrestle the gun from a now wild-eyed and cursing Pete Mac.

For a moment, Sammy thought he had a hold of it, but the barrels were slick with oil and it slipped from his grasp.

Pete Mac jerked it high in the air out of Sammy's reach. But he hadn't reckoned with Sammy's speed.

With his head down, Sammy barged him in the gut.

Pete Mac doubled over. And the gun went off.

Luke jumped out of the car and raced over to them.

Sammy had straightened up and was staggering backwards. The front of his overcoat was covered with blood, but it wasn't him who'd been hurt. It was the girl.

She lay there, face down in the road, with bright red blood puddling around her head and shoulders.

'What the fuck have you done, Pete?' Luke stood over the girl, his arms hanging loosely by his side.

'It wasn't me. *He* did it.' Pete Mac waved the shotgun at Sammy Kessler, who was backing away from them towards the haulage yard, his gaze fixed on the girl sprawled out on the roadway.

'He threw himself at me. You saw him, Brendan. I lost my balance. It wasn't my fault.'

Brendan snatched the gun off him. 'Get back in the motor, you moron, before he calls the law.'

'A Kessler call the law?' Pete Mac did his best to sound bold, contemptuous.

'All right then, before he calls an ambulance. *Just get in that fucking motor.*'

'Brendan, wait.' It was Luke. 'It's Catherine.'

'*What?*'

'Catherine.' Luke swiped his hand across his forehead, pushing back his hair. 'Pete Mac's gone and fucking shot her.'

Why was she bothering? Eileen looked down at the half completed sweater. Conker brown. For one or other of the boys. Not that they'd been seen dead in it. Forty-two years of age and finding ways to pass the time. She might as well be sitting there by the fire like her mother, with her face pinched, her shoulders hunched, and a shawl draped round them. And just like her grandmother before that. Women old before their time. Not like their men, who, except for a few grey hairs and slightly thicker waistlines, seemed to look the same in their forties as they did in their twenties.

Eileen smoothed down her smart navy skirt, and checked the sheen of her stockings as they stretched over her ankles, proving to herself that she was still an attractive woman, a woman who took care of herself.

A woman who might as well have been invisible for all the attention her husband paid her.

'Not happy with the jumper, Mum?'

'If I'm honest, Patricia, not really love. But it keeps me busy.' Eileen smiled, gathering up her pride. 'You know how it is.'

'Yeah, I know.' Patricia nodded, then added casually, 'Fancy coming shopping tomorrow?'

'Don't we always on a Saturday?' What else was there to do when she'd already cleaned the house from top to bottom, and done all the chores during the week, when the men were out and she wouldn't be a bother to them?

'I just thought we might go up West for a change. Selfridges, or Marshall & Snelgrove. Somewhere like that.'

Eileen flashed her eyebrows with interest. This sounded promising. More like her old Pat. 'The Roman Road or East Ham not good enough for you all of a sudden?'

'I never said that. I feel like going somewhere a bit, you know . . .' She cast around trying to find the right word. 'Special.'

'Why not? Let's treat ourselves. Catherine'll be raring to go.' Eileen tipped her head and looked sideways at her daughter. 'Here, you're not getting the old shopping bug back like your little sister, are you? She's more shoes than a shoe shop that one.'

Patricia shrugged. 'I want to get away for a few hours, that's all. Go somewhere different.'

'I know how you feel.' Eileen shifted forward in her seat as she saw the dejected look on her daughter's face. 'All right, love, I didn't mean to upset you. I was only teasing.'

Patricia looked away, unable to face her mother.

'There's nothing's wrong is there? You're not feeling unwell?'

Patricia nibbled at the inside of her cheek. Here goes, saying it made it real, made her have to deal with it. 'Mum, I'm expecting.' There, she'd said it. 'About twelve weeks gone, I reckon.'

'My little Patsy!' Eileen rushed over to her daughter, arms stretched wide.

Patricia accepted her hugs, but Eileen could feel the stiffness, the wariness in her child.

'Don't tell Pete will you, Mum. Not yet. If it goes wrong again I don't want to . . .' She considered her words. '. . . disappoint him.'

'It won't go wrong, love, not this time. I promise. With all my heart. You weren't well before. All that fuss when your dad found out. Then rushing the wedding through so no one knew. And then . . .' She hesitated, tipping her daughter under the chin and looking into her eyes. 'Look, everything's going to be wonderful. And Dad'll be so happy for you this time.'

'I still want to make sure nothing goes wrong before I say anything to him, Mum. Please. Promise me.'

'Okay, but it'll be fine, I just know it will.'

Patricia blew her nose noisily. 'I do love Pete, you know.'

'Yeah, I know, sweetheart. Just like I love your father.'

Patricia's chin dropped. She stared down at the cosy familiarity of the brown and green patterns in the carpet, the carpet she had grown up with, that she'd played on, sat on, stretched out on to listen to all her mum's stories about living 'back home' in Ireland – the carpet that meant home and safety, even during the noise and clamour of the war. The carpet her mum had stubbornly refused to replace. She loved it for all those reasons, but most of all she loved it because it had nothing whatsoever to do with her life with Peter MacRiordan.

Yes, Patricia loved him all right, just as much as she had said she still loved him when she found out before they were even engaged that she wasn't only carrying his

37

child, but also the pubic lice – and the subsequent lies and humiliation – he had given her into the bargain.

If only it wouldn't have hurt her parents so badly she'd have told the selfish, fat-headed pig what to do with their marriage. But, good Catholic girl that she was, she had to get used to the fact: she was married to him. And it was a life sentence.

Patricia sniffed back the tears. It was no good thinking about what might have been, she was pregnant again, carrying a new life inside her. She'd just have to lump it. Especially now she'd told her mother.

And that was that.

Brendan was really having trouble taking in what had happened. It felt as if time had somehow lost its power to move forward, that everything had been cranked down to agonisingly slow motion, making things hyperreal yet dream-like at the same time.

He turned and watched Sammy, who was now running towards the entrance to the Kesslers's haulage yard. His movements were those of a silent film being shown at the wrong speed. His arms pumped up and down – *thwack! thwack!* – but so slowly that they were useless, ineffectual pistons. His head moved from side to side in great wagging nods, and his legs described ridiculous looping strides that were getting him nowhere.

Then Brendan turned back, dragging against an invisible force, and saw his brother kneeling on the ground by Catherine.

Pete Mac was standing over them both – his face distorted, his mouth opening and closing. He might have been shouting or even screaming, but Brendan could hear nothing.

38

Not until his brother broke the spell.

Luke reared up from his knees, grabbed Pete Mac by the lapels and smacked his forehead full into his brother-in-law's face with a sickening, skin-splitting crunch.

The force threw Pete Mac backwards off his feet.

When he hit the ground, Brendan could hear him crying like a baby.

Brendan shook his head like a swimmer emerging from the waves. He had to help Catherine.

'Here, I'm talking to you, Kessler,' a man called to Sammy over the loudly revving engine of a blue Bedford truck. 'Are you listening to me? I said, this lorry needs two new tyres and it could do with something or other to stop this bleed'n' whining. It's gotta be the gearbox. Hark at it, how can I be expected to . . .'

The man continued speaking, but Sammy ignored him.

Without a word, and with his blood-splattered topcoat bundled in his arms, he raced up the wooden steps into the old caravan his father used as an office. He slammed the door shut behind him and paced wildly up and down the grubby strip of carpet.

He had to think.

How on earth was he going to explain what he was doing with Catherine O'Donnell? His old man would kill him.

He could feel his chest rising and falling like he'd just run the four-minute mile.

Or why he'd left her there in the road.

What a bastard.

It was all too much. There were too many complications.

Like what he was doing driving Daniel's new Jag.

And then there was the new coat that he'd bought on his mother's account. How could he return it to the shop now it was all stained? He laughed slightly hysterically. It had been such a good plan: he was going to make it sound as if he really didn't want to take it back off her, but would, as a favour when Catherine realised she wouldn't be able to take it home.

Coats? Why was he thinking about fucking coats? It was Catherine he should be worrying about. And the law.

Shit! As soon as the ambulance crew saw what had happened, they'd be sure to start sniffing about. Danny would go raving mad, his mother would go crazy, and as for his father . . . No, that didn't even bear thinking about.

How was he going to get out of this little lot?

He couldn't help it. He hadn't known when he'd first met her that Catherine was one of *the* O'Donnells. But at least he knew she'd understand why he'd had to leave her out in the road like that. She knew how families like theirs worked.

And he'd make it up to her. Show her he loved her. Find those crap hounds who'd hurt her, and kill them. Or maybe let the bastards know who she was. That'd do the trick all right – finding out the O'Donnells were after you.

And when he finally sorted everything out they'd have the best life together. He'd get them a beautiful house, they'd have lovely kids, and Catherine would be the best-looking wife a bloke could ever dream of.

His hand hovered over the telephone. He should call an ambulance. No. Let them animals out there do it. Let them explain what they'd done, and why they had a sawn-off shotgun in a London street in the middle of the afternoon.

He swallowed hard. He'd better have a quick look round the watchman's door in the yard gates, make sure they'd sorted her out. That they hadn't driven off and left her there.

Then he'd get himself back home.

He had no choice. If he didn't get back in time for the Shabbas meal his mother would kill him before his father had the chance. And God alone knew what Danny would do to him if he realised his car had been missing all afternoon.

What a fucking mess.

Chapter 3

As Brendan screeched out of Brick Lane and onto the Bethnal Green Road, Pete Mac lurched across the back seat.

'Get off her, you stupid bastard,' yelled Luke. 'I'm trying to bring her round and you're fucking suffocating her.'

'That's nice language in front of your sister.' Pete Mac was doing his best to sound casual, but he was very close to losing control of his bowels. Gabe was gonna kill him for this.

'Anyway, it ain't my fault. It's him. He's driving like a bloody maniac.' Pete Mac squeezed himself into the corner, putting as much distance between him and Catherine as the back seat of a Standard saloon allowed. 'And maybe I could see what I was doing if you hadn't smashed me nose open for me, Luke. You've made all me eyes puff up. Patricia's gonna have the right hump when I go home looking like this.'

Luke lifted a blood-stiffened strand of hair away from Catherine's drawn and pallid face, speaking to Pete Mac as he stroked her cheek with the side of his thumb. 'You're lucky that's all I did to you. You couldn't even help me grab that pigeon you dozy, useless bit of crap. If I hadn't chucked me coat over it in time, how would it have looked?'

The soreness in his hands from the beating he had given Joshua long forgotten, Brendan whacked them down on the steering wheel, making the car swerve towards the middle of the road. '*Will you two keep quiet*? I'm trying to get us back to the yard without drawing attention to the fact that my sister is on the back seat with a fucking gunshot wound, and you two just . . .'

A shotgun wound.

Jesus Christ.

Brendan felt the vomit rise in his throat. The bitter taste making him close his eyes and grimace. He had to pull himself together. It wasn't quite dark yet, and now the bloody fog was starting to lift. He should get off the main drag and onto the back doubles before anyone got a look in the car.

Again he pulled the wheel hard to the right, and stuck his foot down on the floor, swerving off the Bethnal Green Road and round into Chilton Street.

Luke cradled Catherine closer, protecting her as the car raced across the busy junction. 'Come on, Cath. Wake up,' he whispered into her ear. 'Give us one of your smiles.'

'*What the hell now?*' Brendan stamped on the brake.

'What's the matter with you? It's only a removal van.' Pete Mac was peering over Brendan's shoulder. 'You could get a bus past that, easy. And this girl needs a doctor, mate.'

'What d'you think I'm trying to do?' Brendan spat the words through gritted teeth as he stuck the car in reverse, and twisted round to see where he was going. Batting Pete Mac out of the way, he roared the car back onto the Bethnal Green Road.

He'd finally urged the complaining engine back into top when he had to hit the brakes yet again. A kamikaze copper had jumped out in the road, right in front of them, his hand stuck in the air, palm outward, in a command to

43

stop. Not exactly what they needed. Not now. Not with his sister bleeding all over the back seat, and with Pete Mac looking like he'd been in the ring with Rocky Marciano.

'What's going on?' Luke tugged at Catherine's coat, doing his best to hide the blood behind the high fur collar, and motioned for Pete Mac to help him kick the pile of weapons under the front seat. 'You don't think they're after us already, do you, Brendan?'

'Dunno.'

Brendan fumbled around, lighting a cigarette. The car had to reek of blood. He puffed on it furiously, creating his own, personal, indoor fog, and then slowly wound down the window. 'Yeah?' he said, exhaling smoke out of the side of his mouth.

The policeman smiled. 'Congratulations, sonny.' He spoke in an agonisingly slow Welsh accent. 'You're my first of the day.'

'Do what?'

The officer held up a gadget that looked like a cross between a Pifco hair dryer and a Martian ray gun. 'Another weapon in the armoury of the crime fighter.' His voice was full of proud admiration for the thing. 'A weapon to stop toe rags like you from making the streets dangerous for law abiding folk –' he jerked his thumb over his shoulder '– like those little old ladies over there, innocently buying their potatoes and greens from the fruit and vegetable stall.'

He sighed contentedly, all shiny uniform buttons and self-congratulation. 'Been brought in specially, I have, to train the locals on the equipment.'

Brendan flicked the barely smoked cigarette out of the window. '*Toerags* like me?' The dangerousness of the situation forgotten, Brendan was frowning hard, as if he

44

were concentrating on trying to understand what the man could possibly mean. 'Do you know who I am?'

'Well, let's see, shall we?' The policeman rested one hand on the roof of the car and lowered his head to get a better look at Brendan's face.

Hurriedly, Luke wound down the rear window to get some fresh air circulating, folded his arm around his sister as if she were a sleeping lover, and told her quietly, 'It's okay, Cath, I'll look after you.'

'With that quiff, you do bear more than a passing resemblance to Mr Presley. But you can't be Elvis, now can you? He's away in the army, isn't he? But there is something a bit greasy about you. Here, you're not him are you? Not gone AWOL or nothing? Cos you do know I'd have to report you if you have? Serious offence, deserting. But, let me think. Are you officially back in Civvy Street yet? Now there's a puzzler.' He tapped his finger on his chin in a sarcastic pantomime of contemplation. 'Tell you what, I'll ask my young Lesley, she knows all about you rock and roll stars.'

'All right, Taff. Just tell me. What's the SP here? What you after?'

The officer's nostrils flared. He straightened up, beckoned for his colleague, who was waiting over by the police car, to join him, and said very slowly, 'What did you call me, *sir*?'

'I think you'd be better off knowing what to call *me*, actually, *mate*. O'Donnell mean anything to you?'

A momentary cloud passed across his face. Why was this little cockney yob so confident? 'No. Nothing.'

'Anything wrong?' asked the other officer as he sauntered over, clearly bored with his lot. This definitely wasn't his idea of a good use of a Friday afternoon.

'Yes, I should say there's something wrong. This gentleman reckons I should know him. Name of O'Donnell.'

'O'Donnell?' the other man repeated, suddenly alert, dropping his head to get a look at the driver.

It was taking Brendan every ounce of willpower not to slam the car into first, shove his foot down on the accelerator, and get Catherine as far away as possible from this swede-bashing idiot and his stupid bloody machine. But he had to be sensible. Keep calm. *Don't create a commotion*.

'Yeah, that's right. I'm Brendan, Gabriel's son.'

The second officer didn't miss a beat. 'Of course, sir. Just see if you can take it a bit easier next time, eh?' He flicked a forefinger against the rim of his helmet. 'Remember, safety first and all that.'

'Thanks, I'll remember. Constable . . . ?'

'Medway, sir.'

'Constable Medway. Thank you. And I'll make sure I remember you and your family at this special time of the year.' He directed a look at the other man. 'And I'll make sure I remember your mate and all.'

'Thank you, sir.' Medway bent closer. 'Sorry for the misunderstanding; didn't recognise the motor.'

As he pulled away, Brendan caught the two policemen reflected in his rear-view mirror. They were still standing in the road, their faces almost touching. The local bloke, now all stabbing, pointing finger and snarls, was very obviously having the better of it. It was amazing how much of a focus the promise of a Christmas bonus – rather than the threat of a punch in the face, or something a whole lot worse – could give an officer.

*

Luke jumped out of the car and shoved back the high, corrugated iron gates of the scrap yard. Brendan drove in, sending the two Alsatians chained up by the lean-to office into a frenzy of barking.

He wrenched on the handbrake. What on earth was he going to tell his father?

He lifted his chin at Luke, signalling for his brother to help him shift Catherine off the back seat and into the office, then snapped at Pete Mac to deal with the blood inside the car.

For once, Pete Mac was glad to do as he was told. He definitely didn't fancy being there while they tried to talk to Gabriel. There was no chance he'd even listen while they explained how it had all been an accident. He never listened. Probably wouldn't even if Catherine herself was to tell him.

No, the best plan was for him to give the car a quick clean, then make himself scarce. Stay well out of Gabe's way for a bit. Give the bastard a chance to have a few drinks and calm himself down.

Brendan stood by his father's scratched and rickety desk, just as he had done a long, bewildering hour and a half ago.

'I swear to you, Dad,' he said, showing the palms of his hands, an innocent man. 'I haven't got any other explanation. It just all went wrong. Kessler's boy started struggling with Pete and the gun went off. And I really, on my life, do not know why Catherine was there. All I know is she was suddenly in the middle of it. And she got hurt. Truly, that's all I know.'

Gabriel O'Donnell covered his still unconscious daughter with the tartan rug that was usually draped over the bulging springs of the battered sofa on which his sons had carefully set her down. He knelt on the floor beside her and stroked his hand lovingly across her blood-caked cheek in an unwitting echo of the gesture made less than twenty-five minutes ago by Sammy Kessler.

In his other hand, Gabriel held a blood-smeared tumbler half full of Jameson's. 'Luke,' he said, his voice gruff and halting from trying to hold his emotion in check. 'Go to the Albion. Get Stonely. He knows to keep his mouth shut.'

Luke's eyes flicked towards the glass in his father's hand. As usual, the whiskey had been the first thing he'd reached for. He knew he had to talk to him before he poured too much more of the stuff down his neck. He looked again at his little sister, willing her to wake up.

'Can Brendan go and get him, Dad? There's something I need to talk to you about.'

Gabriel knocked back the rest of his drink in a single swallow, screwing up his eyes as the liquor hit the back of his throat, and banged his glass down on the floor. Then he took his daughter in his arms. 'For fuck's sake, one of you fill that glass, and the other one of you go and get Stonely. And be fucking quick about it.'

Brendan, as wary as his brother when their father had a drink in him, said softly, 'I'll fetch the doctor, Dad.'

As soon as Brendan had closed the door behind him, Luke tore his gaze away from Catherine, and started talking; the words spilling from his mouth in a tumble of fear of his father and the shame of betraying his sister. 'Dad, she's been seeing him for nearly two months.'

Gabriel didn't react.

'Sammy Kessler. It's why I didn't want us to go over there today. Why I tried to stop us. I didn't want any

48

trouble. I thought maybe we could talk to 'em. Work things out.'

Gently, Gabriel eased Catherine's head onto the arm of the grubby sofa, and scrabbled awkwardly to his feet. 'But you didn't think to stop her?'

Luke stared at the floor, unable now to face either his sister or his father. 'She wanted it kept secret.'

Gabriel walked slowly towards his son. 'Let me see if I understand you right, boy. I knock my pipe out earning a living, making sure you all have the good things in life, everything you want and need, and you keep secrets from me?' He cocked his head to one side. 'You *did* say it was a secret?'

'Yeah.' He could smell and feel his father's whiskey breath on his face, but still he couldn't look at him. 'She loved him, Dad. She showed me this photo. Down the coast somewhere. She knew she could show it to me. Knew I wouldn't shout at her. They'd gone on a day out. Just the two of them.'

'Why didn't you stop her seeing him?' Gabriel's voice was thin, defeated.

'I tried to stop us going –'

'Today. The day I told you to take . . .' Gabriel leaned back against the wall. 'Told you to . . .'

Slowly, Luke raised his head and looked directly into his father's face. 'She's dead isn't she?'

Luke's only answer was the sight of the tears streaming down his father's face.

The bottle of Jameson's in Gabriel's hand was now half empty, and logic was taking increasingly haywire paths through his shock- and booze-washed synapses. There were secrets, and lies, and things that didn't add up.

49

Things he couldn't understand. Luke had kept a secret from him. And so had Catherine. And the boys had let that fucking idiot, Pete Mac, who couldn't wipe his own arse without a map, actually handle the shot gun. All that was bad enough, and he knew he'd have to deal with it all – deal with all of them – but what was haunting him, what Gabriel couldn't get his head around, was Eileen telling him that Catherine was indoors with her and Patricia.

If only she'd told him, he wouldn't have let the boys take that stinking thing with them. And he'd have never let Pete Mac go anywhere near the place.

It was all Eileen's fault.

And now his little girl was dead, and he had to get Eileen out of the way while he cleaned up the mess.

He swallowed another mouthful of whiskey.

He should have had more control over them. Over Eileen, over Patricia, over Catherine . . .

But it was still him who had told them to take the gun. No matter how he tried to make it otherwise.

His tears flowed. Whatever else happened, Eileen must never, ever find out that he was as good as responsible for his own daughter's death.

Never.

He knelt down and tucked the tartan rug round Catherine's now cold, lifeless body, closed his eyes and asked God to take care of her soul.

Then he hauled himself to his feet. 'I walloped you boys once you were old enough to understand,' he said, staring down at the grubby, oil-stained lino. 'Kept you in order after your mother had spoiled you as babies. But Patricia and Catherine, your mother carried on letting them get away with things. And look where it's got them. Pat stuck with MacRiordan. And Catherine . . .'

He turned and looked at Luke, thrusting the glass into his face. 'You listen to me, boy. You do exactly as I say. You go and stop Brendan from bringing that drunken old bastard Stonely anywhere near this place, then the two of you, you get straight back here. And you bring Peter MacRiordan with you.'

As soon as Luke had left, Gabriel picked up his private telephone. 'Rosie, my love. Something's come up. I won't be coming round later. I . . .'

He tried to say something else, but couldn't. Sobs shuddered through his chest.

The woman on the other end of the telephone frantically tried to make sense of what was going on, but his blubbering and the booze were making his voice thick, his words barely audible. 'Gabe, darling, what's wrong? Talk to me, Gabriel, please. You're frightening me. Gabe, has Eileen found out?'

No answer.

'*Gabe. Has Eileen found out?*'

'No,' he managed to say. 'Not yet. God help me.'

Brendan and Luke were back in the office within ten minutes. Dr Stonely had had a win on the horses, and had been as drunk as a ship's rat trapped in the rum store, and Brendan hadn't been able to rouse him from his chair, let alone lure him away from the saloon bar of the Albion.

Their father had just put down the telephone after finishing a second brief, equally confused conversation. He'd been speaking to his sister, Mary, who lived on his stud farm in County Kildare with her husband, Sean Logan. Gabriel had been arranging for his sister to be unwell.

Actually, Mary was far from unwell; she was a tall,

51

strong woman – tough as a jockey's arse, most people would say – but she was always more than willing to help her brother. Sean Logan was a bit trickier, glad of Gabriel's patronage, but not exactly reliable with anything that might involve using his brains. But Mary would sort him out.

Gabriel motioned for his sons to be quiet and dialled yet another number.

'Eileen,' he slurred. 'It's me. Want you to go over and stay with Mary for a few days.'

He paused, listening.

'You know, women's things. Sean's as useless as a two bob watch. She needs you, Eileen. Right away. Brendan'll sort out the ferry tickets. And Pete Mac can run you to the station.'

Luke waved both his hands and mouthed, 'He's not here.'

'Sorry, my mistake. Pete's busy. Luke'll take you.'

Eileen crossed herself. Please, please don't let him tell me to take Catherine with me. From the sound of it, he'd hit the bottle early today and would explode with temper if he found out she wasn't there.

She could have wept with relief when Gabriel said, 'And don't worry yourself about leaving us lot to manage on our own for a few days. Catherine and Patricia can look after us.'

'Patricia's gone home to get Peter's tea ready for him,' she said, glad of an opportunity to tell the truth for once. 'And before you say anything, she didn't go home in the fog by herself. Stephen Shea dropped by with an envelope for you and so I got him to drive her.'

When Gabriel didn't answer immediately Eileen felt the need to say something, anything to fill the gap.

'You're always saying he's the best driver you've ever met.'

'Yeah, he's a good man, Stephen Shea.'

'Are you all right, Gabriel?'

He looked at his daughter's body. 'Me, Eileen? Sure, I'm just grand.'

Eileen went slowly upstairs to her and Gabriel's bedroom, took a small leather case from off the top of the wardrobe and started distractedly filling it with things for her stay at the stud farm. Sweaters, a thick tweed skirt. Then she took a selection of bras, panties and underslips from her dressing table, but paused, clasping them to her chest, as she wondered why she was being sent over to Ireland this time.

She knew it was nothing to do with Mary Logan. Eileen would be the last person her sister-in-law would want around the place if she were really ill. There'd been no love lost between them for years, not since Mary and her mother had accused Eileen of plotting to steal away their breadwinner, when she had started walking out with Gabriel when she was barely sixteen years of age.

Maybe he wanted her to take one of his brick-shaped packages over again – the packages that contained *none of your concern, woman*. But it was obvious to Eileen what they contained. She wasn't stupid, and she'd realised a long time ago that the stud was as much to do with hiding profits from the London businesses as it was about breeding Irish horses. For Gabriel it was a purely practical decision; working on the principle that a middle-aged woman wouldn't draw attention to herself and so was less likely to be searched, it simply made sense to him – regardless of what she might feel.

Or maybe he was planning something big and just wanted her out of the way. It wouldn't be the first time she'd been treated as an inconvenience when he had a crowd around the house to discuss *men's business*.

Patricia would be disappointed, but Eileen knew there was no point in trying to argue with Gabe – there was no point anyone trying to argue with him – especially not when he had a drink in him. So, she was going and that was final. There was always another day to go shopping. And Patricia was learning to understand disappointment as much as her mother.

Pete Mac sat on the grubby, pink, frilled bedspread grimacing each time the iodine-soaked cotton wool made contact with his bloody nose.

'Oi, watch it! Be careful, can't you?'

'Aw, my poor Pete.'

'Poor? I'm not poor. Why does everyone act like I'm some sort of charity case or something? Like they're doing me a favour all the time.' Pete Mac reached into his pocket, pulled out a roll of notes and tossed it onto the pillows. 'I don't think that makes me poor, darling, do you?'

She picked up the money and smiled. 'Course not, Pete.'

'Good. Now get your clobber off, Violet, I need a blow job to calm me down, girl. I've had a right fucking day of it.'

Chapter 4

Pete Mac lumbered into the office, pausing in the doorway to check Gabriel's mood. Seeing his father-in-law with his head in his hands, obviously nearing alcohol-induced unconsciousness, he held up the final edition of the *Evening Standard*. 'Here, see this? I reckon we pulled it off.'

'Where the hell have you been?' Luke, who was standing in the corner of the shabby lean-to, spoke to Pete Mac without once taking his eyes from the tartan rug covering the body of his sister.

'Had a few things to sort out, didn't I.' Pete Mac lifted his chin, proud of himself. 'Picked up a few bob from the girls – Anthony persuaded them back on the street where they belong – and then I . . . But never mind all that, have a listen to this.'

Pete Mac picked up the paper, cleared his throat and began to read – quietly so as not to disturb Gabriel. '"*Following reports of gunshots this afternoon, two police cars attended the scene. Officers discovered evidence of blood on the roadway, but soon established that this had come from a pigeon, which, apparently, had been struck by a passing vehicle.*"'

He winked at Luke. 'Nice touch that, mate, stomping that thing's brains out. Good thinking. Plant the evidence, eh?'

'No thanks to you,' muttered Luke.

Pete chose not to hear him. '"*The police are assuring locals . . .*"'

'I asked you where you've been, Pete.' This time Luke was looking right at him. 'I should have been here with Dad and Brendan, and . . .' His words trailed off as he turned and looked again at the tartan rug. 'But I had to drive Mum to the station so she could get the boat train.'

Pete Mac frowned, pulled his chin into his neck, and looked sideways at Luke. 'She's your mother, mate, not mine.'

Brendan, who'd been sitting on a straight-backed kitchen chair, with his elbows on his knees, his hands dangling between his legs, and his head bowed, sprang to his feet. He snatched the paper from Pete Mac's hand and threw it on the floor and grabbed Pete Mac by the collar. 'Ain't you even gonna ask how she is?'

Pete Mac pulled away from Brendan and glanced nervously over at Gabriel. He was slumped forward, his cheek squashed on the desk, snoring like a hog. 'Yeah, course, I didn't like to, you know, intrude. So, how is she?'

'She's fucking dead.'

Brendan only just managed to swerve out of the way as Pete Mac vomited in a spectacular arc right across the greasy carpet.

'For Christ's sake, Pete, be quiet.' Brendan was staring out of the window into the yard, smoking to cover the stench of vomit.

'But are you sure Gabe knows it was an accident? That I'd *never*, *ever* have intentionally hurt a hair of that girl's head? He's got to believe me.'

Luke, who was spreading sheets of the *Evening Standard* over the mess, paused and turned to Pete Mac. 'Please, Pete. Do as Brendan says. I mean it. You'll only 'make things worse if you don't keep your mouth shut.'

Pete Mac took a breath as if to speak, but just nodded.

Brendan pulled the window down a crack, flicked the cigarette outside then turned to face them. 'Okay. Luke's got Mum off on her way to Aunt Mary, and now we know – finally – where everyone is, and that no one's had a tug or nothing.'

At the mention that he might just possibly have been pulled in by the law, Pete Mac gulped back another rise of bile in his throat.

Brendan raked his fingers through his hair. 'Now, we can get on.'

'So, what we gonna do?'

Brendan shook his head. 'In your case, Pete? As you're told, that's what you're gonna do.' He pointed at his mouth. 'So, zip that and wait till you're spoken to. Right?' He picked up the phone and dialled.

'Hello, Stephen? It's Brendan. I need to see you. Over here at the scrap yard, mate. Soon as you can. All right?'

Stephen Shea was middle-aged, of average height and medium build. He had light brown hair, and a pleasant, if not particularly handsome, face. He wasn't loud, but was willing to have a bit of a laugh. He liked a pint, but wasn't given to getting drunk. He had a wife and a couple of grown-up kids, and lived in a neat terraced house off the Whitechapel Road. In other words, he was a regular, unremarkable sort of a bloke. But what set him apart was that, as far as cars were concerned, Stephen Shea was a genius: the best wheelsman in the whole East End, probably in the whole of the Southeast of England, according to those who knew about such things. That and the fact that he would have killed with his bare hands for his friend, Gabriel O'Donnell. Gabriel had looked after Sheila and the kids – Sheila, his childhood sweetheart, who'd married him despite the fact that she'd become Sheila Shea – when Stephen had been put away for a full handful for his part in a bungled bank job for which he'd taken the entire blame.

He hadn't even earned the gratitude of the two pathetically unsuccessful, small-time crooks who had screwed it all up, and who had since disappeared off the face of the earth – or rather to the south of Spain – warned off, according to rumour, by a furious Gabriel O'Donnell, who had very little time for amateur tosspots messing things up and getting the law sniffing round. Stephen still blushed at the mere thought of his involvement with the pair of knob-headed prats. But that was all in the past. Stephen had learned his lesson, and since that day had been employed by no one but the O'Donnells.

'Sorry, She,' he said, putting down the phone and looking longingly at the plate of corned beef hash, peas and carrots he hadn't even had the chance to taste. 'Got to pop out, babe.'

Sheila nodded with a little smile; she was nothing if not an understanding wife. 'Don't worry, love, I'll keep it warm for you. Make you some nice fresh gravy when you get back.' She touched his cheek with her lips. 'Time for just a quick cup of tea and a slice of cake before you go?'

'Sorry.'

'All right, go on. I'll see you later. And you look after yourself, yeah?'

Stephen Shea walked through the door of the lean-to office in the O'Donnells' scrap yard ten minutes later. He looked worried.

'If you're concerned about the takings from the street pitches, Brendan, on my life, I collected them all as usual, and dropped off the envelope round yours this afternoon. You can phone your mum, if you like. I had intended giving them to your dad like we'd arranged.' He couldn't help snatching a look at Gabriel, who was still sprawled, snoring across the desk. 'But he wasn't there. And then your mum asked me to drive your Patricia home because of the fog. And cos I didn't know how long it would take in this weather, I thought it'd be best to leave the dough there for when your dad got home later on.'

He hesitated before adding quietly, 'You don't have to worry. I told Eileen the envelope was full of receipts from that demolition job over Vicky Park way. And no need to worry about your Pat.' He was addressing Brendan rather than Pete Mac. 'She got home just fine.'

'Thanks, Steve. We appreciate you looking after her. And, as you can see, Dad got held up anyway.'

Stephen took another quick look at his boss. He was obviously out for the count. 'Yeah, and I don't wanna go upsetting him, Brendan. But if I can say – between us like – that Jewish mob what set up the betting pitches opposite ours. They were there again today. Opposite every single pitch. And every one of them had some big bloke minding 'em. West Indian looking some of them. Definitely not fellers I recognise from round here. I didn't know what to do. From what our blokes told me the takings are gonna be well down.'

'It's okay, Steve, Dad knows already.'

Stephen Shea looked relieved, and nodded as though that explained things. 'So, that's what you wanted to talk about.'

'No, this ain't about the takings, mate. Or the Kesslers.

Not even their minders.' Brendan pointed to the tartan rug, rubbed his hand over his eyes, and sighed wearily. 'Stephen. We need a favour, mate. A right big one.'

It was nine o'clock on Saturday morning, yet despite the amount of alcohol Gabriel had consumed in his office the day before, and the half-bottle of Bushmills he had swallowed when he had come round after his sons had eventually got him home last night, Gabriel was now stone cold sober. He was standing in the big, basement kitchen of the family home, a cosy room that would have fitted more easily into an Irish farmhouse than with the 'contemporary' show home look favoured by Patricia and Catherine. He was holding aside the starched, white lace curtain that usually shielded the shallow window set high in the wall.

He looked up, watching the passing feet of people going on their way to do their ordinary, uncomplicated things in their ordinary, uncomplicated lives. The fog was as bad as it had been the previous day, deadening the sound of the passing shoes as they struck the pavement, making them sound as if they were bound in cloth like the hooves of funeral horses, muffled out of respect for the dead.

He let go of the curtain, looked at his watch, and then went over to the blue and white china-decked dresser, close to the telephone. He glanced across at his two boys sitting at the table. They were staring down at their untouched tea and toast: their half-hearted attempt at having breakfast, their failed crack at acting as if everything was normal.

Scrap, Eileen's big tan dog nuzzled up to him, hoping for a treat, a scratch behind the ear, or maybe even a walk, but Gabriel wasn't one to waste time on pets at the best of times, and on a day like this he felt almost murderous. 'For fuck's sake,' he yelled. 'Get this thing away from me, will you?'

Luke grabbed the animal by the collar. 'He's missing Mum.'

Gabriel was about to snap another obscenity at his son, when the telephone rang. Even though he had been expecting it, he still looked horrified.

He checked his watch again, took a moment to compose himself, picked up the phone, listened, and then let it fall from his hand.

As the receiver swung and twisted back and forth on its cord, knocking against his leg then against the side of the dresser then against his leg again, Gabriel closed his eyes, crossed himself and mouthed for God to forgive him.

Luke hurried over to his father and replaced the receiver gently in its cradle.

'Dad?'

'I know it's how it was arranged.' Gabriel's eyes were still closed. 'How we had to do it, but I still can't believe it's over. Not so soon.' He was speaking more to himself than to either of his sons. 'She's gone, God love her.'

Luke tried to steer Gabriel back to the table, to sit him down, but he pushed his son away and picked up the phone again.

Luke looked over at Brendan, but Brendan shook his head.

'Leave him,' he murmured.

Gabriel pressed his lips together, took a deep breath and dialled. 'Sean, it's Gabriel. I need to speak to Eileen.'

There was a pause, and then he spoke again. 'Eileen, I'm sorry to have to do this by phone, but there's some bad news.'

He couldn't go on.

Brendan took the receiver from his father's hand.

'Mum, it's me, Brendan. You'd better sit down. I've got something to tell you. No, please, let me finish, this ain't easy. You've got to come home. Right away. There's been an accident. A bad one. It was this morning. In the fog. It's Catherine. She's –'

He stopped speaking, trying to make out what was going on at the other end of the line. 'Mum?'

'Gabe, it's Mary here, whatever's wrong?'

'It's not Dad, Aunt Mary, it's me. Brendan. What's happened to Mum?'

'Your mammy's fainted. But she'll be all right. Sean's seeing to her right now, getting her a drink of water. Tell me, what's all this fuss about?'

'Aunt Mary, I've got some really bad news. It's Catherine. She's been in a car crash. A serious one. The car burst into flames. There was a terrible fire. And poor little Catherine . . .' Brendan gulped back his tears. 'Aunt Mary, she didn't get out in time. Aunt Mary, Catherine's dead.'

Pete Mac stood outside the door of his house in Jubilee Street, or rather the house that Gabriel had bought for him and Pat as soon as he had found out she was pregnant, and that they were – of course, no question about it, no point even mentioning it – getting married.

A. S. A. fucking P.

He stared at the immaculately black-leaded door furniture and sucked noisily at his teeth. He knew that having a whole house to themselves was a luxury that few couples in the East End could enjoy, especially couples as young as him and Pat. What with all the slum clearances, and the housing shortages that were still being blamed by the authorities on the war, and the overcrowding and multiple occupancy of homes that was simply accepted by most people as a way of life, they were genuinely privileged to have so much space to kick about in.

But Pete MacRiordan loathed the bloody place more than he could say. It was so nice, so tidy, so rotten, well, *just so*. Like Pat and her sodding knick-knacks, her poncy curtains, and her fancy bone china cups with their dinky little saucers.

Why couldn't she just leave the washing-up in the sink for once? Forget about it till he'd gone off down the pub? She could clear up then till her heart's bloody content. Why did she have to fuss about doing stuff while he was still around?

But that wasn't a question he was allowed to ask, because it didn't make sense, not in the world of the O'Donnells it didn't. Because in their world the O'Donnells did exactly as they liked. But they told *you* what to do, and *you* did what you were told.

It was as simple as that.

Take this performance today. He'd said to them at the yard last night: why did it have to be him who had to tell Pat? Why couldn't one of them tell their precious sister the news? He knew she'd take it much better from one of them. But they hadn't even bothered to answer him.

It made him so mad, he felt like telling them what they could do with their so-called 'family business', and with the 'favours' they reckoned they did him all the time. But he couldn't, because now they had him good and proper.

It was bad enough when the only thing they'd had over him was him getting Pat up the duff before they got married. As if he'd have even dreamed of marrying the miserable bitch without them forcing him into it. Why he'd ever let her talk him into playing Vatican roulette, he'd never know, but he'd never do it again, that was for sure. It was French Letters or nothing from now on. Preferably nothing while he had young Violet to turn to. But now he'd made the mistake with the sawn-off, the O'Donnells really had something over him. They'd be on his back for the rest of his natural. It was a fucking depressing thought. He felt really sorry about what had happened to Catherine – she wasn't a bad kid – definitely, the best one of the O'Donnells. But he hadn't wanted to take the gun in the first place. That was Gabriel's fault. But would any of them listen? Course not. And it was why he had to do as he was told. It was a bloody farce.

Last night, when he'd got in, he'd had to tell Patricia some old nonsense about a lump of scrap falling on him to explain away the bloody nose and all the bruising round his eyes. As if he ever shifted any scrap. Then, this morning, he'd had to feed her another load of old cobblers about why he was going into the yard so early. That was stupid in itself; he never went in before eleven. Especially on a Saturday.

As it was, Pat had hardly batted an eyelid over his injuries. Self-centred cow. But she'd had plenty to say this morning all right. She said *he* was selfish, waking her up so early. She didn't feel well. Felt sick or something. Like he cared.

Then he'd had to go to a phone box and call Brendan to make sure they all got their timings right, for when they talked about the 'accident'. After that he'd had to waste nearly half an hour driving around, just to account for the time it would have taken him to get into the yard, and for them to have told him about what had happened.

They reckoned all this palaver gave them all alibis. But if Shea was as bloody clever as they all said he was, then why did they need a cover?

And now he had to face Patricia with the next act in the circus.

He opened the front door, threw back his head and stared up at the pristine whiteness of the embossed paper on the hall ceiling.

Here goes. He puffed out his cheeks then called out, 'Pat, it's me, girl. I've got a bit of news for you.'

'But she can't be dead.' Patricia stood in the hall, shaking her head, refusing to believe it. She was wrapped in a thick candlewick dressing gown and had soft, warm slippers on her feet, but she was trembling as if she were standing there stark naked. 'She's seventeen years old.'

'*Was* seventeen years old, girl,' he said, with a sympathetic pulling down of his mouth.

Patricia felt as if she'd slipped into some strange parallel universe like you saw in the films, where everything was turned on its head, and where nothing made proper sense any more. 'And she couldn't even drive.'

'She could, Pat.'

Her head jerked up as if a string had been pulled. 'What? What're you talking about?'

'Luke had been teaching her.' He sighed disapprovingly, as if this were all his brother-in-law's fault. 'Doing it on the q.t. like, wasn't he. On that bit of wasteland behind the yard. It was his car she nicked to take out on her little jaunt. Silly girl, she wasn't experienced enough to drive in even good weather conditions. Not without supervision, she weren't. But in this fog . . . Well, it was a disaster waiting to happen, wasn't it, girl?' This time his disapproval was targeted on his young sister-in-law. 'Only, lucky she was by herself when she hit that wall, if you ask me. It would have been terrible if she'd hurt anyone else. In the accident.'

Patricia said nothing. She turned away from him and walked along the hallway towards the kitchen. She was going to throw up again, but this time it was nothing to do with morning sickness.

'Here, Pat,' he called after her. 'Any chance of a bit of breakfast, girl? Me belly feels like me throat's been cut.'

Pete Mac sat at the kitchen table. He wasn't exactly thrilled. After getting up so early, he was having to scrape by with a cup of tea and a bit of toast – hardly a breakfast for a man. And he'd had to make it himself. But even he had to admit that Pat did look a bit rough. She was still grasping the side of the sink, staring down at the water gurgling its way down the plughole.

He slurped the last of his tea, smacked his lips, and then wiped the back of his hand across his mouth. 'I'll have to be on my way now, girl,' he said. 'Got to get back into work, cos your lot are gonna be busy with other things today ain't they? Sorting out the funeral and that. So I'll have to be up the yard to take charge of the business.'

Pat stepped towards him. Her breathing was shallow as if she'd been running. 'Drop me round Mum's, Pete.'

'Aw, bugger.' Pete Mac stretched his lips across his teeth, grimacing and tutting at his own foolishness. 'That's something else I was supposed to tell you. Your mum, she's –'

'What?' Patricia leaned back against the sink, sweat

66

beading on her forehead, unsure of how much longer she could stay upright. 'What's wrong with, Mum?'

Pete Mac looked affronted. 'Pat, will you, please, let me finish?'

'I'm telling you, Pete, if you don't –'

'All right. Your mum's over in Kildare with your Aunt Mary –'

Patricia opened her mouth but Pete Mac didn't let her get a word in; he had a story to get right. '– who's ill or something. That's your Aunt Mary, I mean, not your mum. She's fine.'

With that, he stood up and left, leaving his dirty plate and cup on the table.

Patricia turned round, opened the tap and stuck her head under the cold water, letting it rush through her hair and down her neck, not caring that her dressing gown was getting soaked through.

He must have got it wrong. He must have. She couldn't be dead. She couldn't. Not Catherine . . .

Pete Mac stood outside the house pulling in lungsful of damp, foggy air to relieve his suffocation. He lit a cigarette and tapped his knuckles agitatedly against the wall, considering the day ahead of him. Maybe he should nip into the yard and phone Gabriel, let him know he was there, show him he was making an effort at a time of family tragedy.

He drew on his cigarette, holding down the smoke. He was going to have to come up with something to try and get himself back in Gabriel's good books.

Chapter 5

Sammy Kessler hadn't heard a word from Catherine in well over a week. He was getting worried, really worried, and he wasn't feeling very proud of himself. Say she'd been hurt worse than he'd thought? He knew the gun had gone off, and that there was blood. But she couldn't have been that badly hurt. She just couldn't.

Maybe her dad had found out about them and had forbidden her from ever speaking to him again. He knew how his own father would react if he ever found out about them. Worst of all was the thought that she'd been so disgusted with him for leaving her to the mercy of those men, whoever they were, that it was she who never wanted to see or speak to him again – regardless of what her father thought.

If that was the way she felt, he couldn't say he blamed her. But he had to know.

He'd stood in the call box, just around the corner from his dad's haulage yard every night at six o'clock, waiting for the telephone to ring. They'd worked out their system soon after they'd met. Catherine would go to a friend's house, or another phone box, or even use the phone in her own home if the coast were clear, and she'd call him. Then they could speak to each other, like any other young couple, but without anybody knowing what they were up to.

Tonight, Sammy had been waiting for over a quarter of an hour, pretending every now and then to make a call, in a half-hearted effort to placate an angry looking man, who kept banging on the glass with the flat of his hand before finally giving up and stomping off, leaving a string of obscenities behind him. As far as Sammy was concerned, the man could have threatened to punch him on the nose and he still wouldn't have stirred from that phone box. He wouldn't even have let him in if he'd pleaded that he wanted to call 999. Sammy's need was greater. He had to speak to Catherine, to find out if she was all right, and to try and get her to understand why he'd panicked and run away.

Not knowing was driving him mad. He kept waking in the early hours, in a cold sweat, horrified by nightmarish visions of what could have happened to her after those men had taken her away. The dreams were becoming unbearable. Strange hands touching her body, her eyes pleading for mercy because she couldn't scream for help because of the gag they'd tied round her mouth. And the blood oozing around her. It was exhausting him. If he didn't do something soon people would start noticing. His mum would go on about him not getting enough rest. His dad would start accusing him of not pulling his weight. Then they'd start asking awkward questions.

He turned his wrist to catch the dim light from the bulb above his head, and looked at his watch.

Who was he kidding? She wasn't going to call. Not now. Not ever. Not till he explained. So, this was it. His last chance. He'd been putting it off all week, but the only option he had left was to try and contact Catherine through her brother – Luke, the one she said she could talk to. The one who knew that she and Sammy were friends, and that they were sort of seeing one another. But he had to be careful. Keep it light. Much as Catherine might think of him, her brother was still one of the O'Donnell boys.

Sammy flipped up the telephone directory, and searched through the listings for O'Donnell.

Sod it. There were half a dozen of them living at the Stepney end of the Mile End Road. Why hadn't he asked her for her full address? Because he hadn't needed it before, that's why. It wasn't as if her mum was planning on inviting him round for Christmas dinner. He'd just have to call all of them.

He struck lucky on his fourth attempt.

'Hello, can I speak to Luke O'Donnell, please?'

'Who wants him?'

He hadn't thought this through. 'Er, John. John Smith.' *John Smith*? Was he sure?

'Hang on, I'll get him.'

He heard some muttering, then someone said in a flat, dull voice, 'Ta, Brendan,' then, 'Ye'llo? Luke here.'

'Luke, I'm a friend of Catherine's. I think she might have told you about me. My name's Sammy.'

Luke turned his back to the table where Pete Mac was sitting staring at him with unashamed curiosity.

'Sorry, John, but I can't speak right now,' he said. 'Gimme a number where I can reach you and I'll call you later on.'

'Luke, please, listen. I need to know. Has your dad found out, or –'

'Honestly, this really ain't the time for this, John. Just gimme a number.'

The door at the top of the basement stairs opened and Gabriel stumbled down into the kitchen. 'Who's that on the phone?' His voice was thick from drinking.

Luke hurriedly scribbled down the number Sammy gave him and slammed down the receiver. 'No one, Dad.'

'Nothing to do with tomorrow?'

70

'No, nothing.'

Pete Mac folded his arms. 'It was some geezer, wasn't it, Luke? Reckons his name was *John Smith* if you can credit it. Sounds well monkey to me. Who's ever heard of anyone really called *John Smith*? Not keeping any secrets from us are you, Luke? Feller calling you under a false name? What's all that about?'

Gabriel steadied himself with both hands against the table and looked into Pete Mac's face. His eyes were bloodshot and his focus was far from sharp, but his expression was clear enough. 'My wife's upstairs in our bed breaking her heart, while my daughter – your wife – tries to comfort her. And I'm going to bury my other daughter tomorrow morning. And we both know how she really died, don't we? So, do you think this is the time for your ignorant remarks?'

Pete Mac rose to his feet. 'Maybe it'd be better if I left.'

'You got something right for once,' Brendan hissed at him under his breath.

Pete Mac peered out at the world – or rather up at the grubby, cobwebbed ceiling – through swollen slits of eyes. He was on his back, in a lumpy bed, and his head was banging like a steam hammer.

And there was a bad smell, stale and musty, filling his nostrils. It was as if something had been soaked through, and then left in a screwed up heap to dry, far away from even a waft of fresh air.

Where the hell was he?

He heard soft snoring close to his ear, and, raising his head as far as the pain allowed, he swivelled his gaze sideways, trying not to move the rest of his body.

Violet?

He levered himself up into a sitting position, and hunted around for his watch on the clothes-strewn chair that served as a bedside table.

Quarter past eleven.

He wondered, for a brief, self-deluding moment if it was eleven at night, but the pale winter light slanting through the gap at the top of the curtains, where the wire drooped from a single, wonky nail, told him otherwise.

Shit! It was gone eleven o'clock in the morning. He'd been at Violet's all bloody night. And the funeral mass had started over an hour ago. And he was over in fucking Shadwell. He'd have to go straight to the cemetery.

He chucked the bedcovers off him, making Violet, who had still been asleep, wake up and begin complaining indignantly as the cold air hit her shoulders.

She stretched his name to three whining syllables. 'P-e-te. What d'you think you're doing?'

'I'm getting dressed, you daft cow. What d'you think I'm doing, tap dancing?'

'But your shirt . . .' The whine in her voice had levelled off into a sneer of disgust.

He picked it up off the floor and discovered it to be the pungent source of the really unpleasant stench. 'What the hell's happened to this?'

Violet snuggled back down under the blankets. 'Don't you remember?'

He turned and looked at her as if she were stupid. 'If I did, would I be asking?'

She smiled saucily over the edge of the covers. 'You brought a bottle of champagne round last night. And a bottle of Scotch. And after we – well, you – had polished off most of the whisky, you got all, you know . . .' She turned her head and looked sideways at him in what she thought was a sultry imitation of the pictures she'd seen in her film magazines. 'Frisky. You told me to take off my clothes. And then you sprayed the bubbles all over me.'

She nibbled her bottom lip to stifle the giggle that was threatening to erupt. 'Trouble was, quite a lot of it went over you an' all. But you didn't care; you were too busy licking it off me bits to bother about your shirt. I wanted to rinse it out for you, but you were ever so insistent.'

She reached out and cupped his balls in her hand, squeezing them gently. 'Like a wild tiger you was, Pete, you filthy sod. Here, how about coming back to bed for a rematch?'

He pulled away impatiently. 'Leave off, Violet. Can't you see I'm in a hurry? Now get up and run an iron over this for me, while I stick me head under the tap and try and get rid of this bloody hangover.'

Pete Mac abandoned, rather than parked, his car across the gates of the Catholic cemetery. He took a quick squint round, looking for the mourners, but could see only a group of formally clad men from the funeral directors, who were enjoying a smoke outside the chapel.

Bloody hell, not the chapel . . . Hadn't the requiem mass at St Joseph's been enough for them? Probably not, knowing Eileen. She'd be expecting every bit of knee bending, bell ringing and hymn singing that Father Shaunessy had to offer, and – just in case someone missed something – in as many venues as the old ponce could come up with. And, knowing him, he'd be more than happy to oblige. Anything to get a bit of extra wedge out of Gabriel.

Pete Mac puffed his way along the short path to the chapel, swearing that he would get himself back in shape, and stop drinking so much – first thing tomorrow morning. It would, after all, be impolite to refuse a glass or two at the wake. And, as he'd already missed the bit at the church, he'd better be on his best behaviour for the rest of the day. Keep his head down and play the game, do his bit as the caring, dutiful son-in-law.

He paused outside the chapel, pulled out a screwed up handkerchief from somewhere deep in his topcoat pocket and swiped it over his face. Despite the bitingly cold wind, and the heavy, grey-yellow sky, filled with the threat of snow, the short run had made him sweat, and had caused the stench from his shirt to waft up from his armpits like a miasma from some fetid, bodily swamp. Patricia was gonna just love that. Then he smarmed down the orange springs of his still damp hair with both hands, nodded to the undertakers, and wrenched open the heavy wooden door.

The priest was well away, as if he'd been going at it for some time, and the place was packed, including the side and central aisles, where it was standing room only. As busy as Upton Park when the Hammers were playing at home.

Pete Mac looked across the sea of black clad, heaving shoulders, the sobbing women with their veils and hats, and the misty-eyed men in their heavy winter overcoats. On one side of the chapel he noted a huddle of impressively senior coppers; and at the back, a clutch of cute little birds – friends of Catherine's no doubt, *very nice* – and spotted enough flattened noses, chiv marks and cauliflower ears, belonging to faces from both sides of the river, to start a full-blown bout of gang warfare. It was funny how a funeral had the so-called hard men coming over all sentimental; Pete Mac didn't get it himself, he thought it was all a bit effeminate. But, like he'd told himself, needs must. He had to take his 'rightful' place next to his poor, grieving wife.

God help him.

But how was he supposed to get to the front where the O'Donnells were sitting without having to barge his way through and make a right show of himself?

To his surprise, apart from the odd wrinkled nose, and a slight withdrawing as he passed by, most people seemed to be too lost in their own thoughts to bother with Pete Mac's lateness, or even the whiff from his shirt, and he managed to slide in beside Patricia with unexpectedly little fuss. Although a single look from her prat of a brother, Brendan, was enough of a warning to let Pete Mac know that he should expect rather more of a reaction a bit later on.

While Pete Mac was wedging himself between Patricia and Luke, wondering how long he'd have to sit on such an uncomfortable, arse-numbing bench, the three tearful, red-eyed young women at the back, whom he had rightly identified as friends of Catherine, were equally, if differently, preoccupied.

'Wonder which one's her boyfriend then, Jan,' sniffed the blondest of the three.

Janet dabbed at her nose with a soggy tissue and shook her head. 'He won't be here, Paul,' she sniffed back. 'He's Jewish.'

Pauline, taken aback, spoke more loudly than she'd intended. 'So?'

Bernadette, the third of the girls, and the only one of them from a Catholic family – though a long-since lapsed one – nudged Pauline in the side. 'Keep it down you two,' she said. She might not have been to mass for years – actually, not since the day her nan had insisted that her mother have her head wetted at the font – but she retained a fearful respect for religious practices. 'We *are* in a holy place, you know.'

'But what diff—'

'Don't you know anything, Pauline?' Bernadette swiped her eyes with the back of her gloved hand and leaned in closer to her friends so no one else could hear. 'That's what all that secret business was about. If Cathy's family had found out she was seeing a Jewish boy they'd have killed her.'

'Here, maybe it wasn't an accident. You don't think they did kill her, do you? You know, found out about them, and did her in.'

Janet, momentarily forgetting herself, rolled her eyes and sighed irritably. 'You really are dumb, ain't you, Paul? As if her own family would kill her. Bernie meant they'd go mad at her and put a stop to her seeing him.'

'Yeah, but you've got to admit, it is a bit fishy. I mean, she couldn't even drive, could she? So, why was she in the driver's seat of the car?'

Now it was Janet who leaned closer. 'That's where you're wrong again. If you must know, she could drive. I heard someone saying earlier. She'd been learning. With her brother. Luke. Him up there at the front.'

'He's bloody gorgeous.'

Bernadette looked appalled. 'Pauline, I'm sure you don't need reminding again, but we are at a funeral.'

'Yeah, I know, but look at him. I wouldn't say no.' She stood up, following the example of the rest of the congregation. 'I'd love to meet him. Do you think we'll be welcome at the do afterwards, Jan?'

'Oh, yeah, knowing Catherine's dad's views on us three, we'd be about as welcome as a dose of the pox.'

As everyone filed out of the chapel towards the graveside, Pete Mac thought it wise to pre-empt any potential hostilities between him and Brendan.

'Surprised there's no newspaper people here,' he said, drawing Brendan to one side. 'Thought they'd want to at least report the accident, it being so tragic and everything.'

Brendan closed his eyes for a moment, dragging his fingers down his cheeks, then slowly buttoned his overcoat up to his throat. 'They've been warned off.' His voice was as cold as the wind that was now carrying the first flurries of snow, and it certainly didn't invite further conversation, but Pete Mac wasn't one to take a hint.

He flashed a simian grin showing pale pink gums and bits of the saveloy and chip supper that he'd shared with Violet the night before that were still stuck between his teeth. 'What, too many coppers here who want to keep their privacy? Who don't want to be seen at a do like this?'

Brendan felt too wrung out for this. What was wrong with MacRiordan that he didn't get anything right? He shook his head. 'Arse about face as ever, Pete. Why shouldn't police attend a *do* like this? It's a funeral. And Dad's a benefactor to all sorts of charities, and there's all sorts of people who wanna pay their respects to the family. All right? Plain enough for you?'

'Yeah, course. But why worry about the papers then?'

'Who said anyone's worried about them?' Brendan stared at his brother-in-law. Didn't the tosspot understand anything? Did nothing get through his thick skull? 'Clever people don't want their mooeys splashed all over the headlines. Not like them so-called Robin Hood heroes you read about in the *Evening News*.' He curled his lip in a sneer and spoke in a contemptuous imitation of an elderly woman. '*They've always looked after me and my old mum and we never have to worry about leaving our doors unlocked cos the streets are all safe with them around. No. That ain't our style.*' His voice was back to his own. 'And you should fucking well know that by now. We don't want a poppy show, we want privacy. Especially on a day like this. So, if only for the sake of Mum and Pat, break the habit of a lifetime and keep your trap shut. All right? Now get over there and stand with your wife, where you belong, God help her.'

Chapter 6

The hollow-eyed O'Donnells had led the mourners into the Star and Compass, the pub nearest the Catholic cemetery, a full half-hour earlier, but the proceedings were still very subdued. A wake for an elderly person – someone who'd had a good innings, whose life you could celebrate – that was one thing, but for a seventeen-year-old girl? That was another thing altogether. The food had hardly been touched, glasses barely lifted, and not a single note of an Irish ballad had been heard.

Eileen had been sitting in her own private silence. Since returning from Kildare the day after the accident, she had uttered only the words necessary to retain that solitude, to keep others at the distance she needed. But now she had plenty to say.

Ignoring Patricia and her sister-in-law, Mary Logan, she rose shakily to her feet and made her way over to Gabriel.

Pushing her way through the sombre group of awkward-looking men, who were standing with her husband, Eileen grabbed his wrist with such force that his eyes popped wide with astonishment.

'Why couldn't you let her live like other girls?' Eileen's voice came out as a tortured keen. 'Then there'd have been no need for her to tell lies. No need to go driving cars on her own. Going out and about God knows where.'

Gabriel, swallowing back the curses that were filling

his mouth, said, quietly and politely, 'Excuse us, gentlemen.'

The men, putting Eileen's extraordinary behaviour
down to grief – no one, not even his wife, spoke to Gabriel
O'Donnell like that – nodded and muttered a ragged
chorus of: *sure*, *of course*, *we're fine here*, and turned
their attention to their drinks and a discussion of the
racecard at Newbury.

Gabriel gripped her by the upper arm, and steered her
over to a table in the far corner, indicating with a tip of his
head for the occupants to move.

He sat her down with a shove, and stood over her,
keeping his back to the room. 'You dare talk to me about
lies? It was you who lied, Eileen. You knew she was going
out. You told me she was indoors when she wasn't.'

'She was a young girl.' Eileen fumbled at her cuff for
her handkerchief. 'She wanted to see her friends. Have a
bit of fun.'

'What, like Patricia did, you mean?'

She looked up into the green, gold-flecked eyes of the
man she had once loved more than life itself. 'You drove
her to this, Gabriel O'Donnell. And you drove me to lying
to you. You didn't let her move or breathe.'

He shook his head. 'No, Eileen. I won't let you do this
to me. It's you who was in the wrong.'

'So, you were right, were you, making Luke lie to me,
not letting him tell me about teaching Catherine to drive?'
Images of her happy, laughing child, spinning around the
house like a top, were making Eileen giddy. 'I'd never
have agreed to her doing that at her age.'

'Get up.' He cupped his hand under her elbow and
steered her over to the bar, where Luke was standing with
Brendan and Pete Mac.

'Luke,' said Gabriel, 'tell your mother why we kept Catherine's driving a secret.'

Luke gulped at his drink, giving himself time. What should he say? What did his father *want* him to say?

'She wanted to surprise you, Mum.' Another sip of his drink, a bit more time. 'Pass her test so she could take you and Pat out shopping and that.'

Eileen took her son's face in her hands. 'This is your sister's wake, Luke. If you're telling me more lies. If you're . . .' Her words dried up, her legs gave way, and Eileen O'Donnell collapsed on the pub floor: a shattered heap of black wool crepe and bitter tears of resentment.

Gabriel scooped her up as if she weighed little more than a child. 'Luke, get Stephen. It's time me and your mother were leaving.'

'All right, Dad, I'll come with you.'

In less than an hour, Eileen had been persuaded up to bed with a glass of water and a couple of the tranquillisers Dr Stonely had given her on her return from Ireland. Luke and his father were sitting at the kitchen table, much as they had been doing every day and night since what they now unfailingly referred to as the 'accident'. It was as if their denial of the reality of events somehow reshaped the truth of things, made them fit a more comfortable, or, at least, a more acceptable pattern.

Gabriel was in his shirtsleeves, his black tie loosened, and his braces dangling from his shoulders. He was nursing a very large whiskey, staring down into the glass as if it might hold the cure for his broken heart.

'Dad,' Luke said eventually. 'Can I talk to you?'

Gabriel let out a long, slow sigh. 'If you can tell me

how to get drunk, so I can forgot this whole bloody mess, son, then talk away.'

'I'll pour you another drink.'

Gabriel held up his half-pint tumbler. 'I've got about a quarter of a bottle in here already.' He sipped at the liquor then took a bigger mouthful. 'Go on then,' he said, without looking at his son, 'top it up.'

Luke rocked his chair onto its back legs and lifted the bottle from the dresser behind him. He filled his father's glass almost to the brim and poured himself a double.

'Dad, someone told me something this morning. And it's made me think.' He flicked a look at his father. He looked as if his spirit had been drained out of him. His usually arrogantly handsome face was shadowed with loss. He could only hope he was listening, because he wouldn't have the courage to say this again. 'I reckon that since the accident it'd be all too easy for things to get out of control. That they could turn into something really serious.'

Gabriel hadn't shifted his gaze from his glass. 'Serious?' Even his voice betrayed his exhaustion. 'You're right there, boy. Because someone's gonna pay for this. Pay with everything they've got.'

'That's what I mean. And only you can stop it happening.'

Gabriel snorted, a soft roar. 'And, tell me, why should I do that?'

'It was an accident, Dad.'

'If she hadn't been with *him*, it would never have happened.'

Luke, wary of his father, but knowing he had no choice, risked going on. 'I've been thinking that maybe we should call a truce.'

Gabriel let out a humourless puff of laughter. 'A what?'

82

'With the Kesslers.'

Gabriel's hand flashed across the table. He grabbed Luke by the collar of his jacket, twisting it until it was tight up against his son's throat.

Luke could do nothing other than try to catch his breath. His father was capable of hurting people badly enough when he was sober, but, when he'd had drink in him, he was capable of anything.

'When I was younger than you,' Gabriel snarled, his face so close that Luke could see the flecks of saliva gathering in the corner of his father's mouth. 'I took a chance. A massive chance. I left your mother back home and came to this country, a strange place I'd never been to before, to see if I could get us a better life. A decent place to rear a family. And what did I find when I got here? Pubs and lodgings that had signs in the window saying "No dogs, no blacks, no Irish". I wasn't Mr Gabriel O'Donnell, a willing, hard-working man. No, I was Paddy. Mick. A stupid bog-trotting fool. Someone who was only given work because I was so poor I was prepared to do anything, and for less pay than anyone else. I learned my lesson then that nobody was going to make my dreams come true for me, boy. So I showed them all that I'd do it for myself. Every fucking one of them.'

He let go of Luke, shoving him back in his chair. His sudden rush of energy spent.

'And you want me to do deals with the Kesslers? The fuckers who took away my child? The scum who think they can come back here and take away everything I've ever worked for?'

'It wouldn't be like that. They'd be more or less working for us. We'd make sure we kept control of things. Protected our interests.' Luke was speaking quickly, spilling out his words before his courage failed him. 'Have them buy moody scrap off us, say. At the right price. Or something else that'd tie them in. Make sure they were involved, but in a way that they couldn't cause any trouble for us'

Gabriel sniffed dismissively. 'You have been thinking, son.'

'Look, Dad, you of all people, you *know* how this sort of thing gets out of hand. You take that first step and that's it. You can't go back. You're over the line. And then, before you know it, you're at war. Like with the mob over in Bermondsey. Businesses got neglected, some even ruined, but worst of all, people were killed, remember?'

'Remember? Yeah, I remember. People were killed. Just like your sister was.'

'And that's exactly what I'm talking about. Taking the gun with us, it was the step too far. The step that pushed it over the edge.'

Gabriel felt the guilt surging up in his chest. He looked his son directly in the eye. 'Are you saying,' his voice was low, 'it's my fault Catherine's dead?'

'No, Dad,' Luke lied, bowing his head, knowing his father should never have given them the gun. 'What I'm saying is, do you wanna start something with the Kesslers. Have it all go off, and risk the business, and risk losing me as well? And Brendan? And the men who've been so loyal to you – they'd be targets right away. Men like Barry Ellis. Kevin Marsh. Stephen Shea. Anthony. And how about all the other blokes who work for you? And their families. And d'you wanna put Mum at risk? And Patricia . . .'

Luke ran his tongue around his parched lips. Should he be saying this? Why not, it was the reason he'd even thought of such a wild idea in the first place, why he was brave enough to be saying any of these things to his drink-fuelled, grief-maddened father.

'Dad, you know earlier, when I said someone told me something?'

No reaction other than another mouthful of whiskey.

'It was Patricia. While we were waiting to see if Pete Mac was gonna turn up for the Mass.'

'She told you what? That she married a fool?'

'No. That she's expecting.' He raised his hands. 'I know, I should have let her tell you herself. She ain't even told Pete Mac yet. But then nobody's acting exactly normal at the minute, are they?'

'Patricia's expecting a baby?' Gabriel was blinking as if someone had turned on the lights without warning him. 'When?'

'I'm not sure. But we've got to give this a try, Dad. For all our sake's, but especially for Patricia's.' Luke meant it. He wouldn't wait until there were more guns being flashed about and lives being threatened. He wouldn't let anyone harm a hair of Patricia's head. He'd swear to that on Catherine's grave.

'How's Mum?' It was Brendan, trudging down the stairs into the basement kitchen. He looked as exhausted as his father.

'She's resting. Dad got her to take some of them pills that Stonely gave her.'

Brendan dropped heavily onto the chair next to Gabriel's. 'Give us a glass of that.'

Luke tipped back and took another tumbler from the dresser. 'Everyone still down the Star?'

'Yeah, but Patricia was feeling a bit rough, so –'

'A bit rough?' Gabriel snapped. 'What's wrong with her?'

Brendan frowned, Christ the old man was losing it lately. 'Don't worry. She was upset, that's all. Like the rest of us. So I dropped her off home. Aunt Mary went with her to make sure she was all right.' He took his drink from Luke, eased off his tie and settled back in his chair. 'She'll be more use to her than Pete Mac.'

Luke poured himself a refill. 'Brendan, I've been talking to Dad.' He was speaking slowly now, cautious with his words. 'About how we should give it a go – cooling things down with the Kesslers. Before they get out of hand.'

Brendan slammed down his glass, spilling whiskey over the table. 'You *what*?'

'Look, we all know it'd be easy for us to go crazy. But like I was saying to Dad, think how it all went wrong with that team from over South London. They steamed in here with all them war surplus guns that were floating about, and –'

'And then Dad sorted it out.'

'Course he sorted it out.' Luke snatched a quick look at his father. 'Eventually. But how much damage did it do the business? And how many people got hurt in the meantime? Really hurt. It makes sense for us to use our loaf over this, Brendan. We're doing well. Why risk losing any of it? This way we keep the power, and keep them in order at the same time. We'll be in charge, know exactly what they're up to. Plus a good weed out of anything they make. What do you think?'

'I'll tell you what I think, Luke. I think you've lost your fucking mind. On the day of your sister's funeral you reckon we should let them arseholes in on our business. Put our hands up in fucking surrender? Just like that?'

'No, not surrender. More like a truce. But on *our* terms. We say what we want, and what we're prepared to let them do. We set the rules. It's just like they'll be working for us. We win all round.'

'Dad,' Brendan appealed to his father. 'You can't tell me you're thinking about going along with this crap.'

Gabriel spoke for the first time since Brendan had joined them. 'What if I am?'

'Then I don't think you understand what he's saying.'

'Have I got eejit written here?' he asked, pointing to his forehead. 'I'm thinking about it, that's all. If they show proper respect, do what I say, then maybe I'll let them have a few crumbs off our table.'

'But –'

'But let them take a liberty – just once – and that's it. I'll kill every last one of 'em.'

'I'll organise a meet then shall I, Dad?'

Brendan's face was twisted with rage. 'What, they your new friends are they, Luke? Gonna nip round theirs for a cuppa and a chat? And hand over all the business while you're at it?' He turned to his father. 'You're upset, Dad. And you're tired. Wait till the morning and you'll see this can't be right.'

'Is that so?'

'Well, come on. A truce? With the Kesslers? After what's happened?' He leaned closer to his father. 'Please, Dad, don't do this.'

Gabriel drained his glass.

Brendan glared at his brother. 'I'm going out for some fresh air, something stinks in here.'

'Don't bother,' said Luke, unhooking his jacket from the back of his chair. 'I'm going out anyway. You stay and keep Dad company. Believe it or not, there's something he'll tell you, Brendan, that you might actually want to celebrate when you hear it.'

He turned and patted his father on the shoulder. 'I don't reckon Patricia'd mind.'

Luke wasn't sure how long he'd been walking, but it must have been hours. The snow had blown itself out, but a freezing rain now angled down into his face, and had soaked right through the shoulders of his overcoat. His trousers were sodden, flapping about his legs, and his feet were squelching in his thin, Italian leather shoes.

He looked about him, noticing that the streetlamps had come on, and that the shop windows were leaking pools of light out onto the rain-slicked pavements.

Aldgate? How had he wound up here? He checked his watch. Ten to six. For him to have walked for so long and to have covered so few miles, he must have been walking in great blind circles.

Ten to six? He frowned. *Call me at six o'clock*, that's what Sammy Kessler had said.

There was a phone box across the road, on the corner of Mansell Street. Might as well get it over with. It had been that sort of a day.

He pulled out his wallet and searched for the scrap of paper.

'Hello,' said Luke; it was more of a question than a greeting.

'Yeah.' Sammy couldn't hide his disappointment. When he'd stood there in the phone box and the phone had actually rung he'd really believed it would be Catherine.

'It's Luke O'Donnell here.'

Sammy brightened up a bit. 'Tell me about Catherine.'

Luke kicked an empty cigarette packet into the corner of the booth. 'Maybe not on the phone.'

'We can meet then. Now okay?'

'Er, yeah. I suppose.' Luke peered out of the smeared glass of the telephone box. 'Do you know the Tun and Grapes up at Aldgate?'

'I'll be there in an hour.'

Luke sat at the far end of the short, curved bar by the fire. He was glad of the opportunity to dry his clothes, but the seat also gave him a clear view of the only entrance into the small, dark-wood panelled pub. Despite what he'd said to his father and brother, he was as unsure of what he was about to do as almost anything he had ever done in his young life, but if Sammy brought a team with him, at least he'd see them coming. And, if it did all go wrong, he wouldn't have much of an audience. Pubs in this area did little evening trade and always closed early. At this time of the evening, the bar was host only to him and a sparse gaggle of City stragglers, reluctant to go out in such awful weather to catch their homebound trains from Fenchurch Street. And, dressed as he was in his dark funeral clothes – so close to their office uniform – the place also offered him the small comfort of anonymity.

Luke was onto his third drink and spiralling down into the introverted misery of grief when Sammy Kessler appeared in the doorway.

Luke stood up, hand held out in unsure welcome. 'Sammy?'

'That's me.' Sammy looked him up and down as he walked across the pub. 'And you must be Luke. Catherine said she could trust you. Is that right?'

89

'Yeah. We always shared our secrets, even when we were kids.'

Sammy looked around the now almost empty pub. 'So, is she joining us?'

Luke's brow pleated into a tight frown. Christ, the bloke had no idea. 'I think we should get a drink.'

Sammy Kessler looked at Luke as if he were joking, as if he were playing some sort of sick prank. 'You're lying, right? Having a laugh?'

Luke shook his head. 'I wish I was. But I'm not. Catherine's dead, Sammy. We buried her today.'

'No, that can't be right. Why wasn't it in the papers?'

'It just wasn't.'

'Now I know you're lying. A death by shooting in a London street? It'd be all over the front pages. Why are you doing this?' He rose to his feet. 'You think you'll be able to split us up by telling me all this crap.' Sammy loomed over him, his lips turned back in disgust. 'And what are you going to tell Catherine, that I've run off with some Jewish girl because I can't marry a Catholic? Well, you won't get rid of me that easily, O'Donnell. I love her, and she loves me. Got it?'

Very slowly, Luke stood up and stared coolly into Sammy's angry face. 'What shooting? My sister was killed in a car crash. She drove into a wall in the fog. The car burst into flames. She didn't have a chance.'

'She did what? Do you think I'm stupid? Why didn't I hear about it? And anyway,' he allowed himself a knowing smile, 'she couldn't even drive.'

Luke was struggling to keep his voice under control. 'You didn't hear about it Kessler, because people round

90

here know better than to run off at the mouth about the O'Donnells's private business. And, as a matter of fact, she could drive.' He took a deep breath. 'And don't you reckon it was a more dignified way to go than being left in the road to bleed to death, after being shot in the throat with a sawn-off shotgun?'

Sammy raked his fingers through his hair, blinked and made jerky little movements with his head as though he were in pain. 'She can't be dead.'

'I know. But it's the truth. And we need to get our stories straight, Sammy. For all our sakes.'

'For all our sakes? Are you completely spineless?' Sammy stepped back, knocking his bar stool to the ground. 'I swear I'll kill you, O'Donnell. I'll kill all of you.' He stabbed a finger into Luke's shoulder. 'You especially. You were the one who was supposed to care about her. So if you know what's good for you, you'd better fuck off out of it.'

The barman moved hastily to the other end of the counter. The manager would be down to lock up soon, let him deal with this.

'No, Sammy, you listen to me. I cared about Catherine more than anyone'll ever know. And I thought you were supposed to and all.'

'I did. I do.'

'Then why did you leave her there? You didn't have a clue who we were. We could have done anything to her. Taken her away and done what we liked with her. But you ran away and left her.'

Sammy's face crumpled like a wet rag and tears trickled down his smooth, usually untroubled, cheeks. 'I had no choice.' He swiped angrily at his face with the back of his hand. 'It was a secret. No one knew about us.'

He raised his head and looked, pleading, into Luke's eyes. 'No one but you.'

'The trouble with secrets is, Sammy, they come back to haunt you.' Luke's mouth was so dry his tongue was sticking to the back of his teeth as he spoke. 'And denying something don't make it go away.'

'What are you, a fucking nut doctor?' Sammy's face was contorted with rage at Luke, at himself, at the whole, rotten world.

'No, just someone who knows a bit about secrets, that's all, and a bloke whose sister's died for nothing.' He bent down and picked up the stool, setting it back on its legs. 'You've had a shock. We all have. But we can't just go off our heads. We've got to keep a lid on all this or the whole thing'll blow up in our faces.'

Sammy shook his head angrily. 'Why should I listen to you?'

'You'd better listen to me. Now, I don't know what influence you've got with your family, but I guarantee this.' Luke leaned forward and pointed his finger right into Sammy's tear-stained face, meaning every word as he hissed them out through clenched teeth. 'If this ain't gonna end in one big bloodbath then you do as I say. If you don't take the piss, I can make sure we leave you and your family alone. We'll maybe even come to an arrangement to do a bit of business with you. Something in the scrap line. In turn, you get your girls off our patch and move them somewhere else, and the same goes for the betting pitches. Nothing within spitting distance of us, right? But you go crooked on us, or try and have us over, take one step near our clubs, the spielers, or the protection, then I won't be held responsible. All bets'll be off. You got that, Sammy Kessler?'

'You're out of your head.'

'Why, because I wanna make sure we look after our own interests? Because I don't wanna lose any more of my family? Think about it. The same applies to you. These arrangements mean there can be peace between us.' He put down his hand and leaned back. 'For as long as you lot do as you're told.'

'You are mad.' Sammy was looking at Luke as if he genuinely thought he had lost his mind. 'Even if I wanted to, how do you suppose I could ever explain these new *arrangements* to my old man?'

'Something'll come to you, mate. Or it had better, if you don't want all out war. I saw some of that when I was a kid. My dad took on some of the South London hard men, and do you know what, Sammy? He won. Hands down. But the claret that got spilt before it was all sorted out . . . You don't want to know.' He paused, letting it sink in. 'And I suppose you don't really want your family knowing about you and our Catherine either. So, how about you arrange a meet between your old feller and mine? You know my number.'

'You bastard.'

As Luke strode away from the pub he felt bewildered. On one of the worst, if not the worst day, of his whole life, he felt exhilarated.

He had always left most of the tough stuff to his father, to Brendan, and to the various thugs, hard nuts and foot soldiers who worked for them in the less public parts of their business. But that exchange with Sammy had got his heart pounding and his blood racing.

And now he needed a drink, a proper one, not a half-pint in some dodgy old boozer, but somewhere he could be himself and could celebrate. And he knew exactly where he was going to have that drink: the Lagoon Club, on Dean Street, in Soho.

Paulie, a bloke he'd met in the City Arms on the Isle of Dogs, was the barman there, and he'd given Luke an open invitation to pop in and see him any time he fancied it.

Any time at all . . .

Chapter 7

The moment he stepped through the narrow, street level doorway of the Lagoon Club, Luke was overwhelmed by doubt. He'd just buried his sister, for Christ's sake, what the hell did he think he was doing going out to a club? Especially a club like this one.

A deep shame wedged itself in his chest like a brick. But, as he hovered at the top of the grim, South Seas mural-painted stairway, grief took over, usurping the brick with the taste of sour vomit. The grief wasn't only for Catherine, it was for himself – a man who didn't know who, or even what, he was.

He took a few tentative steps down towards the cramped underground space and the soulful sounds of a tenor sax that were soaring up from the smoky darkness.

As his eyes became accustomed to the muted lighting, Luke could make out a flamboyantly dressed, elderly man – floppy, velvet hat; heavy silk cravat, tied in a pussy cat bow at his throat; purple and gold brocade jacket – sitting in the corner facing the stairway. He was petting a pale pink poodle, perched delicately on his lap.

The man lifted his eyes and lazily surveyed the handsome youngster standing on the stairs.

'Varda the dolly old eek on the dish, Poppett,' he trilled to the poodle, wagging the dog's paw at Luke. And then, to Luke himself, 'Fancy a little bevie?' He paused, batting his sparsely lashed lids. 'Or something a bit stronger more to your taste? Me for instance?'

Luke couldn't. He couldn't go any further. Just as he hadn't been able to the last time. Or the time before that.

'Sorry,' he said over his shoulder, as he turned and made his way back up the stairs. 'There's been a mistake. Never realised the time. Got to go. Meeting someone. I'm really late. You know how it is.'

The man expelled a long, drawn out breath. 'Yes, sweetheart, I know exactly how it is. It's the story of my life, lovey. That's what all the good-looking ones seem to say these days. *Sorry*. Makes me feel like a right old meese omi-polone.' He lifted the poodle's ear and said in a loud stage whisper: 'Shame, eh, my little cherry? I was really bonar for him and all. It'll be a lonely old arthur for me tonight as usual. Ah well, let's have another little drinkette then, shall we? And perhaps, Poppett,' he sighed histrionically. 'I'll learn to keep my queeny old polari for them what appreciates it. Or for them what admits it.'

How could going into a room in your own home be this difficult?

Eileen made another faltering reach for the handle then, with all the determination she had left in her, she snatched at it, and threw open the door, waiting for the monster of grief to leap out of the shadows and devour her.

But there was no monster. Just a bedroom with a comforting glow, warming it like a soft quilt, as light from the streetlamp outside filtered through the cream lace curtains. Catherine had so loved that cosy radiance that she would never close the heavy drapes, not even in the heart of winter.

Eileen slipped off her shoes, crossed herself as if she were going into a side chapel for a moment of quiet prayer, and entered in her stockinged feet.

Making sure she disturbed no one else in the house, she clicked the door shut carefully behind her, turned on the light, and immediately felt a heart-leaping closeness to the daughter she would never see again. She looked about her – at the room that was still as much a little girl's domain as it was a young woman's, trying desperately to keep hold of the feeling of intimacy with her child. Then she walked towards the bed, the sheepskin rug soft and yielding between her toes. It was really little more than a raw, unfinished fleece, but Catherine had insisted on bringing it back from one of their trips to Kildare. She must have been what, seven, eight years old? Old enough to know her own mind and to get her own way.

Eileen stopped suddenly, drawing up one foot and sucking in a truncated hiss of breath. She'd trodden on something hard.

Bending down, she ran her fingers through the deep curling pile until she found it: a disc of white plastic, the size of a two-shilling piece, with a brass clip stuck on the back. One of the cheap market earrings that Catherine had collected and cherished as if they were precious jewels. But however cheap they were, Catherine had looked lovely in them, especially when she'd worn them with matching loops of poppet beads wound around her throat and wrists.

Eileen touched the treasure to her lips and slipped it into the pocket of her pale blue, quilted nylon dressing gown.

Moving closer to the bed, she reached out and ran a finger across a poster pinned above the headboard. It had been carefully unstapled from the centre of one of Catherine's magazines, the marks from the metal still clear in the crease. It was an image of Catherine's favourite – the actor who played Kookie in the television programme *77 Sunset Strip*. He was leaning forward, combing his quiff of blond hair. She remembered how Catherine used to make them all laugh, saying how she'd go to Hollywood one day and meet him, reckoned she would sweep him off his feet, probably even marry him.

She'd never meet him now.

Eileen had to look away, unable to bear the thought.

Below the picture was a bookshelf, with chunky, green china rabbit bookends supporting a set of Lang's fairy books.

Eileen smiled through her tears. She practically knew them all by heart. Even when she could read them for herself, Catherine had still loved her mother to tell her the familiar stories over and over again, lulling her into a deep, child's sleep full of magical stories in which there would always be someone there to rescue you.

Eileen, now almost unable to control the whooping, shallow sobs rising in her chest, dragged her gaze away, lighting on the bedside cabinets – and more memories of Catherine, her precious girl. On one stood the Ekco transistor radio Brendan had brought home for her – after she'd driven them all half mad going on and on about how she couldn't live without listening to Radio Luxembourg – and a half-eaten packet of Spangles, its curling ribbon of paper wrapping winding out in front of it. On the other cabinet was her Dansette record player, its pale blue and cream leatherette lid still open from where she'd been playing her records. Catherine had always loved music, dancing about the house and singing at the top of her voice.

Eileen lifted the arm and took the top 45 off the stack

on the turntable. She read the label: The Drifters. She knew them. 'Save the Last Dance For Me'. And knew the tune too. Then the next: 'Itsy Bitsy Teeny Weeny . . .'

A sudden flash of memory. The row she'd had with Catherine about the bikini she'd bought in the summer. She was as crazy over clothes as she was over music, but Eileen had forbidden her from wearing the thing to the Lido. And then, when she found out that it had cost her nineteen and eleven – nearly a pound for those ridiculous few scraps of material – she'd been angry with her all over again.

Why? Eileen wondered. Why had she denied her child such a small pleasure?

She went over to the cream and gold Melamine wardrobe and began sliding outfits along the rail one after the other. She unhooked a hanger and took out a sky blue skirt, stiffened with a froth of net petticoats, so short it had barely come down to Catherine's knees. That had caused another row.

Had they really spent so much of the time they had together arguing?

Next: bright red toreador pants, with figured black ricrac down the outside seams.

Such a tiny waist.

Eileen touched the material to her cheek and then hung the trousers back on the rail.

It was almost too much: the feel and smell of her so close.

As she was about to close the wardrobe door, she spotted the old toffee tin tucked in among the racks and racks of shoes.

She bent down and picked it up, frowning at the brightly painted lid: a cartoon-like spaceman firing his ray gun at an enemy ship. Trying to remember. When had Catherine got this? Two, three Christmases ago?

Whenever it was, she'd still been a child.

Eileen carried it over to the bed, sat down and eased off the lid.

Photographs.

She tipped out a flutter of memories onto the lavender bedspread.

Eileen was studying a picture of a chubby kneed toddler, with a sagging, knitted bathing suit, standing in a tin bath in the back yard that first summer after the war, when the door opened.

'Luke,' Eileen said, anxiously. She didn't know why, but she felt guilty, as if she'd been caught trespassing. 'I never heard you come in.'

'I took off my shoes. I heard Brendan talking to Dad down in the kitchen and didn't want to disturb them. Well, didn't really feel much like joining them, to be truthful. Sounded like Dad's had a skinful.' As he spoke, his eyes were fixed on the empty tin by his mother's feet. 'But then I saw the light on under the door, and I . . .'

'Wanted to feel near her?'

'Yeah. But I thought you'd be asleep by now. You know, the pills.'

'I didn't take them. Didn't want to be packed off into oblivion. I want to remember.' She patted the bed. 'Come on love, come and see.'

Luke sat on the edge of the bed and accepted each picture after his mother had finished putting together its story, drawing from it every possible connection with her youngest child.

'See that one,' she said, handing it to him to look at,

while she carried on sorting through the piles of memories. 'The one with Scrap? She could make that dog do whatever she wanted. That day, she'd got out all her doll's clothes and . . . Oh look,' she interrupted herself. 'Here's a recent one. Looks like it's at the coast somewhere.' She held it at arm's length, turning it to the light, trying to understand. 'Now when was that taken? And who would have –'

'Mum.' Luke slid his hand over the shiny black and white snapshot, just glimpsing a smiling Catherine, her eyes sparkling, as she posed for whoever was taking the picture. 'This is too hard, for me. Too soon. Can we put them away? Please. Just for now?'

Eileen touched his cheek and nodded. 'Of course.'

'Thanks. We'll look another time, eh? In a week or two maybe.' He stood up, helping his mother gently to her feet. 'You get off to bed. I'll tidy these away.'

Eileen nodded, and, with a brush of her lips on his cheek, and a whispered goodnight, she left him to it.

Luke waited, listening for his mother to open then close her bedroom door, and then shuffled hurriedly through the snaps. He slipped a slim stack of them into his back pocket and snapped the lid back on the tin.

The next morning, Luke – like his father and brother – didn't get up for breakfast.

Even though Luke had gone to bed almost immediately after his mother, he'd lain awake for most of the rest of the night, going back, time and again, to the photographs he'd smuggled out of Catherine's room.

As for Brendan, he'd stayed down in the basement kitchen with Gabriel into the early hours, trying to persuade his increasingly incoherent father that letting in

101

the Kessler family was the stupidest thing he could possibly even consider doing, and that grief was clouding his judgement, stopping him from thinking straight. But Gabriel had drunk so much by then that he'd hardly heard a word of his son's arguments and pleas, and had eventually hauled himself up to bed, where he'd passed out on top of the covers without so much as taking off his shoes. Brendan had followed him up not long after.

The only one of the O'Donnell household to be up and about on the morning after the funeral was Eileen.

When Gabriel had crawled his way up to their bed, Eileen, rather than lie there listening to him snoring, had got up and left him to it. She'd considered going back into Catherine's room, but didn't want to disturb Luke whose room was next door, so she'd crept downstairs and sat by herself in the ground floor front parlour, trying to see her baby on that last day – stretched out on the sofa while Patricia did her nails for her.

She'd tried so hard to grab hold of the happy moments – the laughter, the singing and dancing – but the emptiness kept opening up in front of her. And now she was down in the basement kitchen – rinsing her teacup, dressed and ready to go and see Patricia, who was carrying the one beacon of hope in Eileen's life – when the telephone rang.

Eileen answered it and then called up the stairs. 'Luke, are you awake? It's the telephone.'

'Who is it, Mum?' His words were heavy with sleep.

'A friend of yours. Look, you'll have to come and get it, I'm off to Patricia's. I'll see you later.'

Luke padded down the stairs in his underpants, his eyes barely open, and his hair sticking up in black tufts.

'Nnn?' he mumbled into the mouthpiece.

'Luke?'

'Yeah. Who's this?'

'Sammy Kessler.'

Luke was immediately awake. He looked over his shoulder to make sure he was alone. 'What's happening?'

'I've managed to convince Dad it's at least worth having a meet.'

'Right . . .' Luke said the word very slowly, the prospect of an actual, real life meeting suddenly seeming far less reasonable than it had done when it was just an idea. 'When?'

'In two weeks. December 13. It's a Tuesday, okay.' It wasn't a question.

'I'll make it okay.'

Mary Logan handed a cup of tea to her poor brother's aggravating dimwit of a wife and smiled sweetly – a smile that didn't reach her eyes. 'Can I make you a bit of something to eat, Eileen, my love?'

'Thank you, Mary, but I've no appetite for food.' Eileen, who was sitting on the sofa in what her daughter, Patricia, called her 'lounge', took the geometrically patterned, black and white cup and rested it on her knee.

Even on a gloomy winter's morning, the house was bright, stylish and welcoming. Before Pat and Pete Mac had moved in, the inside of the tall Victorian terraced house had been completely transformed. Following Patricia's strict instructions as to what was required, Gabriel had moved in a gang of men from the yard, and told them to get a move on before the wedding.

Their first jobs had been to strip out all the ornate coving and ceiling roses; to cover up the turned banisters and the panelled doors with hardboard – making sure to remove any old-fashioned brass door furniture and to replace it with modern, slanting plastic handles. Then they had concentrated on the basement kitchen, which, under Patricia's eagle-eye, they'd cleared of the deep butler sink, the wooden draining board, the Maid Saver, and the old black leaded kitchener, and had refitted with Formica and stainless steel units and a shiny Ascot heater. They'd then moved up to the ground floor where they knocked out the dividing wall between the front and back rooms, creating Patricia's spacious 'lounge'. The final job, and the one the men all agreed they really had better not tell their wives about in case they started getting any ideas, was to transform the smallest of the three top floor bedrooms into a proper, plumbed in bathroom with a lavatory and a separate wash basin. It was like something out of a film.

Patricia and Catherine had gone mad planning how to decorate the place, and it was the lounge that was to be the centrepiece of the whole project. The floor was covered in parquet – just right to show off the new orange and cream rugs; walls were painted white; Pucci print was made up into curtains; framed prints were selected from the range in Timothy Whites; and G Plan teak furniture catalogues, showing all the very latest in Scandinavian style were pored over, and a dining suite, sofa and armchairs, sideboard and tables were ordered. With the finishing touches of spider plants hanging from the ceiling in raffia containers; primary coloured glass vases full of flowers; ceramic dishes filled with fruit, a brass sunburst mirror over the hearth that now housed the electric fire; heavy pottery lamps with oversized shades; and a television set placed in one corner as the main focal point, the room had been pronounced perfect by the delighted sisters and their admiring mother.

Almost a year later, Eileen would, if asked, have agreed that it still looked as fresh, airy and bang up-to-date as the day Patricia and Pete had moved in, but today it could do nothing to lift her spirits.

'Are you sure you won't have just a slice of toast?'

'Thanks all the same, Mary, but I don't think I'll ever want to eat again.'

'Not that Sean and I have ever been blessed, of course, but it must be a terrible thing, burying a child.' Mary breathed out the words as if in prayer. 'Although you should have something, Eileen; you must keep up your strength. What with Gabriel having you trek all the way over to Kildare to take care of me when there was nothing wrong – it's Sean I blame for that, getting everyone excited over nothing – and now poor Catherine.' She crossed herself ostentatiously. 'May God keep her safe in his bosom. And you still having to cope with the rest of the family.' *If you can be bothered to shift your lazy, scraggy arse, and get your men a decent bit of grub on the table, and find the time to do a few bits of washing for them, you spoilt bitch*, she thought to herself. 'You've got three strapping men at home to think of.'

Eileen said nothing, didn't even bother sipping at her tea. She just sat there, not really listening, while Mary talked and talked, not even noticing the sly, snide remarks that, as always, polluted her every other word.

'Look, Eileen, look who's here,' Mary said, standing up and with a little clap of her hands, finally getting Eileen's attention. 'Here's our Patricia come down from her bed at last. And how are you this morning, my little love?'

Patricia, still in her dressing gown, with purple shadows under eyes, her skin deathly pale against her

105

almost black hair that was plastered flat to her skull, walked into the room very slowly, as if worried that her head might fall off her shoulders. Carefully, she leaned forward and kissed her mother on the cheek.

''Lo, Mum.'

'Sweetheart. Look at you.'

'Sick again?' asked Mary.

'Yeah. Very.'

Eileen put her untouched tea on the floor, stood up and hugged her daughter. 'It was good of you to come back with Patricia yesterday, Mary,' she said, over her daughter's shoulder, meaning it. 'I hope you know I appreciate it.'

Mary treated her sister-in-law to another broad, lips-only smile. 'Glad to be of help, Eileen. Especially as you were in no state to help her yourself, dear.' She stepped forward and tapped Patricia on the back.

Patricia twisted away from her mother to see what her aunt wanted.

'And at least you only have yourself and the baby to think about for the rest of the day,' she said brightly, leading her over to one of the armchairs that stood on either side of the electric fire. 'I shooed that Pete Mac out of the house first thing.' She bent forward and turned on another bar. 'I mean, we don't need men around cluttering up the place, now do we?' *And we certainly don't need Eileen clucking about like a distressed hen if she finds out what happened.*

Patricia flashed her aunt a look of gratitude for hiding from her mother the fact that Pete Mac was, yet again, on the missing list, and yet another night had passed without him sharing her bed, and that yet another day would pass without him finding out about the baby they were going to have.

If she hadn't felt so sick, so desolate at losing Catherine, and so totally and completely worn out by everything – including her well-meaning aunt's ministrations and her endless cups of tea – Patricia would have gone out and found Peter-bloody-MacRiordan. First she would have told him about the baby, and then she'd have told him his sodding fortune, and, finally, she'd have smacked him one right round his ugly, rotten mug.

Still, there was plenty of time for that. Pete, ever the bad penny, would turn up sooner or later. Just as he always did. Just as if nothing had happened. Expecting a smiling, wide-armed welcome, a hot meal on the table, and a quick fumble under the sheets, before he fell asleep as quickly and easily as an innocent cherub.

God he was a pig.

Patricia rubbed her middle protectively. But he wouldn't spoil this for her; she wouldn't let him.

Chapter 8

The big Daimler saloon stood at the front of a line of showily expensive, top of the range cars that had been parked in an otherwise unremarkable little side street. Gabriel had got out of the front passenger seat – Stephen Shea having driven – instructing his sons and son-in-law to stay where they were until he sent someone to tell them otherwise.

Apart from the thin, bluish light pooled around the base of the single lamppost, the street was dark, cold and damp, and Gabriel was dressed accordingly in a heavy, immaculately tailored, navy overcoat, leather gloves and trilby. He looked every inch the wealthy, successful man.

Standing next to him on the pavement outside the terrace of narrow, ordinary-looking houses was Harold Kessler, barely five feet five and weighing in at a good fourteen stone, but as cocky as a six-feet-five, heavyweight champion. He was dressed similarly to Gabriel, but in shades of camel and brown rather than dark blue. Both men were flanked by big, silent minders, whose only moving body parts seemed to be their constantly vigilant eyes.

Kessler ground out his cigarette under the slightly stacked heel of his highly polished shoe. 'Chinatown, Mr O'Donnell? A strange choice of venue.'

'You've been away from the East End for too long, Mr Kessler.'

Mr Kessler. It stuck in Gabriel's throat to show even such superficial respect, but the meeting had been arranged and he would see it through to the end, however it might turn out. In truth, it was only pride that had made him turn up – pride that he was a man of his word. He could kick himself now for consenting to be in this bastard's company. He had only agreed to all this at a time of weakness: Catherine's death, being told Patricia was expecting, and Luke going on and on about the trouble with the bloody south Londoners.

'Far too long.' Gabriel paused for a moment, taking time to pull himself together, as he realised that, as usual, when he was about to lose his temper, his accent had become far less Stepney and more markedly Galway. 'Or you'd know that what with all the bomb damage there's very little left in Limehouse of the old Chinatown.'

He indicated the terrace with a flap of his hand. 'Just odd remnants like this, and the occasional pub like the one across the road.' He clasped his hands behind his back and surveyed his surroundings. 'The gambling clubs and eating-houses are all moving over to Soho.'

Pleased with his show of superior knowledge, Gabriel allowed himself a brief hint of a smile. 'That's why I was able to pick up this place for such a fair price.'

'This place?' Kessler shrugged and spread his hands – an exaggerated parody of a gesture. He didn't get it. A small terraced house near the docks? Who would want such a hovel? 'So, this is where our discussions are to take place? In here?'

Gabriel nodded. 'That's right. Nice and private. Shall we go in?'

As Kessler took off his hat and inclined his head in agreement, Gabriel beckoned for his sons and Pete Mac to join him and his minders. Stephen Shea stayed behind to mind the cars.

Daniel and Sammy Kessler followed the example of the O'Donnell boys, and, along with their cousin Maurice, got out of their car to join their father, Harold.

Maurice was Harold's self-important, swaggering nephew. He had come down from Manchester to stay in London for a few days. That had been nearly a month ago, and he was now apparently staying on indefinitely, having been taken onto work for his uncle – purportedly in the haulage trade. Neither Maurice's mother nor father seemed to have any reservations about these arrangements, even though they were both well aware that Harold's businesses were all a bit on the dubious side to say the least. In fact, this turn of events had answered their unspoken prayers: maybe, at twenty-five years of age, he'd start making something of himself at last – anything, in fact. So long as it was something a long way away from them.

Once through the nondescript doorway, Gabriel was more than gratified to see the look on Harold Kessler's face. From the street outside, the terrace had been left to look like a row of small, individual dwellings, and so, to outsiders, it appeared as if they had entered a little two-storey house. But inside it was a very different matter. All the houses in the terrace had been joined up to form a complex of rooms and stairways running the whole length of the outwardly ordinary side street.

'Bloke called Chen did all this, over fifty years ago,' said Gabriel, indicating the central corridor lined with doors. 'A lot of betting used to go on, on this floor.' He paused to grin. 'Still does. But not on puck-a-poo – that was their game, the Chinese fellers – and there's no opium these days either. But there are still plenty of girls and drinks to keep the punters entertained in the private rooms, where they can enjoy their brag, and their pontoon, and their poker, and, well, you name it they enjoy it. In fact, I'm surprised you didn't know about this place. I thought,' he considered his words, 'people of your religion enjoyed a bet and a good time.'

Kessler's eyes narrowed for the briefest of moments. 'No more than any other religion, *Mr* O'Donnell.'

'Quite so, Mr Kessler. Now, if you'd like to follow me.' Gabriel, slightly nonplussed by his faux pas, but also more than a little put out by the arrogant little fucker's cheeky response, inclined his head in a gesture of more or less apology and led the party of men along the corridor.

Maurice was the only one amongst them to pause and admire the series of black and white erotic etchings that had adorned the otherwise plain walls since the 1920s, before only slightly increasing his pace to join the rest of the group, as they followed Gabriel down the discreet spiral stairway at the far end of the marble floored passageway.

At the bottom of the steps stood a man whose neck looked to be about twice the circumference of his head.

'Thank you, Anthony,' said Gabriel, nodding to the man.

Antony immediately pushed open the heavy sliding door that he had been guarding.

The noise from the other side hit them like a wall.

Again Gabriel enjoyed the look on Kessler's face. 'Chen also joined up the cellars.'

They were in a massive, windowless, low-ceilinged, flagstoned space – a huge, cacophonous arena. The central area, marked off by a rough chalked circle, was quite bare, but around the perimeter of the enormous, brightly lit

111

room stood a double row of metal and canvas chairs. The seats were nearly all occupied by expensively dressed men talking animatedly, but politely, to one another, and handing over large amounts of money to skimpily clad young women, all of whom had satchels slung across their shoulders. Behind the chairs stood more raucous gaggles of men, many of them in sailors' uniforms.

'A favourite place to spend their wages after a long voyage,' explained Gabriel. 'And not a bad choice either – placing your bets with a pretty girl and having her fetch you drinks, while you enjoy the company of your friends, before enjoying more . . . let's say, intimate pleasures.'

'But what are they betting on down here?' Kessler was puzzled – he could see no cards, no roulette wheel, no one-armed bandits, or any of the other illegal gaming machines usually favoured in 'private' establishments.

Gabriel was now really beginning to enjoy himself, having one over on Kessler. Maybe it wouldn't be such a bad arrangement after all.

He smiled warmly. 'Welcome to my boxing club, Mr Kessler.' He paused just long enough to register the man's expression of surprise, and, *yes*, there it was: a brief flicker of admiration. 'The soundproofing was a bit of a job, a nightmare in fact, and certainly not cheap, but worth it if you enjoy your privacy as much as I do.' He let out a pleasant, amused little puff of air. 'And bare-knuckle bouts do have a habit of attracting the wrong sort of attention.'

He looked Harold Kessler directly in the eye. 'The point of the bare-knuckle fight being, of course, to inflict the worst possible damage on your enemy – to kill him if necessary – in order to win. An ugly view of things, maybe, but, as I always say, better to reign in hell than serve in heaven.'

Gabriel held his gaze just a moment too long for Kessler's liking, making sure that the man felt the full discomfort of being in his power then, finally, when he thought he'd held him for long enough, he let him go, smiling at him again.

'Perhaps you'd fancy coming along as my guest to watch a few bouts one evening.' He winked matily. 'I'd make sure you picked the winner, you can be sure of that.'

Kessler returned his smile, and again shrugged and spread his hands. 'I like to do business with a man who knows the winner, Mr O'Donnell.'

Gabriel tried to decide if the little prick was being sarcastic, and was angry to realise that he couldn't actually figure him out. He felt his fists clench. Was he taking the piss or what?

The moment was saved by a pale, wiry man in his thirties. He was quite tidily dressed, but his clothes seemed just that bit too big for him, as if he had lost weight. From the dark smudges under his jittery, darting eyes, it was obvious he had something on his mind. He approached Gabriel with such humility that it wouldn't have been a surprise if he had actually buckled at the knee and gone for the full genuflection.

'Scuse me, Mr O'Donnell. Don't wanna be a nuisance or anything. But can I have a quick word? If you're not too busy, like.'

'Sure, Ted.' Gabriel liked this. 'We're all friends here. Speak freely.'

'I've got a cotchell of groins, Mr O'Donnell. And a few loose diamonds. And some gold bracelets. All good gear. I did a grab in Hatton Garden yesterday cos I need a bit of dough for my old woman. My brief reckons I'm going down for a right lump, and I have to know she's got enough to last her, so she can look after herself and the kids.'

Gabriel nodded benevolently. 'It'll be a pleasure to help you out, Ted. You go over and see Anthony, tell him I said he's to take you through to the cashiers' room, and say I said they're to give you whatever price you say. I know you won't take a liberty.'

Ted did everything but kiss Gabriel's hand. 'Mr O'Donnell, I can't tell you –'

'Don't worry yourself, Ted. And don't worry about your family either. They'll be all right. You have my word on it.' He reached in his pocket and took out a roll of notes. He peeled off four fivers and handed them to Ted. 'Have that on the Scotch bloke in the second fight. My treat. You won't be sorry.'

With that, Gabriel turned to Kessler with a broad, handsome smile. 'Anyway, enough of all this, we're not here for the sport, now are we?' A pause, just long enough for the ambiguity to sink in and aggravate Kessler. 'So, if you and your sons and colleagues would care to join me in my office . . .'

'If it seems satisfactory to me, and this –' Gabriel hesitated, considering his words, '– *venture* goes ahead, I think it goes without saying, Mr Kessler, that we both understand what we know is right and wrong here. What we should and shouldn't be doing. The ground rules – the code, if you like – that we should follow.'

Gabriel was sitting in a leather library chair, at an elegant Queen Anne desk, in a plushly decorated, wood panelled room that wouldn't have looked out of place in a gentlemen's club in Pall Mall. Harold Kessler was sitting on the other side of the desk in a deep-buttoned winged armchair. Both men were flanked by smoke-wreathed family members and their minders.

'We're neither of us stupid men, Mr Kessler, we're not mugs, and we're definitely not fresh in off the boat either. We both realise what I'm talking about. But let me set out the details for clarity, for everyone's sake.'

Kessler inclined his head in a gesture of permission that Gabriel wasn't entirely thrilled with, but he wasn't going to let his irritation show.

'You'll use your vehicle fleet to collect the scrap. There seems to be an endless supply of average stuff around, more than anyone can deal with, but then, Mr Kessler, there's the really good stuff, the stuff people would give their right arm for, the stuff for which you need the right contacts to get access to. A special sort of supply.'

Kessler was beginning to feel that he was getting out of his depth. Scrap wasn't his game. 'Explain.'

Gabriel looked at him, waiting for the show of respect.

'If you will,' Kessler added eventually.

'Okay. We – by that I mean, you, in this case – graciously accept money from an investor – some posh type with more money than sense, who can't wait to get his jollies from the pleasure of mixing with real, authentic cockney villains.' He paused, leaned across the glass-topped desk and mouthed. 'Gangsters. Hoodlums. Faces.'

Kessler couldn't help but smile in recognition, he knew the type exactly, the ones who regularly risked their nice, comfortable lives just for the sake of a cheap thrill. Their preference could be for street corner tarts, illicit gambling, pretty boys, dope smoking in West London blues clubs, it

115

didn't really matter, what mattered was that they thought it was *dirty*. And that was what they liked.

'Then,' Gabriel continued, 'with his money tucked away nice and safe in your bin, you buy something really tasty from a supplier. A very discreet supplier, of course.'

Kessler, intrigued, shifted forward in his seat. 'What sort of stuff?'

'Military scrap. Planes, army vehicles, that sort of top of the range type of gear. You view it whole, and then you collect it. It'll be cut up and stripped down ready – remember this is quality metal we're talking about – and you sell it on. Top dollar. Very nice. Very good profits to be had. Maybe even sell it to me. What with me being an expert in scrap metal . . . But, and here's the beauty of this game, you do not – repeat, do not repay the investor either his original stake or his cut of the profit.'

'What if they call the law? You know that sort, probably knows the Chief Constable personally. Probably plays golf with the feller and fucks his wife.'

'What if he does? A couple of plods turn up on your doorstep, Mr Kessler, and you just straighten 'em out. Give 'em a nice drink. They take the bung *and* they put the frighteners on your investor – "*You wouldn't have anything to do with any illegal procurement of military property, now would you sir?*" The investor will now be shitting himself. He'll deny he's ever heard of you, let alone that he's given you any dough. And that's the beauty of you being the middleman, rather than him doing the deal with a known scrap dealer like me. "*All a mistake, sir. I see, sir. Long as you've not been wasting police time.*"'

Gabriel smiled. 'And did I remember to mention that I'll be the supplier as well?'

At the sight of the greed lighting up Kessler's face,

Gabriel couldn't help letting out a deep, self-satisfied sigh. Was it really going to be this easy taking control of the cheeky little bastard? It certainly looked like it. Perhaps Luke was right after all, this definitely beat going to war with them.

He took a moment to light a long, thick cigar. 'We're not, you see, Mr Kessler, like them ponces who might act like tough guys, but who just take a cut out of every job that's done by all the blokes on their manor, because they're too bloody scared to do their own dirty work. We love taking part, Mr Kessler, we love getting our sleeves rolled up and getting our hands stuck right down in the muck. That way, you see, we always know what's going on. We ensure that no one is taking a liberty. Because we really don't like liberty takers, Mr Kessler. We really don't like them at all.'

Kessler nodded courteously. 'I like the sound of the way you do business, Mr O'Donnell. And I'm sure it can be mutually beneficial.'

'Glad to hear it. Now, if this arrangement is to proceed, this is what you do. You take your toms off our patch. You move them further east, up West, over the fucking river if the fancy takes you, but you do *not* stay on our patch. You can keep the betting pitches on the Shoreditch side, but not on the Whitechapel side, or down towards the docks. There's no shops opening there yet and I intend to make hay, as the old saying goes. You can keep your drinking club in Hoxton, open more round there if you like – again, well away from any of mine. But you'll use my gambling machines. Aw, yeah, and I'll be expecting a straight dollar in the pound on everything you earn.'

'Your machines *and* twenty-five per cent? I thought you said you didn't take –'

'I'm fair, Mr Kessler, but I'm not a fool. I said we don't take a cut from other people's jobs. We do take a cut, of course, from their businesses – the businesses that we might otherwise be running. We do own this manor, after all – and is there anything wrong with twenty-five per cent? Is there something unusual about that?'

Kessler looked at his sons and his nephew and flashed his eyebrows at them – they'd got off lighter than they might have done – and then shook his head. 'No. Nothing at all.'

'Good. But, I'll remind you again. Nothing of yours is to be within spitting distance of ours. And, if you get any trouble, say from the Eyeties over in Clerkenwell, then it's down to you to sort it out. But if you go monkey on us, Kessler, if you try and make a move on the spielers, try putting in a single one-armed bandit of your own in the drinking clubs, touch *any* of the protection – even the soft foreign touches too scared to actually tell me if they're being had for payments twice over – I'll find out about it. And then it's over. I promise you that. So don't give me any agg, because I'm telling you, if you *do* give me any aggravation, I'll have you. War will be declared. And if that happens, you would be well advised to disappear from these parts as soon as possible. And you'd better make it somewhere one hell of a lot further than Notting Hill or even the south of Spain. I have contacts, Mr Kessler. In many, many places.'

Gabriel paused to tap the ashes from his cigar into a heavy crystal ashtray.

'So, what do you think, Mr Kessler?'

'Can we still sell Tanner a Pick straws and work the Shell game down the Lane?'

'Mr Kessler, I hope you're not being sarcastic. I asked what you think?'

'I think, *Gabriel*, that we have a deal. So, please, no more formality.' He beamed beatifically and held out his hand. 'Call me, Harold. Use my name. It's what people do when they're in business together. When they're colleagues. Might I even say – friends?'

'Harold,' said Gabriel, through his teeth, grasping the man's hand, and only just managing to stop himself from punching the squat, little bastard full in his ugly, grinning face. 'Nine o'clock. Time we went to meet the ladies.'

Chapter 9

Hidden away behind an anonymous door, in a street shabby even by Soho standards, and with only a small, dull brass plaque screwed to the wall signalling its existence, the inside of the Dahlia Club was a revelation. With its subtle lighting; blonde, maple wood interior; etched glass privacy panels, and deep leather banquettes, it had the glamorous feel of the Grand Salon of an elegant ocean liner. And even on this bitterly cold winter's evening, the fashionable venue was packed with what excitable gossip columnists would call *an exhilarating combination of high life and low life*. In other words, it was a place patronised by those who could afford it: a rich social mix of aristocrats, business people, and criminals. And with sufficient numbers of pretty young staff, glamorous entertainers, and ever-willing hangers-on in attendance – both male and female – to make everyone very happy to be there.

Yet, despite the crowd, there was one large, round table still unoccupied: the table that had been booked for the O'Donnell–Kessler party. Regardless of Luke's last minute reservations about what he had actually set in motion, and after a not entirely easy discussion with his father about the matter, he had booked the Dahlia so that the families could 'celebrate' their new business relationship after the meeting – if it went well. And Luke was, he supposed, glad to acknowledge that the meeting had gone well, or at least sufficiently well to satisfy his father.

For the time being, anyway.

An obsequious man in white tie and tails, who seemed anxious to show how overwhelmed he was to be receiving Gabriel O'Donnell in such a humble establishment, showed the O'Donnells and Kesslers to their table.

Gabriel was brushing away the maître d'hôtel's attentions with a pantomime of his own: a humble smile, a modest wave of his hand, and a self-effacing inclination of his head.

Both men knew it was all just an act. On his previous visit to the Dahlia, Gabriel had made sure he would be warmly welcomed back – despite the drunken behaviour of the bent-nosed, cauliflower-eared company he had been dining with that night – by palming the man two five pound notes. The man now had only wonderful memories of the privilege of serving Mr O'Donnell, plus the expectation, of course, that he would be equally well rewarded after serving him and his very slightly more sophisticated looking companions this evening. It was the way the wheels turned.

Gabriel, showing he was in charge of proceedings, acted the polite host and remained standing while Eileen, Brendan, Luke, Patricia and Pete Mac were seated. His lips twitched with annoyance as Kessler did the same, fussing around while his wife, Sophie, his two sons – Sammy and Daniel – Daniel's fiancée Rachel, and his nephew, Maurice, made themselves comfortable.

Gabriel insisted that Harold be the next to sit down, and only sat down himself after the various minders were accommodated at a hastily prepared table, which, while it might have been unfashionably close to the kitchens, gave the men a full, unobstructed view of the room. From there they could keep an eye on anyone who'd had a bit too much to drink and thought he might start playing the hard man. It was an occupational hazard for a family such as the O'Donnells that they would occasionally be challenged by foolhardy, drunken show-offs who wanted to impress their companions with their toughness. It was far kinder for a minder to accompany them out to the lavatory and give them a discreet warning or even a light kicking.

On the whole, the party seemed, superficially at least, to be glad to be there, although Eileen, still raw with grief and dressed in a sombre rather than glamorous black crepe, calf-length dress, had only gone along because she was too emotionally drained to argue with her husband. She had managed a stiff, polite smile when Harold Kessler had introduced his family to her, and again when she had been seated next to his wife, Sophie, as part of the strictly gender-divided seating plan.

Eileen found Sophie Kessler loud and showy, swathed as she was in crystal-sprinkled, floor length drapes of coffee chiffon that showed off every line of her handsomely curvaceous body, and with her fair curls piled on top of her head. Large diamonds flashed at her ears and on both hands. But, Eileen had to admit, she also seemed a decent enough woman, and watched approvingly as Sophie made sure that Rachel, her pretty, if over-primped and preened, future daughter-in-law, settled into conversation with Patricia, making sure that both the girls were at their ease.

'Here, Eileen.' She jumped to hear her name. It was Pete Mac, calling right across the table to her, waving his fork about as if he were conducting the band. 'I was just saying to Gabe here that he'd better watch out, cos he looks the right business in that new Italian mohair suit of his, don't he? And if he ain't careful he'll wind up getting captured by one of them pretty little cigarette girls. What a turn out that'd be, eh?' He grinned, looking about the table, checking that everyone was appreciating his wit. 'I mean, he might have forty-four years on the clock, but some of these young girls, well, they like an older man, don't they.'

Gabriel, wishing all kinds of evil on the idiot, closed his eyes for fractionally longer than a blink, and then flashed his teeth at Harold Kessler as if sharing a joke. 'Likes a laugh does my son-in-law.' Then he turned to his wife. 'You all right, Eileen?'

Eileen nodded silently and Gabriel returned to his conversation with the men.

Sophie looked at Eileen, put down her knife and fork, and touched her lightly on the back of the hand. 'Don't you fancy the sole, Eileen?' Sophie jerked her head at her husband. 'Typical of my Harry, barging in and ordering for everyone without even asking what they want. He thinks he's being helpful, but he's not, he's just being a nuisance. Does it all the time. Can't help himself from always having to be front of the queue.'

Eileen had probably been the only one who'd noticed the look of fury that had passed between Gabriel and Brendan, when Kessler had taken it upon himself to take charge of what everyone was eating, but she hadn't much cared, not on her own account. She had no appetite anyway.

'Shall we ask the waiter to fetch you something else? I'm sure it won't take a minute for them to rustle up something nice for you.'

Eileen smiled, more easily this time. So, she too was

used to living with a difficult man. 'That's very kind of you, Mrs Kessler, but –'

'I told you. Sophie. Please.'

'Sophie. Like I say, it's a kind thought, but I'm not hungry. Thank you all the same.'

Sophie closed her hand over Eileen's. 'Harry told me the sad news this morning. I can't imagine what it must be like to lose a child. And in such an accident . . .'

Eileen could manage nothing more than a brief nod. She couldn't trust herself to speak without bursting into tears, and she didn't want to make a fuss, not in front of all these strangers. Gabriel would hate it.

'Children are always such a worry,' Sophie went on with a sigh. 'We try to protect them, wrap them up and keep them safe, but, in the end, we have to let them go, let them make their own mistakes. Take my youngest, Sammy, the one over there, sitting next to . . . Luke is it?'

'That's right.' Eileen's voice was little more than a whisper.

'You should see the way he's been carrying on lately. Girl trouble. It has to be. A mother knows. He's hardly said a word for weeks. But will he talk to me about it?' She tutted, somehow managing to express a mixture of frustration, resignation, and love for her child. 'Course he won't.'

'He does look pale.'

'Pale? That's not the half of it. He's not sleeping, he picks at his food, and as for conversation at the dinner table . . . He might as well not be there. But, please, God,' Sophie picked up her champagne saucer, raising it in salute, 'maybe he'll meet someone at Daniel's wedding.' She took a long draft from the glass before setting it down, then slapped the table, her heavily ringed hand making a

124

metallic clunk. 'Eileen, I've had a wonderful idea. You and your family, you must join us at the wedding. Next Tuesday. Be our guests. I'll send you an invitation. You must come.'

A wedding. Eileen said nothing. She just let the woman talk.

'For us, Tuesday's a lucky day for getting married, and not just because the caterers are cheaper midweek.' She raised her shoulders and winked, trying to draw Eileen into her joke, then reached across the table, tapping a perfectly painted Tangerine Pearl fingernail on the tablecloth by her husband's side plate.

'Harry, sorry to interrupt, but I was saying to Eileen, she and the family should come to Danny and Rachel's wedding. It would be a great way to seal this new business venture of yours. A real celebration.'

'What an idea.' Harry clapped his hands together, and pointed at Sophie, demonstrating to everyone his wonder and admiration for his wife. 'You're a clever woman. But I suppose that's obvious.' He grinned broadly. 'After all, you married me didn't you? And of course they'll all come to the wedding.' He raised his glass. 'The 20th, it's a date.'

Sammy and Luke's eyes met before they hurriedly looked away from each other; Brendan and Gabriel exchanged a tense, snatched glance, with Brendan willing his father to say the right thing.

Maurice noticed both connections with interest.

Then, Gabriel spoke. 'Thanks,' he said. 'And any other time we would have been honoured. But, with our recent unhappiness, it's probably too soon for us to go to a wedding.' He pointed his cigar – that he, like the other men, had been smoking throughout the meal – at Eileen, who was staring intently at her plate as if the untouched sole might have a message for her. 'Especially for my wife.'

Harold Kessler shrugged and spread his hands – a gesture that was beginning to annoy Gabriel in a very serious way. 'I understand,' he said generously, actually not understanding at all – they came out tonight didn't they? But who wanted them at the wedding anyway? He stood up and reached out to Gabriel. 'Still, today, today has been a good day.'

Gabriel also stood up, wondering what the little prat was up to now.

He might have known.

Harry put his arms round Gabriel and hugged him, the top of his bald head only just reaching Gabriel's top pocket handkerchief.

'Come here, come here,' he muttered into Gabriel's chest.

Gabriel stood there stiffly waiting for Kessler to let him go, but instead, he jerked back his head, cocked it to one side, and held Gabriel at arm's-length, exuding all the insincere emotion of a professional mourner hanging around for a free drop of the hard stuff after a funeral.

'We'll have a good future together,' he said, wagging his head up and down. 'A good future.'

Gabriel found a smile from somewhere. Was the little bleeder ever going to let him go?

He could have showered the band with kisses of gratitude when they stopped playing and the drummer performed a complicated roll to get everyone's attention, followed by the bandleader announcing the cabaret.

Gabriel and Harold – apart at last – took their seats as the main lights dimmed and the stage lighting turned from white to a deep, unsubtle mauve. The froufrou curtains lifted and a troupe of high stepping showgirls, wearing towering feathers in their hair, staggeringly high heels on their feet, and a brief scattering of sequins on their bodies, began kicking and wiggling to the Latin rhythms of 'Mambo Italiano'.

'Here, Luke,' snorted Pete Mac, elbowing his brother-in-law in the ribs. 'This is one of your favourites innit? One of the old ones they play down the Lighterman's Arms. At the drag shows.'

Maurice's ears pricked at the mention of the notorious Isle of Dogs pub that he had found within days of arriving in London.

Luke stood up. Christ, Pete Mac got on his nerves. 'Excuse me,' he said, stabbing a thumb in the direction of the lavatories.

Gabriel produced yet another smile. This evening was beginning to give him jaw ache.

A few seconds later, Maurice Kessler was on his feet. He pointed to his crotch, and mouthed to his Uncle Harold, 'Think I'd better join him.'

Maurice stood at the urinal next to Luke and undid his flies. Apart from an elderly attendant, who was busying himself polishing one of the big, three-sided mirrors, they were alone.

'So, feller, you weren't much taken by all them tits and arses flashing about out there then?' Maurice said in his broad, Mancunian accent, while studying Luke's penis as uninhibitedly as if he were considering which slice of porterhouse he fancied in a butcher's window. 'And that's certainly not the last turkey left in the shop,' he said approvingly.

Luke, shocked as much as embarrassed, turned his body away and concentrated on trying to finish urinating.

'That qualifies you as being more than well endowed I'd say. And I'll bet it makes you a right popular one with the boys.'

Luke's head jerked up. 'What did you say?'

'Come on, feller,' Maurice said, his voice low, amused. 'Anyone can see you're as bent as a nine bob note.'

'You what?' Luke flashed a look over his shoulder to check that the attendant wasn't eavesdropping. 'Don't be so fucking stupid.' He fumbled as he did up his trousers – his hands were trembling – and walked over to the washbasins.

'Are you saying you're not?' Maurice's voice was mocking, amused.

'Oh, I get it,' Luke said into the mirror, as Maurice again came and stood next to him, closer this time, his sleeve brushing Luke's back. 'You don't like these new arrangements. You're worried you might lose out, so you're trying to wind me up. Trying to cause trouble between the families so it all breaks down before it's even had a chance to get going.'

'On the contrary, feller. I'm just trying to be friendly.' Maurice winked at Luke's reflection and ran a finger up his spine.

Even through the layers of his jacket and shirt, and despite what he refused to admit even to himself, it made Luke shiver – a feeling of contracting waves that ran from the base of his throat, through his chest, right down to his groin.

He shook his head and pulled away. 'What's your fucking game, Kessler?'

'Game's a good word for it.' He paused, letting a wide

grin spread slowly across his lips. 'You see, while I'm not exactly queer myself, I'm game for anything, me. Threesomes, foursomes. Older women. Younger ones. You name it, and I'm in there, feller. In like bloody Flynn.' He checked himself in the mirror, slowly admiring his own reflection. He liked what he saw – slim, but muscled build, just enough over average height to be described by most people as tall, and with a full head of dark, wavy hair that, because he'd kept it up until now, he was convinced he wouldn't lose. Not like his father and Uncle Harold who had both gone bald in their teens. He licked a finger and slicked back his eyebrows and then turned his attention back to Luke. 'And I've always fancied having a few innings batting for the other team. Something nice and intimate at first. A cosy little twosome. So, with a good-looking, well-endowed feller like yourself on offer – and a Southerner . . . Well, that'd be two new scores on my sheet in one go. And who knows, maybe I'll really like it.'

Luke stabbed his finger at his temple. 'You're sick.'

'Sick? No I'm not. I just think it's why we're here on earth: to learn. And I aim to learn as much as I can before I go. And even if I go young, that'll be all right by me. I'll be England's answer to James Dean. A corpse maybe, but a bloody handsome one.'

'You are, you're out of your mind.'

'I'm glad I've met you, Luke O'Donnell, I've always liked a challenge.' Maurice put a hand on his shoulder.

'Get off me.' Luke shook himself free and threw a handful of silver into the tips plate.

At the sound of the coins hitting the dish, the elderly attendant, moving with surprising speed, proceeded to pump away at a fat rubber bulb attached to a silver-topped, cut glass bottle, spraying Luke's head and shoulders with sweet smelling cologne.

'Stop it. I don't want any.' Luke swished his hand around in the mist as if he could brush it away. Then he strode towards the door, about to leave, but then stopped and half-turned to speak to Maurice, knowing he had to deny those things – again – that he'd said about him.

He stood there, clasping the handle, looking over his shoulder at a whole gallery of grinning Maurices leering back at him from each of the row of triple mirrors that lined the wall opposite the cubicles.

'Here, Luke,' they all said. 'You know what they say about protesting too much, don't you, feller?'

By the time Luke got back to the table, he knew he wouldn't be able to just sit there and join in the small talk. He had to get away. Get some fresh air. Blow away the vile stench of the cologne and Kessler's filthy insinuations.

'I'm sorry, everyone. I don't know what's got in to me, I'm feeling a bit strange.'

The sight of Maurice Kessler smirking at him made his stomach lurch.

'I'm going outside for a bit of air.'

'I'll go with you,' said Maurice. 'Make sure you're all right.'

'No, you stay where you are.' Hearing the panic in his own voice, Luke added more calmly, 'Enjoy your brandy.'

'Brendan'll go with you, Luke, won't you Brendan?' Eileen asked. 'He really doesn't look well.'

'I'm fine.'

'Brendan?'

'Okay.' Brendan frowned, noticing the look of amusement on Maurice's face. There was something about the bloke that Brendan really didn't like, and it wasn't just because he was a Northerner, or even because he was a Kessler. He just made Brendan's flesh crawl.

Brendan and Luke stood outside the club, dragging on their cigarettes, blowing clouds of smoke and steamy breath into the freezing night air. Luke staring ahead, oblivious of his surroundings, concentrating on the pictures in his head; Brendan focussing on the passing punters, nodding at the accuracy of his predictions as he guessed which door each of them would slip into as they sought out their own particular choice of illicit entertainment. Every one of the mugs was ready and eager to be separated from his hard-earned cash in the West End equivalent of the O'Donnells's places in the East End. The sorts of places that were as good as money printing factories, and that they were now planning on letting the Kesslers have a share in. It was like a bad joke.

Luke flicked his cigarette butt into the gutter. 'You know, Brendan, perhaps it wouldn't be such a bad idea if we went to this wedding.'

'What?'

'Mum seemed to manage all right tonight. And we wouldn't have to stay that long.'

'Have you taken leave of your senses?'

'It wouldn't hurt.'

Brendan turned full onto Luke and stared right into the eyes that wouldn't meet his. 'Hold on, I get it. *That's* what all this lark's been about tonight. I wondered why you've been up and down like a bride's nightie. It's the snatch innit? You've lost your bottle.'

Luke dropped his head back against the wall, puffed out his cheeks, and closed his eyes. 'I'm not like you, Brendan. This is all you've ever wanted, but you know I've never been sure about it. And as for this job, I honestly don't understand why Dad wants to take the risk. The streets'll be full of Christmas shoppers, plus we don't even know they'll be delivering the money that day.'

Brendan took his brother's face in his hands, making him look into his eyes. 'First of all, Luke, we're doing the job at seven o'clock in the morning. Not many shoppers around then, not unless they're after lifting a couple of pints off a passing milk float. And second – yes, we do know it's being delivered on Tuesday; the clerk called Dad with the code word this morning. They've definitely brought the delivery forward because of the holidays.' He let go of his brother and rubbed his hands together like a stage villain. 'So, that's the wages plus all them lovely Christmas bonuses. Just think about it.'

Luke rubbed his own hands over his face. He felt as if he hadn't slept for a month. 'Look, Brendan, since the accident, I'm even less sure about how much I want to be involved in the business, it's –'

'Hang on a minute. *You're not sure how involved you wanna be?*' Brendan grabbed hold of his brother's arm, dragged him along the street and shoved him into the darkness of a narrow alleyway.

Luke, slipping and skidding on the muck-strewn ground, only saved himself from going over by clutching onto Brendan. 'Have you gone crazy?'

'Not yet, I've not, Luke.' Brendan pushed Luke away from him, sending him staggering backwards into the rough brick wall. 'But I might, so you'd better watch yourself. For someone who reckons he's not sure how

132

fucking interested he is in the business, how come you were so quick setting up this little lot? Getting us hiked up with them bastards?'

'Brendan, don't do this,' said Luke trying to get past him, and away from the stink of whatever it was rising up from around their feet. 'You've been drinking, you don't know what you're saying.'

Brendan stepped forward, sticking his face up close to Luke's, blocking his escape. His breath stank of booze and tobacco, making Luke turn away. He hated the fact that his brother was getting more and more like their father.

'Don't come this crap with me, Luke. First you cover up for Catherine when she was knocking about with that Kessler fucker, and now, because of you, we're tied up tighter than a duck's arse with his whole fucking family. So you're in it up to your neck, whether you like it or not.' He grabbed Luke's face between his finger and thumb, squeezing his cheeks so hard he could feel Luke's teeth through the flesh. 'Understand?'

Luke shook his head, and Brendan, exasperated, let him go.

'It's not like that.'

'Don't take the piss, Luke. Just because you're my brother, doesn't mean I won't get wild with you.'

'I know.'

'*I mean it*. You're in this with the rest of us.'

'But –'

'No, no buts. It's too late for that. And while we're at it, perhaps you'll explain what all that was about back in there, you getting all chummy with that prick's nephew.'

A noise at the top of the alley made Brendan pivot round.

'Oops, sorry, ladies,' said a mocking masculine voice. 'Didn't mean to interfere in your little lover's tiff.'

'Fuck off,' snarled Brendan.

At that moment, Luke was glad they were standing at the bottom of a dark, stinking alleyway. He couldn't have stood Brendan seeing that his cheeks had coloured up like a schoolgirl's.

'Temper, temper,' laughed the man, and then, addressing someone they couldn't see, said, 'Sorry, Brian, we're too late, darling; someone's got our spot already. But maybe they might like a bit of extra company. How about it? Fancy that do you?'

Brendan spat on the ground in disgust. 'If you know what's good for you . . .'

'All right, sweetheart, hint taken.'

Brendan was ready to punch someone, and Luke was beginning to panic. Getting Brendan annoyed was never a good idea, but with the mood he was in tonight it would have been a really stupid thing to do. He had to calm him down.

'Look, Brendan, I promise, all I wanted to do was stop things getting out of hand. There's no edge to what I did, I swear. And surely you can't want it to be like it was before either – not knowing if there was gonna be axes smashing down the front door in the middle of the night; waking up to see a strange bloke standing over our beds with a gun in his hand.'

'We were kids then, Luke. Things are different now. We're men. Or we're supposed to be.'

'I know, and that's why we should be grown up enough to realise we've got to keep a lid on things.'

'If you're trying to pull that *Patricia's having a baby* old fanny on me, Luke, then don't bother.' Brendan leaned into him, his temper coming very close to turning physical. 'All this bollocks tonight: it's all your fucking fault. All of it. So don't even try that sentimental shit. It might have worked on Dad when he was too pissed and too upset to even know what day it was, but it's bloody obvious he's regretting it now. He's sitting back there gritting his teeth just having to talk to the stupid bastard, let alone being expected to go to his son's fucking wedding.'

Luke spoke as evenly as he could manage. 'Hasn't losing Catherine made you think, Brendan? Made you try and figure out what –'

'I get it. You really are a coward.'

'Thanks.'

Brendan sighed wearily. Rowing with Luke. What was the point of that? He'd had just about enough of this whole fucking night. 'I'm sorry, I shouldn't have said that.' He put his hand on his brother's shoulder. 'I know you're nervous about the snatch. It's only natural, first time being in the front line on a job like this. But you're gonna be all right.'

Luke let out a dry, humourless puff of laughter. 'D'you reckon?'

'Trust me. And it'll be a good opportunity to show me I was wrong, that you're not a coward.'

Luke felt like running a million miles away. 'Yeah?'

'Yeah. And anyway, it's good for you, learning new stuff.'

'What do you mean? Who've you been talking to?'

Brendan put up his hands. 'Blimey, Luke, don't be so bloody touchy. I'm trying to be friends here.'

'Sorry. You're right, I am nervous. But I still don't know why I've got to be part of it. Dad's got plenty of experienced blokes he always uses. So why do I have to go along? Come to that, why does *he* have to be there? He's not been on anything like this job for years. Always prides himself on being the businessman.' He put on a breathy imitation of his father's cockney-tinged Galway accent. 'I'm the brains, not the brawn.'

Brendan, despite his anger and frustration, couldn't help but smile at the familiar impersonation – Luke had managed to defuse his brother's temper by mucking about ever since he was a toddler, saving himself from many a well-deserved clout.

'I'll tell you why, shall I, little brother? It's because this Kessler lark has got to him. He wants to show everyone, anyone who might have even the slightest doubt, that he's still a right tough bastard. Game as a bloody beigel. Heart like a fucking lion. And up for anything. Fuck the risk and bugger the danger. Plus, of course, there's one hell of a lot of dough involved.'

'Hasn't he got enough already?'

'There's no such thing, Luke.' Brendan put his arm round Luke's shoulder. 'Believe me. The more someone like Dad has, the more he wants. It's his nature.'

'I don't get it.'

'No, I know, mate. Different temperaments, eh? But think of the sort of expansion that kind of money can finance.'

Luke had nothing to say, well, not anything that would make sense in Brendan's universe.

Brendan punched him playfully in the guts. 'And, apart from Stephen Shea, Dad's gonna keep this one in the family. So, not only do we not have to divvy it up with any nasty, greedy outsiders, it'll also prove how loyal we all are to our dear old dad. You included, I'm afraid, Lukey boy. Good for his image, see. Show he's still got it – the bottle and the brains to pull off the big blag – and that his family stand by him, shoulder to shoulder, right there in the line of fire. That all enough of an explanation for you, little brother? They good enough reasons?'

Brendan wagged a finger at him. 'And, this is the clincher. It's the best buzz you can imagine. I know you don't believe me, but you wait till you feel the kick you get out of it. Better than sex, some blokes reckon.' He laughed. 'Not that red-blooded O'Donnells would ever agree with them sort of nutters, of course. But close enough for it to be bloody fantastic.' He started walking back towards the street. 'Come on, mate, let's go back in there and put on a show for Mum and Dad. Let everyone think we're loving it. I mean, one more lie can't hurt, can it?'

He looked over his shoulder and saw that Luke had made no attempt to move. 'Come on.'

It took Luke less than a minute to decide to follow his brother back to the club.

The first part of the Dahlia's celebrated cabaret had ended, and the place of the long-legged chorus girls had been taken by couples doing their best to dance the Twist the way they'd seen the new dance demonstrated on television.

No one from the O'Donnell–Kessler party had moved onto the dance floor, they were still seated at their table, their numbers swollen by the minders, who, now that the meal was over and plenty of drink had been taken, had been invited to join them.

Luke distanced himself from Brendan by sitting well away from him, but he still watched as his brother fell so

137

easily into making himself the centre of attention amongst the now substantial group of men. He was making them all laugh out loud and slap their hands on the table.

Amongst the men, only Sammy Kessler seemed immune to Brendan's charms, as he put on joke accents, grinned and gurned, and acted out the story of how he and his friend, Baby Bobby Watts – the well-known son of the even more well-known Big Bobby Watts – carried off a two and a half grand con for the price of just three short trips to a rich but gullible junk merchant out in Essex.

Brendan explained how Baby Bobby had been the first to make the journey east to the salt marsh badlands a couple of miles outside Tilbury, introducing himself to the dealer as a Dutchman over on business in the nearby docks – business involving the disposal of a large quantity of top quality, green glass bottles. If only he could find the right customer, he could bring over unlimited supplies from Holland.

The dealer, rich as Croesus, but described by Brendan as looking like a cross between Fagin and the tramps who hung about in Itchy Park, would hardly give him the time of day. Who the hell wanted green glass bottles?

Disappointed, the Dutchman left.

A week later, Brendan turned up at the bloke's yard saying he could only hope that the dealer could help him. He had the possibility of making a killing, if only he could get hold of some green glass bottles, the *exact* size and shape as per the drawing – coloured in and everything – that Brendan showed him. In fact, he told the man, he could take an unlimited supply of the product, if only someone could get hold of them, but he'd heard that they were only available in Holland. His last hope, before making the trip over the water, had been dealers working in the vicinity of the docks in Essex. He wasn't going to be stupid about it, wouldn't be taken for a ride, but he would offer a very good price.

As soon as Brendan left, the dealer was on the phone. Sadly, he had no contact number for the Dutchman, but how difficult could it be to get bottles? But as he described the product to every contact he could think of, he soon discovered just why the man had been trawling the area with no luck. No bottles of the precise colour and description could be found. Other bottles, certainly, but those exact ones . . .

Then, just a few days later, a miracle happened: Baby Bobby turned up at the yard again. But – and he stressed this more than once – the dealer had to bear in mind that this was now a seller's market. The bottles were, so Bobby the Dutchman had heard, the most desirable commodity in the whole of the county. This meant, of course, that Dutch Bobby would need some money up front to show good-will for the supply of his very desirable product.

He had the wedge in his hand before he could say Edam cheese.

Through that little deal, the boys had earned them-selves a nice few quid, but, best of all, the bit that made them all laugh loudest, was the fact that not only did Brendan not deliver the items as promised, they never bloody existed. And if Baby Bobby – a born and bred Eastender, who got the earache if he even had to cross the river to go over South London for the day – was a Dutchman then Brendan would eat his clogs for him, and maybe have a windmill or two for afters.

'Come on, chaps,' said Kessler, with all the flam-boyance that a short, fat man in his forties could muster. 'More drinks to celebrate our union with a family with such a genius amongst them.' He leaned forward and pinched Brendan's cheek. 'And a special one for this boy. A boy any father would be proud of.'

Glasses were raised and congratulations offered.

While Brendan accepted all the praise with convincingly good humour, Maurice Kessler took the opportunity to leave the testosterone-fuelled huddle to go and sit with Luke. 'So, do you fancy another drink then, feller?'

'No, I don't. I don't want anything from you.'

Maurice's face folded into an expression of knowing, easy amusement. He slipped his hand under the table. 'Sure I couldn't tempt you?'

It took Luke a moment to register that Maurice really was touching the inside of his thigh and that his hand was *creeping up towards his balls*.

Luke pulled away. 'Don't you ever . . .'

Maurice raised an eyebrow. 'Sorry,' he whispered. 'Must have slipped.'

Luke got up and went to sit with his mother on the far side of the table. The increased amusement on Maurice's face infuriated him, but Eileen was unaware of her son's discomfort. She was just glad of his company, especially as Sophie Kessler had been hijacked by an embarrassingly drunk Pete Mac, who was even now draping his arm over the back of the poor woman's chair.

Pete Mac sniffed loudly. 'Brendan's not the only one with stories to tell you know, girl.'

Sophie remained polite. 'Really?'

'And you lot . . .' he paused to belch. '. . . ain't the only religious ones either, you know.'

This time she offered a strained smile.

'I helped out at the church fête once. Even though I

140

ain't really churchified meself. But I go along with it. It keeps the old woman happy.' He put his finger to his lips, joining her in his conspiracy. 'That's her – Pat – over there.' He waved and called across to her. 'All right, girl? You women like all that holy lark, don't you, love?'

He returned his attentions to Sophie. 'Anyway, like I was saying, I like to do my bit. So I helped out. Know what I did?'

Sophie had no idea.

'I put the frighteners on this little kid, who'd won everything all day. It looked like the little bugger was going to win the last race in the donkey derby and get the pick of the last of the decent prizes, the one they'd earmarked for the priest. So, you know the donkey he was riding in the derby?'

Sophie didn't, but thought it best to let him continue.

'I kicked it right up the jacksy. It went raving mad, like a wild bull it was. The kid couldn't get anywhere near it. That stopped him, the little bleeder.'

Pete Mac swigged at his drink. 'Should have given the kid a kicking and all really. Right little toerag he was. Wound up in the nick for doing gas meters. Got a couple of birchings by all accounts.' He smirked as if remembering some private joke. 'Mind you, girl, if the truth was told, I reckon Father Shaunessy would have preferred to have had the kid rather than the box of chocolates.' He nudged her roughly. 'The old goat's always enjoyed the company of the altar boys, if you know what I mean.' He grinned broadly. 'His wrist's so limp he can hardly bless himself.'

Sophie's expression had frozen into a tight, thin-lipped grimace. 'I'm sorry, would you excuse me, Mr MacRiordan.' She lifted her chin and gestured to her husband. 'Harry, would you mind calling me a taxi. I don't want to break up the party, but I'm very tired.'

Pete Mac huffed loudly. Silly tart. There he was being nice, even about to ask her if she needed any help up the synagogue – not that he'd actually intended doing anything, but it was a nice thought - and what had she done? Blanked him, that's what. Well, she knew what she could do, the miserable bitch. He'd show her be rude to him.

He wasn't sure how, not this minute, but he'd show her all right.

Chapter 10

It was bang on 7 a.m. Stephen Shea manoeuvred the simple, workmanlike van, bearing the proud legend: *Thomas Simpson and Sons Plumbers. Estab. 1924. Commercial and Private work undertaken*, into the dead-end service road at the side of the tall, West End office block in a street at the back of Oxford Street. Most of the lights were off at that time of the morning, but, exactly as they had expected, there was a lamp on in the service reception, a plain square room furnished with functional office basics, at the rear of the building.

Inside the room, Gabriel, who was sitting in the passenger seat, could make out a middle-aged man wearing the uniform of the Corp of Commissionaires. He had his elbows on his high, clerk's desk, as he sipped from a green enamel mug, and pored over the back pages of the *Daily Mirror*. He didn't even look up as the van drove past.

'Ready lads,' Gabriel said, as he pulled his full-face balaclava down to his chin, nodding to Stephen Shea to do the same.

Brendan, Luke and Pete Mac, sitting on the narrow benches that had been installed along the insides of the back of the van, followed suit.

'Here we go then.' Gabriel crossed himself, picked up his canvas bag, and burst out of the van and through the door of the office.

This time the uniformed man did look up, momentarily more baffled than scared. He put his mug and paper on the desk and rose to his feet. 'What's all this then?' he asked in the tones of a displeased sergeant major questioning a show of high jinks amongst the new recruits. 'What do you want?'

'To wish you a Merry Christmas, of course,' said Gabriel in a fair imitation of a Glaswegian accent.

Pete Mac couldn't help it, he burst out laughing. 'You a Scotchman? You sure, Gabe?'

Gabriel spun round. 'Shut your fucking mouth,' he spat, his accent now slipping all over the British Isles.

'Look out!' yelled Stephen, who was supposed to be guarding the door, but had been the only one to notice the commissionaire picking up the telephone.

Gabriel was on him with the speed and determination of a lurcher after a hare. He grasped the now terrified man's shoulder with one hand, shoved his face flat on the desk with the other – sending the mug flying across the room and spraying tea all over the lino-covered floor – then pulled out a leather-covered cosh from his pocket and whacked it down on the back of the now terrified man's neck. The combination of fear and the lead-assisted rabbit punch knocked him out cold.

Stephen Shea looked at his watch and called over to them from the door. 'They'll be here in less than half an hour.'

Gabriel nodded. 'Right. Concentrate. You, Pete, you bring the things from the van. Brendan,' he jerked his head at the internal, half glazed door. 'You have a quick shufty round the corridor. The cleaners should have gone by now. But just in case there's anyone nosing around out there who wants to be a hero . . . Stephen, take off your balaclava and get ready to greet the security van.' He paused. 'You sure you're still all right with that?'

Stephen laughed. 'Won't I be one of your victims myself?'

'Good man, Stephen.' Gabriel turned to his son. 'Now, Luke, you get his uniform jacket off.'

Luke stood there, staring down at the man, stomach-churning visions of Catherine lying in the road coming unwanted into his head. 'He's bleeding.'

'And you're a bleeding nuisance,' offered Pete Mac, coming back in with his arms full. 'Move yourself Luke or you'll get us all nicked.'

Gabriel spoke softly. 'Ignore him, Luke. Just do as I say.'

Luke didn't answer, didn't trust himself to speak, he just got on with it.

While his son pulled off the man's jacket, Gabriel set out the ropes, cloths, and the can of petrol Pete Mac had fetched from the van.

By the time the wages van arrived, the commissionaire had been tidied away behind a run of lockers in the adjoining changing rooms, where, in a little over ninety minutes, chattering office workers would be stowing their umbrellas, bags, and heavy outdoor footwear. He was bound to a metal and canvas chair, gagged and trussed up like a turkey, and had just over half a gallon of petrol soaked into his trousers. It had mingled with the urine he had released involuntarily when he had come round and realised what was happening to him; the humiliation, fear and fumes had filled his yellowing eyes with tears he couldn't even move to swipe away.

Seeing the plumber's van that was blocking his way into the service road, the driver of the wages truck tutted impatiently, told his guard he wouldn't be a minute, got out of the cab, and slammed the door angrily. This was a good start. Knowing his luck he'd get held up on every single drop – and he had enough of them to do, what with everyone getting paid early because of the holidays.

'Here, mate,' he called to the man who was leaning against the door, puffing on a roll up.

The man was Stephen Shea. He was wearing a bulky overcoat to conceal his body shape; a flat cap, pulled down hard to his eyebrows; thick, milk bottle glasses shoved up high on his nose; and a chunky muffler knotted about his chin. His own mother would have had trouble recognising him. 'Yeah?'

The driver pointed at the van that was blocking his path, stopping him from getting bloody started for the day, never mind finished. 'You the plumber, are you?'

'Sorry, pal, can't help you. Busy all day, see. Got all my jobs mapped out for me by Hitler's mother back at the yard. I'd love to help you, but she'd have me guts for garters. See, what with this cold snap, and Christmas and everything . . . You know how it is. Sorry.'

The man rolled his eyes. 'Look, mate, I ain't got a leak, I've got a delivery to make. And your van's in the way. So, you gonna move it for us or what?'

'Well, I've not really finished yet. Frozen pipes, see. Terrible mess in the Ladies' toilets.' He wrinkled his nose, making his glasses waggle up and down. 'The governor's fault for turning the boiler down, if you ask me. Like an igloo in some of them offices.'

'Do us a favour, mate, we won't be long,' pleaded the driver. 'Go on. I've got Christmas presents to collect for the missus.'

Stephen flicked his roll-up into the gutter. 'Well, so

146

long as you're not. Cos, to tell you the honest truth, I've not actually even been inside there yet to have a look. Wanted a quiet smoke first, see. But if I don't get in there and get it sorted out before them office wallahs start turning up, I'll never hear the bloody end of it.'

'Thanks, you're a good 'un.' The driver gave him a double thumbs up then trotted back to his vehicle. He backed out onto the public road, and Stephen – very obliging – pulled out after him, peering myopically through the distorting lenses of the glasses, allowing the security van to turn round and reverse back in before him, thus swapping places on the service road.

The plumber's van was now effectively the cork in the bottle, blocking the way out for the wages van until Stephen was good and ready to let them go – not that they'd actually be able to go anywhere. Well, not for a while they wouldn't.

The driver and guard jumped out of their vehicle and made their way into the service reception, both more than ready for a quick, reviving cuppa. Five minutes wouldn't hurt, not now they'd got the van out of the way.

Gabriel was sitting at the desk, with the enamel mug set in front of him. He was wearing the commissionaire's uniform jacket and the balaclava. The two men could see his sleeves – dark serge, buttons and braid – but the balaclava was hidden behind the open *Daily Mirror* that Gabriel was holding up in front of him, and apparently studying intently.

'Morning, Stan,' grinned the driver, winking at his guard. 'If only this lot realised how useless you are, you deaf old git, they'd chuck you right out on your arse.'

Gabriel dropped the paper. 'Is that any way to talk to a man who probably fought in Flanders' poppy-covered fields for the likes of you?'

The guard's jaw dropped in an involuntary parody of cartoon surprise. 'What the –' was all he managed to say before Brendan stepped from behind the door and took hold of him, pulling his arms tight behind his back.

Pete Mac grabbed the driver.

'Don't even think about making a fuss, just answer me nice and even like,' said Gabriel, flicking his eyes towards the door. 'I heard you out there. You were talking to someone.'

The men glanced nervously at one another, but said nothing.

Gabriel sighed, disappointed by such an unhelpful response. 'Take them through to the lockers, lads.'

Brendan and Pete Mac marched them into the corridor.

Their eyes widened as they saw Stan gagged and lashed to his seat. Their nostrils twitched.

Gabriel took a lighter from his pocket and held it to the commissionaire's petrol soaked groin. 'You can smell it, can't you? What is it do you think? Petrol, maybe? Very dangerous that can be, especially with a naked flame around.' He made a show of putting the lighter back in his pocket, picked up the petrol can, and held it in mid-swing as though he were about to fling the contents over the driver. '*Well*?'

The driver nearly lost control of his bowels. 'It was a plumber.'

Gabriel turned to the guard, who averted his gaze before he spoke, ashamed of his own cowardice.

'That's right,' he said. 'There's a plumber out there. Bloke with a cap.'

Gabriel nodded. 'Ah, the truth at last – very sensible.' He tossed Luke a length of rope. 'You. Go out and see to him. Make sure he's not going anywhere.' Then he jabbed a finger at the guard. 'And now it's time to take a look in that vehicle of yours.'

'Wait, please,' the driver pleaded. 'Can't we just vanish? Can't you let us make a break for it and –'

Gabriel interrupted him with a raised hand. He then put his finger to his lips to indicate that the man should keep schtum, and took out his lighter again. But this time he sparked it up, and held it right under Stan's nose. 'Don't think so, lads. Do you?'

With Gabriel directing, it took them less than twenty minutes, a fraction more persuasion, and only the minimum of fuss, to get the van opened up for them; to tie the two men to the legs of the desk; to transfer all the money from the wages van to their own – far more than they'd been expecting, the driver having been contracted for extra Christmas drops – to make sure they'd left nothing incriminating behind – and then to drive sedately out of the service road.

It took just a further half an hour to reach a boring looking Morris shooting break, which was to be the vehicle they would use to drive in a time-consuming, nerve-wrackingly circuitous route, finally reaching their slaughter – the flat in Kilburn where they would divvy up and stash their haul – by about a quarter to eleven that morning.

So far, there had been just the one slight hitch, and even then no one except Pete Mac knew about it.

He had thought that while he was tying up the driver, the bloke had muttered at him a bit sarcastically, and so

149

Pete Mac had taken against him. When they were all outside, packed and ready to leave, he had starting running back towards the office, patting his supposedly empty pockets, calling over his shoulder that he was sure he'd had a packet of fags with him, and had better just check. Evidence and all that.

Safely inside and out of earshot of the others, Pete Mac had given the driver a right bollocking about manners, called him a cunt, and had then struck him round the side of the head with a knuckle-duster, catching him on the temple.

Picking up presents for his wife was now going to be the least of the van driver's worries over Christmas. The fractured skull, internal bleeding, and subsequent brain damage would be of far more concern.

Pete Mac's only response to the bloodied and unconscious man, who had flopped forward as far as his bindings allowed, was a slightly giggling, 'Ooops!' But when the guard's bowels gave out in terror, dreading it would be him next, Pete Mac wafted a hand in front of his nose, and gasped.

'You dirty bastard. What is it with you two's manners? And what the hell did you have for fucking breakfast?'

Pete Mac was just about to escape from the stench, disappear out into the fresh air, but he couldn't let the guard get away with it, or else he'd think he'd one over on him. So he turned round, walked back over to the desk, and stamped his heel as hard as he could, full in the man's crutch.

Eileen and Patricia were struggling through the bustle of bag-laden Christmas shoppers in Oxford Street. Neither of them looked very pleased to be there.

'God, I've not got the heart for this, Patricia. Not this year.'

'Look, Mum, it's nearly quarter to twelve. These crowds are only going to get worse. How about calling it a day?' She pulled her mother gently out of the way of a hot chestnut seller's glowing brazier. 'We've got the turkey ordered from Marston's, Alfie Simms is delivering all the veg, and you made the cake and the puddings ages ago. I can pop out tomorrow and get the last few bits down the market.'

Eileen slipped her arm through her daughter's and drew her close. 'You're a good girl, Pat, but come on, let's get this done. The men won't just be expecting a Christmas dinner with all the trimmings and everything else we can cram on their plates. Big kids that they are, they'll be expecting something to unwrap waiting for them under the tree.'

Patricia knew that her mother was kidding herself, that all their efforts were actually nothing to do with what the men wanted, but were about her feeling the necessity to go through the motions, to do what they did every year, to make the house and table look the way Catherine used to love at a time of year she used to adore. 'If you're sure you're up to it.'

Eileen's lips compressed in sadness as she held back the tears. 'Hark at you in your condition worrying yourself about me. It's me should be looking after you, darling.'

'You're letting us stay round your place over the holiday.'

'*Letting* you? I couldn't think of anything I'd want more.'

'Except having Catherine back, eh, Mum?'

151

That did it, the tears spilled over onto her cheeks. 'Yes, love, apart from that.'

'Come on, Mum. If we're brave enough to put up with those men of ours, we're brave enough to face the crowds in Selfridges.' Patricia took out her hankie and dabbed away the dampness on her mother's face. 'Might even have a quick look at the maternity dresses, eh?'

Her tone didn't carry the conviction of her words.

While Eileen and Patricia half-heartedly compared the length of men's cashmere scarves, just a few miles away, in an historic synagogue on the edge of the City of London, Daniel Kessler was bringing down his foot on a linen wrapped glass, shattering it with a loud, satisfying crack.

Cries of 'Mazel tov!' echoed around the ancient walls as Sophie Kessler, tears of joy rolling down her cheeks, threw her arms round her husband's neck.

'Harry, our little Danny, a married man – how can it be possible?'

'I'll show you the bills for the wedding if you really need proof. Now, come on, let's get to the hall and get some of that food and champagne down us before your sisters guzzle it all.'

As the wedding party bustled around outside, getting into the fleet of cars waiting to take them to the reception, Kessler sniggered to himself like a schoolboy who'd just heard a grown-up talking about willies. He hadn't thought that much could have topped O'Donnell falling for the idea that he'd brought his family back to escape the threat of more riots, rather than realising he'd had little choice but to leave Notting Hill once Rachman had decided to take over. But today was special, his eldest son was now a married man, a man who would one day be more than capable not only of taking over the family businesses, but the O'Donnell bastards' businesses into the bargain.

He couldn't have been a happier man.

Patricia had, after not much argument – she hadn't the energy for it – allowed her mother to pay for the late lunch they had both done little more than pick at. The excitement and enthusiasm of everyone surrounding them had done nothing to lighten their mood.

Patricia stood up and began buttoning her coat. 'Mum, can I say something?'

'You know you can say anything to me, love.' Eileen wasn't looking at her daughter, she was concentrating on easing her gloves over her fingers.

'I know I've got to try and think of the baby as a new start, but it's Pete, Mum. He's just so . . . Aw, I don't know how to explain it.' She flapped her hands in exasperation. 'I know it sounds daft, but he's just so flipping *big*. Like a great big bull crashing about and making a mess, and not listening, and always doing what he wants and never thinking about telling me when he's coming home, and . . .' Her arms dropped to her side as her words ran out. Her chin dropped almost to her chest. 'It's like he just doesn't care about anything but himself.'

'I know, love.' Eileen gave up on her gloves and shoved them into her pocket. Her youngest might have been taken from her, but she still had a duty to her other children. She couldn't abandon them by allowing herself to wallow in self-pity; she had to try for their sakes. Be it by buying them silly gifts or trying to help them make the best of a not very good situation.

153

'We all have our burdens to bear, darling, but, when you think about it, we're better off than a lot of women. At least our men provide for us, look after us, and protect us. They might not always be the most sensitive to what we're feeling, and not bother much about asking what we want from life, but they do work hard. That's why they need to relax, have a few drinks – maybe even a few drinks too many. Let their hair down. And we . . . we just have to try and understand them. It's the price we pay.' She paused, summoning the final justification. 'And better than living in some hovel in Ireland with no water or electric.'

Patricia bent down and began gathering up her bags from under the table, not as convinced as her mother apparently was as to what was worth the sort of price they were paying.

When Gabriel had led them into the slaughter earlier that day, they had all – even Luke – been chuckling like monkeys, with their arms full of shopping bags: an ordinary group of chaps paying someone a visit at Christmas time. Luke had been surprised, to say the least, by the inside of the pleasant, little two-bedroom flat.

On a highly polished dining table there were muslin-draped plates of sandwiches, cheese and biscuits, and fruit. And around the plates were neatly laid out tins of beer with an opener and glasses, and four thermos flasks – which they soon discovered where filled with whiskey-fuelled coffee and tea – and even a home-baked cake, complete with jolly, if amateurish, Christmas icing showing a snowman standing next to a lop-sided fir tree.

They had dumped the bags on the floor – all carrying the names of high street chains, department stores and even one or two from Dublin, just what good Irish lads coming over to England to see their families in Kilburn would be carrying – and threw themselves onto the armchairs and sofa.

'Jesus, Stephen,' grinned Gabriel. 'I thought I was getting too old for all this.'

Stephen grinned back at him. 'You too old, Gabe? Never.'

Gabriel opened one of the glossier, string-handled bags and lifted out a brick of bank notes. He tossed it over to Stephen. 'Just that would be enough to finance opening that drinking club I've been thinking about over Plaistow way.'

Stephen clapped his hands around it, weighing it appreciatively. 'Happy Christmas, Gabe.'

'And to you, my friend. Now let's have a drink. I might make my living out of crime, Stevie, old son, but I am passionate about me leisure. I just need a glass in my hand and a fucking great wedge in me bin. What more could a simple man like me ask for?'

Luke, who, up until now, had said very little, opened one of the cans and poured the cold beer down his throat. The excitement of the robbery had both shocked and excited him, disturbed and thrilled him. He had beamed like a tickled baby one minute, and had shaken like an abandoned one the next. But now he just felt drunk from the combination of adrenaline, too many slugs of warm, hip flask whiskey in the van, the two cups full of thermos flask toddy he'd gulped down without it barely touching the sides – now all topped up with the beer.

'Here, Brendan,' he said, 'who was that copper? You remember, the one who helped us out when that other one stopped us for speeding?'

'Medway,' said Brendan without a pause.

'Yeah, Medway, that was his name.' Luke put down his can, ripped a stack of notes from one off the bags, tore off the paper binder and threw the money in the air. 'Happy Christmas, PC do-us-a-favour Medway. To you and yours. Have a Happy-bloody-Christmas, mate.'

'Good thinking, Luke, very good,' said Brendan, smiling indulgently as he took the opener from the arm of his brother's chair. 'I told you coming on this job'd be good for you.' He popped a can for Gabriel and then one for himself. 'That'll be a sensible thing – showing him our appreciation.'

'You're not really gonna bother treating him are you, Brendan? I reckon he was a right flash fucker.'

Brendan looked coolly at his brother-in-law; he spoke quietly, slowly, his restraint not hiding his disdain. 'He did us a favour on a very difficult day. And we're going to say thank you. You see, that's the problem with you, Pete. You don't get it, do you, the old back scratching bit? Or the idea that you should keep your word?' He paused, sipped at his beer. 'When it's in the interest of the family, you act nice. It keeps things sweet.'

'What, like I tried being nice to that Kessler's old woman? The ungrateful, stuck-up cow.'

'What're you going on about now?'

'That Kessler bitch. She didn't want to know in the Dahlia Club, did she? Making conversation with her I was, all polite and everything.'

Gabriel wasn't really listening to what they were talking about – something to do with coppers and polite conversation, or something – but he was confident Brendan could handle it, whatever it was. And, anyway, he had other things on his mind. He looked at his watch and smiled as the telephone rang, right on time.

'Here, Gabe,' said Pete Mac, all saucer-eyed. 'You don't think that that's Danny Kessler calling us for advice about what he should be doing on his honeymoon tonight, do you?' He pumped his elbows and waggled his hips suggestively. '*Go on my son, give her one!*'

Gabriel didn't respond to Pete Mac, instead, he calmly checked his watch again, and with a deep, satisfied sigh, he stood up.

'It's for me,' he said, and went out in the hallway to answer the phone.

'Gabriel, thank God you're all right.' It was a woman's voice, soft and concerned.

'I'm just fine and it's good to hear from you, my love. It's been quite a day.'

'Is everything at the flat okay for you? Enough to eat and drink for everyone?'

'Couldn't be better. Everything's perfect as always, my angel, except of course that you're not here. It's empty without you.'

There was a contented pause as the praise was accepted with pleasure. Then, 'I'm glad.'

'Glad you're not here?'

She heard the smile in his voice. 'Don't tease me, Gabriel O'Donnell. Now, are you managing without me?'

'Rosie Palmer, how could I ever manage without you, my darling?'

He put down the receiver and went back into the boys with a warm smile on his face.

They all knew better than to question him, but he spoke before they even had the chance.

'Pete Mac was right,' he said, now sternly straight-faced. 'It was the Kesslers. But they didn't want my

157

marital advice, they wanted my blessing. So, I think a toast is in order, lads.' He raised his can, using it to make the sign of the cross in the air, and said very solemnly, 'To Danny Kessler, his lovely bride and her new family.'

When the others burst out laughing, Gabriel tried to hold his serious expression, but failed totally. He threw back his head and shouted out loud, 'May they all behave themselves or rot in hell like the dogs they are!'

Chapter 11

Brendan pulled on the handbrake and smiled. It was a fine, bright afternoon, the kind of day that lifted your spirits, with the sky the sort of inspiringly cloudless blue that, when you looked out at it from behind the car window, made you think it might just be July, that you could walk outside with rolled up shirtsleeves and feel the heat of the summer sun on your back.

But appearances can be deceptive. Outside it was still winter, so cold and crisp that, as he got out of the car and breathed in, Brendan felt as if he were taking down great gulps of iced mountain water, making his lungs contract from the shock of it. Although, it had to be said, what he was inhaling on Shoreditch High Street, was a very long way from the pure air he'd tasted during his childhood stays in Galway and Kildare. Because the high street on which Brendan was standing was on the 'wrong' side of the ancient wall – the old Roman barrier that, while no longer visible, was still most definitely there, dividing the world of wealth and privilege that was the City, from the shadowy streets of the East End that occupied its backyard – a place where working people spent their lives manufacturing goods and providing services for their privileged neighbours.

As always, when Brendan parked so close to the City boundary, he wondered if, one day, he might cross that divide, and make it meaningless, be accepted for who he was, and not just because he had a thick roll of notes in his pocket. But, for now, he was satisfied with taking his neighbours' money in exchange for providing them with the means to meet their three seemingly inexhaustible needs – booze, betting, and whores.

He issued a final instruction to the two men inside the car, then crossed the pavement and stood outside a busy builders' merchants.

As if summoned by a bell, a brown-overalled assistant appeared by his side.

Brendan slipped him two pound notes and the man smiled and nodded. 'Course,' he said. 'Don't you worry about a thing, Mr O'Donnell. It'll be a pleasure to keep an eye on your motor. A real pleasure.'

The exchange was also a pleasure for Brendan: a further strengthening of his reputation as being a man with enough scratch in his pocket to be generous, and confident enough in himself to know that his bidding would be done.

He patted the assistant on the shoulder, turned and beckoned for Luke and Pete Mac to get out of the car and join him.

Brendan was now striding along, with his brother and brother-in-law flanking him, heading east towards a narrow alley, which threaded through to a cobbled cul-de-sac that anyone unfamiliar with the area would probably never have realised was there.

At Brendan's signal – a raised, leather-gloved hand – they came to a halt at the top of the short, block turning, and, despite their familiarity with the street, stood and weighed up the situation, taking their bearings as carefully as if they were on a military reconnaissance.

The roadway was flanked on one side by the high, almost windowless walls of a sweet factory; the other by the wide-open front of a furniture finishers, where they could see bow-backed men and boys working in a way that they never would. At the bottom of the street, was the dull brick façade of the incongruously named Bellavista club.

Being mid-afternoon, the little street was busy with the traffic and sounds of manufacturing, and the air was filled with the sweet, heavy scent of boiling sugar, mixed with the equally sweet, yet somehow acrid stench of toxic polishes and glue. The labourers and craftsmen in the furniture workshop, used to such comings and goings, flashed envious yet cursory glances at the three men standing at the top of the street in their expensive, unstained clothes, presuming they were just more lucky buggers who could chose to spend their afternoons in the Bellavista Club rather than having to worry themselves about the finer points of veneers, finishes, and rotten lacquered brass fittings.

They were right in one way, the three men were going into the club, but they weren't being seduced by the bold neon light over its door that winked its saucy, candy-floss pink come hither, promising as it did a business very different from the production of cough candy twists and dining-room suites. The trade in which the club specialised was, in actual fact, quite prosaic: the sale of alcohol to those whose thirst could not be satisfied by the everyday licensing hours extended to drinkers in other more 'regular' establishments – and that wasn't what attracted them either. Well, not exactly.

'Right, lads,' said Brendan, shooting his spotless French cuffs and smoothing down his thick black hair, which was no longer greased into a quiff, but was allowed to fall forward in a fashionable, more natural style. 'Let's get ourselves inside and explain the new arrangements to Mr Johnson.'

Brendan put his palms flat on the brick wall on either side of the door, rocked back on his heels, judged his distance, and then rammed one chisel-toed Chelsea boot, square and flat footed – *smack!* – against the hinge side of the door. It would have been easier kicking in the lock side, but he knew kicking the hinge side would cause more damage, make more impact, lend more drama to their entrance.

It took him two more goes to send the door splintering in on itself with an at first slow creak, and then with a swift, dusty *whhhump!* as it finally surrendered and hit the floor.

Luke threw a look over his shoulder. Not one of the workers – being used to some of the club's drunker customers acting very badly indeed – had been foolish enough to show even a hint of curiosity.

As Brendan brushed any stray specks of grime from his sleeves, he tutted with concern. 'Not much care being taken of these premises, is there, lads? Shame, prime location like this. Think we'll have to explain our insurance policy to Keithy Johnson all over again, don't you?'

Pete Mac grinned. 'Here, that was good, Brendan – *insurance policy*. You make us sound like the men from the Pru.'

Despite its grandiose name, the Bellavista was little more than a very large, low-ceilinged room, having once been the workroom and store for a gown manufacturer who had long since retired to Hendon. It was no longer packed tight with whirring industrial sewing machines, and hissing Hoffman presses, but was fitted out with plain wooden tables, kitchen-style Windsor chairs, and a functional, undecorated bar from which over-priced, unbranded drinks were served in not very clean glasses. There was a single, evil-smelling lavatory that was generally ignored, the customers preferring to risk the elements rather than the stench, and to relieve themselves in the corners of the alleyway outside.

And yet most of the tables were occupied, and by surprisingly smartly turned out customers; some were playing cards, one was flicking through the early afternoon City Prices edition of the evening paper, but most were happy to be simply drinking, smoking, talking and laughing, passing their time with like-minded men.

There were no women in the room.

And no one except the man behind the bar seemed all that disturbed or interested, as Brendan, Luke and Pete Mac entered the place, walking over the kicked-in door with as little heed as if it had been the unpolished doorstep of the mother of their worst sworn enemy.

Why should the customers have cared? If it had been a police raid they'd have known about it, would have been given plenty of advance warning to get out, as more than a few of the customers were in the force themselves. So, best just to keep their heads down, keep their eyes on their drinks, and maybe get a bit of free entertainment thrown in. Let sleeping dogs lie and all that. That's the ticket. Have another sip. Chin, chin!

The bystanders had it right; the object of the O'Donnells's visit wasn't anything to do with any of them. The O'Donnell boys and their knuckle-headed brother-in-law were there to see the man behind the bar –

Keithy Johnson, the sole owner and proprietor of the Bellavista drinking club.

Keithy was an overweight, crop-headed man in his fifties, who looked as if he hadn't seen daylight for at least the past thirty years, and had not exerted himself physically for the past forty. But who now, from the panic in his eyes, the sweat on his top lip, and the way he was wringing the grubby glass cloth through his hands, looked as if he couldn't decide whether he should run like the clappers or just give in and cack his pants right where he stood.

'Keithy, old son,' said Brendan, hoisting himself up onto a cheap, bamboo barstool, and nodding for Luke and Pete Mac to stand either side of him. 'I know we could have rung the bell and all that, but I thought I might do you a favour, let you know the sort of mood I'm in before we begin.' He smiled his handsomely disarming smile – Keithy's new best friend. 'Just so you wouldn't make the mistake of going and upsetting me, like.'

Keithy gulped – a stranded codfish with no way back to the sea – took out a bottle from under the counter and held it up for Brendan's approval, careful to shield its well-known label from everyone else in the room. 'This suit you?'

Brendan shook his head.

'It's okay,' Keithy assured him. 'It's the proper gear, not the shit I serve them lot.'

'We're not here to drink, Keithy,' said Brendan, offering the man a sad downturn of his lips and a regretful shake of his head, all the while holding poor, distraught Keithy's gaze without so much as a blink. 'We're here to chuck you out.'

'You're here to what?' Keithy Johnson looked from

Pete Mac to Luke and back to Brendan. 'You're having me on, right?'

'Not really, mate. No.' He leaned forward. 'Look, you saw how we came steaming in just now. Well, what sort of protection could you ever hope to get that could insure you against that? And as you know, Keithy, we're the only insurers round here anyway, so what's the point you trying? And – I dunno – we just want the club. Simple as that. So now it's ours.'

'But you can't –'

'I'm sorry, Keithy, but we can. And, let's face it, let's put our cards on the table and be honest here, you've got no one to blame but yourself. Pete Mac came round here only last week offering you all sorts of extra protection, all kinds of help, but would you accept it? No, course you wouldn't. Thought you could have one over on us, didn't you?'

'That's not what happened. You know I couldn't afford the sort of money he was talking about.'

'Yeah, course I know. I ain't fucking stupid.' Brendan leaned back from the bar and grinned. 'Good plan of mine, eh?'

'Please, Brendan . . .'

'Anyway, perhaps you could have afforded it if you'd stopped playing the gee-gees.' Brendan put on a suitably rueful expression. 'Betting always was a mug's game.' He leaned forward again and whispered. 'But don't you go telling no one I said that, will you Keithy? Don't want me profits going down, now do I?' He winked as he settled himself back on the stool and folded his arms.

'Now, you either tell everyone a nice little story – I dunno, your wife's dying or something. Ask them all to leave nice and quietly, and say the club'll be closed for a day or two. Then you follow them out that front door – or rather, what was the front door. That, or we have to help you on your way. And you wouldn't like that, Keithy, old son, you have my solemn word on it.'

Keithy grabbed the edge of the bar as if it would give him safe anchor. 'Brendan, please.'

'*Sorry?*'

He shook his head, getting his words right. 'I mean, Mr O'Donnell, please. Don't do this to me. It's the wife, she's –'

'Ugly?' suggested Pete Mac.

'Nice one, Pete,' said Brendan, still staring unflinchingly at Keithy, who was now sweating as if it really were July.

'Come on, gentlemen, please.' He held up the Scotch again. 'Why don't you let me pour you all a nice drink?'

'Because we don't fucking want one,' said Brendan. He snatched the bottle from Keithy's hand and tossed it over his shoulder, an unwanted chip wrapper thrown into the wind. 'Time to get to work, lads.'

It took just a few minutes of bottle smashing, table kicking, and chair launching for even the most hardened drinkers amongst the Bellavista's clients to get the message that they were being invited by the O'Donnells to vacate the premises as soon as their booze-decelerated bodies could manage.

Only Keithy and Herbie – the dozy, elderly potman who had only just returned from the ripeness of the lavatory – were left behind to defend their territory, and once Pete Mac had raised a splinter-ended chair leg to Herbie's face, it was just Keithy.

Keithy hadn't been expecting Brendan's first punch, a right jab straight to the cheek. But he did try to avoid the

166

second. No chance. It threw him off balance, sending him windmilling into the shelves of glasses behind him.

He staggered to his feet, the blood pouring down his face from a split eyebrow sending rivulets of red into the deep creases of his podgy cheeks. He leaned back on the lower shelf, not even noticing the shattered glass. 'Please. Leave now, chaps. Before some of the customers come back to see what's going on. Some of them are coppers you know.'

'Coppers? In an illegal drinking bash? Never! Next thing you'll be telling me is that some of them were kaylied.' Brendan, his hands still gloved, reached in his pocket. 'Go and stand by the door and keep an eye out, Luke.'

Luke hesitated, guessing he was being got out of the way. He wasn't entirely sure whether he was pleased or not.

'Now, Keithy.' Brendan turned back to the bloody, frightened man, smiling at him with just his mouth – all white teeth and steady, emotionless gaze. 'Do you know what I always love about Christmas time? Have done ever since I was a nipper? Any idea?'

'No Bren . . . Mr O'Donnell.'

'Well, I'll tell you, shall I? Having all that fruit, that's what. The grapes, and tangerines and nuts and that. Smashing. A real treat. In fact, I love the nuts so much I've kept my very own pair of nutcrackers in my pocket, just in case I should ever be lucky enough to come across any on the off chance. Then I'd be ready, see. I mean, you know how it is, it'd be a bit of sorry situation if I didn't have me equipment with me, now wouldn't it?'

Keithy gulped and nodded, blinking back the blood that was trickling into his eye.

'Trouble is, I'm a bit out of practice, not had any nuts since what, must be Boxing Day. Weeks ago. So maybe I should get in a bit of practice, eh, Keithy? Reckon that'd be a good idea?'

Keithy's mouth felt as if it had been glued shut.

'What's that Keithy? Can't hear you, mate. Here, tell you what, you can give me a hand. *Your* hand. And it won't only be a bit of practice for me, it'll be a little reminder for you and all.'

Brendan grabbed Keithy's hand, and yanked him across the bar. His eyes narrowed and his voice dropped. 'A reminder to do as you're fucking well told.'

'No, Mr O'Donnell, please.'

'Don't do this, Keithy, don't get me wind up, or I might just have to practise on your fucking nuts and all.'

Luke heard Keithy Johnson's screams and felt an involuntary, shameful stirring in his groin. Brendan was right: despite what Luke had always protested, there was an excitement in this business that he was beginning to get used to. And to like.

It was a fact of which he wasn't proud.

Brendan put his arm round Luke's shoulders, guiding him back towards the car. 'All right, Luke?'

'Yeah.'

Brendan squeezed him. 'Good, good. Now,' he said over his shoulder to Pete Mac who was tacking along behind, swigging from the bottle of single malt that he'd liberated from under the counter. 'Nip round Charlie Taffler's and tell him we're ready for him to start the refurb. And tell him quick as he can, Pete. He's got two weeks tops.' Brendan turned back to his brother. 'I right fancy the idea of having a bit of a do after we've sorted out the scrap deal with the Kesslers.' He grinned nastily. 'Be good to have somewhere nice and new to take our nice new friends, eh, lads?'

Harold Kessler wasn't a fool, he understood the value of good quality scrap in a still scarce market, but he looked about him and wondered what the hell he was getting himself into. This place didn't feel right.

Here he was on a dark, miserable afternoon – one of those days when the sky was like a dull, heavy lid, not letting more than the feeblest of the last of the dying light in through the cracks – with the bitterly cold weather doing its worst to freeze his arse off, and the slicing, icy wind slanting the rain down between his neck and collar, and squelching into his shoes. And what was he doing? Standing on a tiny airfield in the open mouth of an arc lit, corrugated iron hangar, somewhere out beyond North London, in a place where the suburbs had finally petered out, leaking into a scrubby, brown-grassed countryside. It was a place Harold Kessler didn't recognise, hadn't been to before, and didn't much want to come to again.

And then there were the men. There must have been nearly a dozen of them. They made Kessler really nervous. He'd been told by O'Donnell to bring along no one but family, that it was to be hush-hush, too important to risk anyone else finding out about it. Yet all these dungaree-clad men, clambering about on an aeroplane that filled up almost the entire space inside the hangar, could get a good enough look at him to identify him and grass him up anytime they felt like it.

Then there was the more immediate threat the men presented: they could come running at him right now if they had the mind to, with their spanners and hammers

169

waving above their heads, knock him to the ground and take everything off him as easily as picking an apple off a tree. Kill him even. He might as well have had a target painted on his arse by way of invitation. And here he was, standing there like a fucking lemon, while his car, his one means of escape, was parked deep in the shadows where he couldn't even see it.

He wished he was somewhere else, somewhere that was warm and dry, maybe sitting by a fire with a double Scotch in one hand and a nice little bird in the other. In point of fact, he would have been quite happy to have been sitting indoors with Sophie. Anywhere that meant he didn't have to look at Gabriel O'Donnell's self-satisfied mooey, as he stood there, looking down from his six feet bloody two, or whatever he was, pretending not to notice the cold and rain.

'Isn't this a bit, well, how can I say . . .' Kessler looked around him as he searched for the right word. '. . . casual?'

'Trust me,' said Gabriel enjoying the man's discomfort. 'Just be said and led, Harry. Just be said and led. Casual's a good thing to be.' He chewed at the damp end of his cigar, which, he'd made a loud point of promising Harold Kessler, would remain unlit while they were in such close proximity to the aircraft; speaking to him as if he were a nervous, elderly relative who needed to be reassured.

'I promise you,' Gabriel continued, 'casual's a *very* good thing to be.'

Kessler hated this, hated feeling like a lost tourist being offered obvious, patronising advice by a know-all bastard of a local.

'See, when you act casual, Harry,' Gabriel said, now in smiling, benevolent parent mode, 'no one's suspicious.

170

It's the jumpy ones that interest them, the ones they watch. It's the nervous ones what become their prey.' Still smiling, he sighed, studying the unlit cigar with a show of regret for the smoke he wasn't able to enjoy. 'Now, shall we get down to business? You look like this weather's getting you down.'

Gabriel's smile didn't last very long. He had gone from patronising to bloody annoyed in a few brief moments. And now, after nearly fifteen whole, perishing minutes of wasted time, his lips were twitching with irritation, and he was feeling something that was a very long way from casual.

They were still standing outside the hangar, but were no further forward with the deal, despite Gabriel having patiently run through the details – again and again.

What was this fool Kessler expecting from him? He was doing the bloke a massive favour even letting him get a sniff of this deal. *And he had the cheek to question him*?

He hadn't liked the rude, arrogant little runt before this had happened, but now . . . Now he would happily have pulped his stupid face for him, taken real delight in feeling his knuckles smash into the bones behind his smooth, fat, baby chops.

Why had he listened to Luke's old fanny about truces and deals with these bastards? He must have been out of his head. The boy had little more than an amateur's experience of the inside running of the business, and yet he'd let him talk him into getting hiked up with this load of crap.

He was having to stand here, like a spare prick at a wedding, going over the details of a deal that anyone with any brains would have blessed him for, would have snatched off his hand to have been even a little part of. Did Kessler really not get it? Or was he just acting like the aggravating little turd he really was? If it wouldn't have meant losing face, he'd have walked away. Left him there, done up like the kipper he was: no guts and two faces.

Kessler's lips were moving again, and Gabriel knew he'd better listen, even if he had long since realised that whatever the fool was going to say would be about as much use as two penn'orth of fucking tripe.

'So, tell me, Gabe, how do I know that the scrap I take away in my trucks is the metal that they've cut off that plane in there? Where's my guarantee that justifies my investment here?'

Back to this.

Okay . . .

Gabriel breathed out slowly and drew his fingers down his face, doing his best to hold his temper. 'Like I said, Harry, one of the reasons I brought you along this afternoon was so that you could test the goods in whatever way you chose – magnets, chemicals, filter papers, you name it. That testing's for all our sakes. You do it before you give me half the dough you got from your investor. And before I pay that half over to my contact to seal the deal. Right, so far so good. Then, when my contact's team've got rid of all the identifiable parts, and cut it up, and it looks nothing like the plane it once was, *then* it'll be nice and ready for your trucks to collect, and you can test it again. Just the same way. Or different. Up to you. If you're happy with it, my contact gets the other half of his payment. Then you deliver it to me and I sell it on. If we do get stiffed in that last part of the deal, I'll suffer as much as you do, Harry, because that's when me and you get our bit of poke out of it. That's why I'm leaving the testing to you.' He stabbed his cigar at Kessler, wishing it was alight and that he could stab it in the arsehole's eye. 'As a matter of goodwill.'

'How do I know I can trust the cutting team?'

'How do we know we can trust anyone, Harry? Because we believe someone's word, that's why. And because the team know I'd kill them if they tried to have one over on me.'

Kessler turned down his mouth, jerked his head to one side, and flashed his eyebrows. He then leaned back, still keeping his eye on Gabriel, and whispered something to Daniel and Maurice. Then he nodded and said to Gabriel, 'Okay. We test twice. Agreed. My boys know what to do. And if they're satisfied – *if* – then Sammy's sitting over there in the car,' he inclined his head towards the shadows thrown by the beech hedge that ran the length of the hangar, 'with the first half of the investor's money on his lap. But, remember, we'll still be testing when we collect.'

Gabriel found a smile from somewhere. Even if the little tosspot still didn't seem to have fully grasped who was on whose side and what they were actually doing, why couldn't they have got to this point a quarter of an hour ago?

'Of course, Harry. That's understood. That'll benefit us both. Now, Brendan, Pete, you two go with Daniel and Maurice. And Luke, you go and sit in Harry's car. Keep Sammy and the money company till its time to fetch it over.'

With the testing finally completed to Harold Kessler's idiosyncratic satisfaction – he still had only a cursory understanding of what they were actually checking for, his attention and business acumen not really extending to anything more complex than straightforward blags, pimping, and bullying of various kinds – he and Gabriel stood outside the hangar. They were making falsely chummy conversation, both, in their different ways, relieved that this first deal was at last about to get off its backside, and both eager to get back into the warm.

And Maurice, good nephew that he was, had volunteered to trot off into the shadows to tell Sammy and Luke that Uncle Harold was at last ready to hand over the money to the O'Donnells so they could pay the supplier.

Ten feet away from the car, Maurice slowed down. He could make out the two figures sitting in the back seat, and a finger being jabbed angrily into someone's face. But which of them was doing the pointing? And why was he so upset?

He crept forward. From five feet away he could see – and hear – quite clearly.

Sammy was *very* upset with Luke.

Maurice stood there, watching. And listening.

He smiled, enjoying himself as voices were raised and he heard some very interesting references to someone called Catherine, and how much Sammy had loved her, and how it was all the O'Donnells's fault she'd died.

Catherine?

Wasn't that the O'Donnell girl who'd wound up fried to a crisp like an overdone fish supper?

He listened a bit longer.

Yes, it was her all right.

His cousin Sammy had been going with young Catherine O'Donnell?

Who'd have thought it?

And the O'Donnells were somehow involved in her death?

This was good. The sort of information that could prove useful in all sorts of ways. He'd definitely file this away for future use.

When Maurice eventually stepped forward and tapped on the car window, Sammy Kessler and Luke O'Donnell sprang apart in shocked surprise, guilty as two monkeys caught with their paws stuck in the sweetie jar.

'All right, fellers?' Maurice beamed down at them, as he opened the back door. 'Nice and cosy in there are you, while we do all the work?'

Sammy was about to protest, but Luke beat him to it.

Pushing the door open wide, he shoved Maurice out of the way. 'Piss off, you flash, Northern bastard.'

'Hold on there, feller. Hurrying off like that, anyone'd think you've got some nasty secret you don't fancy sharing.'

Gabriel didn't so much as blink as Brendan took the bag from Sammy Kessler, and nor did he intend to show himself up by checking that the brown, leather attaché case contained the full, agreed amount. That sort of behaviour was for mugs: men who didn't consider themselves frightening enough to know that the likes of Harold Kessler wouldn't dare try to take the piss.

Kessler was finding it a bit more difficult to hide his feelings. He had just handed over half of a very big wedge that he had acquired – admittedly with unexpected ease – from his investor: a posh, self-important City type, who had become a regular user of Kessler's whores, but who, on their first meeting, had treated Kessler with little more respect than he had the toms.

But when Kessler had 'accidentally' engineered

another meet, and had explained his proposition to him, the man had suddenly become his friend, slapping him on the back and explaining what a good chap he'd always found Kessler to be, and how he was never averse to a little tax free investment if any should come his way. He'd acted as if they'd known each other since their days at prep school, rather than from a chance encounter a few weeks before, when Kessler and Daniel had been collecting the takings from one of their street brasses.

It might have been easy for Kessler to get the money off the bloke, but why had he just gone and handed over half of it to O'Donnell? For the promise of a pile of scrap that, although he was paying for it, he was going to hand back over to O'Donnell, who was then, supposedly, going to sell it on and share the profits with him?

He must be out of his mind. If this went wrong he'd make O'Donnell wished he'd never heard the name Harold Kessler. He'd show O'Donnell mess him around. But he had to keep up his image, even with this lanky Irish schmuck. Needed to take control of the situation. Show him what was what.

'This is a good day's work we've done here, Gabriel,' he said, as they walked back towards the cars. 'The first of many such deals, God willing. So, how about we all meet up to celebrate one evening next week? My treat. We can go to Marlino's, a restaurant I know on Greek Street. Owned by good friends of mine. They'll look after us, give us the best of everything.'

Gabriel, who had decided that this was the perfect moment to light his cigar, puffed rhythmically, staring at the slowly burning tip, indicating with a lift of his chin that Brendan should answer for him.

'Good idea,' was Brendan's response. 'We can take the

ladies out to dinner at your mate's gaff, whatever it's called, and then us chaps can go and visit our new club. You might have heard of it: the Bellavista.'

Kessler actually stopped in his tracks. 'The Bellavista? I thought that was Keithy Johnson's place.'

Pete Mac came in with the timing of a pro. 'It was,' he said.

Chapter 12

Eileen O'Donnell and Sophie Kessler settled themselves into the soft, cream leather upholstery in the back seat of the Daimler. They were waiting for Stephen Shea to go back inside Marlino's restaurant so he could find out what was keeping Patricia and Rachel.

'Pretty girl, your Brendan was with tonight, Eileen.'

'She seemed nice.' Eileen was vague, preoccupied in the way she often was these days.

'Serious, is it?'

'Sorry?'

'Wake up, Eileen,' Sophie laughed gently. 'Brendan and his girlfriend?'

Eileen gave a tiny shrug that barely disturbed the sapphire mink stole she was clutching round her shoulders. It was now four months since she had buried her child, and she was wearing black, but this dress was floor-length, stylishly fitted, and adorned with a glittering ribbon bow of diamonds at her shoulder. 'They never last long,' she said, turning to Sophie, doing her best to be sociable, 'not with Brendan.'

'Daniel used to be like that: different girl every week. You don't know the relief when he settled down with Rachel. I only wish my Sammy would do the same. Since he broke up with that nasty little madam who broke his heart, he's been moping about like he'll never meet any-one ever again. I keep telling him: you're young, you'll find plenty of girls. But will he listen? Kids, eh, Eileen?'

Sophie peered out of the window of the parked car onto Greek Street, wondering if they were ever going to get away. She was getting to like Eileen, like her far more than she'd ever expected, but trying to have a conversation with her wasn't exactly easy. She wasn't blaming her, she couldn't begin to imagine what it must be like to bury your child – mad as they drove her at times.

She tried another tack. 'Your Luke seeing anyone?'

'No one I know about.'

Another dead end.

Sophie patted Eileen's hand. 'I really am sorry about this.'

'It's okay, I've only the dog to worry about.'

In the darkness, Sophie could just make out the tears brimming in Eileen's eyes. 'You know,' she said briskly, 'I'll bet it's that Rachel titivating again. But why bother? With Harry and Gabriel taking the boys off to this drinking club, Rachel'll be tucked up fast asleep in bed before any of them start thinking about making their way home.' She looked at her watch and tutted impatiently. 'Quarter to eleven; this is getting silly.'

'It's all right. I know what girls are like.' Eileen's voice was small, distant, as her mind filled with the familiar pictures of Catherine, sitting in the big, cosy basement kitchen with scrunched up toilet paper twisted between her toes, tongue nipped between her teeth, as she painted her nails the latest startling shade. Her hair – before she and Patricia had their outrageous urchin cuts that Eileen thought were more suited to little boys than to young women – wound over big, fat rollers to straighten out its pretty, natural curl, and a thick white paste of face pack smeared over her lovely features.

She would have been eighteen years old on New Year's Eve.

Sophie gave a little laugh. 'Not having been blessed with daughters, Eileen, I'm having to learn – fast – about modern girls. Like why Rachel dyes that beautiful hair of hers that auburn colour. And, for goodness sake, why she's started going on at Daniel to get his hair straightened. Straightened! Can you believe it? Honestly, tell me, Eileen, what's wrong with a head full of tight fair curls?' Her smile broadened as she remembered. 'When he was a baby, he was like an angel. People used to think he was a little girl. Him and Sammy get it from me, of course. My ringlets were nearly white when I was a toddler.' She chuckled throatily. 'I tell them to think themselves lucky that they never got their hair from their father.'

Eileen wasn't really listening, but she heard enough to murmur her agreement.

'Who knows, perhaps Danny and Rachel will have some good news for me one day soon. And maybe I'll have a granddaughter to fuss over. And then I'll become an expert on modern girls, and begin to understand Rachel at last.'

Eileen let out a long sighing breath. 'I don't think any of us understands anyone. Not really.'

Sophie didn't know what else to say.

Stephen Shea was waiting in the restaurant's lobby, casting self-conscious glances at a fancy-handled door displaying a plaque of a woman wearing a wide picture hat, a crinoline dress, and carrying a parasol over her shoulder.

He would do anything for Gabriel – had done things he

180

wouldn't be prepared to speak about to anyone, not even to Sheila – but hanging around outside a ladies' lav like some dirty old man?

What on earth was taking them so bloody long?

Inside the powder room, Rachel leaned into the gilt framed glass and tidied her plucked and arched eyebrows with a tiny, tail-handled tortoiseshell comb, while Patricia – barely five months pregnant but feeling like an overheated, shapeless sack of spuds next to the slender, boyishly-figured, Rachel – perched uncomfortably on the edge of a dinky brocade chair that wouldn't have looked out of place in a kindergarten.

Patricia picked up one of the many lipsticks that had spilled from Rachel's bag and widened her eyes as she wound out its metallic lavender core. She hadn't seen anything like that colour before. It was gorgeous. Catherine would have loved it.

'Rachel . . .'

'Take it, I've got loads.'

Patricia dropped the lipstick as if she'd been caught trying to pocket it. 'No. It's great, but I didn't mean –'

Rachel lowered the miniature comb, and narrowed her eyes at Patricia's reflection. 'What's wrong?'

Patricia cast around for the right words. 'Rachel, do you ever talk to Daniel? About his work? Well, not his work exactly. But when he goes out. And stays out late. You know, like tonight. With the men going onto Dad's club. Do you ever wonder what he's getting up to?'

'No.' Rachel drew in her chin, looking at Patricia as if she were stupid. 'Why should I?'

'You know. In case he's . . . Aw, you know.'

'No, I don't actually.' Rachel paused to stuff the little

181

comb back into her make-up pouch, and to scoop all the lipsticks back into her handbag, her pretty lips stuck out in a not very attractive pout. 'I get all the money I need. I've got a house that he's letting me get done up however I want. I have a great life. What's to wonder about?'

'I know all that,' said Patricia, wishing she hadn't started. 'I've got all that too, but, I mean, Daniel. Himself. Isn't he sometimes –'

'He's the best part of it all,' Rachel gushed. 'And that's why I always make sure I look good. Dye my hair the colour I know he loves. Wear the sort of clothes that drive him wild.' She let her glance slide up and down Patricia for a long, embarrassing moment, her expression clearly implying that it wouldn't do any harm if she made a bit more of an effort – maybe a nice tight roll-on. 'And that's why I've decided not to have kids. Well, not for a long time yet.' Her words were as pointed as her look had been. 'Because my Danny is wonderful. And more than enough for me. I'm not like a lot of girls, you see, Patricia. I don't need a houseful of brats to make me happy. And nor does Daniel. I'm everything he needs. Everything.'

Rachel turned back to the mirror, and Patricia watched her as she teased out the Jackie Kennedy flicks of her glossy, tinted hair, part of her wishing that Pete Mac was *really wonderful* too. But another part of her was wondering if maybe Rachel was a fool. Or a liar. Or just hard as nails, and prepared to put up with anything for her *great life*.

'That was good of you, getting Shea to take the girls home,' Kessler said, as Gabriel ushered him through the door of the Bellavista. 'But we could have put them in a cab. I'd have paid.'

'That's a generous offer, Harry. But Stephen's a loyal servant, and I like to feel there's someone I know and trust taking care of my wife, and that she has a safe journey home.'

Kessler swallowed the insult, and changed the subject. 'Well, will you look at this?' As he stepped inside the completely refurbished club, he whistled as if he were genuinely impressed. 'This has certainly changed.'

He waited for Gabriel to walk ahead, leading them into the once bare barn of a place that had now been transformed – with the help of a team of brickies, plumbers, carpenters and electricians, many yards of crimson velvet and gold netting, and some very clever lighting – into a passable likeness of a galleried, turn of the century bordello.

Satisfied that Gabriel was out of earshot, Kessler whispered under his breath to his son. 'This really has changed, Daniel.'

Daniel refused to be impressed by the new, glitzy décor, or by the fact that the place was so busy. 'Don't make any difference to me, Dad. Never been here before. Never felt the need to.'

'Take my word for it, son, it's changed, all right – a lot. Just look at it.' He did the wide-armed, shoulder-shrugging thing, and said quietly, 'It's not just some rotten old bash any more, where you can come along to pour cheap turps down your throat until you get sick to your stomach. It's a place where you can have a drink, fuck a whore, and get a dose thrown in for luck.'

Daniel held his arm to his face and snorted his laughter into his sleeve.

'Mind you, Dan, even I wouldn't mind having to make an appointment with the pox doctor's clerk, not if it was the price of having a taste of that one over there.' Kessler pointed to a raised, padded bench, where a row of young women in various states of revealing dress were sitting smiling prettily for the mug punters.

Daniel followed his father's gaze and grinned. Of course, the little one with the heavy breasts, and the wild halo of gorgeous red, wavy hair – a pint-sized Rita Hayworth just like she was in the old films he loved to watch.

'Just look at the body on her,' marvelled Kessler. He puckered his lips and kissed the bunched tips of his fingers. 'She'd make a blind man see, that one. You should get in there, Daniel. God knows, it's not as if you'll be fighting off your brother, the miserable sod. I don't think he could get it up if you played the national anthem, the mood he's in.' Kessler leaned closer to his son. 'Here, why not try and get Sammy to enjoy a bit of company, eh, Dan? Cheer the little fucker up a bit.'

He shook his head – a man bewildered by his youngest son's behaviour – and began making his way over to join Gabriel and the others at the bar. He tossed a departing thought over his shoulder. 'For your mother's sake, Dan. She's been worrying about him. You know how she gets.'

Daniel looked around for Sammy and spotted him sitting alone at one of the little gilt tables set around the edges of the room. He had the expression on his face of a man who sucked lemons for a living, but that apart, he had a drink in one hand and a cigarette in the other.

He was all right; and it wasn't as if he was being held prisoner.

Daniel turned his back on his sour-faced brother and

eased his way through the crowd of men smooching with the smiling come-on girls. He stopped in front of the bench where the rest of the girls sat waiting to be selected – items on a shelf, barely one step away from meat on a slab – and fixed the redhead with a smile.

'What's your name then?'

'Nina. What's yours?'

'Daniel. Drink, Nina?'

'Love one,' she said, sharing a quick look with her companions. This was a touch; the customers were usually at least twenty years older than this one, and not nearly as attractive. And even though blonds weren't really her type, and, if she had a choice, she preferred them to be really tall, he did have a great body. And she'd always liked fit-looking men. That was why she *really* liked the O'Donnell boys: tall, dark and hunky. Perfect. But from the day she and the other girls had been brought into the revamped club, it was made clear that the O'Donnells were not going to bother with the likes of them. So this one was a real bonus.

'Friend of Mr O'Donnell's are you?' Nina said, running a fingernail down Daniel's cheek.

'Business associate.'

Bingo! Loaded!

'I've not seen you in here before.'

'No, my wife don't let me out much,' he said, taking her by the hand and leading her towards the bar.

'Cheeky.'

'No, just honest. I'm a married man.'

'That's nice.'

He shrugged. 'It's all right, I suppose,' he said, helping her up onto a stool, well away from where his father was sitting – not because Daniel had anything to hide from him, but because he didn't want to be anywhere near the O'Donnells or that idiot Pete MacRiordan.

He put his hand on Nina's back, and pulled her close, fantasising about the heavy, creamy breasts that bulged out over her neckline tumbling out into his hands, and thrilling at the touch of the slippery red satin dress against his skin.

Rachel was going to be a good little wife, and a good little mother – his own mother would make sure of that – but if Daniel had had a choice in the matter, Nina was far more like he'd have chosen for himself.

She leaned into him, her arms pulled together to accentuate the swell of her breasts. She had used the same move ever since she'd been thirteen years old and had realised the power of her body. When, after some misdemeanour or other, rather than sending her on the dreaded trip to the headmistress's office, her flushed-faced geography teacher had let her off with nothing more than a garbled warning and a not completely unpleasant grope after the final bell. That had all happened a full, incident-packed, and instructive three years ago. Nina had learned that one school lesson very well indeed.

She giggled prettily as she sipped the sickly fruit punch that Daniel had bought her, the only drink she and the other girls were allowed – so they would keep sober and their minds on their work.

'Look,' she said, 'look at these little see-through sticks. I love these.' She tossed her thick red hair over her shoulder, swishing it against the satin, dropped her head to one side and held a plastic cocktail stick up against one of the crimson shaded wall lights.

'See,' she said, her small, childlike teeth pearly white against her pink, smooth gums. 'It's a naked lady; look, you can see her little titties. Not as big as mine though are they?'

Daniel cupped one of her breasts in his hand. 'You're right there, sweetheart,' he murmured, burying his face into her neck under the thick curtain of her hair.

'I collect these and cash them in,' she said, moving so that her knee slipped in between his thighs. She heard him moan softly.

'It's how I get paid. I love the lime green ones best, they're worth more cos they're the ones what come in the champagne cocktails. Do you like champagne cocktails, Daniel?'

'Love 'em.'

'Shall I order you one then?'

She felt him nod against her throat.

'Champagne cocktail over here for the gentleman,' she said to the barman with a knowing look.

'Champagne cocktails? In a near beer joint?' It was Maurice.

Daniel jerked upright and looked over Nina's shoulder into Maurice's grinning face. 'How long have you been standing there?'

'Do you mind?' Now it was bloody Brendan O'Donnell standing behind Maurice. What were they doing, forming a queue?

'Our Champagne's the genuine article.' Brendan wasn't happy.

Maurice half turned, looked at him and grinned. 'Can we have a steward's enquiry on that, feller?'

'Look, Maurice.' Brendan really didn't like this bloke. 'We're meant to be having a nice evening here.'

Maurice turned right round and inclined his head. 'So, you got yourself a proper licence for this place then, eh?'

Brendan snorted like a pony let loose in a field; surely even an idiot like him knew it was impolite to ask that sort of a question – any sort of a question – when it was none of your business. 'I have friends.'

'Friends?' Maurice smiled. 'I'll say you do. That one having dinner with you tonight at Marlino's. Very nice arse. How much does she charge an hour then?'

Daniel, seeing the expression on Brendan's face, stepped in. 'What is this?' He peeled Nina's arms from round his neck. 'It's like having a fucking audience, and a bloody noisy one at that.'

Maurice spun back round to face his cousin. 'Audience, eh? Well I wouldn't mind watching if you're up for it.' Then back to face Brendan. 'What do you think Brendan? You game?'

Brendan looked at Maurice as if he was as funny as a bit of string, and then said to Daniel, 'I'm sorry to interrupt you – and Nina – but I want to talk to you. Privately. About business. D'you mind, Maurice?'

'He don't mind,' said Daniel. 'Maurice, go and get yourself a drink. Nina, I'll have to make it another time, darling.'

Nina did her big eyed, imploring little girl with big breasts thing, and Daniel crumpled. Her expression was just like Rachel's when she wanted him to buy her something. And he was a sucker for it.

Bloody birds.

'Hang on.' He dipped in his pocket, whispered something in her ear, and slapped her on the backside.

She nodded, smiling up at him as she accepted the money he slipped into her hand, kissed him on the cheek, and snatched the precious lime green stick from his drink. Then she wiggled her way over to

Sammy Kessler with a cute, bye-bye jiggle of her fingers.

'This had better be good, O'Donnell,' Daniel said to Brendan. 'I was ready for that.'

Brendan leaned back on the bar, and folded his arms. 'You didn't have to pay, you know, Daniel, you're my guest here this evening.'

'It's okay' he said, his eyes following her across the floor, 'I only gave her enough to make sure she puts a smile on my brother's face. Sammy's been a bit down lately.'

'Yeah, well,' said Brendan hurriedly, 'families can be a worry.'

'Right,' he agreed, pulling himself together. 'You said you wanted to talk business.'

'I do. There are two more planes coming our way. It's all happened a bit on the quick. If you're going to be involved, we need the money by Monday night. Can you produce?'

Daniel nodded calmly. 'Sure.'

Brendan hid his disappointment. He'd intended catching him out, have a reason to row the Kesslers out of the deal. Show his father how useless they were. It would have been a good first step towards getting rid of this ridiculous arrangement – which he fully intended to do before he took over the business. And, at the rate his father was drinking, that wouldn't be too far into the future.

He looked into Daniel's eyes, wondering if he was telling the truth, whether he really could get another investor willing to cough up enough of a stake by Monday.

Daniel Kessler was also wondering: about why Brendan had put the deal to him, rather than Gabriel

O'Donnell speaking to his father? He disliked the O'Donnells as much as he reckoned they disliked him and his family, and he didn't trust a single one of them. But, for now, he reckoned it made sense to pretend that he couldn't have been happier than being in the bastards' company. It'd give him a chance to watch and learn. Figure out what the fuckers were up to.

Daniel looked about him. 'The club looks like it's a big success, Brendan. Congratulations. You must be very pleased.'

The compliment caught Brendan off guard. These Kesslers were as slippery as bloody eels. 'Thanks. Let me get you another drink.'

As Brendan turned to catch the barman's attention, his own eye was caught by something else. Maurice – the slipperiest of the lot as far as he was concerned – had taken himself over to Luke, and was grinning like a wolf as he made an exaggerated show of pointing out to Luke that Nina was draping herself all over Sammy Kessler. As for Sammy, he obviously wasn't interested in the girl, and was making a right song and dance of trying to get rid of her.

Brendan shook his head. Why had his dad done this? He should have known that inviting the Kesslers to the club would cause nothing but trouble.

Nina was now taking Sammy's refusal of her services as a personal challenge, especially as that mate of the O'Donnells had paid her so well to entertain his brother. She'd bloody well entertain him if it killed her – the other girls'd take the right piss if she couldn't at least get to sit on the dozy bugger's lap.

'What's wrong, handsome? Bit shy are you?'

Sammy flicked her hand off his neck. 'I said, just get away from me . . .'

'Don't be like that, lover, your brother gave me a little present to be nice to you. Wasn't that kind of him?' She rubbed her hand over his fly, smiling broadly as she felt his erection. 'Here, you! You might pretend you're not interested, but this little chap can't lie, now can he?'

Sammy was on his feet. 'Keep whatever he gave you. And here.' He stuck his hand in his trouser pocket and pulled out a roll of notes. He licked his thumb and peeled off two fivers. 'Take that *little present* and all. From me. But just piss off. Got it?'

Nina was disappointed, and a bit scared. This weirdo was a friend of the O'Donnells after all, and pleasing him certainly wouldn't have done her any harm, but displeasing him would be a very big mistake.

'I'm sorry, I just thought you wanted to have a bit of fun.'

Sammy straightened his tie, and combed his hair back with his fingers. 'Forget it, all right?'

She smiled. As always, she'd quickly bounced back and was looking on the bright side. She didn't really mind that much. The O'Donnells were good to work for – she reckoned she earned them anything from £50 to £400 a week – and they not only allowed her to keep a tenner for herself, they looked after her as well, always had plenty of minders about the place, *and* they didn't have too many disgusting sorts for her to deal with. So, as long as she kept getting paid, they could do or not do as they liked. In fact, it actually made a nice change. Before the Bellavista, she'd only ever worked as a come-on girl before, satisfied with her bit of commission on the drinks, but since she'd been here there hadn't been a single evening when she hadn't been expected to go upstairs to the private rooms with at least half a dozen different men, and sometimes

191

with a lot more. Not that it bothered her, not really, but it could get boring.

Still, she'd better give it one more go. 'Are you absolutely sure, sweetheart? I can do anything you fancy, you know. I'm very versatile.' She looked up at him through her heavily mascaraed lashes. 'Well, so I've been told.'

Sammy sucked in his breath through gritted teeth. What was it she didn't understand? He wanted Catherine. Not some cheap tart.

He took her by the shoulders and started shaking her. *'Will you. Just. Leave. Me. Alone?'*

'Jesus.' Daniel slammed his glass down on the bar.

Brendan put up his hand to stop him. He didn't want the Kesslers and their minders getting upset over one of his girls. That would be a right show up. 'It's all right, Daniel. If she's upsetting your brother, I'll sort it out. Okay?'

Brendan was over by Sammy and Nina before Daniel had a chance to reply. A few curious eyes followed him, but men getting angry at tarts wasn't exactly big news to the sort of punters who used the Bellavista.

Brendan put on a concerned expression. 'You don't look very happy, Sammy. Anything I can do?'

Sammy said nothing, he just dropped his hands from Nina's shoulders and stared at Brendan as if he could kill him.

'Not upset you has she, mate? Or maybe you prefer a brunette. Or a blonde. Whatever you fancy.'

'No thanks.'

'Suit yourself, but it would be my treat.'

'I'm not interested in your whores. Got it?'

Brendan raised his hands. 'Fair enough. Just being friendly.'

Nina had her head bowed, but she was sneaking looks at one man then the other. What now? What should she do?

Maurice was watching the three of them. He was enjoying himself. The O'Donnells and the Kesslers doing business together? How was that ever going to work? And knowing what he knew about Catherine O'Donnell and his cousin Sammy, that could make the situation explosive. And then there was Luke: he was convinced he was right about him. He grinned happily. Why had he ever thought that coming down to London was going to be dull?

He went and stood beside Luke, and said quietly, 'That's an interesting little scene, eh, feller? A man who won't take a beautiful woman. Even as a gift.'

'Fuck off,' muttered Luke, and barged his way over to his brother.

'Here, let me help you out here, Brendan.' Luke grabbed hold of Nina's hand and dragged her across to the stairway that led up to the private rooms. 'That's one less problem to worry about,' he called over his shoulder.

She giggled with relief, feeling as if she'd just won the Littlewood's jackpot. Not only was her problem of what to do next solved for her, but she was going upstairs with *Luke O'Donnell*. Perhaps she'd really cracked it this time. This could put her into a different league all together. Make her practically one of the family.

'You all right now, Sammy?' asked Brendan.

'Yeah. Terrific.' He sounded more angry than relieved as he edged past Brendan. 'If you don't mind I'll go over and say goodnight to me dad.'

Brendan sighed wearily as he joined Daniel Kessler

back at the bar. This was getting to be like a game of pass the sodding parcel, with little Nina as the prize.

He picked up his glass and took a swig of whiskey.

'Good job you dealt with that,' Daniel said. 'Don't want a reputation for trouble in a new club.'

Brendan downed the rest of his drink in one. 'Just didn't want your brother Sammy making a fool of himself.'

Daniel bristled. 'It was your brother what surprised me.' He said it tonelessly.

'What?'

'Luke. Going upstairs with that bird.'

'She's a good clean girl. All our Bellavista girls are.'

'No, not that he's gone with a tom – I was thinking about giving her one myself – but that she's a bird. According to our Maurice, Luke's the other way.'

It took every last bit of Brendan's self-control to stop him from kicking Daniel Kessler until he'd never be able to go with another woman again. Instead, he snorted as if he'd just heard the funniest joke ever. '*Luke?* That's a laugh,' he said. 'Right comedian your cousin.'

Chapter 13

Sammy found his father still sitting at the bar with Gabriel. 'Dad.' His voice betrayed his weariness. 'I'm going home.'

'All right, wait for me outside, son.' Harold Kessler had had quite enough of O'Donnell's club and his drunken ramblings, and was glad of an excuse to escape.

'Gabriel, the Bellavista, it's a great place.' Harold clapped him on the shoulder. 'And I've had a wonderful evening. It's been a real celebration. But you'll have to excuse me. It looks like my youngest has downed one too many of your very generous cocktails.'

Gabriel screwed one eye tight to help his focus, and nodded, unclear as to what he was agreeing to, but mellow enough to want to make everyone happy – until someone upset him.

'Oi, Sammy!' Harold Kessler spotted his son just as he turned into Folgate Street, heading in the direction of Bishopsgate.

'I'm getting too old for this,' he puffed, catching up with him. 'Forty-one and the body of a sixty-year-old. Maybe I need some exercise.'

'Or learn how to say no to fried fish,' Sammy snapped back.

'What's wrong with you?' Kessler took hold of his son's overcoat, stopping him. 'I told you to wait for me outside the club.'

He twisted round, snatching his coat from his father's hands. 'I'm not drunk, no matter what you think, or said to O'Donnell. But I am angry.'

And he was. Sammy Kessler had a burning resentment that he was stoking up ready for it to burst into raging flames. He loathed the O'Donnells and their fucking idiot of an in-law Peter MacRiordan more than he'd hated anything or anyone in his whole life.

Since Catherine had died, their brief time together as a couple had taken on more of a reality than it had ever had when she had been alive. He had completely rewritten those few weeks, including forgetting that he'd left her bleeding and alone in the road. And that, if he were honest, he had known deep down that even in his dreams they would never have wound up together. His family would never have stood for it. But right now, with the mood he was in, Sammy Kessler was fit to blame anyone for his having lost her. Anyone except himself.

Sammy, taller than his father, loomed over him. 'Why should we put up with this, Dad? Why?'

Kessler backed away, his hands at his chest, his head to one side. 'Don't go getting upset with me, son.'

'I'm not upset with you. Well, maybe I am. But what I wanna know is why we have to listen to them O'Donnells. It's like we're a bunch of twats hanging about waiting to be told what to do.'

Kessler sighed. This was just what he needed: Sammy getting all emotional. The boy was turning out to be too much like his mother. Always getting worked up about something or other: where they lived, girlfriends, and now the bloody business. Like he knew anything about it.

He reached up and put an arm round his son's shoulders. 'Bide your time, Sammy. Just bide your time.

Things'll work out. You see if they don't. Your brother Daniel'll see to it.' His face creased into a chubby baby's grin. 'He's already organised a new deal for us. Tonight. Two more planes. How about that? And, when we're ready, we're gonna –'

'We're gonna what? Let 'em piss all over us? What's happening to us?' Sammy was snorting like a bull, as the familiar images of the sawn-off shotgun, Catherine sprawled out in the road, and what he now knew to be the O'Donnell boys, sliced into his brain.

He couldn't work with the O'Donnells. He wouldn't.

'Dad, we should be cutting proper deals. Of our own. Like back in Notting Hill. Ones that work for us. Nothing to do with them Irish cunts.'

Kessler looked at his youngest child as if he were missing one or two links in his chain. 'Look, Sammy, son, you did a good job at the airfield the other day, a very good job, but that doesn't mean you can –'

'I did a good job?' Sammy could hardly believe this. 'What, sitting in a car with a bag of money on my lap? How hard's that? You must really think I'm stupid.'

Kessler was getting fed up with this, and he was cold. Even the thought of going back to the Bellavista was beginning to seem inviting. 'No, not stupid, Sammy, but when you decided you didn't like it round here, what did you do? You went running back to Notting Hill. What was I supposed to think? You made a choice then. A choice that went against what I thought was best for you. And what happened? You came running right back. I was right. Of course I was. I'm your father. I know. Just like I know now, by the way you're acting, that you're not happy. You hardly speak, you don't eat. And back there in the club – you didn't join in. This is business, Sammy. You need to

197

change your attitude. Then perhaps I'll listen to you. You can't be half-arsed in our line of work. It's too dangerous. Especially with the O'Donnells breathing down our necks.'

'But that's exactly what I'm talking about. *Why* do we have to have anything to do with them?'

'Because, like it or not, son, this is their toby, and they're the ones with all the power.' He reached out, patted his boy's cheek and winked. 'For now, eh.'

Sammy clenched his fists. Why couldn't his father see what he was doing? 'Look, Dad, say I come up with something that'll get us a real stake; enough for us to be able to ignore the O'Donnells?'

Kessler smiled benevolently. 'Sounds good, son.'

'I've got plans.'

Kessler pulled his collar up round his throat and looked up at the sky; it was starting to rain again. 'I'm sure you –'

'Please, will you just listen to me? There's these people; they're bringing them over the channel. From India. Like our family came from Russia.'

'So they're rich? These Indians?'

Sammy hesitated. 'And there's other stuff we should be getting into. The strip clubs and near beer joints. They're earning hand over fist.'

Kessler smiled, a picture of the compassionate elder. 'Of course they are. All over London. But d'you really think there's room for more?'

Sammy dropped his chin. This was getting him nowhere.

Despite himself, Kessler couldn't help feeling sorry for his son. 'Listen, Sam, it's good to know you're taking an interest. I've been worried about you. So has your mother. All this moping about. But what's the rush? Let's just bide our time, eh? Take it easy.'

Sammy's head flicked up. 'But say I come up with something that'll knock that arrogant bastard O'Donnell right off his perch?'

'Do that son, and you've got my ear.'

Sammy could feel his excitement rising. He had his father's interest at last. 'I'm meeting a man tomorrow afternoon.'

Kessler's magnanimous smile dissolved into condescending nodding and patting. 'Good for you, son, good for you.' Then he shrugged down into his coat, more than ready to get out of the rain, and away from such a pointless discussion, even if it really did mean going back to the Bellavista. 'Now, if you don't mind, I think I might nip back to the club. Dry off and have a drop of brandy to keep out the cold. But if you don't fancy it, don't worry; you get yourself off home. Go up on the main road and find yourself a cab.'

Kessler was handing over his damp coat to the hatcheck girl, when Maurice appeared at his side.

'All right, Uncle Harry? Sammy calmed down now has he?'

Kessler rolled his eyes. 'You know how he's been, Maury. I don't know what's wrong with the boy. One minute he's shooting off to West London, then he's back. Now he reckons he knows what's best for the business. What does he know? He can't even look after himself.' He rolled his eyes. 'Hark at me, I sound just like his mother.'

Maurice flashed his teeth. 'I think it's nice you care about your son. I hope he knows how lucky he is.'

Kessler – the perfect father – looked suitably modest. 'I know one thing: he's going to take forever getting a cab at this time of night, especially in this weather. And if he doesn't manage to find a cab, and he gets home soaking wet, and then he gets himself a cold, I'll never hear the end of it. Your Aunt Sophie'll nag me till I become a scientist and find a bloody miracle cure for him.'

Maurice was still smiling, but inside he was urging the old windbag to shut up. 'Uncle Harry,' he jumped in, while Kessler was taking a breath. 'I'll go after him. Keep an eye on him for you.'

Maurice was treated to the triple bonus of a shrug, a patted cheek, and a hug. 'You're a good boy, Maury, a very good boy. Your parents should be proud.'

Maurice accepted the praise with appropriate humility and left the club at a trot with a cheery, 'See you later, Uncle Harry.'

Kessler was a man blessed. He'd tell that piss tank Gabriel O'Donnell how his big-hearted nephew had given up the rest of his evening just to sort out his cousin. That'd show him what a fine family the Kesslers were.

Luke was sitting in one of the Bellavista's upstairs rooms on a clean, but hard and narrow bed – punters weren't encouraged to spend too long up there – with Nina's child-sized arms wrapped around his neck.

He had only taken her upstairs to prove a point to Maurice, and would have been less than happy to know that Maurice had disappeared into the night in pursuit of Sammy Kessler, without giving Luke O'Donnell so much as a second thought.

'It's okay,' Nina cooed into his ear. 'It happens sometimes. But I won't tell no one.'

'Tell no one what?'

'That you can't . . .' She flicked her eyes downwards. 'You know.'

'Who said I can't?'

'Well, you've not even undone your –'

'Just shut up!' Luke fired the words at her through clenched teeth, ripped open his flies, grabbed Nina by the hair, and shoved her face down into his lap. 'Now do your job.'

Despite the shock at his sudden violent change of attitude, Nina did her professional best.

As she eventually managed to get his flaccid penis to show interest in the ministrations of her tongue and lips, tears poured down Luke's face, falling onto her glorious red hair in sparkling rainbow droplets.

He threw back his head, his eyes pinched tight – from humiliation, but also from passion – not wanting to watch the back of her head as it worked up and down, yet finding himself unable to resist her attentions.

Why was he doing this to himself, and to this girl who didn't even look as old as his little sister?

Luke shuddered to a squalid, unsatisfactory climax, wishing he could wipe away his disgrace and degradation as quickly and easily as he knew the girl would be spitting his semen into one of the scratchy paper handkerchiefs, which she'd snatched from the bedside table before she gagged on the indignity of having a stranger's taste in her pretty young mouth.

He'd known ever since he could remember that this was just one of the ways his family made the money that gave them their nice, comfortable life, but Luke swore to himself that he would never do anything as sordid as this again. But, somewhere deep inside him, he knew he was kidding himself, and that one day he would do something far worse than having a paid tart suck on his dick. One day, he would step over the line that marked the end of all the lies, but that also marked the point of no return.

And that thought terrified him.

Her work done, Nina tried to make conversation with him; he might be a bit strange, what with all that crying and carrying on and that, but his family did own the place, and she didn't want to seem unsociable. But Luke would have none of it. He just tidied up his clothes, blew his nose and stumbled out of the room and down the stairs, leaving Nina on the bed to count her spoils and to hide a few of the notes in her roll-on. It was all so confusing tonight, and what with all the comings and goings, nobody would miss the odd couple of quid.

As Luke took the last three stairs in a single stride, he crashed into Pete Mac.

Pete Mac waggled his eyebrows and grinned. 'Saw you coming down, Lukey boy, and thought I'd take your place. Money that little whore's been raking in for nothing tonight, she might as well do us both a favour, eh?'

Luke felt just about ready for the likes of Peter MacRiordan. 'If you take even one step up them stairs, Pete, I'll tell Dad. Then you'll really be in for it. We all know about your bit of stray, but going with toms, with our Pat being in the family way? Who knows what you'd be risking?'

Pete Mac clicked his tongue against his teeth. This was bloody typical. The whole bloody family could get their end away with any scrubber they fancied, and no one would say a word. But if he felt like having a bit on the side, all hell broke loose. Bleed'n' hypocrites.

Good job Violet was always ready and willing. In fact – he looked at his watch: ten to one – he might as well go round there now. Nothing more was happening here tonight, and Gabe was too pissed to notice who was in the club and who wasn't. So, he'd just say his goodnights to Brendan, and explain that he was off home to check on his beloved, pregnant wife.

As Pete Mac ambled along in the now sheeting rain – there wasn't much that had him moving at more than strolling pace – to pick up his Zodiac that he'd parked under a streetlight in Folgate Street he suddenly sped up. There, just a few yards in front of him, up on the corner, was Maury, the only Kessler he had any time for – a right comical bugger. He was holding open the door of a taxi for that miserable fucker, Sammy. And he was telling the driver to take them to the Drake, a late night drinking spot off Gerard Street. A right bloody hole, but where you could drink twenty-four hours at a stretch and no one said a word, a bit like the Bellavista before Brendan had persuaded his old man to spend all that poppy doing it up. Pete Mac wouldn't mind a bit of that before going round to Violet's.

'Here, Maurice,' he bellowed, far louder than necessary. 'I'll have some of that, mate. Wouldn't mind a few more swift ones before getting off home.'

'Sorry, feller,' said Maurice with a wink. 'Got a bit of family business to sort out.'

Rather than being offended, Pete Mac grinned. Maurice, the cheeky Northern bastard, was obviously up to something.

Maurice presented Sammy with a second extortionately priced triple 'Scotch' that smelled more like something you'd use to strip varnish with than enjoy drinking, and

203

treated himself to another small sip of his pint of vile, supposedly imported lager. Maurice planned to keep his head clear – it was Sammy he wanted drunk and loose tongued. And from the swivel-eyed look on his face, the plan was working. So much so that if he didn't jump in now, there'd be no point, Sammy wouldn't be able to tell his arse from his elbow.

'I know all about you and Catherine O'Donnell.'

Sammy's head jerked up. 'Me and Catherine?'

'That's right, feller. Luke told me.' He was only partly lying, as he had heard the words from Luke's very own mouth, when they'd been at the airfield. Even if he had been speaking to Sammy rather than him at the time.

Sammy suddenly felt very sober. It was bad enough that the O'Donnell boys knew he had been seeing their sister, and that he'd left her bleeding in the road. But now Luke was blabbing to Maurice – Sammy's own cousin. What would the rest of his family do if they found out? Not only a Catholic, but an O'Donnell. His mother would never forgive him. And as for his father . . .

Sammy tapped his thumbnail against his bottom teeth. He had to straighten things out with Maurice, make sure he kept schtum. And he had to bring his father to his senses. Make him realise how stupid it was to do business with the O'Donnells. And do it quick – before one of them opened his mouth and dropped him right in it.

'You look shocked, feller.'

'Not shocked, disgusted. I can't believe he told you about me and Catherine.' He picked up his drink and swallowed down a mouthful, squinting at the taste and the burning in his throat. 'That family, I'm gonna have 'em.'

Maurice patted his cousin's shoulder. 'You need a plan, Sammy, lad. And money. It always takes money.'

'Tell me something I don't know.' Sammy went to pick up his glass again, but shoved it aside in anger. 'I need a proper stake. Big enough to show Dad he's gotta take me seriously. And enough to make people take notice of us, show 'em we're a family to be reckoned with. Then we get shot of them bastards, and have nothing more to do with them – whether we stay in the East End or not.'

Maurice leaned forward and spoke quietly. Not that anyone in the Drake was interested in anything other than the contents of the glass in his hand. 'We could do a bank.'

'Who could?'

'Me and you. That'll show your old man what you're made of. And start priming the pump.'

'What, us two?'

'Listen, feller. It's easy. In the morning, we stroll into any boozer on the Bethnal Green Road, and see who fancies working. Get ourselves a little team together. Then, one of us goes in the bank, pretending to change a note, and checks out the place – makes sure there's no coppers hanging about or anything, checks the lie of the land. That kind of thing. Then he comes out, gives the others the SP and they steam in with pickaxe handles, make the bank clerks shit themselves. Then they hand over whatever we want.'

A bank job? With Maurice? Sammy was now feeling that while he might have sobered up a bit, he had probably gone off his nut at the same time. 'You're having a joke, right?'

'No.' Maurice sounded as if he didn't understand Sammy's problem with the plan.

'Look, Maury, that sort of thing might still work up in Manchester, but we've moved on a bit down here. Ever heard of bandit glass?'

205

'Don't get flash with me, feller.'

'I'm not getting flash. I'm just wishing I'd kept my mouth shut.' He covered his face in his hands. 'What a fucking mess.'

'Blimey, Sam, calm down, feller.' Maurice shuffled his chair closer to the table. 'How about this? You lived over in Notting Hill. They reckon there's a fortune being made in property over there. Say we go and get ourselves some of that?'

'Right. Course. Property. I'll get myself a pin-striped suit, a bowler hat, and an umbrella shall I? I'm sure Mr Rachman won't mind.'

Maurice looked blank.

'It's all tied up already. Like everything else that's worth any dough.'

Maurice didn't look pleased. He leaned back in his seat and took his time lighting a cigarette. 'Well, if you're not interested. And you don't mind that slag Luke shooting his mouth off about you and his sister to anyone'll listen. Then what can I say?'

Sammy studied his cousin, watching him as he flicked his cigarette lighter – on, off, on, off – feeling sick at the thought that if the whim took him, Maurice could bubble him anytime he wanted.

He took a deep breath, letting it out long and slow. It killed him to do this, but now his monkey, two-faced cousin knew about Catherine he had to keep him sweet, on side.

'Sorry about that, Maury. Nothing personal. I'm just a bit jumpy, that's all. And I am interested, as it happens. I might even be one step ahead of you.'

'Come on then, feller, I'm all ears.'

Was telling this to Maurice as stupid as he thought it was?

Probably.

'There are these two blokes. Blokes I've been thinking about going to see for a while now.' *Yeah, when I was thinking about how I was going to set up somewhere a long way away so I could be with Catherine.* 'And I reckon now might be the time. Come along if you like. Say we leave around noon tomorrow?'

Chapter 14

Sammy sat in the passenger seat, barely registering the twists and turns of the country lanes, as Maurice struggled to manoeuvre his sleek, silver Jensen at worryingly fast speeds through the wintry countryside.

When he had made the decision that he was going to stay long term with the London branch of his family, the car had been bought for him by his parents. It was probably as much a bribe to leave Manchester for good, as a gift to wish him well, Sammy thought, because, as far as he could see, the showy vehicle was the one single thing about his cousin that was of any worth or interest. And he couldn't even handle *that* properly.

Sammy lit a cigarette. Perhaps they were trying to get rid of their son in a more permanent way than just moving him to the other end of the country. He, of all people, knew that car crashes were a good way to get rid of something embarrassing.

He wound the window down a crack to take the smoke, and stared out at the twiggy, almost leafless hedgerows, wondering what it would have been like to have made this journey with Catherine.

Or even alone. Maybe he would have taken some pleasure in having a break away from the East End, from the O'Donnells, and from Maurice and the rest of the bloody family.

It now seemed the accepted thing that his dad and brother treated him as if he was as useful as an arse with a headache, while his mother apparently saw him as someone to be fussed over as if he had some terrible disease. It was driving him off his head.

And now he had to sit here, listening to Maurice's boring bollocks as he babbled on and on. The sound of his nasal northern vowels was bad enough, but if he said: *So, you and Catherine O'Donnell then, eh, Sammy, feller, that's one for the book, that is, a right turn up, a Catholic girl and an O'Donnell* just one more time, Sammy honestly thought he might lose control, and tell his cousin: *Okay, that's it, tell whoever you like about me and Catherine, because I don't care any more. I loved her. And I still do, and there's nothing any one can do about it.*

Then whatever happened, surely it couldn't hurt him any more than he was hurting already.

He ground the heels of his thumbs into his eyes, trying to wipe away the visions of Catherine's body sprawled across the filthy tarmac.

Why *not* throw Maurice that additional little tit-bit? Tell him how she was murdered by her own family? How could telling the truth make things any worse than they were now?

Sammy almost laughed. Because he was weak that's why. A grown man who couldn't face up to his own family. But he would face Catherine's family, the ones who'd made him admit that terrible weakness in himself. That was why he was sitting here, being driven by a maniac through the Kent countryside, on the way to meet some people who, Sammy could only pray, would help him get rid of the O'Donnells from of his life. And maybe, who knew, with a bit of luck, would help him get rid of the O'Donnells – full stop.

'Oi, Sammy lad, are you listening to me, or what? I

asked you, who are these blokes we're meeting? I don't want to look like a prick when we get there, now do I?'

In Sammy's opinion, Maurice couldn't look like anything other than a prick, but he wasn't going to start getting lairy with him. Not yet, not while he needed him to keep his mouth shut.

Sammy aimed his cigarette butt out of the window at the trunk of an ivy-covered oak. He missed.

'They're two cousins.' His voice was weary, almost defeated.

'Like us, eh, feller.'

'Yeah, like us. Their name's Baxter. Joey and Chas. They're Londoners, but they got this place out in the country a few years back.'

'Why the move to the country?'

'Got to like the area, so the story goes, when they used to come down here as kids, hop-picking with their nan.'

'What they like then, these Baxters?'

'They run a small, South London outfit. They're hard –'

Maurice snorted loudly, interrupting him. 'You're having me on, right, Sam?'

'How d'you mean?'

Maurice flashed Sammy a disbelieving look. 'Why would a cockney want anything to do with South Londoners? My old feller always said you lot north of the river prided yourselves on being,' he put on a mock posh accent, '*superior* to the likes of them.'

'I might have been born in the East End, Maury, but Notting Hill was always my home. Where I felt I belonged. Until I met – Here, slow down.' Sammy stopped himself from saying any more. Maurice had enough on him already.

He consulted the roughly scribbled map he'd had propped up on the dashboard like a party invitation since they'd left Stepney Green. 'If this is right, I think we're getting close.'

The Four Aces roadhouse was a large, single-storey, wooden building with broad, shallow steps leading up to the veranda, which ran along the whole front elevation. It was painted a dark, sludge-like green that helped it blend almost organically into its idyllic riverside surroundings. The only thing that made it stand out as being something of a cuckoo in its verdant nest was the blue and pink neon sign, fashioned in the shape of the eponymous hand of cards, flashing on and off over the door. But even that had an odd, cheerful charm in the gloomy, grey light of the February afternoon.

Maurice sent up a shower of gravel as he sideslipped the Jensen into the car park, and came to a scrunching halt in the lee of an ancient-looking arched stone bridge, which spanned the foamy, rushing waters of a chilly-looking weir below.

Apart from a battered, open-backed truck, and a few small family saloons, the car park was empty, but it was easy to imagine such a spot being packed out in fine weather, as day-trippers took their refreshment, while watching their laughing, splashing children playing in the river.

'This looks a right dump,' was Maurice's only comment as he locked the car. But as he followed Sammy inside the Four Aces, Maurice had to admit that it was an intriguing sort of a place. Homely, but chaotic.

It was filled with an apparently random mix of furniture: scruffy leather armchairs; slightly wonky, overstuffed sofas; assorted wooden tables and chairs; low, three-legged stools; long carved benches; and what looked like old church pews. Any of the dark stained floorboards not hidden under furniture, were covered by scatterings of threadbare rugs. And with the quirky ornaments and lamps, cushions and tasselled drapes, stuffed creatures under glass domes – all sizes from a tiny wren on a willow branch, to a large, barrel-chested monkey dressed in a smoking jacket and matching braid trimmed hat – it seemed the owners must have spent much of their time scouring markets and auction rooms. Either that or they had a lot of elderly relatives who had chosen to leave them all their old junk in their wills.

It took two massive log fires to heat the big space, one at either end of the long, single bar that ran along the back wall, and they were doing their job well, the place was as cosy as an intimate front parlour.

A pair of lurchers, stretched out in front of one of the fires, with their chins resting on their long elegant paws, opened their eyes and pricked up their ears as they observed the visitors. They appeared too lulled by the warmth to spring to their feet and make a stand. But anyone taking their apparent passivity for granted might have come unstuck, as they were as ready as any snarling Alsatian to protect their masters' territory.

'Okay, boys, *stay*,' snapped a whip-thin, frail-looking man.

The lurchers sighed in whispery canine unison, relaxed their ears and closed their eyes, returning to their twitching doggy dreams.

The thin man was sitting at an old kitchen table. He was playing dominoes with a man who, if he hadn't been so fat, could have been his identical twin brother.

212

The thin man focussed his pale-eyed gaze on Sammy.

'The name's Sammy Kessler. I'm here to meet Chas and Joey Baxter.' He was well aware that he was talking to Joey himself, *and* that his fat cousin Chas was sitting there across from him; Sammy, like a lot of people, knew these two by reputation.

'Mind pointing me in the right direction?'

'You've found them,' said fat Chas, flicking a double blank high into the air, and catching it with a chubby knuckled snatch, his South London accent grating on Sammy's nerves almost as badly as Maurice's Northern one. 'Who's the other bloke?'

'This is my cousin. Maurice Kessler. He's down from Manchester. Living with us in London for a bit.'

Chas's face folded into a thousand creases. He was smiling. 'Best thing to do with Manchester – leave it.'

Maurice's eyes narrowed very slightly. *The cheeky fat fucker.* But he didn't like anyone thinking they could upset him – not that easily. So he winked at Chas. 'A sense of humour,' he said. 'I admire that in a feller. Just like I admire this place. Very original. Shows imagination.'

Chas and his skinny cousin looked at each other, weighing up if the Northern git was taking the piss. It wasn't easy for them to tell. They weren't accustomed to such exotic company.

They stood up. 'We like it,' Joey said. 'Right, business. We'll go somewhere private.'

Chas nodded for them to follow Joey, who, moving with surprising speed for someone who looked so physically frail, was already over by the door.

They went outside, round the back of the roadhouse, where barrels and crates and empties were stacked in apparently disorganised chaos, but there were no weeds sprouting, or bits of broken glass, so it was all, no doubt, in businesslike readiness. It was beginning to look like a bit of a trademark with the Baxter boys – things looking chaotic.

'Hands against the wall,' puffed Chas, winded from the effort of their short walk.

Sammy and Maurice didn't move, instead they just stared, questioning what they'd just heard. *Hands against the wall*? Was he sure?

Joey laughed and shook his head as if he were dealing with a pair of daft five year olds. 'You didn't think we'd let you onto our turf without searching you, did you?'

This was going well. Maurice wanted to join in with his laughter – but not because he was amused. If it took the Baxters's fancy they could put a bullet through the back of their skulls, drag them into the woods, and have them safely buried all within the hour. Have fucking daffodils planted on top of them ready for Easter. And no one would know any different.

Because no one knew they were there.

So much for Sammy and his big fucking plans.

Maurice wasn't so much relieved as genuinely taken aback when all they got was a very professional frisking.

'Clean,' said Joey to Chas, snapping Maurice back to attention.

'Fair enough,' said Chas, 'let's go.'

'Hang on,' said Sammy, grabbing Joey's arm, and flashing a worried look at Maurice. 'We came to talk to you.'

Joey stared at Sammy's hand on his shirtsleeve. Despite the cold, and him being such a slight man, he hadn't bothered with a jacket, and didn't appear at all uncomfortable even with the wind whipping across from

214

the water meadows on the other side of the river, but he *definitely* appeared put out by the fact that Sammy had taken the liberty of touching him.

'I know, Mr Kessler,' he said, eyes still fixed on Sammy's hand. 'That's where we're going – somewhere we can talk. We keep our business private.'

Sammy withdrew his hand, sticking it deep into his overcoat pocket. 'Right. Good.' He spoke as if it had been his idea all along to go off somewhere.

Chas sniffed loudly and spat a great gob of green snot into the grass. 'Follow us. And make sure you keep up.'

As he put the Jensen into first, Maurice was about to make a smartarsed remark to Sammy about the state of the beaten up flat-back truck that Joey and Chas had clambered into, but when it took off at a gravel-spraying lick, he turned down his mouth and nodded his approval. 'Souped up. Nice touch. Full of little surprises them two, ain't they, feller?'

They drove at speeds that made their earlier drive look like a Sunday afternoon jaunt with the Mothers' Union. After forty or so stomach-churning minutes they arrived at a little boat yard on an estuary. It was a long way from the main road leading them back to the safety of the Blackwall Tunnel and the 'right' side of the river.

Maurice parked the Jensen next to the truck on a piece of rough ground, hurriedly locking the doors so that he and Sammy could keep up with Chas and Joey, who were already halfway along a short jetty against which a tatty-looking boat had been moored.

Sammy was beginning to have serious doubts about all this. The other craft in the tiny marina were clean and spruce, their brass gleaming even in the thin, afternoon

215

light, and their natty little flags flapping and snapping proudly against the wintry sky. It seemed a miracle that the rust bucket they were about to climb onto could actually sit in the water, let alone sail anywhere.

Maurice held back a snigger as Chas heaved himself down through the hatch after Joey, like an over-sized cork being shoved into a bottle, and then gestured for Sammy to be his guest and go next.

As Sammy's feet hit the floor of the cabin, he stared about him in surprise and didn't feel too bad at all.

Maurice landed next to him. 'Here, this is a bit of all right, feller.'

That was an understatement. Compared to the exterior, the inside of the four-berth motor yacht was a palace, decked out with highly polished cherry wood, and with subtle tones of soft pink and grey in the immaculate upholstery.

'Don't like to have anything too flashy looking on the outside,' said Joey matter-of-factly. 'People get to thinking you're rich, and then they wonder where you get your few quid from.'

Maurice looked about him, nodding his approval. 'Very clever, feller. And this is a right handy bit of kit. Take it wherever you want, carry whatever you like, and all without attracting too much attention.'

Chas and Joey exchanged one of their glances, and Chas signalled for their guests to sit down. 'Niceties over,' he said. 'When we heard you wanted to see us, I must admit we were surprised. From what we understood, you Kesslers are all nice and cosied up with the O'Donnells.'

Sammy didn't hesitate. 'My family are doing some business with them.'

'The O'Donnells are a powerful outfit.'

'I know, and I know you had trouble with them a few years back.'

'When we was only based in Bermondsey.'

Maurice sniggered. 'What, before you went international, feller, and came down to Kent?'

Chas steepled his fingers over his great, fat belly. 'It was a nasty business. People got hurt.'

This time Sammy paused for a moment, looking right into Chas's puffy, piggy eyes. 'People died.' Another pause. '*Your* people.'

'They did.'

'And that's why I thought you'd be the perfect choice for me to do business with.'

'What business?'

'One or two bits of business actually, jobs that'll earn us enough of a stake to put a stop to the O'Donnells thinking they can act as if they own us. Enough to really shock them into realising who and what they're dealing with. And you can be in on it.'

'What sort of jobs?'

'All sorts.' Sammy had promised himself he would bide his time, wouldn't say too much too soon. 'I'm talking big money. And –' he added the clincher '– I'm talking about you helping us destroy the O'Donnells.'

'Sorry, but I think you're wasting our time. We've got our own interests to think about.'

What was going on? This wasn't what he'd expected. 'But –'

'But nothing. We don't need to start messing about with all that old Wild West fanny again, do we, Joe?'

'No, Chas, we don't. I had enough of all that shooting lark a long time ago.'

217

'In fact –' Chas hauled himself to his feet and jerked his head for Joey to do likewise '– I think we've gone far enough with this conversation.'

'You don't understand.' Sammy was now standing next to him. In spite of the cold, he could smell his own nervous sweat. 'There'd be plenty in it for you.'

'We're doing all right as it is, thank you. Come back another time maybe. When you've actually got something to talk about, something that don't involve playing Cowboys and Indians. And make sure it's something that's worth the agg.'

Maurice was close to exasperation. Some big scheme this was turning out to be. He tried to think of something to say that might repair some of the damage, and that might recover a bit of their self-respect.

Sammy beat him to it.

'I've got something to talk about now. And it would just be the beginning. On my life, when I said about you helping us destroy the bastards – I meant help us destroy their businesses. I wasn't expecting nothing else.'

More exchanged looks between Chas and Joey.

Chas sighed theatrically. 'We'll listen for two more minutes.'

'Right. It's a warehouse. It'll look like it's been stuffed full of furs. *After* it goes up like a rocket display on bonfire night. A warehouse that you two could have shares in. And . . .' He let the words dangle for a moment or two. 'In the future, let's say, I might also be looking for a way of disposing of some unwanted remains.'

Joey grinned, flashing more gold than teeth. 'So, *you're* gonna do the O'Donnells?'

'I'm not saying that.'

'Sorry, perhaps that was jumping the gun.' His grin spread even wider. 'As you might say.'

Sammy held up his hands. 'No, you're right, Joey. Cards on the table. You two know how them bastards work, which might prove very useful to me. And you two've also got a grudge against them.'

'True,' Chas said, plonking down on his seat – back in the chair in every sense. 'And?'

'And . . .' Sammy was speaking slowly but thinking in overdrive. 'That's where I might be useful to you. And if I maybe did want to get rid of some unwanted rubbish at some point in the future . . .'

'I don't think we'd be averse to lending a hand then – *after* the event, like – do you, Joe?'

'No.'

'In fact, we might know a man you might wanna speak to.' One of Chas's already piggy eyes disappeared in a wink. 'Posh bloke. Goes hunting and that. Mate of his runs the kennels for the hounds. They feed 'em on raw meat; make sure they keep their hunting instinct. So, if you ever did want to dispose of that rubbish . . .' He let the idea sink in. 'Please, let us know. We'd be happy to make the introductions. That's right, innit, Joe?'

They were the most words that Chas had said in one go since they'd met him. He was obviously excited.

'Chas. Joey.' Sammy held out his hands in open-palmed gratitude. If this went the way he hoped, it might just be the answer to his problems. 'You've almost embarrassed me now, making such a kind offer. Thank you. I'll remember your words. And, I swear, once I've got the stake together, I'm gonna finance the plans I've got that are gonna show up the O'Donnells for the two bob merchants they really are. And by the time we've finished, we'll be the only people anyone'll do business with in the whole East End.'

Chas and Joey exchanged another glance, while Sammy stared into the middle distance visualising bits of the Irishmen disappearing into a mincing machine. That would definitely get his father's attention, show him what his son was capable of. And maybe revenge on the O'Donnells might just begin to wipe away some of his guilt.

Just over seven weeks later, on a dull but dry Saturday evening in late March, Sammy and Maurice sat in the Jensen in a deserted side street in the East End's garment district. They were watching through binoculars as a colleague of Joey and Chas Baxter expertly set fire to a warehouse off the Commercial Road, a warehouse which the Baxters and the two Kessler cousins now owned in everything but name. The name on the papers being that of Susie Farlow, the young, widowed sister of the barmaid from the Four Aces.

A month after that, Mr Walter Jenkins, a bored, unhappily married, middle-aged loss adjustor, was sympathising with the young and lovely Mrs Farlow as he stared down the front of her blouse at her very attractive bosom. He told her how sorry he was that everything she'd inherited on the sad and premature passing away of her husband – the money which she'd invested in the warehouse – had literally gone up in smoke, when all the contents and fabric of the place had been destroyed in the devastating fire. But he hoped that the cheque would be of some compensation.

Susie Farlow, looking suitably mournful, but ever so grateful, didn't mention that the late Mr Farlow had been beaten to death by one of her boyfriends, a man who'd taken exception to his girlfriend being a married woman. And Mr Jenkins – oblivious of such complications – became quite excited at the thought of the charming, grateful, available young woman, and of the nice big cheque that she held in her dainty little hand.

He even began to wonder if he might perhaps offer her a more personal kind of comfort.

So smitten was he, in fact, that even if he *had* discovered that the few valuable contents of the warehouse – a couple of low grade mink coats, a box of squirrel stoles, and a half a dozen very old-fashioned musquash capes – had actually been removed and sold before the fire had happened, and that all that was left in the store at the time of the 'accident' were a few scraps of offcuts and a load of burnt rabbit skins, he would probably have ignored the evidence of his own eyes. For Mr Jenkins was a man fuelled by a dream: a fantasy of escaping from the insurance industry and from his dismal marriage.

As for young Mrs Farlow, who had been well paid for her work, she was actually tempted to go on a second date with Mr Jenkins. The first, which she'd initially seen as a necessary chore to prevent him from becoming difficult, had actually turned out to have been rather pleasant, unused as she was to men like Mr Jenkins. But, on reflection, she thought that doing so would probably have been pushing her luck with the Baxters. And so she did as they told her, and disappeared out of the country for an extended spring holiday, going to stay with one of their business associates who lived in a little Spanish fishing village called Fuengirola.

Mrs Farlow had made a wise choice, striking it very lucky indeed by choosing to go and stay with the Baxters's colleague.

221

Billy the Brick – so named for his early apprenticeship in famously daring smash-and-grab raids, before his graduation to more sophisticated, not to say much better paid, crimes – had been lying low in his charming, newly purchased, seaside villa, and was missing female company; well, female company of the sort that had blonde hair, a saucy laugh, and a reassuringly familiar, South London accent.

And the widow Farlow fitted the bill perfectly.

She soon settled in, and the holiday just seemed to go on and on. It wasn't long before Susie had plans for their little fishing village retreat. Using her pay off from the Baxters, she opened a real novelty of a place, a genuine English pub complete with a dart board on the wall, plenty of Red Barrel on tap, and roast beef and Yorkshire pudding on the daily menu.

Billy the Brick thought she was gorgeous, but bonkers, but Susie had an idea that it might just catch on.

Back home in England, the money that Susie Farlow had accepted in the form of Mr Jenkins's compensatory cheque had been tidily laundered and divvied out. Sammy Kessler had thanked the Baxters, and told them he was looking forward to doing business with them again very soon, and popped his share into a thick manila envelope.

The next morning, he waited for his mother to start clearing the breakfast things, and then asked if he could have a quiet word with his father.

Expecting yet more nonsense from his youngest son, Harold Kessler very reluctantly followed Sammy and Maurice into the front parlour, leaving Sophie to her chores.

*

Making sure the door was tightly closed, Sammy handed his father the envelope full of money, plus an edited explanation of recent events – playing down the role of the Baxters somewhat, but playing up the fact that this was only the first of the many scams that Sammy was planning. Scams which would get them a big enough pot to get them right out of the O'Donnells's circle of influence once and for all.

'I mean it, Dad,' Sammy said, tapping the bulging manila. 'There's gonna be plenty more where that little lot came from.'

Maurice had been right: this time Harold Kessler *was* listening to his son. He was listening very closely indeed.

Chapter 15

It had been a week since Sammy Kessler had handed the envelope full of money to his father, and now, with an eye to his plan of severing every last tie with the O'Donnells, and of repaying every bit of hurt they had inflicted on him, Sammy suggested that he and Maurice should pay a visit to the Bellavista.

They arrived at the club accompanied by two dishevelled looking men, who appeared to have had more than their fair share of booze before washing up in the narrow Shoreditch cul-de-sac.

One of the two bullet-headed, but immaculately dressed, door minders, put out his hand to stop them entering, looking Sammy and Maurice's companions up and down with obvious disapproval.

'These chaps with you, Mr Kessler?' The doorman couldn't keep the contempt from his voice.

'These gentlemen,' said Sammy with great solemnity, 'are my personal friends.'

Had the two strangers not been with members of the Kessler family, they would never have made it through the door – the O'Donnells were clear on this: mysteries weren't welcome anywhere near the new Bellavista – but the bouncer had a problem. He could just wave them in and risk them making nuisances of themselves. But that wasn't a good idea, not when his bosses kept stressing that they were trying to make the place *more classy*. He could insult them by keeping them on the pavement like idiots, while he checked with Brendan whether he should let them in or not. But that would upset the Kesslers – and maybe the O'Donnells. Or he could refuse them entry, point blank.

In short, he could start a fight by doing anything other than letting them waltz right in. And that might cause a fight anyway.

Great.

The bouncer puffed out his cheeks. It was no good asking his colleague, his brains stopped in his ham-sized fists. No choice but to take a chance and hope that the Kesslers would keep an eye on their mates. And so, with his metaphorical fingers crossed, the minder ushered the four men through. But, just to be on the safe side, he waited a few diplomatic minutes, and followed them into the club so he could warn Brendan about what he had done, and to promise him that he only had to shout and he and his mate would be right by his side.

Brendan took in the information without a word, not even bothering to get up from his bar stool to go over and greet them. He could see all he wanted from where he was – for now.

But it soon became clear that the strangers were not exactly respectful guests. Their voices were loud; their gestures over-extravagant, and their attitude towards the O'Donnells' bar staff was dismissively arrogant. None of that would have been too much of a problem for Brendan – not in normal circumstances. In fact, treating the bar staff with a measure of disdain was as good as an established business policy of the O'Donnells. But when it was tanked up pals of the Kesslers, who thought they could come bowling into his club and act that way, it made Brendan start twitching.

Finishing his drink, he checked his tie and hair – peering ostentatiously in the mirror behind the bar – and strolled over to where the four men were standing in the middle of the dance floor. As he passed by, customers nodded and smiled at him, eager to show their companions that they knew one of the owners – one of the notorious O'Donnell family – *in person*.

Brendan extended his hand to Sammy Kessler.

'Evening chaps,' he said, cracking a handsome grin at Sammy. 'You and your friends are more than welcome to come and join me and my brother for a drink at our table.' The grin softened into a warm smile; he was the good-natured host, gesturing with a lift of his chin to where Luke was sitting by himself sullenly nursing a very large whiskey.

One of the Kesslers's drunken companions slapped Brendan hard on the shoulder. 'Thanks all the same, moosh,' he yelled, turning heads all round the bar. 'Rather sit with a bird, if you don't mind. I mean, this *is* a fucking knocking shop, ain't it?'

He folded an arm round the other drunk's shoulder and they staggered over to the girls' bench to check out what was on offer.

Brendan just managed to keep his lips stretched into a thin approximation of a smile. 'Your mates are a bit Brahms, ain't they, Sammy? Sure they ain't had enough?'

Sammy returned Brendan's mouth-only smile. 'Thought that's what clubs like this were for, selling over-priced booze, renting out whores, and generally having one over on the mug punters. But maybe you're right, maybe I had better make sure they at least stay upright. I mean, wouldn't want the Bellavista getting a bad reputation and forcing the law to make an official visit, now would we? That'd be bad for business wouldn't it, eh, Bren?'

Brendan wanted to punch Sammy Kessler right in the face, but this wasn't the time or the place to do it. Especially as he had a very strong hunch that starting a ruck was exactly what the swaggering little twat wanted him to do. And even though every time he looked at the bloke he wanted to hit him – just the thought of him having been anywhere near his little sister made Brendan want to put his hands round the bastard's throat and shake him till his brains rattled – he wouldn't give Kessler the satisfaction of letting him know he could upset him.

He managed to keep what was left of his smile plastered to his face. 'No one ever likes to get an official visit, Sam,' he mugged.

'You're right there, Brendan.' Sammy turned to his cousin and winked. 'So, reckon I'd better get over to them other two, Maury. Case they do something silly. But there's nothing to stop you from joining Brendan and Luke *at their table*. Go on, go and enjoy yourself.'

'You know, Sammy, I think I will.' Maurice flashed his eyebrows at Brendan, and rubbed his hands together in eager anticipation. 'Right, a taste of the O'Donnell hospitality . . . I'll have a large Scotch, please, feller. And make sure it's Scotch, eh? Cos I can't be doing with the Irish.'

Brendan walked over to speak to the barman, knowing he had to get away from that saucy, big-mouthed fucker before he landed him one right in the middle of his sneering, Northern gob. Sammy Kessler was bad enough, but there was something about his toerag of a cousin that Brendan could feel crawling all over his skin like a slime-trailing bug. He was a nine carat piece of shit.

227

Maurice, on the other hand, had a very different opinion of himself – he was feeling rather pleased with what he'd achieved: winding up Brendan O'Donnell like an over tight clock spring without so much as breaking sweat. Nice.

Time to move on and see what he could do to his little brother.

Maurice snatched up a chair, set it down close to Luke, and straddled it like a horse. 'So, how're you doing then, feller?'

No answer.

'Fair enough.' Maurice began whistling along to the crackly recording of Bobby Darin singing 'Mack the Knife', enjoying the knowledge that he was making Luke feel uncomfortable just by being there.

Still accompanying Bobby, Maurice linked his fingers and stretched out his arms, right under Luke's nose, cracking his knuckles loudly.

He stopped whistling abruptly, pointed at Luke and said, 'Just out of interest, don't you ever feel like asking our Sammy about, you know – him and your sister?'

Luke stared about him, gathering his words, his lips stretched tight across his teeth. He then returned to studying his drink. 'I ain't got the first clue what you're talking about.'

'It's all right, Luke, me cousin's told me all about her.'

Luke lifted his head and looked directly into Maurice's smug, mocking eyes. 'What are you on about?'

Maurice paused, the little smile playing about his lips somehow making the silence suggestive. 'I hardly mean your Patricia, now do I? It's Catherine I'm talking about.' He looked over his shoulder. 'So, where's this drink I was promised then, eh, feller?' He turned back to Luke. 'Mind you, I don't know if you'd really want to hear what he's got to say. Not really. Some of the things he told me about her . . .' He narrowed his eyes, pouted his lips and shook his head. 'Like how she loved to get –'

A sudden, loud squeal, as one of the two drunks pushed a young brunette off the bench, sending her crashing backwards into the wall, distracted Maurice for a brief but crucial moment.

Luke swung back his arm and punched him – hard – on the side of the head.

'Are you sure?' Maurice, clutching his temple, spun round. He stuck his face right into Luke's and grabbed him by the lapels. 'Have you lost your fucking mind? I could rip your head right off your shoulders with just this one hand, you pathetic little queer. I like a grin with the best of them, but you have just overstepped the fucking mark.'

'Leave it, Maury.' It was Sammy. He was pulling Maurice to his feet. 'I think it's time we joined the others.'

Maurice let go of Luke, but poked him hard in the chest. 'Touch me, would you, you Irish ponce? I'll have you later.'

Brendan was standing in the farthest corner from the door looking fit to detonate with temper, as Kevin Marsh and Barry Ellis sprawled on the floor in front of him, grappling with Sammy's two companions. Fists were flying and girls were screaming. It was like a scene from a Saturday morning Western at the fleapit.

There was a sudden explosion of glass and a chorus of high-pitched yelps from the girls, as one of the drunks managed to pull off Barry's shoe and aim it at the row of optics behind the bar.

At the sound of the bottles smashing, the door minders were inside in a flash.

'That's it,' hollered Brendan. 'Out.' He grabbed the shoe thrower by the hair and dragged him to his feet, pushing him towards Sammy Kessler. 'And it might be an idea if you and your cousin go with them and all.'

'You're chucking us out?' Sammy shook his head pityingly. 'That would be one big mistake, O'Donnell. Our two families are trying to be friends here, and what are you doing? Mugging us off. Treating us like punters. What would your old man have to say about that d'you reckon?'

'He's not here is he?'

Luke, still rubbing the sting from his knuckles from where he'd punched Maurice, joined his brother in the middle of the chaotic scene. 'All right?'

'Fine,' said Brendan, not taking his eyes off Sammy. 'Kessler, you and your cousin and your two piss artist mates, get out. Now.' Then he put out his arms, and, with the minders flanking him, began marshalling the four unwanted guests towards the exit. He turned his head and called to his brother. 'Now the cabaret's over, make sure everyone's got a drink, Luke.'

Barry and Kevin, their shirt tails hanging out, their hair in their eyes, and with only three shoes between them, stood on either side of the door like glowering ushers at a shotgun wedding.

'Come on, lads,' said Sammy, seeing the other three out onto the pavement, as he straightened his collar, 'let's get away from here. We don't have to put up with O'Donnell's old guyver.'

Once Sammy had stepped outside, Brendan tried to shut the door on them, but the drunk whose hair Brendan had grabbed had other ideas. He moved with unexpected speed, sticking his foot in the jamb, and lurching back inside.

Before Brendan knew what was happening, the man had raced through the lobby and back into the main part of the club, and was clambering over the girls, hauling himself up onto their bench, scattering them around him like a frightened flock of screaming, multi-coloured gulls.

'You O'Donnell fuckers,' he hollered over the music, waggling his outstretched arms like a tightrope walker as he battled to keep his balance on the narrow seat. 'You wanna watch your arses. Cos I'm coming back here, and I'm gonna set fire to this bastard place. I'll show *you* throw *me* out.'

With that he lurched off the bench, shouldered his way back through the crowd and fell through the front door, slamming it loudly behind him.

Outside on the pavement, Maurice put an arm round the supposedly drunken man's shoulder and hugged him warmly. But the man was no longer drunk, he was, like his supposedly equally intoxicated mate, completely sober. The four men walked steadily and calmly towards the top of the cul-de-sac.

'Regular little fire brands you South London lot, ain't you, feller?' said Maurice. 'And not bad actors, eh, Sammy? They should go on the telly, shouldn't they? There's good money in that.'

'And there's good money in causing aggravation for them Irish cunts and all. Here lads.' Sammy gave each of the two men a wad of notes. 'Give my regards to Chas and Joey, and tell them I'll be in touch.'

'Very nice job, fellers,' said Maurice, pulling open the

door of a phone box on the corner of Folgate Street. 'I'll only be a minute, Sam. Just got a quick call to make. Might as well wind them right up, while we're at it. Here, hold on.' He beckoned the two men to come back. 'Can either of you two show me how to do an Irish accent? Just for a laugh like.'

While all hell was breaking loose at the Bellavista, Gabriel was sitting in front of a frill trimmed, kidney-shaped dressing table, taking sips of Jameson's in between knotting his paisley tie. The drink was supposedly an alibi, his cover to convince Eileen that he'd been in the club with the boys. But even he was beginning to wonder if he was getting to be as dependent on the stuff as his father had been – and that was a long time before he'd finally run off for good and left them all to fend for themselves.

He stood up and slipped his arms into the jacket Rosie was holding up for him. Then he turned and pulled her close.

'I don't know what I'd do without you, Rosie Palmer.'

'So long as I make you happy, love, that's all that matters to me.' She dropped her chin, her heavy dark hair falling about her face. 'And Ellie, of course.'

'I know you miss her, Rosie,' he said, stroking her soft, pale cheek, 'but she's better off over there. She couldn't be at a better school than St Anne's. And you know Mary would rather have her eyes plucked out than have anything bad happen to her. It's for the best, my angel, you know that.'

'I know, and I'm not complaining, honest, Gabe, but . . .' Rosie gently pulled away from him and fetched his cigarettes and lighter from the bedside table.

He tucked them into his pocket. 'Tell you what, Rose, how about if I get Mary to fetch her over next week?'

Rosie's eyes welled up with tears. 'Really? Next week?'

'Why not?'

'You're so good to me.'

He smiled down at her, loving her in his own way, but knowing he'd never understand why she was prepared to sacrifice so much for him. He hadn't wanted the bother of another child, so what had she done when she'd fallen pregnant? She'd as good as given her up. For him.

He could never care so much about what someone else wanted. Never.

Rosie undid her wrapper and let it fall to the floor, showing off her ripe, plump body, the body that made Gabriel forget all the everyday nonsense that drove him mad and that, he would say, justifying his thirst, drove him to drink. 'You deserve a proper thank you for that.'

Gabriel felt himself harden. 'You're a beautiful woman, Rosie Palmer, a truly beautiful woman.'

The next morning, Gabriel went into the yard early. He wanted privacy, so he could speak to his sister about organising the trip over from Ireland.

He had just put the receiver back in its cradle, when the door was pushed open and Gabriel saw Brendan and Luke framed in the opening. They were staring at him, eyes wide with surprise, as if they'd been caught burgling the place.

Brendan spun round to say something to someone behind him, but he was too late.

'You should have heard the piss-taking accent.' Gabriel heard Barry's voice saying from outside, and then sliding into a mocking Oirish lilt. 'See, dey weren't punters, dey weren't even our mates. Sure wasn't it all –'

'All right Barry,' Brendan cut in.

'Let him finish.' Gabriel was on his feet, looking over his sons' shoulders. 'Come in here, Barry. You too Kevin. Now, what were you saying?'

Barry and Kevin sloped up the steps into the shabby lean-to office like schoolboys caught smoking behind the girls' lavs. Barry looked at Brendan, pleading with his eyes for a signal to tell him what to do.

'Go on,' Brendan said flatly.

Luke could barely stand to listen.

Barry gulped then said, all in a rush and in his own cockneyfied Dublin, 'Them blokes who turned up at the Bellavista. They weren't really drunk; they were just there to cause trouble. Show us up. They were paid to do it. They work for them blokes that the Kesslers owned that warehouse with.'

Gabriel tipped his head to one side and held out his hands – totally confused. 'What blokes? When? And what warehouse?'

Barry looked at Brendan again. Knowing he'd said too much, but what could he do – risk a good hiding from Gabriel? At least Brendan would only give him a bollocking for shooting his mouth off.

He lowered his eyes and began, very slowly. 'There was a bit of a ruck in the club last night.'

'Tell me you don't mean the Bellavista.'

'Sorry, Gabe.' Barry dropped his chin. 'Sammy Kessler, and that flash cousin of his, they came in with these two blokes. Then, right after they left, one of the arseholes phoned the club. I answered it. He was taking the piss, putting on some stupid accent. But I know it had to be that Northern ponce.'

'I said, *Barry*, what blokes and what warehouse?'

'The fur warehouse. The one that got torched. The one they say Sammy Kessler bought with the Baxters. And the blokes last night, they work for the Baxters and all.'

'*The Kesslers and the Baxters are working together?*'

Barry nodded miserably, but did his best to limit the damage of the bad news. 'Only Sammy and his cousin though, Gabe. Not Daniel or the old man.'

Gabriel stared. 'Aw, so that's all right then, is it?'

'Well, no . . .'

'Anything else I should know about? Anything else you weren't planning on telling me if I hadn't been here early?'

Barry was wishing he was in a damp, dark cell somewhere having lighted matches poked down his toenails. 'When we threw them out of the Bellavista, one of them came back in, shouting the odds about how he was gonna torch the gaff.'

Gabriel dropped down into his seat. 'That's it, we've lost control. Why did I ever think them whoresons would know how to behave? I should have known they'd take my kindness for fucking stupidity.' He smashed the side of his fist onto the desk. 'And if *anyone's* going to set light to my fucking properties it's going to be fucking me.'

He fumbled around trying to get a cigarette out of his packet, his hands were shaking with temper.

Luke lit one of his and gave it to his father. 'What you gonna do, Dad?'

'Do? I'm gonna tell that fucker Kessler his fucking fortune. That's what.'

Brendan was tempted to urge him on, get him even

235

wilder, make him realise that this was the moment they should break with the Kesslers once and for all. Even get another dig in about the drugs he was sure the Kesslers would start dealing, if they didn't shift themselves and get the business sewn up first. But one look at his father's face, and Brendan knew it was best to keep quiet.

Gabriel's cheeks and throat had gone a lurid, purplish red and the veins in his neck were bulging and throbbing as if he were about to have a seizure.

Brendan judged it right: he would have to bide his time.

Luke, on the other hand, had more immediate plans.

While Gabriel was coming close to boiling point in the scruffy lean-to in Bethnal Green, the objects of his fury – Sammy and Maurice – were in the Jensen speeding along peaceful country lanes. This time it wasn't wintry, rural Kent they were driving through, but the Essex country-side, and the hedgerows and trees were in their full spring glory.

'Easy there, feller.' Maurice was beginning to regret agreeing to let Sammy drive. They were racketing along a rutted farm track that the dry spell had rendered as solid as jagged chunks of concrete. 'This isn't a bloody truck.'

Sammy's face didn't give away a flicker of irritation, he just dropped down a gear and lowered the speed. Anything rather than let Maurice back behind the wheel.

After a few more minutes being tossed and bucketed around they came to a straight stretch of metalled road that led directly to a beautifully proportioned, red brick Tudor farmhouse.

Chas and Joey Baxter – resplendent in vests and braces, with a variety of fresh cuts and slightly older scabs standing out against their pale skin in the slightly chilly, but clear morning light – were waiting in the magnificent front porch to welcome their guests like a nightmare parody of a pair of postcard seaside landladies.

'Thought it was Kent you two fellers liked,' said Maurice, sitting back in a huge carved oak armchair and looking around the great hall with undisguised admiration. 'What with all that jolly London hop-picking with your old gran and that. So, what brought you out here to Essex?'

'Pea-picking. Near Ongar,' said fat Chas.

'What, with your nan again? She sounds a good old girl.'

'All right, Maury,' said Sammy, 'we're not here for family reminiscences. Let's listen while Chas and Joey tell me how they're gonna double my money for me.'

Joey did something with his skinny weasely features that was the closest they'd ever get to a genuine smile. 'Only way to guarantee that, mate, is to fold it in half and stick it back in your britch.'

Sammy laughed politely and looked to Chas for a sensible answer.

'Come and see our barn,' was his unexpected reply.

They eventually reached the traditional Essex barn by fighting their way through a tangled spinney, with briars and brambles lashing their faces – the explanation for the Baxters's scratches and scabs.

Chas, in his usual laconic way said that they used a different route each time they went to the barn so as not to beat a single, detectable path from the house. But that there were plenty of tracks for four wheel drives, as well as a whole series of anonymous little lanes crisscrossing along the back that could easily be accessed by the trucks, and plenty of quiet spots to transfer their loads into the Jeeps.

Joey heaved open one half of a pair of tall double doors and flicked a switch. They all blinked as a fluorescent glow lit up the whole, triple height space. As with the Baxters's boat, first impressions of the barn had been deceptive. Outside a piece of architecturally interesting agricultural history, inside a thoroughly organised system of alphabetically labelled, well-lit, open metal shelving with corresponding filing cabinets and rolodexes: all in all, a well-thought out system for delivery and distribution.

Joey pointed into the air with a bony finger. 'This, chaps, is set to be the biggest porn warehouse in the Southeast. We fitted it out using our cut from the warehouse. Always good for business to put some profits back into the firm.'

'Why Essex?' asked Sammy, adding hurriedly, 'And I'm not talking about the pea-picking. Why not Kent? Surely the sort of gear you're talking about comes over from France.'

'Good point. A lot of it does. And that's why everyone would expect us to bring stuff in over the Channel, what with us being based in South London and Kent. But we decided the Harwich route in from Holland is the way forward. There's a lot of gear available over there. A lot of the real hard stuff.'

Sammy could feel the excitement. This was smelling just right. He knew the sort of money that the dirty bookshops brought in in Soho. If he could start supplying them direct . . . 'Okay. Say we provide as many lorries as you want, maybe even organise ourselves a few regular runs taking stuff out to Holland or Belgium. Good, legit cover plus some extra bunce into the bargain.'

Chas and Joey shared a look. 'Sounds very possible,' said Chas.

Sammy took a breath. 'Like I say, I can provide the vehicles and drivers, as many as you need. But there is one slight problem. I'm going to have to ask for a bit of help financing the first run. That's why I'm offering you a sixty–forty cut on this one.'

'Eighty–twenty,' said Chas without missing a beat.

'Seventy–thirty.'

'Done.' Chas spat into his fat palm and slapped it against Sammy's.

'But, after that, fifty–fifty, okay?'

'Fifty–fifty,' said Joey. 'And, when this takes off and starts bringing in the dough like I know it will, there's something else you might be interested in.'

Chas had settled himself down to enjoy the sun on a circular bench under a huge mulberry tree on the lawn at the side of the house, while Joey escorted Sammy and Maurice back to the Jensen.

'And it's got other benefits,' Joey said, as Maurice unlocked the car. 'It looks a nice, straight down the line business. But it's a very useful way of rinsing through the profits from trade like this.' He turned and looked in the direction of the barn. 'And a good way of shifting the merchandise about. We're setting up in South London as we speak. And just think how nice it'd be for you to set up something so visible in the East End, before them O'Donnell cunts get a look in. Hit them where it hurts. Their pride, their pockets, and their fucking balls.'

'Kesslers's Cabs, eh?' Sammy raised his hand in goodbye to Chas, and then shook Joey's bony claw. 'It's

239

a thought. But I'll have to think about it. See how much we get out of this film and book lark first. Then see if I can afford to diversify.'

'Sammy, mate, you won't be able to afford not to.'

Gabriel snatched up the phone from his desk. 'What?'

'It's me, Gabe, Eileen.'

'Not now.' His voice was full of pained exasperation. 'I've got –'

'Sorry, Gabe, this is important. Patricia's round ours, and she needs Peter to take –'

'Hang on a minute, Eileen. Calm down.' He put his hand over the mouthpiece and rolled his eyes. 'Stephen, where's Pete Mac got to?'

'I'd put money on him being round that Violet's drum again,' said Stephen, avoiding Gabriel's gaze by concentrating on folding his *Sporting Life* into a neat oblong.

Gabriel nodded wearily. 'Me too.' He took his hand away from the phone. 'Sorry, Ei, he's out seeing a bloke about a contract.'

'Well, can someone find him? Patricia's gone into labour.'

'Don't worry about Pete Mac, I'll send Stephen.' Gabriel put down the phone. 'Stephen, get round my place and get our Patricia to the hospital, will you.'

It wasn't a question.

Stephen stood up, and shoved his paper in his jacket pocket as he made for the door. 'I'll take me five minutes.'

'Steve,' Gabriel went on with a sigh. 'When's he going to get rid of that little scrubber? It's all beginning to seem a bit too serious.'

'You want my genuine opinion on that, Gabe? It's not

240

serious at all. He's just a lazy bastard, who can't even be bothered to sniff out a fresh bit of skirt to mess around with.'

Gabriel put his elbows on his desk and buried his face in his hands. 'All I've ever asked is that my family should be happy. Is that too much for a man to ask?'

Chapter 16

'I don't think I'm going to able to get in tomorrow afternoon, Pat,' said Eileen softly, smiling down into the hospital cot, as she gently tucked the blankets around the new love of her life, her baby granddaughter, Caty. 'Got a few errands to run. But I'll be here in the evening to see you, okay?'

Patricia, who hadn't said much during the visit, grabbed her mother's hand. 'Mum. Will it get better now I've had the baby?'

'Better? Course it will, darling. It's not even been a week yet. All that soreness and pain'll soon be nothing more than a bad memory now you've got your precious little bundle.'

'I'm not talking about that.' She pressed her teeth into her bottom lip, biting back the tears. 'I mean with Pete. Will he grow up a bit now he's a dad?'

Eileen sat down on the high-backed bedside chair and squeezed her daughter's hand. 'I honestly don't know, Patsy, love. I don't know if men ever grow up, not in the way we have to. Now you have a child, you'll soon realise, it's women, mothers, who keep things going. We might only be quietly in the background, while it's the men making all the noise and fuss, but really we're the strong ones – we have to be. We keep it all together. We don't just clear off down the pub if the mood takes us, or if things get too much, like they do. We just get on with it.'

Patricia buried her face in her hands. 'What have I done?'

'Ssshh, love, don't cry. It's not all bad.'

'No?'

'No, course not. It's the way we get what we want. Our home, and our life with our family. And it's the way we get to keep it.'

Patricia dropped her hands and looked pleadingly at her mother. 'I'm sorry, I'm just so miserable. And I keep thinking about how much Catherine would have loved the baby. Mum, I miss her so much.'

'So do I, darling,' said Eileen, wiping her daughter's tears with her fingers. 'Every single minute of every single day, God love her. And when I think of some of the people on this earth who wouldn't even be missed . . .'

'She was so funny, wasn't she? Always mucking around, making us all laugh. She could get Dad to do whatever she wanted, remember?'

'She was our baby.'

'And she really would have loved little Caty wouldn't she?'

'Yes, darling, she would.' Eileen kissed her daughter on the cheek and stood up. 'I'd better be off now, or the nurse'll be after me. We've already had an extra ten minutes.'

'Do you think Dad'll be able to get in tomorrow afternoon if you can't?'

'I'm not sure, Pat.' Eileen took one more look at the baby. 'I think he might be a bit busy. You know, what with work and everything.'

As she walked out of the ward, Eileen had to keep her lips pressed tightly together to stop her screaming to the world, 'Of course he won't be able to get here tomorrow afternoon. *Of course he bloody won't.*'

Eileen had told her daughter the partial truth: Gabriel was busy the following afternoon. But not with work. He was sitting on the sofa in the front room of the neat, ground floor, two-bedroom flat in Kilburn with his mistress, Rosie Palmer.

'You seem edgy, Gabe,' Rosie said, throwing him a glance over her shoulder, as she rearranged the table full of cakes and sandwiches yet again. 'Is it seeing Ellie? It'd be understandable if it was. It's been what? Three months since you last saw her?'

'No,' he said, 'it's Eileen.'

'She'll be caught up with the new baby.'

'She's that all right.' He rubbed a hand over his chin, absent-mindedly checking for signs of stubble. 'The first time we went in to see Pat, we were driving home after, and she said how glad she was that the baby was a girl.'

Rosie repositioned a plate of glossy pink cupcakes and turned to face him. 'You can't blame her for that, can you, love? Think about it. She lost Catherine, and now she has a new baby to fuss over. A little girl. I can't begin to think how I'd feel if anything ever happened to Ellie. It's hard enough not having her here with me all the time. But to lose her forever . . .'

Gabriel stood up, his soft towelling dressing gown flapping open, showing a body that, despite his boozing, was still well muscled for a man in his forties. 'You're a good woman, Rosie,' he said, pulling her to him. 'Good and generous. That's why you don't understand the way a woman like Eileen thinks. She said she was glad the baby's a girl, because it means she won't be involved with

244

the business. She was looking down on me. Looking down on what I do.'

'Don't condemn her, Gabe. Women don't always realise what you men have to put up with. Or how hard you work. But it's not our fault we don't understand.'

'Eileen understands all right. She knows where the money comes from, and she's only too happy to let me pay all the bills. She doesn't say no to that.'

Rosie reached up and stroked his neck. 'Don't upset yourself, Gabe, not today. Please. Why don't you go and get dressed? Ellie's going to be here soon.'

Rosie was ready and waiting on the front step when the taxi arrived twenty minutes later.

She ran down the path and wrenched open the back door.

Mary Logan, Gabriel's sister, stepped out onto the pavement, followed by a pretty little girl in a school uniform, her hair braided into two shiny, blue-black plaits.

Rosie's hand flew to her mouth. 'Sweetheart,' she sobbed, and bent down to fold her in her arms.

Gabriel came up behind the little group.

'Say hello to your daddy,' said Mary, removing the child from her mother's hugs and guiding her towards Gabriel.

'Hello, Daddy,' said the little girl, peering up at him from under the brim of her bottle green hat.

At the corner of the street, hiding like a sneak thief in the shadow of a red and white striped watchman's hut by a hole in the road, Eileen O'Donnell stood watching the touching scene of family reunion. Tears were flowing unchecked down her face. But it wasn't because she was watching her husband scooping up his supposedly secret daughter, making her pigtails swing around her head, while his whore stood beaming, full of happiness, by his side, and her bitch of a sister-in-law, Mary Logan, encouraged the pair of them.

No, it was looking at the child that tore her heart apart.

Eileen hadn't had a glimpse of her for nearly two years and knew that she must now be almost ten years old – the whore had had her when she was little more than seventeen years old. And now she was a schoolgirl in her sweet, convent uniform, so full of life, yet so shy with her daddy, a man she rarely saw.

And she was the living image of Catherine.

It was all Eileen could do to stop herself from rushing over and snatching the child up in her arms, to cover her little face with kisses, to steal her away from that woman.

She watched as her husband's whore suddenly held up her hand, and said with such a joyful smile, 'Hang on, darling' – *darling* to *her* man – 'I can hear the phone. You and Mary sort out the taxi and get Ellie's bags, and I'll go and answer it.'

Ellie, her name was Ellie.

Such a pretty name for such a heartbreakingly beautiful little girl. She hadn't known her name before. There'd been no one to ask. Everything Eileen knew about her had been found out by standing behind half-closed doors when Mary was over from Ireland to see Gabe, sneaking looks at notes in pockets when sending clothes to the laundry, and listening to whispered phone calls.

The worst part of it had been all those other people knowing. It didn't bother Eileen that they were probably laughing at her stupidity and foolishness. No, it was knowing that they could tell her so much about the child, but that she wasn't able to ask them. And it hurt even more

246

since Catherine had died. Hurt so much it drove a knife through her heart; made her ache like she had a stone in her chest and a lead weight in her stomach.

A brief moment later, the whore was back outside on the step, and this time not looking nearly so happy. In fact, she looked as if she had just been slapped around the face.

'It's for you,' she called to Gabriel, who was taking his change from the cab driver. Her voice was low, measured, but Eileen could still make out every single word.

'Me?'

She nodded. 'It's Luke.'

'*My* Luke?'

She nodded numbly and stepped aside to let him into the hall.

'Sorry to call you when you're round there, Dad.'

'I don't want to even start discussing the ins and outs of that right now, boy. Just tell me what the fuck you want and then get off this phone.'

'You said you wanted to talk to Harry Kessler.'

'I said I was going to tell him a few things.'

'That's right. To sort this all out.'

'Luke –'

'Dad, I've contacted him for you.'

'*You've done what?*'

'And he's agreed to come to the yard to see you. Half ten, Monday morning.'

'He's *agreed?*'

'Dad, I bet he's as wild with those boys of his as you are.'

'Luke, I don't think you begin to realise what someone being wild really means. But if you don't get off this

247

phone, *now*, you'll realise a lot sooner than you could imagine. Now don't you ever, ever, call me on this number again. Do you understand?'

'But Dad –'

'Listen to me, Luke, because I don't intend repeating myself. I'll swallow seeing the no-good bastard now you've arranged it. Because I don't want one of my family being made to look a fool. And I'll even give him a fair hearing, waste time listening to his crap and his lies. But, I swear on this, son: if you tell anyone about me being here – *anyone* – I promise you, you'll regret it for the rest of your life. *Got it?*'

Gabriel sat alone in his office, his face set like a hollow-eyed Celtic carving. Harold Kessler had just smarmed and shrugged and spread his arms through a ridiculous two hour meeting.

Kessler was going to give his boys a talking to, tell them what was what, sort it all out, and everything was going to be hunky-fucking-dory . . .

Brendan had stormed out in disgust, and Luke had gone running after him, calling for him to stop, but Brendan wouldn't listen. He just jumped in his car and screeched out of the yard.

Kessler had made some smartarsed comment – *boys, eh!* – that made Gabriel want to stub out his cigarette on the man's fat, smug face. Then he'd laughed, and he'd fucking shrugged – again – and he and his poxy sons – flashy, over-confident Daniel, and the shifty looking younger one, Sammy – and that aggravating arse of a nephew of his, Maurice, had left.

And now what was he left with? Another compromise for the sake of so-called peace. That's what.

Gabriel could hardly believe he'd actually agreed to give them another chance.

And why had he done it? Because he'd let a tearful Rosie, *Rosie of all people, for Christ's sake*, persuade him that peace was better than the alternative, and that she wanted the father of her child, the man she loved, to stay safe.

Well, if this was peace, he'd hate to see what war with the bastards would be like.

He should have talked to Mary about it, not Rosie.

No, hang on, no he shouldn't. What the hell was he even thinking? He shouldn't have talked to anyone. He never used to; never used to take any notice of anyone but himself. He was Gabriel O'Donnell, head of the family, the boss, number one, a law unto himself.

And now he was giving that stupid fuck another chance.

For the sake of peace . . .

He reached for the Jameson's. He hardly knew what to think any more; all he knew was that he needed another drink.

A bloody big one.

September 1961

September 1951

Chapter 17

The man dug his fingers deep into the rigid knots of muscle in Gabriel's neck, and then worked his hands up and down his soap-slicked back.

Gabriel didn't flinch, didn't swear, didn't even try to make himself more comfortable on the marble massage slab. He was too incensed to be able to register anything other than his hatred of the Kesslers and his anger at what they had done – what they had so contemptuously dared to do. After he had given them that final opportunity to behave – an opportunity in the name of fucking peace . . .

When the masseur indicated that he had finished his routine by stepping away from Gabriel and collecting up his sponges, soaps and scrapers, the seven men – Gabriel, Brendan, Luke, Pete Mac, Barry Ellis, Kevin Marsh and Stephen Shea – secured their towels around their waists, and made their way through to the refreshment room of the municipal baths. Gabriel visited the baths every Wednesday morning, because he could. Because he, unlike lesser mortals – the mug punters, who spent their Wednesday mornings in factories, workshops and offices – was the one who decided what he did with his time. But on this particular Wednesday morning his sense of superiority, his knowledge that he was in control, while others were being controlled, had been shat on from a very great height. By the Kesslers.

And he didn't like it. He didn't like it one fucking bit.

The seven men sat on wooden loungers waiting for

the tea and toast they had ordered. Their toast would come topped with the various combinations of eggs, beans and tomatoes offered by the baths' tiny kitchen. Usually, the snacks were a simple but enjoyable treat. And usually, the post-steam relaxation time would have been easy and companionable, interspersed with occasional jokes and wise cracks, and maybe with coded discussions about bits of business that had to be attended to, but not today. Today felt drawn out. A void waiting to be filled.

It was, as it was so often, Pete Mac who cracked first.

'Well, you know what they say, Gabe.' His voice echoed round the high, white and green tiled walls of the bathhouse like that of a Tyrolean yodeller in full throat. 'After the Lord Mayor's show comes the shit cart. And this time it looks like it's Kessler who's driving the fucker.'

Gabriel was just about to shout at his son-in-law to stop his non-stop, bloody aggravating, idiotic, bollocks-for-brains, smart mouthing, but a man came into the room, unknowingly saving Pete Mac from Gabriel's temper.

The man was wearing a white knee-length apron over baggy shorts and a vest, and was holding two plates of double poached eggs on toast, decorated with dainty slices of tomato and sprigs of cress. He smiled pleasantly and held out the plates for inspection so that they might be identified and claimed by their rightful owners.

Slowly, and without fuss, Gabriel took a deep breath, rubbed his hands together then folded his arms and jerked his head at the door for the man to get lost.

The man hesitated for a brief moment. Tentatively, he experimented, putting down a single plate of food on one of the wooden side tables.

Still without a word, Gabriel swiped at it with a sweep of his arm, sending it crashing onto the duckboarded floor. Soft, orange-yellow yolk dripped down between the slats.

The man decided, pretty sharpish, that discretion was definitely the better part of valour, and he left, taking the remaining plate with him, closing the door with the faintest of clicks.

At last, Gabriel spoke. 'Almost a year he's been back here in the East End. And for nearly all that time I've tolerated the donkey's arse. I've let him get away with his stupid, niggling little tricks, turning a blind eye, pretending I've not noticed his pathetic, two-bob scams. Nearly a whole. Fucking. Year.' Gabriel sat on the edge of the wooden lounger shaking his head. A man disappointed by his own stupidity. A man proved right in his own misgivings about his misplaced generosity.

No one in the room felt like disagreeing, or even agreeing with him for that matter. Not even Pete Mac.

'I've put up with them and I've kept my mouth shut. I must have been out of my bloody mind. I can't believe I've been so stupid. I let that bastard have the world. And what thanks do I get for it? How does he repay me? He pisses all over me and takes a fucking, diabolical liberty. That's how.'

Gabriel's forehead furrowed into a deep frown, as if he were trying to make sense of it all. 'I even cocked a deaf ear when it was obvious he thought he was tucking me up over the betting shops. And then there was all that shit about why he came back to Stepney. Worried about more riots? Bollocks he was. I knew all along he was scared off when Rachman moved in. Well, he's gonna be in for a shock. He's gonna think that that bloke and his henchmen are fucking nursemaids by the time I've finished with Harold Kessler.

'Kevin, pour me a whiskey, and go through it again. Properly. Bit by bit. I don't need figures, just the ins and outs.'

Looks were exchanged between the other men in the room as Kevin fetched a bottle and Gabriel's preferred Waterford crystal tumbler from a black leather holdall in the corner of the room.

They often enjoyed a snifter stirred into their tea after a steam, but this was different. And if Gabriel was about to get drunk and go potty about the Kesslers, then it was probably best he did so in private. Brendan stood up quietly, went over to the door, stuck his head outside, and said something that the rest of them couldn't make out. Then he shut the door again and wedged a chair firmly under the handle.

Kevin handed Gabriel his drink. 'Right, let's see,' he said, 'we all know that there's been plenty of whispers, talk about the Kesslers thinking of branching out, that they fancied making money from this new game, this mini-cabbing lark –'

'Tell me,' Gabriel cut in, 'did I stop his fucker of a son getting into bed with the Bermondsey lot? Did I say a word when they opened their betting shops? Complain they were taking away my business?'

'No, Gabriel,' said Kevin automatically.

Pete Mac's mouth was open before anyone could stop him. 'No, that ain't right, Kev. Once the betting shops started coming in, Gabe said he didn't want anything to do with them. He said the street pitches were okay – no books, no taxes, no betting duty. But the shops . . .' He turned to Gabriel. 'I remember it clear as day. You weren't interested. Said they could get on with it. They could have them. And anyway, if you ask me, the shops'll never amount to anything. Not in the long run. Dingy rotten holes. You wait and see, most people'll agree with me in the end. Everyone prefers the street corner pitches or going down the track. Nice day out, few drinks, something to eat. Much –'

Brendan was on his feet. '*For Christ sake, Pete.*'

'What?' Pete Mac looked hurt.

'First of all, it was you what said –'

'*Shut up. All of you.*' Gabriel threw back the rest of his drink. 'Listen to Kevin, will you. I don't care about the fucking shops. I just know I never gave them permission to do this minicabbing. And I want to know what's behind it. There must be some reason they'd risk upsetting me. There must be something. Something I should be having.' He held out his glass for a refill. 'I know Kessler's got lairy, but not even asking my permission . . .'

Kevin poured him another drink and waited until he was sure that Gabriel had finished speaking. Only then did he continue.

'The honest truth, Gabe, is that I've heard it's gonna turn out to be more than a good earner.'

Gabriel looked to Stephen. 'What do you think?'

'Sorry, Gabe, I can do whatever you want me to do with a motor, but you know what I'm like on the business side.'

'Take a guess then.'

'All right, if you really want my opinion, and if I'm being honest, I can't see it. I mean, would you trust some bloke you didn't know, in a motor you don't even know was his, or insured, or in decent nick, to take your wife home from shopping up the West End? Course not.'

257

Kevin ventured on. 'But that's not the half of it. You've got to think it through, to understand how it can work.'

'Have we?' Pete Mac sneered and was ignored by everyone.

'You see,' Kevin continued, 'it's not only the cabbing itself that brings in the dough – although that shouldn't be overlooked. There's plenty of money out there. Times are good. So there's more and more call for taxis and that. But it's the sidelines that can be *really* profitable – and useful. That's why I reckoned it wouldn't do any harm to consider it as something we should be getting into.'

Gabriel stretched out on his lounger, the whiskey beginning to relax him – just as it always did until he went over the edge of drinking too much of the stuff. 'Tell me, Kevin, these sidelines. What would they be now?'

'There's all sorts, Gabe. Cabs taking the high-end tarts to their punters –'

Pete Mac grinned. 'Tell you what, lads, I'll volunteer to drive that shift meself.'

Again they paid no attention to him. 'Moving the strippers round the circuit, making sure they don't moonlight – we all know the serious sort of dough the strip joints are bringing in these days. Then add in shifting the blue films and dirty book stock about. And we all agree that's gonna be bigger than any of us ever dreamed of, a right bloody goldmine. And then there's collecting the takings from the spielers and the drinking clubs. Very discreet, nice and quiet.' Kevin laughed, unable to believe the beauty of it. 'Can even do that with legit punters on board. And the cab office itself, that's sweet as a nut. That could be used as a sort of central office. Use it for taking "bookings" if you like, for any of the other businesses. Good cover for all kinds of things – even setting up the odd long firm. Especially as you've been talking about wanting to get out of using the scrap game as a front, Gabe. So, I reckon, whatever way you look at it, setting up a minicab office is not only a good idea, but it's got the added bonus that you could close the yard down, soon as you like, and not miss it one little bit. And that's why it's all the more important to have it all tied up, nice and watertight, right out of Kessler's thieving hands.'

Kevin hesitated, weighing up whether he should carry on.

Why not? Gabriel was wild with the Kesslers, not him. He was only being helpful, and he'd be doing Brendan a favour by planting a few little seeds . . .

'And, of course, there's the final icing on the cake, the cabs could give us a very tasty little screen for delivering drugs.'

Gabriel narrowed his eyes. 'I've never had anything to do with that filth, and I never will. You know that, Kevin Marsh.'

Kevin added hurriedly. 'I know what you've always said, Gabe, but this is different. It's not any of that bad stuff, it's just these pills and that. Bet it's not much different from that blood pressure gear you get from old Stonely. And it's all the go in the clubs and dance halls and that. I'm telling you, straight up, it ain't nasty. I mean, even my old girl takes it. Brilliant stuff. Me dad says it cheers her right up. You can –'

Gabriel spoke over him, staring into the middle distance. 'A bit of respect, that's all I expected from them. If they'd have asked, it might have been different. I might have said, open the business. Not big time, but go ahead. But what do they do? They think they can fucking mug me off without me saying a word.'

259

He stood up and started pacing. 'I don't know who they think they are, but I'm telling you this. We're going in to this minicabbing, and they're getting out of it. We're having it all. Every single bastard bit of it.'

He hurled the half-empty tumbler at the wall, smashing it off the tiles. 'I'll show them break my rules. I'll break their fucking necks.'

Luke's mouth had gone very dry. 'Dad, do you really want to do this?'

Gabriel's answer was to turn to Stephen Shea. 'Did you drop Eileen anywhere today?'

'No, Gabe. When I phoned, she said she was taking the little 'un out to the park.'

Gabriel looked at Barry Ellis. 'Go and find Mrs O'Donnell, Barry. Get her home. Now.'

Stephen Shea stood up. 'I can get her if you like.'

'No, you're all right, Stephen. I've got something I need to discuss with you.'

Pete Mac couldn't resist it. 'Why send anyone, Gabe? Why don't you just call her a minicab? I bet Kessler would do you a good deal.'

As had become their habit, whenever the weather was as fine as it was on this lovely late summer day, Sophie Kessler and Eileen O'Donnell were spending a couple of hours in Victoria Park, enjoying the fresh air and the rare luxury in the East End of a green, open space. They were sitting on a bench in the children's playground. Eileen was holding onto the handle of a high-wheeled Silver Cross pram as she and Sophie watched three young children busily working away in the sandpit with their swirly-patterned rubber buckets and spades.

'When Harry first said I should meet up with you,

Eileen, that I should make friends, it'd be good for business – you know what he's like, organising everyone – I really wasn't sure about it. I thought we might go shopping once or twice. But this,' she smiled fondly, 'this isn't what I expected at all.'

'A lot of things haven't turned out how I expected in life, Sophie. Do you know, my Catherine's been gone nearly a year.' She closed her eyes and crossed herself. 'May God rest and keep her soul.'

Sophie took Eileen's hand. 'Let's hope you see no more trouble.' She craned her neck to peer into the pram at the sleeping baby. 'And, thank God, you have the gift of young Caty.'

Eileen took a pack of du Maurier's from her handbag and offered it to Sophie. 'Cigarette?'

Her hand hovered over the packet. 'I should be getting back, to do a few jobs, but it's such a lovely day. Oh, go on then.'

She and Sophie lit up and, sat smoking in companionable silence, watching the children playing.

'Is Rachel feeling any better about her news yet?'

Sophie blew smoke out of her nose and huffed. 'Hardly. All she keeps going on about is losing her figure and turning into an old woman before her time. Why does she think my boy married her – to be a fashion plate? He wants children, a family. I'm telling you, she needs a lesson, that one, on what it means to be a Kessler. On what it means to be a proper wife. But I don't think she'll ever be like one of us.'

'Young women think differently nowadays.'

'Differently? You're right there. Honestly, Eileen, since the day she found out it's probably going to be twins, she's been acting like she's lost her mind. A blessing like that and she weeps and wails like a mad thing.' Sophie bent forward and stubbed out her cigarette on the gravel. 'I'm popping in to see her later this afternoon.'

'Give her my love, and tell her I'm thinking about her.'

'I will, Eileen, thank you. Right after I've given her a good talking to about the ridiculous names she's coming up with. You should hear them. What's wrong with traditional names? Proper names? And I know she needs her rest, but I think she might be turning out to be lazy. She could be getting things ready, but she just sits about doing nothing and then complains the time's dragging.' She shook her head. 'It's not fair, is it? For her it's dragging, but me, if I had another twelve hours a day, I still wouldn't have enough time to do everything I have to.'

'But you'll find plenty of time for those babies.'

'Course I will.'

Eileen stood up to adjust the blanket over her sleeping granddaughter. 'You should see the boys with Caty. Not six months old and she already has them eating out of her hand. I worry sometimes that we might be spoiling her.'

'You don't spoil your children by loving them, Eileen.'

'No, but you should see the things they bring home for her. I reckon it would be good for her to have a brother or sister, so she could learn to share. And Patricia shouldn't wait too long before thinking about the next one. It's not good to have too big a gap.'

Sophie laughed. 'So, you fancy another grandchild, eh, Eileen?'

Eileen wrinkled her nose good-naturedly. 'I admit I do keep hoping. And a grandson would be nice. Still, there's plenty of time and it's her and Peter's business. I'd never interfere.' Her smile broadened as one of the children in the sand pit, a little fair haired girl, wagged a chubby finger at the two small boys she was playing with, instructing them on the proper way to create a sandcastle even though she was barely big enough to lift the sand filled bucket.

'But it doesn't stop me from hinting that I think she should get a move on. Still, I'm lucky that Patricia lets me have Caty as much as she does.'

Sophie chuckled – a light, girlish sound for a woman who was now officially in her forty-first year. 'And our children are lucky having mothers who are happy to mind their children for them. I know I'm lined up for having the twins as soon as Rachel brings them home. Giving her time to go to the hairdresser's and to the gown shops – or whatever they call them these days.'

'Mrs O'Donnell.'

Eileen and Sophie both turned round.

Eileen frowned. 'Barry? Is something wrong?'

Barry Ellis gate-vaulted the metal railings and strode over to the pram. He smiled down at the sleeping child and picked her up. 'I'm taking you and Caty home, Mrs O'Donnell.'

The baby's eyes opened and her face began to crumple into trembling, teary folds.

Eileen tried to take her from him, but he wouldn't let her go.

'Barry, what's going on? You're frightening her. You're frightening me.'

'Sorry, Mrs O.' Barry started striding away. 'Orders from the boss.'

'How about the pram?'

'Sorry, it won't fit in the car. We'll have to leave it.'

Eileen spoke to Sophie over her shoulder as she hurried after him. 'I don't know what this is all about. I'll give you a call.'

Sophie was on her feet. 'You get off, Eileen, I'll wheel the pram round to mine and you can collect it later.'

'But it's a long way,' puffed Eileen, trying to catch up with Barry and her granddaughter.

'A long way? What d'you think friends are for?'

Chapter 18

Brendan checked his now collar-length hair in the rear view mirror, pausing for a moment to admire his new look, then threw open the driver's door, got out of the Jag and took a lungful of autumn air. He smiled – a man pleased with himself and his lot. 'All right, lads, time to put on the show.'

Luke, Pete Mac, Kevin and Barry followed him round to the back of the car, and waited while Brendan opened the boot and handed each of them a meat cleaver and a short-handled lump hammer. The last in line was a reluctant-looking Luke.

Pete Mac narrowed his eyes at his brother-in-law and released a sharp, disdainful breath. 'Not got the wind up have you, Luke?'

Luke wasn't so much scared as terrified – not by what they were about to do, but by where it all might end – the almost inevitable outcome of more blood being shed, and war being declared between the families. 'We shouldn't be doing this.'

Brendan put his hand on his brother's shoulder. He was a man who wasn't going to let anything or anyone stop him. Not even his brother. Not now. Nor would he have him sowing seeds of doubt in the minds of the others. 'Hold up, Luke, what am I thinking of, mate?' His voice was light, almost playful. 'Give us them things here.' He took the knife and hammer from his brother and tossed them – *who could care less*? – back into the car. 'I'm so revved up, I'm getting myself all confused. We've got to have someone make them calls. Might as well be you, eh?'

Pete Mac looked from Brendan to Luke and back again in slack-jawed amazement – *you what?* – while Kevin and Barry avoided looking anywhere but down at the pavement.

'Here, cop this.' Brendan took a canvas bank bag full of coins from the boot. 'You're on phone box duty while we sort out the drivers on the late shift. All right?'

'Brendan –'

'I said, *all right*?'

Brendan bowled up the black and white tiled path of the tall, three-storey house in Burdett Road. He was followed by Pete Mac, Barry and Kevin. Not one of them made any attempt to conceal the tools they were carrying.

Brendan rat-tatted nonstop on the knocker until the door was opened by a woman wearing a crossover apron and a turban; she was carrying a scrubbing brush in her chapped and reddened hand.

'What the bloody hell d'you think you're up to –' she began, her words drying as she saw the cleavers and the hammers that the four men were holding as nonchalantly as if they were knives and forks.

'Get your old man out here,' said Brendan. 'Now.'

'But he's having a kip, he's on –'

'Lates. Yeah, we know, darling. Just get him.' He stuck the hammer in the jamb and pulled his lips back in a travesty of a smile. 'And don't even think about trying to shut that door on me.'

The woman disappeared along the passage, and they heard some mumbling and cursing from a room at the back of the house, and then some accusatory screaming in reply.

Brendan was just beginning to grow aggravated by the delay when a man appeared in the hallway. He was wearing a tatty striped dressing gown that didn't quite meet across his gut – a belly that must have cost him a fortune to have cultivated to such proportions – and which gave them a full, unwelcome view of his greying Y-fronts, his sagging string vest, and his hairy, drooping breasts.

'So, Mr Wade,' Brendan began politely. 'You're doing the late shift for the Kesslers.'

The man, not the brightest of souls, smiled craftily, showing a set of brown and rotten teeth that made Brendan take a step backwards even though he was well out of reach of the man's no doubt stinking breath. 'Why d'you wanna know? Got a bit of private for me, have you?'

'No, I've not got a bit of private for you, I've got a warning. This time it was your tyres . . .' Brendan used the paper-thin, sharpened cleaver to point over his shoulder to the man's Consul that was parked on the street behind them. 'Next time . . .' He flicked the knife forward and hooked it into the web of the man's string vest. 'Who knows what might get slashed? And I'll tell you what, a little tip for you. If I was you, I'd be careful if you've been claiming on the sick, or on the old Nat King Cole, while you've been driving for that mob, because you know what people are like, don't you. They get jealous and the fuckers go and grass you up.' He shook his head sadly. 'People, eh, Mr Wade. It'd be a right bugger though, wouldn't it, if you did get bubbled? I mean, I can just imagine how hard it must be to survive on them poxy handouts in the first place, but being nicked cos you was claiming, and all . . . Well, that'd be a double dose of bad luck, now wouldn't it?'

Brendan shook his head in sympathetic solidarity, and then turned to address his three menacingly silent companions. 'Here, I've had a great idea.'

He turned back to Wade, who had finally cottoned onto what was happening, and was just about ready to fill his Y-fronts. 'I reckon if you wasn't working for the Kesslers, then you'd probably be all right. And,' he grinned happily, a man with a brainwave, 'you're never going to believe this. I might even know of a proper cabbing job you could have. With a decent firm and everything. Our firm. The O'Donnells. I'm sure you've probably heard the name. *And* I might be able to get you a deal on four new tyres.'

'Look, mate –' Wade began.

'Mate? I'm not your fucking mate.' Brendan was on the man before he knew what was happening – drawing the blade of the cleaver down his cheek with one hand and aiming the two-pound hammer through his front window with the other.

Wade's wife, who had been spying on events from behind the net curtains, screamed and bawled in terror as the glass exploded into the room, and the hammer went whirling past her and smashed into the radiogram that stood against the far wall.

Wade swiped his hand down his face and looked stunned at all the blood. 'I've got kids in there.'

'And I said, *I'm not your mate*. All right?'

'But if I . . .' he whined, his words petering out as he realised he had no idea how he was going to finish his miserable, feeble sentence. In fact, Wade was so slow that, until he felt the blood trickling down his belly, he hadn't even cottoned onto the fact that Brendan had swiped the cleaver down his string vest, slicing off his left nipple like an unwanted blemish on a ripe fruit.

'What the fuck have you done to me?' he bleated.

The four men answered him by turning away and walking off down the path.

Brendan paused at the gate as he heard Wade's wife begin cursing and yelling at her husband.

He looked over his shoulder at the now shocked and blood-streaked man, who was still standing on his doorstep as if bidding farewell to his unexpected visitors.

'She's got a right gob on her, your old woman, ain't she, Mr Wade? So, if you do make the sensible decision and come and work for us, you will make sure she don't ever come near the office or phone us up or anything, won't you? Cos we don't want her spoiling the tone of our business, now do we?'

Just as the young woman looked up to see what all the noise was about, the door flew off its hinges and came smashing into her desk; it was immediately followed by four aggressive looking men barging into the tiny Brick Lane office and surrounding her.

Her eyes were wide with surprise and alarm, but when she spoke there was a tough confidence in her voice that she'd learned from being dragged up in a family where any sign of fear could earn you a battering.

'Oi, you,' she demanded, looking from one man to the next. 'What the hell do you think you're up to? Mr Kessler'll skin your arses for you when he sees that door.'

'Fuck Mr Kessler,' said Brendan evenly. 'Now, if you know what's good for you, get out.'

'But I've got cabs to send out.'

'Are you stupid?'

'No, I'm not actually. Here . . .' She stood up, sticking her little fists into her waist. 'Are you anything to do with these calls I've been getting all afternoon?'

Brendan put on a mocking, puzzled face. 'What calls would they be then, sweetheart?'

'For moody jobs, that's what. *All bloody afternoon* I've been getting them. I've been sending cars all over the bleed'n' shop. And there's never any passengers when they get there. *And* two of the drivers got jumped when they got to the addresses I was given.'

'What a shame,' said Brendan shaking his head. 'Now fuck off.'

'I said, I ain't stupid. It was you, wasn't it?' She gathered up her things, pushed past a grinning Pete Mac, and tottered out of the office on her black patent heels – *keep looking confident*. 'And I'm telling you,' she shot over her shoulder. 'Mr Kessler's gonna go raving mad when I tell him you kicked that door in, and what you did to his business today.'

Brendan winked at her. 'Aw, I do hope so, babe. And you won't forget to tell him it was Brendan O'Donnell what did it, will you?'

'No, I won't forget.'

'You sure you got the name right? Brendan O'Donnell. And take a good like at me mooey and all, while you're at it. I want you to be able to pick me out when Kessler shows you me picture in his photo albums of special friends.' He walked over to her, grabbed her by her upper arms and gave her a shake. 'So, let's see how really clever you are, shall we? What's me name?'

'Brendan O'Donnell.' She was in pain, but she kept her chin up high and her voice strong and steady.

'Good. Very good. And remember, tell him that

270

Brendan O'Donnell said: Challenge us would you, you cunts? Excuse my language, darling. And say we've had a little chat with most of his drivers, cos we're running the minicab business in this toby from now on.' Another wink. '*O'Donnells's Car Services*. Got a nice ring to it, ain't it? And we've got a nice office and all. Not that far from here as it happens. Just round on the Bethnal Green Road. A sight better than this shithole.' He let her go, and shoved her staggering backwards, smack into the filing cabinet. 'But then what would you expect from the Kesslers?'

'You bullying pig,' she muttered, rubbing her shoulder.

'Save your breath, love, and, if you know what's good for you, you wanna wire in and get out of here.' Brendan turned to Kevin Marsh and held out his hand. 'Petrol can, please, Kev.'

Brendan took his pint from Barry, and raised it in salute to him and Kevin. The three men were elated, and the only three men in the whole, tatty Hackney Road pub not even glancing at the blank-eyed girl on the stage, who was see-sawing one of her grubby, stiff-footed black stockings back and forward between her legs in a desultory imitation of bringing herself to a climax.

They had far more exciting things to get off on.

Kevin took a long slow swallow of his Guinness and decided it was time to introduce a note of caution. 'You really are stone-bonking positive Pete Mac and Luke don't know about this, are you Brendan?'

Brendan raised his glass again, closed his eyes and lifted his chin – a grin illuminating his handsome face. 'I told you, Kev, I'm absolutely fucking positive.'

'I'm sorry I'm being so twitchy, but you know I've

never felt right about Pete Mac. It's the same with all them MacRiordans. Mouths bigger than the Blackwall Tunnel, the lot of them. And as for Luke, he's got no, you know, interest in this sort of thing . . . Aw, you two know what I mean.'

'We do, Kev, we know all too well, mate. But don't worry, it'll all be fine.' Brendan couldn't stop his grin widening. 'And if this supplier is as good as he reckons, we're going to be busy boys – very rich, busy boys. So, drink up, lads.' Brendan's voice was now artificially stiff, formal. 'I need to sort out a few things with Dad for the morning. And we've all got an early start.'

Pete Mac threw back the covers, plonked down his feet on the sticky, matted surface of the bedside rug with its faded image of a collie dog, and raked his fingers up and down his stubbly pink chops.

'Come back to bed, Petey. Please?' She dragged out her words through, what were for him, her almost unbearably sexy, pouting lips.

'Don't do this to me,' he whimpered in reply as she rubbed her chubby little hand over his stiffening penis. 'You know I've got to get back home tonight.'

Violet was a dookie mare, didn't even know the meaning of housework, but she had the sort of round, soft body on her that Pete Mac had always dreamed of, and she never, ever complained about anything. *And* she loved him, the dozy cow.

'And I've got to make some business calls, Vi. You know they can't manage without me.'

'You are so clever, Pete.'

He kissed her lightly on the top of her bleached and matted beehive and padded over to the phone that was half hidden by all the lidless bottles and jars that cluttered up her dressing table.

His call was answered almost the moment his finger left the dial. 'What's going on tomorrow, then, Brendan?' he said, only half paying attention, as Violet was now stretched out on the bed in front of him. She licked her fingers and then slowly and deliberately began massaging herself to a far more convincing climax than the stripper had managed in the pub where Brendan had been drinking with Barry and Kevin just an hour before.

Pete Mac gulped.

'You still there, Pete?'

'Er, yeah. Anything I need to know about?'

'You're joking, right? And while we're at it, where did you disappear to tonight?'

'Thought I deserved a break. After all the effort I put in today. Fifteen drivers' houses we went round.'

'Right, and so you decided to spend a bit of time with your wife and little girl, did you?'

'Yeah.' Pete Mac's voice had reduced to a low, ecstatic groan.

'Yeah, sure you did, you lying fucker. Now, you just kiss that soapy tart Violet *night, night* and get round ours. Right away, Pete, I'm warning you. We've got plans to go over for the meet tomorrow.'

Violet was now using both hands.

'But, Brendan,' he said thickly, 'it's nearly ten o'clock.'

'Are you arguing with me? Do you really want me to have to tell Patricia what you get up to when you go amongst the missing all the time?'

Pete Mac slammed down the phone and stared at it. He was fed up with being treated like an idiot by them hypocritical fuckers.

He strode over to the bed, pulled Violet's hands away from her crotch and rammed himself into her.

Two minutes later he was getting dressed.

'Sorry, Vi, got to go, darling. Duty calls. You know what it's like. And I've gotta pop home for a bit, or she'll only get the hump if I don't show me face again.'

Violet sat up and pulled the creased and grubby sheet up to her chin. 'That wife of yours is so mean to you, Pete. So spiteful.'

'Yeah, I know, girl. She's a right bitch. Here.' Pete Mac put his hand in his pocket and chucked two fivers on the bed. 'I know it's not the same as me staying over, but you treat yourself tomorrow to one of them baby doll nighties I like you in.'

He pulled open the bedroom door. 'And make sure it's a red one. One of them you can see through.'

Chapter 19

Gabriel O'Donnell blew on his hands, rubbing them together to get them warm, as he led the way through the stable yard. He strode past the row of ragmen's pony stalls, his breath vaporising in the air, and on past the grander trotting racers' boxes, then along the path, and out onto the open marshes.

Although they were no more than a few hundred yards away from the traffic on the A13, the early morning Thames-side scene that stretched out before them could have been set in the heart of the countryside. The sky was a muted, duck egg blue, tinged on the horizon with pink and yellow, and the mist lay low over the soft, tufted grass, making the elegant trotting horses that were being exercised in their full, gleaming rigs look as if they were wading their high stepping way through a pale grey sea.

As one of the big-wheeled sulkies sped past them, Gabriel raised his eyebrows in approval. 'Nice bit of kit that, Stephen, light and fast. And the bay pulling it, he's a real beauty. Worth keeping an eye on for the next big race.'

Stephen Shea nodded. 'That's Micky Lee's rig, one of the travellers who winters over Canning Town way. They've got some good horse flesh between them all right.'

Gabriel and Stephen came to a halt by a line of vans that had all been parked facing in the one direction to form the edge of an improvised flapping track. Halfway along the line, a wiry youngster in his early teens was perched on a stripped down, lightweight scrambling bike, ready and eager to rev up and drag the lure for the assorted lurchers and greyhounds that were howling and yelping through the wire-reinforced windows in the backs of the vans. Even the existence of the lures – dead and bloodied rabbits, safely stowed away in a sturdy wooden chest on the back of a flat-back truck – wouldn't be apparent after the event, the bodies having been thrown to the dogs both as a training reward and as a means of disposing of the evidence. If everyone did their job – and they would – there wouldn't be a single clue that the illegal meet had ever taken place at Burton's Farm. Although such thorough precautions were probably a bit excessive, as no one without relevant business of some kind or other would be visiting the place, and that included the police.

Run as it was by a loose network of characters – best avoided unless you were either family, an invited guest, or, at the very least, known to be 'sympathetic' to their way of life – Burton's was a very private place. And the likelihood of some innocent civilian stumbling on it by mistake wasn't exactly likely. Especially not with the size of the bull mastiffs that were chained to the main gate.

By the vans, huddles of men were standing around smoking, talking, and placing bets with Kevin, who had arrived an hour earlier, when the mist had been more like a fog, and when it was still barely light. Some of the men were smartly dressed like Gabriel and his companions – suits, shirts and ties, velvet collared overcoats, neat, freshly brushed hats – while the others were more casually attired in rough working clothes, but with flashes of gold on their hands and wrists, and across their ill-matching waistcoats. And every one of them seemed to have plenty of money to place on the first race of the morning.

Gabriel pulled his collar up about his ears and stamped his feet. 'It's a grand morning, Stephen, and more fun than hanging about in some betting shop. More profitable too. Nice big bets, no records, no taxes.' He looked about him, savouring the fresh air. 'But I can't say I'm not worried about leaving things back at the yard and the cab office.'

'Don't worry, Dad.' It was Brendan, who had just strolled over, with a smile on his face and a lurcher straining on its leash. 'Anthony's at the yard with some of the lads and Luke's keeping an eye on the cabs. And not even the Kesslers would be stupid enough to try anything with the blokes I've left there watching the place.'

He jerked the yelping dog back to heel with a sharp rip of the lead. 'And Luke's got young Sherry to look after him if things get really rough.'

Gabriel snorted. 'It's not a joke, Brendan.'

'I know, but as well as the heavies, there are at least half a dozen drivers in and out of there who could throttle a bloke with one hand if they had a mind to.'

'Maybe.'

'Come on, Dad, relax, have a bet, pretend you don't know what hound's gonna win.'

'Talking of hounds, where's that Pete Mac got to again?'

Brendan was wondering that himself. After the ear bashing he'd given him last night he thought even silly bollocks MacRiordan would have got the message to toe the line for once. 'Probably spending a bit of time with Pat and the little 'un.'

'Yeah, course he is, son. And Kessler's gonna just ignore the fact that we torched his cab firm yesterday afternoon.'

*

277

Pete Mac had actually been up and dressed since seven o'clock that morning, unusually early for him. Since becoming a father he rarely stirred before nine, making sure he left all the baby lark to Patricia. But today, as he parked his car near the synagogue at Stepney Green, it wasn't even a quarter to. He was parking there because it was just a short stroll from where he was going to prove to the O'Donnells that he was a man who could handle himself, and that he deserved a bit of respect for once. In fact, after he'd finished today, they wouldn't be able to ignore him or laugh at him – not any more they wouldn't.

He left the car and walked round the corner, stopped a few yards from his target and pulled out a packet of Capstan Full Strengths from his coat pocket.

A big, serious looking bloke was standing by the gate. He'd expected some sort of minder, but this one was a great big bugger. Typical that, little blokes making up for their own shortcomings with oversized foot soldiers.

As casually as he could manage, Pete Mac stuck one of the cigarettes in his mouth, and then made a performance of patting his pockets with his left hand. It made him look as if he were putting out some weird, peripatetic fire that had taken hold in his clothing.

He then walked on, but paused by the man at the gate, leaned forward slightly, and said, 'What an idiot, eh? Forgot me matches. You ain't got a light on you, have you, mate?'

The man narrowed his eyes for a brief moment, weighing up the situation, and judging Pete Mac to be just a passing prat, said in reply, 'Sure.' He pulled out a sizable Ronson lighter that looked like a toy in his huge hand, and charged it up.

Pete Mac knew he had to act quickly, before the man

278

realised what was going on, and before he, Pete Mac, had the chance to bottle it. He pulled his right hand out of his pocket and smacked the man full in the face with a heavy brass knuckle-duster.

Automatically, the man raised his arms to protect his head, and Pete Mac slammed him in the kidneys, sending him staggering into the railings.

Pete Mac started speaking at Olympic speed before the big bastard had a chance to gather his wits about him. 'I'll mark your card, mate. We can do this one of two ways. You either piss off and disappear, or I'll lift my right hand like this –' he began to raise it '– and ten big angry Micks'll be by my side before you know what's hit you. Oh, and nine of them think you've been screwing their old woman.'

The man spat, aiming the gob right by Pete Mac's feet. 'Think I'll leave you white folks to it.'

Pete Mac, the adrenaline kicking in, ushered him grandly onto the pavement – 'A wise choice, sir' – then swaggered up the path and smacked the flat of his knuckle-dustered hand, just the once, on the front door.

Sophie, who was sitting at the kitchen table drinking tea with her daughter-in-law, was immediately on the alert. Harry had warned her that there might be some sort of trouble, and had insisted that Daniel and Rachel came to stay with them. And Rachel hadn't stopped moaning since she'd shifted her lazy arse out of bed . . .

Another knock.

'Who's that at this time of the morning?' wailed Rachel. 'Daniel said Lincoln would knock three times if he wanted to speak to us.'

Sophie pulled her housecoat around her and lifted her finger to her lips. 'Just keep schtum for me, all right?'

Another single knock. 'Sophie, I'm scared.'

In truth, so was Sophie, but her pride and her protective instincts were stronger. 'Rachel, darling, don't worry yourself, all right? It'll be Lincoln wanting the lav or something. If you're really panicking, pop upstairs to my bedroom. There's a phone on the bedside table. Give Danny a call. And I'll go and have a look round the front room curtains and see who it is. Then I'll be right up. Go on. Hurry yourself.'

The knocking grew more insistent.

Sophie smiled. 'There, I knew it'd be Lincoln. But you go on up anyway. It's time we got ourselves dressed.'

She saw Rachel safely up the stairs and walked along the hall towards the front room where she could get a good look at what was going on, and see if it really was Lincoln making so much noise.

She made it halfway along the passage when one of the glass panels of the front door at first cracked and then shattered inwards.

She ducked and screamed, but then her hand flew to her mouth to stop her noise, as a man's hand covered in gingery hairs, reached inside and flailed around searching for the latch.

Not knowing where she found the courage, Sophie sprang forward and shot the bottom bolt before the man could undo the latch.

'For fuck's sake,' she heard him complain. 'If that's the way you want it.'

Sophie stood there, appalled, now convinced she'd never be able to move from that spot, as he kicked and shouldered the door.

It soon began splintering around the lock, and then, as if it were little more than matchwood, it crashed back against the wall, wood and glass shards gouging into the embossed wallpaper like knives.

Pete Mac grinned happily to himself. Brendan wasn't the only one who could bash in a door.

Sophie took no more than a few seconds to register the face of Eileen and Gabriel's schlub of a son-in-law coming towards her, and her power of movement rapidly returned.

Deciding she would be better off making a dash for the safety of the front room and it's heavy, panelled door, rather than trying to reach the stairs – *please God, he might not even realise Rachel was up there in the bedroom* – she flung herself back along the hall.

It was the wrong decision.

She crashed into the pram that had been cluttering up the hall waiting for Eileen to collect it, and went sprawling onto the floor. Pete Mac grabbed her by the arm, dragged her to her feet and shoved her into the front room.

Now he was in there with her, and it was him who was shutting the door. Locking her in there with him. And he was undoing his flies . . .

Sophie grabbed hold of the mantelpiece, not sure if she was going to vomit or pass out.

Pete Mac saw the look on her face as he released his penis from his underpants.

'Don't kid yourself, you silly old cow,' he sneered as he released a dark, steaming stream of urine into the dried flower arrangement adorning her carefully polished fireplace. 'As if I'd want to dip me wick in what you've got to offer,'

Pete Mac sighed contentedly. 'That's better,' and tucked himself back into his underwear. 'Now, where shall I begin?'

'Why are you doing this?' Sophie's voice cracked with fear.

He was about to tell her to shut her mouth when he thought about how Brendan had behaved yesterday, about what he'd said to the bird in the Kesslers's cab office. How it had made him look the right business.

He folded his arms – the big, brave man. 'The name's Peter MacRiordan. Remember me, do you darling?'

Sophie shook her head, pretending she didn't. Hoping that was the right thing to do.

It wasn't.

He looked angry. 'Well, you should, you stupid mare. We met at that posh club, Gabe took us to. And I was really nice to you. Talked to you and everything. But you offended me. Do you know that? Treated me like I was a prick. But I suppose that's just natural for the likes of you; that you think I'm just the oily rag.' He stuck a finger in her face. 'Well, I ain't. And you'll remember me now though, won't you? And you'll tell your aggravating little squirt of an old man that no one, *no one*, ever messes with Peter MacRiordan.'

'Please, I don't feel well.'

'You don't feel well? What is it with you women? Always fucking moaning about something or other. I'll show you don't feel well.'

He paced around the room, picking up things and letting them fall to the floor.

He hated the fucking place. It was the sort of front parlour he'd never had as a kid, but that people like this always had. The sort of place that was so *nice*. Stuffed full of poxy photos and little fancy, stupid ornaments and all that shit; chairs you weren't allowed to sit on in case you squashed the sodding cushions; and a bastard piano. Who the fuck needed a piano when you could have one of them hi-fis? It wasn't as if the arseholes couldn't afford one.

He knew the type of kit he'd get himself if he had their sort of money – he'd have one of them bachelor pads. But while he wasn't exactly short of a few bob, he had expenses. A lot of expenses. Violet's flat for a bloody start.

Maybe when Gabe saw what he was capable of he'd start giving him a fairer whack, a decent cut in the business. When he'd finished here, Gabe'd have to take him seriously then, all right.

Quite calmly Pete Mac strolled over to the piano and lifted the lid. He reached inside his overcoat and took out the hammer that Brendan had given him the day before to put the frighteners on the drivers. Then, with his tongue poking out between his lips to aid his concentration, he began to systematically work his way along the keys.

Sophie, trembling in the corner, and with her back to the wall, knew this was her chance.

Keeping her eyes fixed on him, she felt her way slowly along the wall towards the door. Waiting for the hammer to fall, to disguise the sound of the handle turning, she slipped out into the hall and shot up the stairs.

Pete Mac, absorbed as he was in trying to destroy the piano, kept his focus on the job, but he did speak, or rather he shouted. 'Don't worry, darling, I ain't stupid. I'll be up to see you later. And perhaps you might look a bit more attractive in a different nightie. Red's me favourite colour if you was wondering.'

It took Sophie an agonisingly long couple of minutes to persuade Rachel to open the bedroom door to her, and, when she eventually let her in, Sophie was ready to strangle her. But when she saw the fear on her daughter-in-law's face she could only hug her.

'Have you phoned Danny yet?'

Rachel shook her head. 'Couldn't.'

'That's all right,' Sophie sounded relieved. 'Now don't worry.' She put her hands on Rachel's shoulders and looked her steadily in the eye. 'Now, you sit yourself over there.' She steered her gently in the direction of a pink Lloyd Loom chair by the window. 'Okay?'

Rachel nodded, her lips pressed tightly together.

'Good. Now I'm going to move the dressing table in front of the door, and then I'm going to work out what we're going to do. Okay?'

Another nod. 'Yeah.'

Thank God someone was.

Despite it being barely a quarter past nine in the morning, Gabriel had already swallowed almost a whole hip flask full of whiskey, and had really started to relax, especially as everyone seemed to be having such a good time. The big men over from Ireland were already asking when the next meet was going to be, and Kevin had taken a sack full of dough. Not bad for a few hours enjoying yourself in the fresh air on a fine autumn morning.

Maybe he should think about retiring or at least spending more time over in Kildare at the stud farm. He could get Rosie a little cottage somewhere close by and she could see more of young Ellie.

It wasn't as if Eileen could care less if he wasn't around so much. All she cared about was Patricia, the baby, her precious boys, and visiting the bloody cemetery all the time. It was morbid, that's what it was. The way she carried on, it was like she was the only one who had ever loved Catherine. The only one who mourned her. What had she said to him when he'd told her to stop being so miserable? He thought for a moment, but couldn't quite remember – it would have been something nasty and bitter. But he was clear on one thing: he was a man, a successful man, and a man with needs. He didn't have to put up with her selfishness. In fact, he might pop round Rosie's later, have himself a few drinks and get himself a bit of affection for a change.

'There,' puffed Sophie. 'That should do it.'

Unused to any work heavier than stripping the beds ready to be collected by the laundry van, Sophie was out of breath from the exertion of dragging the dressing table, her husband's tallboy, and the bedside tables, over to the door.

She'd have felt more secure if she'd have been able to add the wardrobe to the barricade, but she knew her limitations. 'Now, let's think. What next?'

Rachel was cowering in the chair, her shoulders hunched, her knees up to her chin, and her arms clasped round her legs. 'Listen to all that noise he's making. Why don't the neighbours do something? Why doesn't someone come and help us?'

Sophie knew exactly why. This was the sort of neighbourhood where the likes of the O'Donnells and the Kesslers weren't interfered with. And if one of the O'Donnell mob had the hump with the Kesslers, then that was their business. Sensible people stayed well out of it.

'They must be out, love,' she said brightly. 'You know, shopping and work and that. But someone's bound to be back soon. Here, you're looking a bit pale, why don't you stretch out on the bed and try and get a bit of rest? Stop worrying yourself, I'll see to everything.'

Sophie stretched the phone lead as far away from the bed as it would go, cupped her hand over the receiver and whispered, hoping that Rachel wouldn't be able to hear the fear in her voice.

'Eileen?'

'Sophie, I'm really sorry. I know I should have come round for the pram –'

'Eileen –'

'Really. I hope it's not in your way, but Gabe's practically had me and Pat prisoners, these past –'

'Eileen, this is *not* about the pram. It's Peter MacRiordan. He's downstairs, and he's –'

'He's what?'

'Let me finish, Eileen, please. I'm telling you, he's downstairs destroying my home. And me and Rachel are stuck up here in the bedroom, with the furniture blocking the door. And I can't phone Harry. He'll just come flying home and kill him stone dead. You know how he is. And then he'll kill me for letting him in after what happened yesterday.'

'You'll have to slow down, Sophie, I don't understand. What happened yesterday?'

'There was a bust up. The boys set fire to the cab office –'

'No, that can't be right. Luke's there right now.'

'No, Eileen, *your* boys set fire to *our* office.'

'Jesus, Mary and Joseph.' Eileen crossed herself. 'How about Danny? Can't he stop him?'

'I thought of that. But can you imagine what he'd do to him when he realises how he's upset Rachel. Eileen, I can't have my husband or sons getting in trouble over him. Please, just get someone round here to come and take him home. Please.'

'Okay, I'll –'

'Oh, Eileen,' Sophie interrupted her. She sounded close to tears 'I've just had a thought. Say he recognises the pram down in the hall, and thinks I've got Patricia up here with me.'

'He wouldn't recognise his own daughter unless she was in her mother's arms.'

Sophie flinched as another loud crash reverberated through the house and Rachel started whimpering like a baby. 'Eileen, the man's going mad. Just get us someone round here. *Please*.'

Chapter 20

Eileen was shaking as if she had a fever. She didn't understand what Pete Mac was up to, but she knew she had to stop him. He might have been a fool, but he was a big fool. And the thought of the sort of damage he was capable of inflicting made her feel sick. And the trouble that he'd cause if either Harold or his and Sophie's boys turned up and caught him there.

But Eileen didn't want her boys involved either. This whole business was complicated enough as it was. She'd just have to get hold of Gabriel.

But finding him was another matter.

After phoning everywhere else she could think of, all Eileen had left was the cab office. It was a long shot, but maybe Luke knew where he was.

'Sherry, put Luke on.'

'Sorry, he's not here at the minute, Mrs O. Try a bit later.'

'Listen to me, Sherry, I need to get in touch with Mr O'Donnell.'

'Sorry, can't help you.'

'I'm not messing around, Sherry.'

'Give us a break, Mrs O. You know what he's like. He'd go off his head.'

'And *I'll* go off my head if you don't tell me.'

'But he'll sack me.'

'Sherry, who do you think got you that job in the first place? And how many chances do you think an unmarried mother like you would have of getting a decent little number like you have there? Sitting in a nice clean office, answering the phone, and chatting to big handsome drivers all day. Think about it, Sherry.'

Sherry Driscoll rolled her eyes. If only Mrs O. knew the half of it. She'd been in the job just one week, since the day the cab office had opened, and she'd already witnessed all sorts of goings on. There were the toms and the betting – they were obvious – but there were other things, things she hadn't quite worked out yet. And that was without the four great big blokes Eileen's old man had posted outside the office because of something – again, she didn't know what – that had kicked off yesterday.

But none of that was Sherry's business, so, of course, she'd never mention it. And anyway, she didn't want to upset Mrs O. She was all right. She'd known Sherry since she was little, and had never looked down her nose at her like the other neighbours. Not even when she had the baby. In fact, it was Mrs O'Donnell who'd persuaded her husband to give her the job in the first place . . .

She took a deep breath. 'He told Luke that if anything happened, he'd be over the flapping track.'

'Right. And where's that?'

'That's all I know Mrs O. I swear on my little one's life.'

'Okay, Sherry, thank you. You're a good girl.'

She laughed. 'But not as good as I should have been, eh, Mrs O'Donnell?'

As Sherry put down the phone, Luke came into the office swinging a carrier bag from the baker's next door. 'Breakfast,' he announced, holding the bag up for inspection. 'What d'you fancy?'

Sherry giggled, flapping tracks and the threat of

Gabriel going bonkers at her temporarily forgotten. 'Anything'll do me, Luke, you know that.'

Luke smiled at her. 'Got just the thing,' he said, fishing out a white paper bag from the carrier. 'Two lovely, big fat doughnuts.'

His smile widened as she took them from him as eagerly as a child. He felt great, so much better than he'd felt for ages. Brendan had promised him that he'd kept his word yesterday – that not one of the Kesslers' drivers had been hurt. Just warned off till it was all sorted out. And Luke couldn't have been more pleased. He'd said all along that that was the right way to go about things. Beatings and slashings got them nothing but more violence. But now it was looking as if Brendan had come round to his way of thinking at last, and could see that things could be dealt with by acting like civilised adults rather than mindless animals.

And who knew, maybe, eventually, Harold Kessler could be persuaded to cut his losses, and pack up and take his family – including that prick Maurice, with a bit of luck – back over to West London.

Luke was even looking forward to getting more involved in the business if it could be more like this minicabbing lark.

And there was another reason to feel pleased with the world. He liked spending time with young Sherry. She was funny, clever, and certainly much better company than he usually had to put up with.

He looked at her, as she smiled up at him, licking her sugary lips with the flickering tip of her little pink tongue. She was pretty, really pretty. And nice. He couldn't help wondering if, with someone like her, he might feel different.

If it was an illness, like they said it was, then surely it could be cured. It wouldn't be like it was with Nina, that brass from the Bellavista. Sherry was different.

She giggled at him over the top of her doughnut as jam oozed out and dripped onto her chin.

His smile faded.

Who was he trying to kid?

Eileen was still trembling as she dialled the number, praying it would be Sean Logan and not Mary who answered.

'Hello, there.'

She instantly recognised the ponderous tones of her husband's slow-witted brother-in-law. Thank goodness for that; he wouldn't even think of questioning her.

'Sean, hello, it's me, Gabriel's Eileen.'

'Eileen! How are you, love? Well are you?'

'I'm just grand Sean, but –'

'I'll get Mary for you, shall I?'

'No, no you're all right, Sean. You don't need to go bothering Mary. It's just that me and young Luke here are trying to think of that place where you all went flapping that time you were over.' She put a light little laugh into her voice. 'Sure, isn't it driving the pair of us mad trying to remember.'

Silence.

'You know, Sean.' For Christ's sake did the man have spuds for brains? 'The flapping track, with the lurchers and the betting.'

'Oh, the flapping. Of course. I remember. Wasn't that a great day?'

'And it was *where*, Sean?'

'Burton's Farm, down on the marshes. Beckton way.

Where they keep the ragmen's horses and the trotters and pacers. Nice feller that Gerald Burton. A real gentleman. Came from over here originally, you know. Kerry, I think it was. Or it might have been Wexford. No, I tell I lie, it was –'

'Sorry, Sean, I have to go.' She had the receiver back in its cradle before he had the chance to take her any further round the map of the Republic.

Her mind was on places closer to home, but far more inaccessible. How the hell was she going to get to Burton's Farm?

She let out a humourless breath of laughter. She'd take one of their bloody cabs, that's how.

Yeah, they'd be queuing up to take her to interrupt their boss while he was doing business.

She'd just have to be careful how she went about it.

She picked up the phone again.

Sophie could hear Pete Mac moving along the hall towards the living room at the back of the house. She could only hope he had enough things left to smash, that he wouldn't grow bored and come up after them before someone came to stop him.

She stared at the phone, willing it to ring. Why hadn't Eileen called back?

She called her number again, but it was engaged.

She flicked a quick glance at Rachel. She was so pale it was beginning to frighten Sophie. If something happened to her or the twins she'd never forgive herself.

It was no good; she'd have to call someone else. But who? It had to be someone who could calm the situation.

Harry or the boys would go stark raving mad at such a

lack of respect, and she really didn't want them involved, but what choice did she have?

Downstairs, Pete Mac had decided that all his exertions had made him a little peckish, so he stomped through to the kitchen that led off the living room at the very back of the house.

He opened the pantry in the corner, and tossed a few packets of this and that over his shoulder, scattering their contents over the blue and white vinyl floor tiles.

'What the hell's all this shit?'

He lumbered back along the hall to the bottom of the stairs and shouted at the top of his voice. 'Don't suppose you've got any pork pies have you, darling?'

This was it. He was at the bottom of the stairs. She had to do something fast. She snatched up the phone and rang the haulage yard.

Eileen dialled the cab office again. 'Sherry, it's Mrs O'Donnell, I –'

'Mum. Is that you? It's me, Luke. Are you crying? What's wrong?'

Just twenty minutes later, Eileen had been grabbed by the shoulder and was being steered by a very angry Gabriel away from the track towards the stable yard at Burton's Farm. Groups of men cast sly glances at them, wondering what possible reason a wife could have for turning up at the flapping, and why O'Donnell didn't have better control of her.

Brendan, Kevin and Barry just made sure they busied themselves with other things.

'Did you send Peter over to Sophie Kessler's home?'

she demanded, as she tripped over the hummocky grass in her totally unsuitable court shoes. 'She has Rachel with her for God's sake. A young pregnant woman. And he's going mad round there, smashing the place to pieces. I had no choice, I've had to send Luke to see what he can do, but you'll have to go round there and –'

He stopped suddenly and swung her round to face him.

She could smell the booze on his breath, could see the high colour of his cheeks. His blood pressure would be through the roof again. She wondered how she could have been so foolish as to think there was any point in coming here, in even trying to talk to him.

'You're a stupid woman, Eileen.' He was walking towards her, looming over her, driving her backwards into the stable yard. 'First of all for even thinking I'd send Pete Mac to do something like that, when we all know he has shit for brains, but worst of all, you're more than stupid for sending Luke round there after him.'

'What else could I have done?'

'Why would you think a pathetic mummy's boy could do a man's job?'

'Don't speak about him like that.'

'Stop protecting him, we all know what he is.'

'What, a decent boy, who hates all your bullying and lies?'

Gabriel shook his head. 'He's the one who's living a lie.'

Eileen felt years of resentment bubbling up inside her. 'What lie's that then? That he has a secret mistress just like his loving daddy?'

Gabriel grabbed her again, this time with both hands. 'What filth has that boy been telling you?'

294

'Nothing. Neither of the boys has told me anything. Neither of them even realise that I know about the dirty slut. They've been protecting you for all these years. Don't you understand?'

'You're lying to save him as usual.' He pushed her away from him, sending her staggering sideways into a stable door, and causing a ripple of whinnying alarm through the horses. 'Now, get out of my sight. I've got work to do.'

Eileen felt her mouth go dry. He couldn't mean it. 'But what about Sophie? And Rachel?'

'I'll sort it out when I'm good and ready.'

The telephone calls that Sophie and Eileen had made to their sons were just minutes apart, but Luke's Mini had been no match for Daniel's Jaguar – or for his incandescent rage at the thought of Peter MacRiordan going anywhere near his mother and his pregnant wife.

Daniel reached the house a good ten minutes before Luke. He jumped out of the car, leaving the engine running and the door swinging on its hinges without so much as a backwards glance.

Pausing for a teeth-gritting moment by the smashed front door – *the door to his parents' home* – he took in a deep, angry snarl of breath and barrelled into the hall.

He found the bastard sitting at the kitchen table – *his mother's table. And he was fucking eating*.

As Luke hovered on the front doorstep he could hear loud, male hollering and grunts from somewhere at the back of the house, and female screams and wailing from somewhere upstairs.

With the first prayer he had uttered since Catherine's

295

funeral playing on his lips, Luke ran along the hall towards the kitchen.

Pete Mac was curled up on the floor, moaning in pain, as he tried to protect his head from the tyre lever that Daniel Kessler was using to beat him.

Luke launched himself across the room at Daniel. 'Stop it. Leave him alone. You'll kill him.'

Daniel whipped round and smacked the lever across Luke's shoulder.

'Don't, Daniel. Stop! There are women upstairs. Can't you hear them screaming? Stop it.'

'I'll give you fucking women upstairs.' Flecks of saliva showered from Daniel's mouth and his arms flailed around as he lashed out again at Luke.

Biting his lip to stop himself yelling from the pain, Pete Mac dragged himself over to the table, and hooked the lump hammer from off the chair, where he had left it while he was eating. Then he hauled himself back across the floor, and, using all his remaining strength, he swung it back and caught Daniel right behind the knees with the full length of the handle.

Daniel roared in anger and surprise, and went down like a prize fighter with a glass jaw.

Luke wasn't sure how he managed it but, somehow, he heaved Pete Mac out to the Mini, and got him away from Daniel before his adrenaline had him back on his feet and he started attacking them again.

'Honestly, Mum.' Luke flinched as Eileen dabbed iodine-soaked cotton wool on his bloodied cheek. 'Sophie and Rachel are both fine. They never even came downstairs. I swear they didn't.'

She glared at Pete Mac who was slumped in the carver

chair at the head of the kitchen table. His face was a pulpy bloody mess, but she had no sympathy with him. 'Fine? How can they be fine with that maniac on the loose? If I was a man I'd –' She froze at the sound of the street door opening upstairs, and Gabriel and Brendan chatting and laughing about the money they'd made and how they could do with a decent fry up after their morning on the marshes.

'At least try to sit up straight,' she hissed at Pete Mac. But he was in too much pain to listen.

Gabriel stopped at the top of the stairs and stared down into the kitchen. 'What the fuck's happened to you two?'

'I tried to tell you,' said Eileen, collecting up the basin of bloody water, the cotton wool and the iodine off the table. 'I knew there'd be trouble.'

He moved slowly down towards them. 'Who did this to you?'

Pete Mac lifted his head with a groan; one of his eyes had closed completely, and there was a wide gash across his eyebrow like an open, rosebud mouth. 'Danny Kessler.'

Gabriel dropped down onto a chair, leaned forward, and banged his tightly curled fists on the table. 'So, stopping their cab firm wasn't enough of a message for them. And they think they can get away with this do they? Making a fool of me.'

He looked over his shoulder at Brendan, who had sat himself halfway down the stairs. Brendan knew his father well enough to understand that, when he was in a temper, being well out of arm's length was the most sensible place to be.

'Brendan, go and find Stephen Shea. Tell him to drop whatever he's doing. Say that the job I talked to him about

– the plans have changed. I need it seeing to right away. *Right away*, got that? And tell him I haven't had the chance to go and get the gear off Welsh Billy. He'll have to collect it himself.'

Brendan was immediately on his feet and heading back up the stairs, glad to be getting away, but with no idea as to what was going on.

Why didn't he know about this job the old man was talking about? And Welsh Billy? He was the bloke who supplied the explosives and detonators for all the big blags; he got quality stuff from his old contacts in the mines and sold it all over the country. Everyone in the game knew Welsh Billy.

But no one had even so much as mentioned anything about a bank job to Brendan.

The reason no one had mentioned the job was because Gabriel wasn't planning one. He had other plans for Welsh Billy's specialist supplies.

Chapter 21

'Look, Rach,' moaned Daniel. 'I know it's gonna take a while to get over the shock, but can't you at least *try* to get some sleep?'

He was on his side, rolled up tight as a winkle in its shell, with the bedclothes pulled up over his head, trying to shield his eyes from the light, while Rachel sat there next to him, bolt upright, drinking yet more tea, and with yet more tears spilling down her pale drawn, cheeks.

He didn't get it. They were back in their own home, on the far side of Stepney Green, well away from Harold and Sophie's place. They had Joshua and Winston sitting outside the house in Joshua's car, ready and waiting to deal with any trouble – and still she couldn't bear the thought of having the lights out, even with Daniel there beside her.

And now he was seriously in need of some sleep.

'Look, love, you know Joshua ain't like that Lincoln – who I swear I will kill if I ever set eyes on again. And Winston, he's a right good bloke and all. Sweet as a nut, the pair of them. You're safe. Trust me. Now come on, you must be as knackered as I am. Why don't you close your eyes for a little while? You'll feel much better if you get a bit of kip. And it'll be good for the babies and all.'

Rachel's chin wobbled. 'It's not just being scared,' she said, putting down her cup, and turning her head so he couldn't see her fresh crop of tears. 'And I am tired, but . . .'

'So, what is it? Why don't you tell me?' He was no longer bothering to hide his irritation. 'Come on, Rach, what the bloody hell's the matter here?' He threw back the covers and dragged himself up against the headboard. 'Just tell me. What the fuck's up?'

Rachel began weeping loudly and miserably.

Here we go, more snivelling; Daniel was really getting annoyed now. All right, she'd been scared stiff by that fucker MacRiordan, but, when all was said and done, he hadn't gone anywhere near her. The prat probably never even realised she was there. So, what was wrong with her?

He rubbed a hand across his sore, red-rimmed eyes. 'Rachel. Please. I'm sorry I swore at you.' He put his other arm round her. 'And, I promise, I won't *ever* let anyone scare you again. All right? And when I've finished, they're not gonna know what's hit them. And, may I drop down dead if I'm lying, they will never, ever go anywhere near you again.'

'I told you,' she whimpered, swiping at her tears with the back of her hand. 'It's not just that horrible pig breaking into your mum's.'

'Then what is it?' He was now really having to fight to keep his voice even and his temper under control.

'You don't . . .' She paused for a big snotty sob. '. . . fancy me any more. You're always out.' She was now wailing loudly.

'Yeah, out working.' He put his hand gingerly on her swollen belly. 'Working for you and the babies.'

'That's not true, Danny. You can't stand the sight of me any more. I'm all fat and ugly. I know I am.' She drew in a deep, shuddering breath. 'And you don't love me.'

'Course I love you.' Daniel pulled her close, desperate to stop her noise. 'I've just been busy that's all.'

'Do you really love me?'

'Yes.' He pressed his lips to her forehead. Even though he was exhausted, he was also a bit ashamed of himself. It wouldn't hurt to pay her a bit more attention. She was such a pretty girl; a bit dopey maybe, and certainly not much cop indoors as far as cooking and cleaning was concerned. But that was okay, he hadn't married her for her brains, and they had the money to get someone to do the cleaning and that for them.

'Here,' he breathed into Rachel's ear, tickling her and making her smile through her snotty, juddery tears. 'You still getting them cravings for, what was it? Cream cheese platzels?'

She shook her head. 'Chopped herring beigels,' she said, somehow oddly shy with her husband. 'The ones they do at the top of Brick Lane.'

'All right,' he said, pinching her cheek as if she were a baby. 'I'll go down Brick Lane and get you one right now. No, two. How about that?'

Panic flashed across her tear-stained face. 'No, Danny. Don't leave me here by myself. Please.'

'All right.' He stroked her hair gently. 'Stick your coat on over your nightie and come with me.' He smiled and winked. 'So long as you don't tell Mum I was out driving on a Friday night.'

'But it must be nearly midnight. And how about your knees?'

'My knees are just fine,' he began, punctuating his words with little kisses planted all over her face. 'And if my beautiful, sexy, gorgeous wife wants a beigel . . .'

Daniel guided Rachel tenderly down the stairs, out of the front door and along the path to his Jaguar. It didn't cost anything to be nice, did it? And if it meant he could get some shuteye into the bargain, well, that was a right win double wasn't it? All bets paid, everybody happy, thank you very much, ladies and gentleman, and goodnight.

He was just about to nip across the street and have a word with Joshua, to let him know where they were going, when Rachel let out a little yelp of anguish. 'It's my bag! I forgot my bag!'

'Blimey, Rach, you gave me a right turn. And what d'you want your bag for? I've got money on me.'

'It's not my handbag I want, it's my other bag.' Her eyes were pleading with him. 'My special bag. For the hospital. It's got all the things they said I've got to take with me.'

He stepped back in alarm and goggled at her stomach. 'Here, you've not gone and . . .' He lifted his gaze and looked into her eyes. 'Have you?'

'No, course I've not. I've got weeks to go yet. But say I do go into labour? Please, Daniel, get my bag for me. *Please*? They said I had to have it with me. Just in case.'

'All right.'

She smiled, relief flooding through her. 'It's up by the bed.'

'You don't have to tell me, Rach. I've tripped over the bloody thing every night for the past three months.' He handed her the car keys and pecked her on the lips, even more relieved than she was. Her going into labour – that would have put the right bloody tin lid on the night, that would. 'You get yourself inside the car in the warm, beautiful, and I'll be one minute. Okay?' He pointed to a metallic blue Zodiac parked discreetly across the street, well away from the glare of the streetlights. 'Josh and

Winston are over there, keeping an eye on things.' He flashed a double thumbs-up at the car. 'Okay?'

She nodded. 'Okay.'

Rachel eased herself slowly into the passenger seat of the Jaguar and shivered. The bright, cloudless day had left a really chilly night in its wake. She'd have to see if Daniel could get them that central heating put in before the winter started, like her Auntie Becca had up in her new flat. Some people moaned about being moved into the tower blocks, but Rachel couldn't understand why. The flats were fantastic, all light and airy, and the council certainly hadn't skimped on the mod cons. She wouldn't mind a nice new place for herself, once the twins were born. Somewhere out in Essex maybe. Anywhere would do, really, so long as it was a long way away from Danny's family – especially his interfering old cow of a mother.

With much huffing and grunting Rachel stretched across and slipped the key into the ignition. She'd get the heater running and have the car warmed up in no time, all ready for Danny. And she'd try and be a bit more understanding about his job. It wasn't his fault his dad made him work every hour God sent. And if she gave in – just a bit – then so would he. And they'd have everything worked out to suit them for once. Instead of his rotten mum and dad.

As she turned the key, something on the floor caught her eye, making her pretty forehead crease in bewilderment, but, before she had a chance to organise her confusion into coherent thought, there was a blinding flash of light followed by a loud whoosh of air.

The explosion could be heard over half a mile away.

Rachel and her unborn babies hadn't stood a chance,

and, despite Daniel's belated, guilt-driven good intentions, her marriage hadn't either. The last thing Rachel had seen in her short, not very fulfilling life, was a skimpy pair of scarlet, lacy knickers poking out from under Daniel's seat.

They belonged to Nina.

What Rachel – or Daniel for that matter – hadn't seen, was that both Joshua and Winston were slumped back in their seats in the Zodiac, and that both of them had had their throats slit from ear to ear.

Stephen Shea went out to the car to fetch the last of the shopping, while Sheila put the kettle on. He knew they'd needed piles of food when the kids were still at home – there had always been a houseful of their mates wanting something to stuff into their teenaged empty caverns of bellies – but five bags full for the weekend, just for the two of them? She'd bought enough grub to feed the street.

He smiled to himself. She'd always liked to keep a good table had Sheila, and, he had to admit, he was looking forward to one of her classic belt busters of a Sunday dinner tomorrow. Roast fore rib of beef with all the trimmings, Yorkshire pudding, and a nice little dob of horseradish on the side. Smashing.

It made his mouth water just thinking about it.

He was bending down with his head stuck in the boot, making sure that nothing had escaped from the final two bags, when the hand clapped over his mouth.

'Let me mark your card for you, Shea,' someone hissed into his ear. 'No fuss or the boys'll have to go in and have a word with your missus. A serious word. They're behind me, ready to go in there right now to *make sure* you don't make a fuss. Got it?' As he spoke, the man was stroking Stephen's throat with a long, thin blade.

He nodded carefully.

'Very sensible. Good. Come on then, we're going for a little ride.'

Sheila looked up at the kitchen clock. What was Stephen up to now? If he didn't hurry up the tea would be stewed and he hated that. He'd either be chatting to some kids playing outside, handing over all his loose change for them to go and buy sherbet dabs from the corner shop; or one of the neighbour's motors would be playing up, and he'd be out there with his head under the bonnet getting his decent clothes covered in grease, fixing it for them. The trouble with her Stephen was he couldn't say no to anyone.

Well, she'd have to say no for him. She took off her apron – Sheila wasn't the sort to go out in the street looking untidy – and went outside to bring him indoors.

She didn't get it. What was going on? The car boot was wide open, the last of the shopping had disappeared, but there was no sign of him.

'Michael,' she called over to a blond-haired, scabby-kneed ten-year-old, who was standing with a group of boys all trying to peep up the skirt of a girl who was swinging herself round a lamppost from a length of rope. 'Have you seen Mr Shea?'

'I never seen him,' said Michael, blushing the colour of a scarlet lollipop. 'And I never nicked no shopping either.'

'I don't care about the shopping.' She marched over and grabbed hold of him by the sleeve of his jumper. 'Tell your mother you can keep it. All of it.'

'I never give it to me mum.'

'Just tell me, Michael. If you know what's good for you, and you don't want me to call the coppers, *where's Mr Shea*?'

Michael looked to his friends for support, but they'd all scarpered. His bottom lip started wobbling, as he thought about the hiding he was going to get from his mother for showing her up. 'There was these men. One of them had a knife. And we went and hid behind Teddy's dad's car till they'd gone, and I sort of took –'

'Michael.' Sheila started shaking and she felt her knees begin to buckle under her. 'Help me indoors. There's a good boy. To the phone. It's in the back room.' She summoned up all her strength. '*Now*.'

'I swear on my life that I had no idea that girl would be in the car.'

'That *girl* was my fucking wife.'

'I'm sorry, it was a mistake.'

'A mistake? So, it would have been okay if you just blew me to fuck, would it, you cunt?'

'No. It was on a timer. Set for the early hours. Something must have tripped it. Maybe the spark from the ignition.' Stephen was doing his very best to keep still; every time he moved, the ropes binding his naked body to the hard metal chair just seemed to get tighter. But he couldn't stop himself.

He gulped hard, trying to get some moisture into his dry, claggy throat. He had to try to work himself loose.

He'd worked out that they were in some sort of a lockup – bare brick, no windows, freezing cold. And from the noise over head, it was possibly in a railway arch. Or maybe down by the docks. But he didn't have a clue where.

'And it was all right for you to slit Joshua and Winston's throats was it?'

'I never –'

'Used something like this did you?' Daniel held up an old-fashioned cut throat razor.

Stephen felt totally humiliated as a hot stream of urine gushed from him, pooling on the indented seat of the metal chair, and soaking his legs in reeking degradation.

Daniel wrinkled his nose, flipped out a handkerchief from his top pocket and held it to his face. 'Here.' He handed Maurice the razor. 'Get him talking.'

Slowly and deliberately, Maurice began slicing a thin layer of flesh from the inside of Stephen's thigh.

The blade was so sharp that, at first, Stephen felt no pain, but then, as the urine trickled down onto the exposed tissue, he couldn't stop himself from crying out, from letting them know they were hurting him, that they had got to him.

Daniel paced up and down the small cramped space. 'Pain. Not good, is it?'

'No.' Stephen managed to gasp.

'So, how about the pain I feel? You murdering my wife? Killing my two babies before they was even born? Don't that count? Was that all right?'

'*No.*'

Daniel spun round and stuck his face up close to Stephen's. 'Tell me, I'm really interested. If it wasn't all right for you to do that, was it all right for that slag O'Donnell to order you to do it?'

'It was nothing to do with him. It was me. I did it.'

'But you said you never did Josh and Winston.'

'I didn't. I don't do things like that.'

'Then who?'

307

Stephen said nothing.

Maurice held up the blade to the bare overhead bulb, examining its edge. 'He's loyal, Dan, you gotta hand that to the cunt.'

'This is a waste of time.' Daniel turned his back on them and walked towards the door. 'Do him. We'll have the others later.'

He reached for the handle, but still not quite able to leave, he turned and watched as his cousin calmly and precisely removed his top clothes and put them on a hanger, which he then hooked onto a nail, before slipping into a pair of brand new pale blue overalls. He then began searching through a full-sized, carpenter's tool box.

Without turning round, Daniel opened the door just wide enough to leave, and said only loud enough for himself to hear, 'I'm glad you're my cousin and not my fucking enemy.'

Maurice whistled tunefully as he unloaded the newspaper-wrapped packets from the back of the van, and ferried them over to the high corrugated iron fencing that surrounded Gabriel O'Donnell's scrap yard.

He grinned and winked at Sammy, who had collected him from the lockup in Silvertown, and who was now sitting, ashen-faced in the driver's seat.

'Not exactly them posh hounds that the Baxters told us about, eh, feller? Shame really. Still, the Alsatians'll just have to do, won't they?'

He lobbed another package over the fence, and peered through a small hole round a rusted rivet holding two of the sheets together.

'Pity I never thought to bring a camera, Sam, I bet your Daniel would have enjoyed a memento of this little scene.'

Chapter 22

Barry Ellis wrenched on the handbrake, and yawned: his head shuddering, and his jaw pulled down until it nearly touched his chest. 'Won't be long, Sand.'

'Good. You look worn out.'

'It was worth it.'

Sandy played it coy. 'D'you think so?'

'You kidding? How randy were you last night?'

'Been nice if we could've stay a bit longer, wouldn't it?'

'Babe, you know I promised Gabe I'd feed 'em this weekend . . .' Barry reached across and began stroking her thigh.

'Oi, you. Less of that. Get a move on and we can get home and have a little –' She lowered her chin and looked up at him through her lashes '– *sleep* before I get the dinner on.'

'Now look what you've done to me.' He took her hand and put it between his legs. 'How am I meant to get out of the car with this?'

Sandy smiled: a crooked, saucy leer. 'Who's gonna be around to see you at this time of a Sunday morning? In fact . . .'

Sandy had his flies undone and had her face in his lap before he even had the chance to answer.

'Blimey, that sea air certainly got to you, girl. But you're gonna have to let me go, or them dogs'll wake up starving and start barking their heads off. Then someone'll complain, and Eileen'll get to hear about it. Then she'll have a go at Gabe cos she's always saying he's cruel to 'em. Then he'll bloody slaughter me for not being here to feed them last night, and for getting him in trouble with his missus.'

'All right, Bal, you don't need to write a list. I know. But you remember.' She winked and clicked her tongue at him. 'It's my turn when we get home.'

After what Barry Ellis saw when he went in to feed the dogs he wasn't exactly in the mood to pleasure his wife. Not only did one of the Alsatians turn on him, ripping at his forearm, as it protected what was left of the freshly butchered meat it had been thrown the night before, but the sight of the other dog gnawing at what remained of Stephen Shea's half-eaten head was an image that would haunt Barry Ellis's dreams for the rest of his life.

Sandy Ellis beckoned frantically for Anthony to get himself over to the car and to help Barry up the steps to the O'Donnells's front door. She had no idea what had happened – her husband certainly wasn't in a fit state to tell her anything. But she knew enough about his life to realise that, when things looked as if they'd gone as wrong as this, she had to get herself into the driving seat and get him round to Gabriel's as fast as she could. She'd driven once or twice before. She could manage. She had to.

'Whatever now?' Eileen, red-eyed and white-faced, was sitting at the kitchen table in her dressing gown, when she heard the urgent banging on the door. She lifted

Scrap's head from her knee and went to see who on earth would be calling before eight o'clock on a Sunday morning.

'Really sorry to bother you, Mrs O'Donnell,' sniffled Sandy, as Anthony eased Barry onto a chair.

'That's okay, Sandra. You sit yourself down.' Eileen was distracted by the look on Barry's face. What was it? Fear? Disgust?

'I'll be outside, Mrs O,' said Anthony, happy to be leaving Eileen to it. 'Bang on the door if you need me.'

'Right, thank you.' Eileen sat down, unable to tear her gaze from Barry's wide-eyed stare, waiting for him or Sandra to explain, as she absent-mindedly fussed Scrap, scratching him behind his silky ears.

But no one said anything.

'All right, Sandra,' Eileen said eventually. 'Are you going to tell me what all this is about? Or do you want to give me twenty questions?'

Sandy flicked a nervous glance at Barry. 'Is Mr O'Donnell up yet?'

'He's not been to bed, Sandra. None of us have.' She lowered her eyes, making a show of concentrating on Scrap. 'The boys're all out looking for Stephen Shea.'

A shadow clouded Barry's eyes. He covered his face with his hands and began weeping silently.

Sandy didn't know what to do, she just knew she wanted to give the responsibility of all this to someone else, to make this nightmare go away.

'Me and Barry, Mrs O'Donnell, we've been away for a couple of days. Down Eastbourne – only one night, mind – and we came back really early this morning, so's Barry could feed the dogs up the yard. Like he'd promised Mr

O'Donnell he would. And . . . I don't really know how to say this. But, from what Anthony got out of him when he was helping him in from the car, I think Barry might have found him.'

From the top of the kitchen stairs, there was a loud cry of delight, as Sheila Shea, gasping with relief clapped her hand over her mouth. 'You've found my Stephen,' she said, through shaking fingers.

Eileen leapt to her feet, and Scrap – put out to lose his tickles yet again – lolloped over to Barry in search of a bit of fuss.

The animal-like scream from Barry Ellis, as soft old Scrap licked his hand, was the most heart-rending sound that Sandy would ever hear in her life.

Brendan tossed down an envelope on the battered desk. 'There you are, Dad.' His voice was full of quiet rage. 'A nice tidy death certificate from Dr Stonely. And only a pony. Not a bad price to cover up the murder of a good and loyal friend. And I've told Ernie Carson we want a closed coffin. Not that there's much left to go in it.'

Gabriel, his head bowed, looked at his hands. 'These have dug holes, carried lumps of metal most men couldn't even lift, and they've beaten respect into people. They've earned us a good life. But what good is all that when your friends suffer?'

'No good at all, Dad. We've gotta finish this shit with the Kesslers once and for all, corner the pills market, and –'

Gabriel's head snapped up. 'So, it's drugs talk again is it? At a time like this?'

'Times are changing. It's you who always says that if we're not looking after the customers then someone else

312

will be. And there's plenty of customers for this sort of gear. If we're not careful, we'll be leaving the way open for them cunts to step right in and take the lot. Believe me, Dad, I've –'

'Oh, I believe you, boy, but don't you dare start trying to get clever with me. I've said no, Brendan. Over and over again. And I mean no. When I'm dead and buried you can run this business whatever way you want. Sell whatever shit you like to whoever you like. But while I'm alive, I'm in charge of this firm, and you'll do as you're told or you'll get out.'

'Maybe I will get out. I've just about had enough of all this.'

'Don't talk bollocks, Brendan.'

The Star and Compass was playing host yet again to a wake where the O'Donnells were in attendance. Although this time the funeral hadn't been for one of the family, it had been for what was left of Stephen Shea, and a lot of serious drinking had been done.

Brendan O'Donnell was sitting with Kevin Marsh and a hollow-eyed Barry Ellis.

Brendan was still fuming at his father's refusal to even give him so much as a proper hearing. 'So, it looks like we'll have to carry on as we are. Keeping it from him like we was fucking kids doing something naughty. I just don't get why he's so fucking pig-headed about it.'

'It's simple.' Kevin tipped his head back, and watched the smoke ring he'd just blown rise and disappear. 'He's getting on, Brendan. We're young. We can see the future. He can't.'

'Yeah, I suppose. But it means we'll have to think about other ways of getting ourselves bankrolled.' He reached across and helped himself to one of Kevin's cigarettes. 'I heard a whisper that Sammy Kessler and that clown of a cousin of his have set up some sort of a porn deal. That it's really earning. Perhaps it's time we thought about moving in on it. Taking it over. How do you fancy that?'

Barry Ellis took a deep breath and spoke for the first time. 'I'll do anything – anything it takes – to have them bastards.'

Brendan stood up. 'Time for another round, I reckon.'

Brendan went over to the bar and clapped his hand on his brother's shoulder. 'All right, Luke?'

'Great.'

'No need to be sarcastic. Now, what'll you have?'

'You're very chirpy, considering we're at a funeral. What you up to?'

'Nothing that need bother you, Luke. But you might like to know that I had a little chat with Dad the other day, and he said I've got to either do as I'm told or get out. You might like to remember that the next time you start whining.'

Luke put down his drink, turned to face his brother and looked him directly in the eye. 'Well, why don't you get out? Before it's too late. I don't know about you, Brendan, but I've had a bellyful of this. We're burying Stephen for Christ sake. *Stephen*. A week after the Kesslers buried that poor girl and her babies. And what happens next? Who's gonna get blown up? Chopped up? Shot to bits? What other lies are we gonna be expected to tell? What shitty story about how someone's died?'

'Luke –'

'No, I'm not listening any more. I think getting out of

314

all this is about the most sensible thing any of us could do.'

'Fine. Go on then. Do it. Go and earn peanuts. Wear cheap clothes. Go to the only clubs you'll be able to afford. The clubs where you won't be safe, where you'll get nicked.'

Luke could taste the bile rising in his throat and the sweat gathering in his palms. 'What rubbish are you talking now, Brendan?'

Brendan looked at him pityingly. 'And you've got the neck to talk about lies? You're a one-off, mate, you really are.' He shook his head in wonder, tightening the grip on his brother's shoulder. 'Listen to me, Luke, I know about you. Tumbled you years ago. But I don't care. You're my brother, and I love you whatever you are, whatever you do. But I ain't having you acting like some hedge-crawling tinker. You're an O'Donnell, Luke. Have some pride in yourself.'

'Let go of me, Brendan, before one of us says something he regrets.'

'Fuck you. You please yourself.'

'I will.'

'Good. Piss off then. Go on.'

Luke shoved past his brother and swerved his way through the crowded pub and out of the door.

Pete Mac, glass in hand and head still bandaged from his beating from Daniel Kessler, sauntered over to Brendan with a concerned smile on his face. 'You know what you've gone and done now, don't you, Brendan?' He sounded regretful, almost sad.

'*What?*' Brendan barked at him.

'You've gone and upset your brother.'

It was only the presence of Pete Mac's mother-in-law,

his wife, and the grieving members of the Shea family that saved him from getting a good kicking and an even more serious head wound than he already had.

'Are you sure he's in there, Maury?'

'Sammy, feller, I followed him here from Shea's funeral do meself. I sat outside the place in a cab, and watched as he came running out of that pub like he had a pack of hounds up his arse. Then his big brother Brendan started off after him. But then he gave up – just stopped chasing him, like he couldn't be bothered any more. But he did shout up the street after him. Hollered out that he could fuck off and get on with it. Then young Lukey boy disappeared round the corner and slipped into a phone box, made a call, waited a bit, then got picked up by a car – one of their firm's I suppose – and I said the immortal lines to my driver, *Follow that cab*. The driver didn't even crack a smile, the miserable bastard. He just gave me a lecture about how minicabs are *killing his trade*. Like I give a fuck now our business is finished.'

Sammy Kessler slid his gaze in the direction of the club doorway. 'But you're sure he's in there?' He was sounding nervous. 'I don't want to go inside if he's not. That'd just be wasting our time.'

Maurice did his best to hide his smile. 'Sammy, I told you, Mr Luke O'Donnell esquire arrived here in Dean Street precisely twenty minutes ago, when I phoned you from that phone box right there on the corner of Old Compton Street. And he has not left the premises since. Okay?'

Sammy nodded, breathing heavily and shifting about like a boxer waiting for the bell to tell him to come out fighting.

'So, do you want me to come in with you then, feller?'

Another nod.

'Thought you might.' Maurice smirked with amusement, but he didn't really get it, why some fellers would rather face a grizzly bear than enter a room full of nice peaceable men all having a quiet drink and a bit of a dance, in happy, friendly preparation for having a bit of something else later on.

Sammy was on the defensive. 'What d'you mean, you thought I might?'

'Nothing. Don't be so touchy. Come on, feller, welcome to the Lagoon Club.'

'Thanks Maurice, I couldn't think of a nicer way to spend the evening.'

Sammy edged his way around the dimly lit room until he was standing just a few feet away from Luke.

Luke was by himself, staring at the dancers, self-consciously tapping his toe to a booming recording of Johnny Kidd and the Pirates blasting out 'Shaking All Over'.

Sammy eased up right behind him and hissed in his ear, '*Oi, you, O'Donnell*'.

Luke jumped as if he'd just been plugged into the mains.

Breathing like a long-distance runner with a bad case of asthma, Luke turned slowly to face his tormentor. He didn't find it easy to swallow, but knew he had to if he was going to spit out the single word that would probably be all he could manage. 'Yeah?'

'I just wanted to catch up with you, that's all, Luke. Let you know that I'm gonna have you. All of you. I'm gonna ruin your lives. Just like your lot ruined mine,

317

when you murdered Catherine. And I'm gonna have you for killing Danny's Rachel. And their babies. Then I'm gonna ruin your brother's life. And your brother-in-law's life. Your mother's life, and your father's, and your big sister –'

'All right, Sam.' Maurice tutted at him with about as much passion as someone who'd made a mildly bad choice from his sock drawer.

'Fuck off, Maury.' Sammy was shouting now, his eyes wide and shining with anger, oblivious of being in the club and of all the men who had turned to watch as he stabbed his finger into Luke's terrified face – the men who were wondering if the strangers were about to raid the place, and whether they'd be wise to make themselves scarce.

'And I'm gonna start by telling your old man your dirty little secret. Tell him that his big brave son's nothing more than a shirt-lifting nonce.'

Luke drew back his fist, but Sammy grabbed his wrist before he could unleash the punch. 'I don't think so, do you, nancy boy?'

Tears began to brim in Luke's eyes. 'Please, don't. Please.'

'You stinking coward.' Sammy shook his head in disgust and let go of him. 'What you gonna do to stop me? Get down on your knees and beg?'

Luke did the only thing he could think of. He shoved Sammy away from him as hard as he could, and fled into the crowd of gawking onlookers, disappearing, unseen by him or Maurice, through an open door at the far end of the room. The second time he'd run away from the truth in one night.

Sammy looked slowly around him, sneering at every

gaze he met. 'And what d'you lot think you're fucking looking at?'

'Don't know, sweet lips,' said a flamboyantly dressed, elderly man sitting in the corner by the stairs with a pale pink poodle on his lap. 'Hasn't got a label on it.'

Even Maurice winced as Sammy barged over and smashed his fist into the old man's nose – shooting up the stairs before anyone could stop him.

'Well, dearie me,' said Maurice, with a flash of his eyebrows, but then made sure he took the stairs two at a time, hightailing it after his cousin, before anyone had the chance to start anything.

The more perverse part of Maurice was tempted to stay behind, to charm his way out of being associated with Sammy and Luke, and maybe make a proper night of it, but with the mood Sammy was in, he thought there might be a bit more action on the cards elsewhere, and he didn't want to miss out on the fun.

But, as he stepped out onto the pavement, Maurice saw that Sammy was far from up for it. He was leaning against the wall, his head back and his eyes closed.

'You all right there, feller?'

'I couldn't help myself down there, Maury. Hitting that old bloke. The way he looked at me made me feel sick.'

Maurice thought for a moment. 'Hang on, Sammy, lad,' he said, holding up a finger to his cousin. 'How about if you wait here, and I go down and straighten it out for you? Make it all right.'

'Would you?'

'I'll be two secs.'

Sammy lit himself a cigarette, and Maurice sprinted back down the stairs into the club.

A group of men were fussing around the man with the

poodle, dabbing at his nose with wet handkerchiefs, and pressing refills on him for his Gin and It.

Maurice had a quick shufti round. No sign of Luke.

'Let me through,' said Maurice firmly.

A hefty man in his thirties – more than a match for Maurice – stepped forward. 'Why?'

'I wanted to have a private word, to apologise for my friend. Explain why he was so nasty to that poor old bloke.'

The man with the poodle spoke, gesturing with a jaded flap of his hand. 'It's okay, let him through.'

Maurice squatted down in front of him, and patted the little pink poodle gently on the head. 'Nice dog,' he said, and then sighed dramatically. 'Look, feller, sorry about that. You just got yourself in the middle of a lovers' tiff that's all.' He held out his hands, throwing himself on the mercy of the man's understanding. 'He is so jealous.'

Then he leaned right up close to the man and whispered. 'If you even think about sending one of these goons up after us, I'll wait for you, and rip this fucking mutt's head right off it's scrawny neck and shove it up your arse. Then I'll kick you so hard in the crutch that your dick'll be sticking out of that filthy old gob of yours. Okay, feller?'

The man's chest heaved in a weary sigh as he dabbed at his still bloody nose. 'I've heard it all, and suffered it all before, sweetheart. So I'm not going to change the habit of a lifetime, and start worrying about nasty boys, who think they've got to duff me up to prove what fine strong men they are, now am I? And I certainly don't want to get any of my dear friends here in trouble with Lily Law. We have enough of that just trying to walk along the street minding our own business.'

Maurice almost smiled in admiration. He had to hand it to the old poof; he certainly had balls.

Back upstairs on the pavement, Sammy was drawing heavily on his cigarette, and glaring at passers-by, daring them to say just one word to him.

'All done,' said Maurice. 'I told the old feller you was sorry and dropped him a score for his trouble.'

'Thanks, Maury, I appreciate it.'

'It was a pleasure, Sam. Anyway, I see it as my job. Spreading joy and happiness. In fact, let's spread a bit more, let's phone Lukey's old man for him.'

The barman at the Star and Compass gasped in disbelief. 'If you think I'm passing on *that* message, after the amount of booze that's been swallowed in here since they came in this afternoon . . . No, what am I saying? I haven't even *heard* any message. I haven't even had this phone call.' It was hardly news about Luke O'Donnell being the other way, but saying so to his old man? What was this bloke on the phone, out of his bloody mind?

'Wait, please, don't cut me off, feller. Just get Gabriel O'Donnell to the phone and there's a fifty in it for you.'

A fifty? That got his interest. This bloke was serious. 'Make it a ton.'

'All right, a ton.'

The barman couldn't believe his luck. A hundred sovs, just for answering the phone? 'I'll get him right away.'

'Hang on, what's your name. So's I know I'm giving the money to the right bloke.'

'Lawrence.'

'Lawrence. All right, Lawrence. The reward's as good as yours, feller.'

The thought of the hundred pounds had imbued Lawrence with a reckless courage, and he found himself persuading Gabriel O'Donnell that the caller had stressed how it was a private matter that no one but Mr O'Donnell could deal with.

Gabriel's immediate thought was that it was something to do with Rosie, and he was behind the bar with the phone in his hand, demanding to know who was speaking, before Lawrence had even finished.

'It doesn't matter who I am, O'Donnell. Just think of me as a friend.'

Gabriel cupped his hand over his other ear to block out the noise of the drunken mourners singing their sorrowful ballads from the old country. 'Kessler, I know that's you. What do you want, you Northern ponce.'

'Sorry, O'Donnell. Never heard of no Kessler. Northern or otherwise.'

Maurice felt a bit miffed; he'd thought he sounded just like one of the soft, Southern nancy boys from the Lagoon Club, thought he'd done a really clever accent. 'My name's Oliver, if you must know, but my friends call me Olive. And that's what I'm calling you about. Friendship. You see, your lovely boy Luke, he's a friend of mine. A really special sort of a friend.'

When Gabriel had stopped yelling obscenities at him, Maurice carried on in an admiring lisp, 'You're very butch aren't you, Mr O'Donnell. Oh, by the way – no, wait, hang on, don't go, Mr O'Donnell. One of the barmen there, Lawrence, that's his name. He's one and all. As a matter of fact he was the first one to give your Luke a seeing to. Make sure you look after him, won't you, Mr O'Donnell, because you do know it's illegal, don't you?

And I'd hate to think he could blackmail your son. I mean, it'd be terrible if the law was to find out his dirty little secret, wouldn't it? And if it got in all them naughty Sunday papers . . . That'd be horrible, wouldn't it?'

Maurice was still speaking, but Gabriel wasn't listening. He had dropped the phone and was moving slowly towards Lawrence – who was pulling yet another pint of Guinness as he daydreamed about the motor he was going to buy himself with his hundred notes.

Lawrence's body was found two months later by a gang of kids. They'd been experimenting with their first packet of Player's Weights, in the privacy of a derelict house on the Barking Road, and had been unfortunate enough to investigate where the disgusting stench was coming from – anything rather than having to persevere with the fags, which had been making them feel seriously unwell.

The association between their queasiness from the taste of the cigarettes and their first sight of a dead body – and a badly decomposed one at that – had been enough to make lifelong nonsmokers of them all.

The body itself was never identified, probably because Lawrence's wife never reported him missing. It suited her too well, him being out of the picture. She'd always fancied being a landlady of her own pub, having her name up over the door. And the owner of the Star and Compass wasn't *that* bad looking. Not really. And, as for the landlord – at his age, he was delighted, not to say surprised, to have a woman back in his life. Any woman.

It was just a shame he'd lost such a good barman.

Chapter 23

When Luke finally got home, it was nearly half past four in the morning, and he was shattered. He had hidden away for hours, like a frightened, cowering animal, in a cubicle in the Lagoon Club lavatories, waiting until the music had died down, and he'd heard the bar staff clearing away for the night. He had spent the next hour or so wandering around the streets of Soho, eventually going to sit in a twenty-four hour greasy spoon, where he nursed cup after cup of dark orange tea.

The thought of going home any earlier and having to face people had been too much for him to bear – especially if Sammy Kessler had done what he'd threatened, and had actually called his father.

It was just impossible to think about.

It would be easier in the morning, when he'd had a rest, time to pull himself together.

Or perhaps it would make more sense to pack a bag right now and leave for good.

Unfortunately for Luke, he didn't have the luxury of making that choice; as he let himself in through the front door, he heard his father yelling at him from the basement.

Luke stood in the hall, his eyes closed, accepting the inevitability of what was going to happen to him. But dreading every moment of what he was about to face as he made his way down to the kitchen.

He stopped halfway down the stairs, and took in the scene below him. His father – sitting there in just his vest and trousers, lids half-lowered, hair falling over his forehead – had obviously carried on drinking long after the funeral had finished.

'Get down here,' he snarled, banging his glass on the table.

Luke moved slowly down towards his fate. 'Where's Mum and Brendan?'

'In bed. So don't think they can protect you.'

'What from? More of your bullying? Your fists?'

'I said, get down here.'

Luke did as he was told, too scared of his father not to, but also because this was it: this was when he would say the things he'd never dared say before. Things he had to say before he lost his courage and started despising himself even more than he did now.

Gabriel rose unsteadily to his feet and took a step towards him. 'Why couldn't you just keep it a secret?'

'What, like you keep your whore a secret? Not much of a secret when everyone knows, is it Dad?'

'So it was you who told your mother about Rosie. I knew it was, you miserable, snivelling little shit.'

'No. It wasn't me. I'd never hurt Mum like that. Don't you understand? I'm not like you.'

'No, you're not like me, more's the pity. You're a vile, stinking pervert.'

Gabriel's hand lashed out.

Luke flinched, thinking his father was going to strike him, but he didn't. Instead, he seized Luke by the collar, dragging his son towards him, making him wince with pain, his body still sore from the beating he'd had from Daniel.

'Why couldn't you be a man?' Gabriel was shaking him.

325

'What, and follow your example? No thanks, Dad. I don't want to be a bully. Or a drunk. Or a womaniser.'

'Shut your mouth, you . . . you abomination.'

'Abomination am I? Been listening to that old hypocrite Father Shaunessy again, have you, Dad? That beast'll tell you anything so long as you keep giving him money.'

Gabriel raised his hand, but Luke stood his ground, refusing to lower his gaze.

'Do you know what, Dad? Hard as it is, this thing about me that I'm gonna have to somehow come to terms with – and all the lies I've had to tell; the fear of being caught out; or being put away by some little creep of a copper with a grudge – I'm glad I'm different. And shall I tell you why? If I hadn't realised how much you despised what I am, I'd have hero-worshipped you. And then I'd have turned out like you: a self-obsessed animal. Just like you're making Brendan into. Believe me, you disgust me far more than I could ever *begin* disgusting you.'

That was it, it was too much for Gabriel; he clenched his fist and laid into his child.

As he kicked and beat his son, tears poured down Gabriel's face. 'I have to do this. Do you understand me, boy? It's for your own good.'

When Gabriel had finished with him, Luke was lying unconscious and bloody on the kitchen floor.

Gabriel gave him a final departing kick, and then hauled himself up the stairs, bellowing at the top of his voice: 'Get that piece of shit away from me, I can't stand the sight of him.'

Eileen and Brendan were down in the kitchen before Gabriel had slammed the street door behind him.

'Mum, please don't make me say it again. I don't need to go to the hospital. And I definitely don't want Dr Stonely anywhere near me.'

'But you were unconscious.' She turned to Brendan who was sitting next to her. 'Tell him.'

'Luke, why don't you let me take you to casualty?' Brendan didn't sound very convinced about what he was suggesting. 'You can say you got jumped in the street.'

Luke shook his head, and wished he hadn't. It hurt. A lot. 'Please, Mum, don't worry. I'll be fine.'

'Luke, I want you to see someone.'

'Okay. Tell you what, I'll see the law. He's gone too far this time. I'm gonna have him over this. I'm gonna drop him right in it.'

Eileen couldn't look at him, didn't know what to say, but Brendan did. 'Don't talk stupid, Luke.'

'Stupid? Is that what you think I'm being?' He put his hand to his lip that had split open and had started bleeding again. 'Give us that flannel, Mum.'

Eileen handed it to him. 'Don't you two start your arguing as well, don't you think I've got enough to worry about?'

'And why do you think you've got so much aggravation, eh, Mum? It's him. And I can't bear to see the way you all put up with it. The covering up for him. The way nobody ever dares –'

'Luke,' Brendan was on his feet, his anger about to tip over. 'Like Mum said, don't start.'

'Why not? Why not tell some truths for once about the great Gabriel O'Donnell? Start letting everyone know what –'

'Don't listen to him, Mum, he's not thinking right.'

327

'*Me* not thinking right? I've never been clearer.' He turned to his mother. 'Why do you put up with him?'

'He's my husband.'

Brendan grabbed his brother by the arm and dragged him to his feet. 'Luke, you're knackered, mate. Let's get you up to bed, eh? Sleep it off. Stephen's funeral's upset us all. And we're –'

'Let go of me, Brendan.' Luke shook him off. 'You're getting as bad as him.'

'He's our father.'

'Her husband. Our father. What a wonderful man! And I'm meant to be proud of that fact, am I? When he brags about what he does just like it's any other business. And how he's so kind and generous to everyone.' Luke threw back his head. 'We all *know* it's just a load of bollocks.'

'Luke!' Eileen crossed herself. 'Will you mind your language?'

He took hold of his mother by the shoulders. 'A bit of swearing, is that what really worries you, Mum? Not the violence, and the fear, and the bullying? Look at you, you're terrified of him. Terrified. Just like all the little boys, who're too scared of that other stinking hypocrite, Father Shaunessy. Too petrified to tell people what he does to them. How they put up with all his crap because they're so scared of him. Just the same as you with Dad. And just like you haven't said anything over all these years, when you've known all along that your husband's had another woman, and that –'

Even as the words came spilling out, Luke was regretting them. And he was almost glad when his mother whacked him round the face with the back of her open hand. But he still couldn't stop himself from saying all the things he had bottled up for so long.

328

'Where d'you think he is now, eh? Who's bed has he run off to?'

Another slap. 'I said, *he's your father!*'

'Oh, yeah, and I'm so happy about that. So glad to be the son of a man who as good as killed his own daughter.'

Eileen recoiled as if Luke had slapped her back. 'What did you say?'

'You'd better sit down again, Mum, there's a lot more you need to know.'

Brendan stepped between them, and closed his hands round his brother's face, forcing him to look into his eyes. 'No, Luke. No. Don't do this. Please.'

'It's too late, Brendan. I told you, I've had enough.'

Chapter 24

When Gabriel eventually came home on Monday morning – three days after knocking his own child to the floor and kicking him senseless – Eileen calmly set a place for her husband at the breakfast table, and told her sons to make themselves scarce as she needed to speak to their father.

Gabriel was sitting with his chin propped on his fists, unshaven, stinking like a rancid brewery, and still, very obviously, drunk. Wherever he'd been on his bender, it was clear that he hadn't bothered taking along clean clothes or a razor.

Luke, his face puffed and bruised, and his eyes peering out of yellow and purple slits, was happy to leave; he couldn't stomach the idea of spending any more time with the arsehole of a man who called himself his father, and had only agreed to stay at the house at all over the past few days because his mother had been so mad with grief. But she'd calmed down now, and he was satisfied that he'd done his job: he'd told her the truth. At last.

Brendan wasn't so sure about leaving them alone. According to what Anthony had told him, Gabriel had lost his temper during Stephen's wake at the Star and Compass, and, for some unknown reason, had taken it out on the barman. He had dragged him out from behind the counter, punching, kicking and threatening him, right there, in front of everyone, not caring who saw or heard – miles away from their own manor.

Then, when he'd got the bloke outside, Gabriel had beaten him unconscious. And, as if that wasn't enough, Gabriel had bundled the bloke into the boot of his car, and had driven off with him.

And all that before going home and starting on Luke.

Brendan really did need to find out what had happened. And why. And if his father had made any other stupid mistakes. Stupid mistakes got you in trouble with the law. And he definitely didn't want the old man ballsing things up for him. Not now. Not when he'd got Kevin and Barry ready and primed to fuck over Sammy Kessler for his porn business. The business that was going to fund their move into big-time supplying.

But Eileen wouldn't hear of Brendan staying, and she led him over to the stairs as if he were a little boy. 'Go on, son. Leave us. I'll be just fine. I'm not a fool, I can see he's drunk. But there are things I have to discuss with him. You can ask him all the questions you want, *after* I've had a chance to talk to him.'

Brendan looked at his watch. 'All right. I've got one or two things to do. But me and Luke'll be back at dinner time, around twelve, to make sure everything's all right. Okay?' He turned to his brother. '*Won't* we, Luke?'

'If you say so.'

'And, Mum, don't go winding him up, will you?'

Eileen pushed a cup of weak tea liberally laced with whiskey towards her husband. She had no intention of helping him to pull himself together. For once, she didn't want him sober. So, as soon as he had finished drinking that, she gave him another one, this time not even bothering with the pretence of including any tea.

She sat and watched him as his eyelids began to flutter,

knowing what she was going to do, knowing what she had to do.

Eileen looked at the clock. Nearly half past ten. The boys would be back by noon. Maybe earlier.

She shook him roughly.

Gabriel came to, groaning pathetically. He staggered to his feet; his bladder bursting.

'I want that glass filled when I get back from the lavatory,' he said, stumbling across the room.

'You're very flushed, Gabriel,' she said gently. 'You really don't look well. I'll get you your pills.'

'I don't need that crap,' he snarled from the top of the stairs without even bothering to turn around to look at her.

'Gabe, you've not taken them since we buried Stephen. You don't want the next funeral to be yours do you?'

When he returned from the lavatory, Gabriel's flies were still open, and his shirt was hanging outside of his trousers. He looked a mess.

Grudgingly he took the pills from his wife and swallowed them, downing them with the half-tumbler of Jameson's she'd set in front of him.

'Get me a refill.'

'Are you sure you really want one, Gabe?'

He lifted his head and glowered at her. His eyes were out of focus and sweat was trickling down his face. 'I'm your husband, woman. The man of this house. Now fetch me another fucking drink before you feel the back of my hand.'

Eileen had to steady herself as she got up to fetch the bottle from the dresser. She had never feared him physically before. Not once. Not even over at the flapping. She'd just put that down to the drink.

But then he'd never beaten his own child into unconsciousness before either.

During the past few days she'd learned a lot of things she hadn't known before about the man she'd been married to since she was barely sixteen years of age.

'The drink, woman. Now.' His words were sliding into one another in a drawl of increasing incoherence, and he was blinking as if the light were hurting his eyes. 'I said. Woman. Drink.'

'I'm fetching it.' Eileen had her back to him, as she stirred the liquid around the glass with her finger, which she wiped on her skirt.

'Why? Why did he have to turn out like that?' he wailed as Eileen handed him the glass, as if his lack of understanding had lent him momentary lucidity. 'Look at the life he has. Here. Beautiful home. Money in his pocket. You're blessed. All you. I've given everything. All you. This what happens. How yer pay me back. Pathetic little queer.'

He gulped greedily at the drink, then stopped and spat it out over the table. 'Wass wrong? Tastes like muck.'

'That'll be your breath. You stink like a hog.'

His head jerked up, he couldn't believe he'd heard her right. 'What did you . . .'

'Nothing. Nothing important.' She took the glass off him. 'Here, I'll get you another.'

Gabriel held the palm of his hand to his head. He didn't feel right.

She gave him the glass, folding his fingers around it. 'And as for me being blessed, I suppose some would say that I am. But me, I think of myself more like a bird in a cage. Sure, I love that I have my food and water and a nice clean place to live, but do I want my babies to live in the cage with me? No. Freedom, that's what I want for them. It might be too late for Brendan, but Luke might still have a chance.'

'Freedom?' Gabriel swallowed another mouthful of his drink then paused to look at the glass. Perhaps it didn't taste too bad. He knocked back the rest of it.

'Yes, Gabriel, freedom. From you.'

'Eileen, I feel –'

'Tired?'

He tried to shake his head, but it was too heavy.

'Well, you should be after all the stuff you've got inside you.'

She sat down, putting a small brown bottle on the table in front of him. 'Brendan got me these tablets. Well, more like capsules I'd suppose you'd call them.'

'Ehhh?' Gabriel could barely make sense of what she was saying.

'They're drugs. You know, those things you hate. They were meant to help me sleep. As if I'd ever sleep again. It was our little secret, because we knew you wouldn't approve. You swallowed three of them, when I told you I was giving you your blood pressure medicine. And now I've been mixing more of the insides of the pretty little things into your drinks. Sure, don't they say that mixing your drinks is bad for you?' She laughed. 'Another secret. So many in one house. And I put up with all of them. And with your lies, your drinking, and your whores. All our married life. But this, I can't take this. I won't. Not any more.'

'I don't . . .' His mouth had stopped working, and his head was lolling forward.

'You know, when I was a girl I used to ask my mother to tell me stories about the old days, but she wouldn't. She said they'd make me too sad. That they were stories of even worse poverty than we were living in. Stories about families fighting one another for nothing more than a few crumbs from the rich men's tables. And stories of things that went on behind the closed doors of so-called decent people. Stories that hid secrets behind lies. You know, I really thought I was going to have a better life living here with you. My God, I was a fool.'

He managed to raise his head and slur a few barely intelligible words: 'How 'bout your lies, Eilee . . .'

Then his head flopped forward onto the table and he began to snore through his wide-open mouth.

With quiet dignity, Eileen rose to her feet, picked up the cushion she had been sitting on – the one she had fetched especially from the front parlour – lifted his head by the hair, and slipped the thing onto the table. Then she pushed his face into the cushion, and held him down – in his drunken, drugged, disgusting stupor – until she was sure he was dead.

As she held him there, she was crying, but it wasn't for Gabriel O'Donnell that she wept, or even for what she was doing, it was for her children, and for Sophie's daughter-in-law, and for her unborn babies.

Eileen rinsed out Gabriel's glass under the tap, poured herself a measure of whiskey into it, and sat herself down by the dresser to make the first of the telephone calls.

'Is that Rosie Palmer,' Eileen asked, surprised at her own composure.

'Who is this?'

'I can hear you're a Dublin girl from your accent.'

'I said, who this is?'

'In good time. There's a question I want to ask *you* first.

335

How could you let him send your child away from you? How could you do that? You're that child's mother. And you act as if she's of no more value to you than a dog that's being sent to the kennels.'

'I don't have to listen to this, I –'

'I thought you wanted to know who I am.'

There was a silence at the other end.

'Well, I'll tell you, shall I? I'm Eileen, Gabriel O'Donnell's widow.'

She heard a gasp.

'That's right, you heard me, his widow. I've just murdered the evil bastard. Killed him stone-cold dead. Just like he as good as killed Catherine, may God rest her. And all those other poor souls. I stopped him. Before he could kill anyone else. I really think I've done everyone a favour, don't you – Rosie Palmer?'

As she put down the phone all Eileen could hear was a sound like a cornered creature screaming in pain as it was being ripped apart by dogs.

She took a moment to think and to sip at her drink, and then she made the other calls.

Satisfied that she had accomplished all she could at home, Eileen put on her coat and left the house, fixing a note with a drawing pin to the front door, and then closing it securely behind her.

Eileen knelt down and crossed herself, taking in the familiar, slightly damp fug of the confessional.

The grill went back and she said, 'I appreciate you coming here for me, Father Shaunessy.'

Then she crossed herself again. 'Bless me, Father, for I have sinned. It is one week since my last confession, and nearly twenty-five years since I last told the truth. And now I've killed my husband.'

She laughed, a blank humourless sound. 'Don't bother to absolve me from that last one, Father. That wasn't a sin, that was a duty. But now, let's get on shall wc? We don't have much time.'

Eileen stepped out of the confession box, and looked the priest levelly in the eye. She could see he was stunned. Well, he was about to be totally and completely bloody horrified.

'And while we're at it, Father – you know, telling the truth and all that – maybe it might do your own soul a bit of good if you confessed to a thing or two.'

Father Shaunessy was as white as a freshly laundered altar cloth. 'Whatever's got into you woman?'

'What's got into me *Father* Shaunessy, is that I'm sick to my stomach with lies. I'm up to here with hypocrisy, and God forgive me, I think I'm even sick of life itself. I've seen and heard too much. But I know what really sickens me most of all. It's you. For what you did to those little boys.' She held up her hand. 'Don't even try and deny it. My son told me everything. Do you know, the poor boy's even wondered if what you did to him had anything to do with the way he's turned out. God love him.'

'I don't know what you think you're doing –'

Eileen ignored him and just kept on talking. 'I thought very carefully about whether I should tell the police about you. But when I thought it through, I realised that it wasn't the answer, that it wouldn't do any good. They'd call me, or rather the children, liars – those who'd be brave enough to come forward, that is; those who wouldn't feel too

337

ashamed to speak about the wicked things you'd done to them. The things you'd forced them to do. And it would all be covered up. And they'd send you off to some other parish, where you'd just get up to your filth there instead. Well, I'm warning you, Father, if you do it again – ever, to any child – I'll find a way to kill you too. You have my solemn word on that, Father Shaunessy. My solemn word. So, it's up to you. You decide what happens. And, as long as you behave, you're safe. For now. But put a foot wrong and I swear, you'll be sorry.'

'Eileen, I won't have you speaking to me like this.'

'Won't you now? Is that so? Do you know, Father, I think there should be an eleventh commandment – thou shall not bully. I mean, just think what the world would be like if there was such a thing. Think how much better it would be. All the control and the power the likes of you have over fearful people and children weaker than yourself – it would just disappear.' She snapped her fingers. 'Whooof! Up like a puff of smoke. Now wouldn't that be a more Christian sort of a world?'

'I think you've lost your reason, woman.'

'No, Father, I've just found it.' She pointed to the stained-glass window high above the altar. 'Take a look at that beautiful picture up there. What does it say to us? The meek shall inherit the earth. And isn't that what we're supposed to believe? Words that'll keep us down. Under control. But we know, don't we, deep down, that it's all rubbish. And sure, it's not much of a place to inherit anyway, now is it? Meek or otherwise. I mean, honestly, Father, who'd want to inherit a shithole like this?'

'Eileen! Remember where you are.'

He reached out to take hold of her arm, but she stepped away from him, putting a row of pews between them.

'Don't you dare touch me.'

He held up his hands. 'All right. Keep calm. You can't be feeling well, Eileen, that's what it is. You're unwell. Now, why don't you sit yourself down? I'll go and tell the housekeeper to make us both a nice cup of tea, and we can have a little chat.'

'Don't waste your time thinking about slipping away to call the police, Father.' She held her arms wide. 'There's no point. Sure haven't I already done it myself? I told them they could find me here at half past twelve. Made sure I gave myself just enough time to get my last few jobs done. Like my confession and like telling you a thing or two.'

'Mum?'

It was Luke calling to her.

She turned around to see both her sons, hurtling down the aisle towards her and Father Shaunessy.

'Let me talk to her, Luke,' puffed Brendan. 'Before you say anything to anyone, Mum, don't worry. We can sort this out. It's gonna be all right. Nobody needs know.'

'What, like nobody needed to know about Catherine seeing Sammy Kessler? Or about how she died? Or about Luke and the way he is – God forgive him. Or about your father and his whore. And your little half-sister, Ellie?'

Brendan's face contorted like a wax mask held in front of a fire.

'Don't look at me like that, son. I know you knew everything all along, and that you thought I was a fool. And you were probably right. But I have to believe that although I might be a foolish person, I'm not a *bad* one. I have to believe that I'm better than he was. That there's a chance for children to be better than their fathers. If they really want to be.'

'Thank God!' shouted Father Shaunessy, as two men in police uniform and two men in plain clothes strode into the church.

The uniformed men were fiddling awkwardly with their helmets, knowing they had to wear them when they were on official business, but they were in church. So, what were they supposed to do?

The plain-clothes policemen just looked generally embarrassed by the whole situation.

'Sorry, Mr O'Donnell, sir,' said one of them, waving his identification at Brendan. 'We had a phone call. But I'm sure there's been some sort of a mistake.'

'No, there's no mistake.' Eileen turned to the altar again and crossed herself before turning back to the policemen. 'It's all true. I've killed my husband, and I'm giving myself up.'

All four policemen looked as confused and astonished as if she'd just started speaking in tongues.

The officer who'd spoken was the first to pull himself together. 'I'm sure . . .' he began. But his words petered out. He genuinely had no idea what to say next.

Eileen smiled at him. 'Please, let me say a few words to my boys?'

The police officers stepped away, relieved for even a momentary respite.

Eileen nodded her thanks and then touched her youngest son on the cheek. 'Luke, I want you to look after Patricia and little Caty for me. And Scrap, he'll be needing his walk when you get home. Will you do that?'

Luke could barely speak. 'Course, I will, Mum.'

'And keep an eye on the father here as well. You know why. And I want you to promise me you'll take care of yourself.'

This time Luke's tears got the better of him. He could do no more than nod. She took his face in her hands, reached up and kissed him gently on the forehead.

Brendan grabbed his mother's hand away from his brother. 'How about me?'

Eileen sighed long and loudly, and looked her other son steadily in the eye. 'Why would I worry about you, Brendan? You can look after yourself. Just like your father.'

'But he's –'

'Dead? That's right. He is. And I killed him. So maybe he wasn't such a big tough man after all. And maybe there's a lesson for you.'

She lifted her chin, turned, and held out her hands to the policemen.

'I'm ready now,' she said.

Make Us Traitors

May 1963

In a dramatic climax to the trial that has been gripping the nation, Eileen O'Donnell, 44, was today sentenced to life imprisonment for the murder of her husband, Gabriel, a crime to which she freely confessed in September last year.

Gabriel O'Donnell, long suspected of being the driving force behind one of the two powerful criminal mobs that have been terrorising the streets of the East End, was never indicted on any of the many charges brought against him and his family. O'Donnell, like his sons, Brendan and Luke, and his son-in-law Peter MacRiordan, had always claimed to be a legitimate businessman.

Sources, who had to be promised anonymity, so great is the fear stalking east London, spoke to this paper about the sham of their so-called businesses, claiming that they are nothing more than a cover for the O'Donnells' nefarious dealings.

In the run-up to the trial, continual attempts were made to persuade Eileen O'Donnell to admit to the involvement of not only her own family, but also of their associates, the Kesslers, in the crime wave that has been sweeping London, but she was only prepared to speak about her own culpability in murdering her husband.

The police are understood to be very disappointed by Eileen O'Donnell's refusal to cooperate, as they are believed to view the halting of the activities of these two families as the only way forward in making the streets safe again for decent people. A campaign that this paper not only supports, but which it promises to pursue.

See page 5 for your chance to add your name to our petition demanding government action.

November 1973

Eileen O'Donnell, 55, who, 11 years ago, sensationally confessed to the murder of her husband, Gabriel, the notorious East End gang leader, was released from prison early this morning.

Wearing a cream-coloured suit, and looking arrogantly ahead of her, O'Donnell was met by her wealthy businessmen sons, Brendan, 35, and Luke, 34.

Luke O'Donnell, bachelor, drove his mother away in a luxury Daimler saloon. Surprisingly, they were accompanied by Sophie Kessler, 53, the wife of millionaire Harold Kessler.

After the trial, a source close to the O'Donnells and the Kesslers linked the murder of Gabriel O'Donnell to a feud between the two families. But whatever its cause, his death was the final horror in a series of terrifying and brutal events, which shook the East End and appalled the country as a whole.

7

At the time of Eileen O'Donnell's conviction, unsubstantiated rumours about the families were buzzing through every London pub. The most often heard was that the troubles between them began when Gabriel O'Donnell found out that his youngest daughter, Catherine, was in a secret relationship with Samuel, Harold Kessler's youngest son. There was further speculation in the underworld, when the body of Catherine O'Donnell, aged just 18, was pulled from a blazing car, that her death was a result of something far more sinister than a road-traffic accident. Everything from sawn-off shotguns to the involvement of one of her own family was suggested. One of the most sickening events was the sudden death and hurried burial of Stephen Shea, one of Gabriel O'Donnell's closest associates. There was much fevered speculation at the time, confirmed by those in the know, that Shea had been assassinated as part of the appalling gangland grudge match between the families, and that, in a shocking gesture of power, his body parts had been fed to Gabriel O'Donnell's Alsatian guard dogs.

Bad feeling escalated between the families, finally reaching crisis point, when Rachel, 21, Daniel Kessler's heavily pregnant wife, was killed in an explosion, which was never satisfactorily explained, although whispers were heard, and fingers were pointed in the direction of the O'Donnells.

It was O'Donnell's death that saw this newspaper launch its ground-breaking campaign to bring safety back to our streets. Since then, matters have been mostly quiet between the families, with word among the criminal fraternity that the O'Donnells agreed to 'tolerate' the presence of the Kesslers on 'their' patch, providing no 'rules' were breached.

Many are now wondering if the release of Eileen O'Donnell will open old wounds, and if terror will return to our streets.

Additional comment and pictures pages 3, 4 and 5.

Chapter 1

In the early-morning gloom, the tall, darkly hand-some man opened the boot of his car, and took out a plain, blue nylon shopping bag. It would probably have looked more at home on the arm of a bargain-seeking housewife than in the hands of the driver of a sleek, black Mercedes.

Brendan O'Donnell shut the boot with a heavily expensive clunk, and set off through the car park of the motorway service station. Head angled down-wards, he pulled the collar of his sheepskin coat up about his face – apparently avoiding the rain – and moved fast and confidently towards the café, with its dim, improvised lamp lighting. The unions were on strike again, playing havoc with the electricity supply, and although, as a rule, Brendan had no time for the bastards, right now he could have kissed the shop stewards bloody personally. These blackouts made the conditions for what he had planned just about perfect.

Halfway along the pedestrian path, Brendan stopped. He secured the bag between his feet and, snatching a glimpse over his shoulder, bent low as if to tie his lace. Satisfied he wasn't being followed, he picked up the bag before heading towards the tall, conifer windbreak that shielded the area where the lorries and rigs, and their slumbering drivers, were parked up from the night before.

'Half four and packing already? We'll be sorry to see you go, hen. Made a nice change, having a lady down here among us lowlifes.' The brass-yellow blonde squinted through the darkness, baring her tobacco-stained teeth in an unpleasant smile. 'Even if you are a no-good, murdering whore.'

Eileen O'Donnell didn't flinch. In her eleven years inside she'd learned her lesson well on how to react to such remarks – or rather how not to react. The resulting isolation had at least saved her from further beatings after the initial attacks that had been her payment for daring to act in a way that the other prisoners had decided was snooty and stand-offish. Paradoxically, it was the reputation of the man she had killed – her husband – that would, in the past, have been her protection. But Gabriel O'Donnell had done too many things, to too many people, and Eileen had paid many times over for his crimes as well as her own.

The blonde heaved herself up to a fleshy crouch, folded her beefy arms across her cerise nylon nightdress, and watched as Eileen collected together the last of the few possessions she had allowed herself to put on show. The trinkets and photographs, she knew, had only added to her vulnerability with the likes of the Glaswegian witch with whom she had been forced to share so much of her meagre living space for the past twenty months.

In some ways, the last few of those twenty months had been the most difficult to endure of the whole time that Eileen had been in prison, because she knew what, and who, waited for her on the outside.

Brendan O'Donnell stopped halfway along the hedge, took a gold cigarette lighter from his coat pocket, held it at eye level and sparked it three times. On the third flame, two men appeared at his side.

Brendan was immediately on the alert. 'Where's Barry?'

Kevin Marsh stared down at his feet and let out a long, slow breath. 'Sorry, Brendan. Barry never showed. Them guts of his must be playing him up again. Probably didn't wanna risk it.'

'Fair enough.' Brendan's face betrayed nothing. 'So, it's down to me and you then.'

'What? I'm not here, I suppose?' It was Peter MacRiordan, Brendan O'Donnell's red-headed lump of a brother-in-law.

Kevin nodded as if the exchange between Brendan and Pete Mac hadn't happened. 'Yeah. And I brought Pete Mac along just in case.'

Brendan looked at his brother-in-law, sighed with resignation, and then opened the nylon bag. From it he took three pairs of department-store driving gloves, the sort that would soon be being gift-wrapped, ready to be placed under family Christmas trees all over the country to surprise dads and grandpas.

'Here you are, lads, these'll keep your hands nice and warm.' Brendan took the empty cellophane packaging from them and then pulled on his own pair before dipping back into the bag.

This time he took out a length of lead piping bound in cloth. 'And this'll open the truck door quicker than any set of twirls.'

'But ain't the driver expecting us?'

'Not this time he ain't, Kev. No.' Brendan jerked his head towards the line of lorries. 'Because this is not a usual pickup. This time we're gonna help ourselves to the load in that nice big green truck down there. The one with *Kessler* written on the side in pretty red letters. See, I've had a whisper that it might be worth our while.' He shrugged down into his sheepskin. 'In more ways than one.'

Kevin's response was a tight frown, but Pete Mac, working as ever from a different agenda, came out with one of his usual, annoying comments. 'Fucking Barry Ellis. Bad guts? D'you reckon? There's me out here in the pissing down of rain, freezing me goolies off, while he's tucked up indoors, nice and warm with his Sandy. And Kevin's still making excuses for him. Everyone knows the bloke's off his nut, so why do we all keep on pretending?'

Kevin grabbed the lapels of Pete Mac's trench coat. 'Just shut it for once, will you, Pete? He's been a good and loyal friend to me, and to the rest of us.'

'Brendan?' Pete Mac was clearly offended. 'You gonna let him treat me like this?'

Brendan looked at him coolly. 'We're meant to be working here, Pete, not rowing like bloody schoolgirls.'

'I still don't think it's right. Barry gets away with murder just because he can't face the fact that he found Stephen Shea's body – well, the bits that was left of it.' He snorted, a derisive mix of laughter and contempt. 'Big fucking deal. That was over ten bloody years ago. More, when you work it out. So why don't he just get over it?'

'Pity it wasn't you what got chewed up by fucking dogs.' Kevin was now very close to punching him.

'Have you two finished?'

Pete Mac looked at his brother-in-law for as long as he dared, then shrugged non-committally. What was the point in arguing? He never listened to him anyway.

'Good. Now let's get going.'

Brendan led the way over to the Kesslers' truck, and then climbed up the steps to the cab and rapped on the steamed-up window.

Jimmy Harris looked at his watch and groaned. Half four in the bloody morning. What now? It was bad enough the trouble he'd be in when he got back

14

home as it was. Nancy was bound to say it was his fault that he'd been told at the last minute to make an extra pickup in Spain. And his fault that the wait had sent him over his driving hours. Course it was his fault – even though the contact had never shown and so he might as well have kept on the road as originally planned. Everything was *always* his fault. That was to say, everything Nancy didn't like was his fault. Anything that went the way she wanted, well, that was an entirely different matter. Mind you, the stopover had been worth it. He'd had a right laugh with that bunch of Paddies he'd got talking to while he was hanging around. He still had the hangover to prove it. But Nancy'd never believe him even if he told her the truth. And as for trying to explain that it wasn't possible for him to push on because of the hours – good as useless. But he couldn't drive legally for another three hours, and that was that, because, as always, Daniel Kessler had warned him: don't do *anything* to draw attention to yourself or the rig, just do as you're told and you get the extra wedge. It was funny how she never complained about that.

And now some bugger was knocking on his window, disturbing his sleep. He couldn't move until at least half seven, and here was this arsehole about to tell him he had to get out of the lorry park. Well, he was just about ready for him.

Jimmy wound down the window. 'What?'

It took him no more than a split second to register

15

the face, but it still didn't make sense. 'O'Donnell?'

'Got it in one, moosh. Now we're gonna move this rig somewhere nice and private.'

'I don't think so.'

'Sorry?'

'Daniel and Sammy'd kill me stone dead. And if their nutty cousin Maurice found out, I'd be better off dead.'

'And you really think you should be more afraid of the Kesslers than of me?'

'Look here, O'Donnell –'

Even in the quiet of the early morning, the cloth wrapping on the lead pipe did its job, the contact with the man's skull making little more than a dull thwack.

Jimmy slumped sideways across the bench seat, a thin trickle of blood running from his nostril.

Brendan tossed the lead pipe into the cab and turned to Kevin. 'I'll go and get the Merc. Then I'll drive by here nice and slow and lead the way. You follow me in the truck, but not too close, all right? And, Pete, you bring up behind in the other motor.'

The black Mercedes, followed by the Kesslers' green truck, and then Kevin's maroon Cortina, were soon heading along a rural byroad that had become little used since the building of the nearby motorway. It was now almost enclosed, tunnel-like, by the overhanging branches of the trees that shielded it from the fields on either side.

Brendan flashed his lights twice then killed them as he pulled into a cinder-surfaced lay-by.

The others drove in behind him.

'Let's have the keys.' Brendan took the driver's keyring from Kevin and started working through them, searching for the one that matched the locks on the back of the truck.

Kevin stood beside him, watching silently.

Pete Mac leaned against the cab and lit a cigarette, kicking the back of his heel against the wheel rim. Why couldn't he have driven the truck? Brendan was treating him like a spare part again, and Pete Mac was getting really pissed off with it. Thirty-eight years old and still being treated like the fucking van boy.

It was then that he spotted the car. It was swerving all over the lane as if the driver had lost control.

Now here was a chance to show Brendan he deserved a bit of respect, and that he was just as capable as the others. He threw his unsmoked cigarette to the ground, searched hurriedly through the cab for the lead pipe, and then scrunched his way round to the back of the truck.

'Ssshh!' he warned the others. 'There's a motor coming.'

The three of them stepped back into the shadows just as the car skidded into the lay-by, scraping across the cinders as it came to a juddering halt. The driver either wasn't in the best of moods or was drunk. Maybe both.

'Shit,' spat Brendan. 'What does he want?'

Then the passenger door was flung open and a young woman in her late teens, wearing hot pants that barely covered her buttocks, got out and wobbled towards the lorry on thigh-high platform boots. She was followed by the car's driver, who was dressed rather more soberly in a heavy, floor-length army-surplus greatcoat.

'I gave you so many chances, Neil,' the girl gasped through her tears. 'I told you, if you so much as looked at one more girl, I never wanted to see you again. And what do you do? You go and snog my best friend.'

'How many more times? No, I didn't.'

'And how many more times have I got to tell *you*, you horrible pig? She told me, Neil. She told me what you did.' Her words started to catch as her sobbing grew louder. 'And I know it's true, because she said you had really wet lips.'

'But, Sookie . . .'

Sookie? Pete Mac stifled a laugh.

'You know it didn't mean anything. We'd all been drinking and smoking and messing about. It was nothing. Look, how about we get back in the car?'

He reached out to her, but she wouldn't let him touch her. He was getting seriously annoyed with this. They'd been driving around all night as he tried to explain that nothing had happened at the party, while she grabbed at the steering wheel and

18

demanded to be let out. Well, she'd got her wish now – they were standing in a lay-by in the middle of bloody nowhere, in the pouring rain.

Why couldn't that stupid Marsha have kept her mouth shut? It wasn't as if he'd screwed the silly cow. Mind you, if she'd have been up for it, he wouldn't have said no.

The girl threw back her head and wailed theatrically. 'I loved you, Neil Barrett.'

He dredged up his last bit of patience from somewhere very deep inside him. 'This has gone beyond being silly. Look at you, you're soaked through. And you must be freezing in that outfit. Come here, Sook. Come on.' His voice was now soft and cajoling. 'Let me give you a cuddle. Warm you up.'

'A cuddle? You must be joking, you animal. I've got no intention of ever getting back in that car with you ever again.' She pointed accusingly at the vehicle as if it were somehow as guilty as its driver.

'I know,' she went on, her chest rising and falling with temper. 'Why don't you go back to college and *cuddle* Marsha? I'm sure she'll be only too happy to oblige. Everyone knows she's the bloody common-room bike.'

Neil snorted dismissively. 'So how are you going to get home?'

'I'll hitch.'

'Fine, if you really want to be on the front page of

the papers tomorrow. *Student murdered by maniac.*
Just because she was too bloody stubborn to admit
she was wrong.'

'If you cared about me, you wouldn't have kissed
her in the first place.'

'Tell you what, I agree with you. So let's just
forget it, shall we?'

They heard the car door slam, and the window
being wound down, and then his sharp, angry voice:
'It's your bloody funeral.'

The car revved away into the early-morning
darkness.

Pete Mac was about to say something, but Brendan
slapped a hand over his mouth.

'Pig,' they heard her snivel, as she came round the
side of the truck and walked slam into them.

It was bad luck for Sookie that Kevin had decided
to bring Pete Mac with him, and also that Pete had
had just about enough of being told what to do.

This was the moment when he would prove, once
and for all, that he was more than capable of handling
difficult situations.

He tore Brendan's hand away from his mouth,
barrelled forward and smacked the girl across the
back of the neck with the lead pipe.

Her knees gave way, and she folded up on herself,
all neat and tidy like a pop-up book being closed after
a child's bedtime story.

Brendan dragged Pete Mac back into the hedge.

'Are you completely off your fucking nut?'

Pete Mac could barely speak with the injustice of it all. 'But you just whacked the driver.' He spat belligerently at Brendan's feet. 'What was I supposed to bastard do?'

They'd just finished hauling the girl up into the cab, shoving her in from the passenger's side, and wedging her fast against Jimmy's body, when a horsebox reversed smoothly up to the front of the Kesslers' truck.

'What the fuck's going on now?' Kevin was beginning to sound as agitated as he felt. This wasn't going well. And he couldn't help wishing that he'd left Pete Mac back in Stepney, or, better still, that he himself had stayed at home like Barry.

'It's okay,' said Brendan. 'Calm down. I'm expecting her.'

'*Her*?' Pete Mac wasn't agitated, he was furious. Left in the dark as usual. Why hadn't Brendan told him about any of this?

A young woman in her early twenties, wearing jeans and a waxed jacket, and with her long dark hair caught up high in a ponytail, jumped down from the driver's side of the horsebox and made straight for Brendan. She kissed him on the cheek and asked in a whisper: 'Where's the lorry driver?' Her accent was Irish, cultured.

'Don't worry about him.' Brendan winked, his

own gruff cockney sounding harsh in comparison. 'Dab of chloroform. Sleeping like a baby in the cab.'

She nodded to Kevin and Pete Mac and then turned back to Brendan. 'And where's Luke? Didn't fancy putting his hand to a bit of manual labour, I suppose? Or maybe this is too exciting for him.'

Her smile broadened into a grin, folding her cheeks into the dimples that made her look the image of Brendan's kid sister Catherine. And that had his stomach flipping over as his head filled with images of Catherine dying on the filthy couch in his father's scrapyard.

'Well?' she demanded.

'All right, Ellie, keep it down. We just didn't need him – okay?'

Pete Mac let out a grunt-like laugh. 'Why lie to her, Brendan? You know Luke's picking up Eileen later this morning.'

'She's coming out of prison?' asked Ellie, her eyes fixed on Brendan. 'Today?'

'Yeah.' Brendan returned his attention to the driver's keyring. 'Now, are we going to get this lot unloaded or what?'

Ellie reached up and touched his cheek. 'Are you going to meet her?'

Brendan bowed his head. 'I'm not sure.'

'She'll be expecting you.'

Brendan shrugged. 'Maybe.'

Pete Mac muttered something under his breath.

Brendan rounded on him. 'What did you say?'

'I said: it's not right having birds involved. They're too fucking soft for this sort of work.'

'If you must know, Pete, *Ellie* is driving some merchandise back over to Ireland for me.'

Ellie stared at Pete Mac, her eyes suddenly hard, as she pointed at the horsebox. 'There's a beautiful, sorrel bay filly in there. A truly gorgeous creature. And I'm responsible for that vehicle's safe delivery.'

'I don't get it.' Pete Mac screwed up his nose as if someone had just farted. 'If she's just moving horses about, then what's she doing here?'

'Because I've got a little surprise.' Brendan slapped the flat of his hand against the truck. 'Not only all the tobacco and hash that I hear the Kesslers have packed in nice and tight among these loads from Spain, but a little something extra that I had slipped in, while the driver was being entertained by friends of mine down in Fuengirola.' He chucked Ellie under the chin. 'And you're going to give it a lift over the water for me in the horsebox, ain't you, sweetheart?'

Brendan was pleased with Ellie, he knew she was bright, but she was also willing. She'd immediately done as she was told, keeping watch on the roadside, while he, Kevin and Pete Mac unpacked the avocado-green lavatories and washbasins from the back of the truck.

23

Ellie glanced over her shoulder every now and then, to check on their progress, noting the look of increasing puzzlement and then pleasure on Brendan's face as they searched carefully through the straw packing in the wooden crates. As he pulled out yet another of the plastic-wrapped parcels, each the size of a flattened bag of sugar, to add to the growing pile at his feet, he weighed it in his hand, and prodded it experimentally with his fingertip.

'Looks like my information was out of date, chaps. Seems like the Kesslers have been branching out.'

'There aren't just chaps here, you know, Brendan.'

Brendan grinned at Ellie's cheek. He hadn't seen much of his dad's 'little mistake' when she was growing up – though, God knows, just her very existence had irritated the hell out of his mother – but once Eileen had gone inside, Ellie had been able to get closer to her half-brothers. She seemed to fancy herself as a chip off the old O'Donnell block, and had become increasingly desperate to get away from the stud farm in Ireland, where she'd been kept hidden away all those years with his dad's sister Mary.

A life in London and a chance to work with Brendan, that's all Ellie wanted these days. And maybe if she carried on being as useful as this, perhaps Brendan would have no objection.

Satisfied that they had finally cleared out the whole lot, the three men stowed the packages in the boot of Kevin's car. Then Brendan rubbed his hands together to warm his fingers, and took a small, pencil-slim torch out of his pocket.

'And now for the little surprise I *was* expecting. The one I had planted. Ellie, you keep a lookout, girl.'

Holding the torch between his teeth, Brendan knelt on the ground, apparently oblivious of the damage the soaking wet cinders were doing to his trousers, and felt under the chassis, seeking out the clips he knew he would find there.

'Gotcha!' he said round the torch, as he released the smooth, cold metal.

What looked like the fuel tank suddenly came loose and dropped down on two sturdy brackets.

But it wasn't a fuel tank.

He opened the hidden lid of the metal container and stepped back, letting the other two men see inside.

'They're fucking guns,' gasped Pete Mac.

'Nothing gets by you, does it, Pete?' Brendan shone the torch so they could get a better look. 'And better to risk the necks of them bastard Kesslers bringing them over from Spain than risking our own, eh, lads?'

Brendan and Ellie worked together clipping the truck's dummy fuel tank to the underneath of the horsebox, Ellie occasionally breaking the silence with soothing noises to calm the filly whenever it spooked.

'Good girl,' said Brendan when they'd finished, in unconscious imitation of Ellie speaking to the horse. 'That was a nice job. Now drive carefully and smile at any nice man from customs who wants to have a talk with you, all right?'

'Sure, and don't I smile at all the fellers?'

'And you've got the address for the drop in Wicklow?'

'*Yes.*'

'Go on then. They'll be expecting you.'

The three men watched as Ellie drove off.

Pete Mac, not best pleased to have been left out of so many of the plans, edged closer to Brendan. 'Fancy getting your own sister involved in gun-running,' he needled. 'All them bad boys with all them bombs and that going off over there. It don't seem right to me.'

'Far as I can see, Pete, there's no more bombs over there than there are over here at the minute. And anyway, Ellie's my half-sister, not exactly the same, now is it?'

'Jesus, I've gotta hand it to you, Brendan. People reckon I'm a nasty bastard, but you've got no sentiment in you whatsoever.'

'Interested as I always am in your opinion, Pete, why the fuck don't you shut up and let me think? I've had it up to here with you and your fucking screw-ups.'

'*My what*?'

'Well, it ain't my frigging fault that we've got a dead girl on our hands, now is it? But it is up to me, of course, to come up with a way of dealing with it.' Brendan checked his watch again.

'It's gonna start getting light soon. So I want that truck torched before anyone starts nosing around. And make sure you rip the tart's clothes up first, and rub one of his spanners, or the wheel brace or something, in the blood. Make it look like he's tried it on with her and they've had a fight.'

He took out his car keys, tossed them in the air, and snatched them into his fist. 'Anthony's waiting for you over at the flat in Bow Common, so get over there and unload the gear with him, have yourselves some breakfast, and see me back at the cab office at, say, half ten, eleven.'

With that he walked over to his car and drove off as casually as if he'd just finished another ordinary day's work.

Chapter 2

Eileen O'Donnell stepped through the prison gate, threw back her head, and let the cold, fresh rain fall on her face. She crossed herself as she breathed the same prayer she'd uttered every day since she had finally got rid of Gabriel. She wasn't asking for forgiveness for what she had done – no, she had no regrets about that – but she desperately wanted guidance for her family. Because Eileen had plenty of regrets about them.

But now at least she was free. Or as free as a woman could be who had murdered her husband, and who had refused to let her children see her while she had done her time in prison.

Despite her greying hair and her much slimmer, almost skinny frame, Brendan spotted his mother straight away. If Ellie hadn't have said anything, he didn't know if he would actually have come, whether he'd have decided to wait until later, but he was here now . . .

He got out of the car and took a single step towards her. But then he stopped. There was a cluster of what could only be journalists making towards her.

Then someone else, a woman, calling his mother's name – *Eileen!* She was running towards her with an umbrella held out ready to protect her from the rain.

He could hardly take in what he was seeing. But it was her, he was sure of it now. It was Sophie Kessler, Harold Kessler's old woman. And Luke was running right along beside her.

Like they were together.

Brendan started running too, and, as he drew closer, he heard Sophie Kessler talking to his mother.

'Eileen,' she was saying, her face full of pity – *damn the interfering old cow*. 'I know all about my Sammy and Catherine. He told me everything. And I wanted you to know that I understand what you did.'

Brendan barged past her and grabbed Eileen's arm. 'My mother don't need your fucking understanding. Come on, Mum, come with me. I've got the motor over there.'

A burst of flashbulbs exploded in the grey morning air, followed by a barrage of questions.

'Mrs O'Donnell! Over here! Do you have any comment about your time inside?'

'Did you have special privileges because of who you are?'

'How did the other prisoners treat you, knowing you murdered Gabriel O'Donnell?'

'Eileen! Here! Are you worried about your sons following in their father's footsteps?'

Eileen didn't seem to notice them, nor did she look

at Brendan, she just stared down at his hand resting on her arm. 'Let go of me.'

She turned to Sophie Kessler. 'I'm very grateful for your words.'

Then she turned to Luke. 'You'll give Sophie a lift home, will you?'

Luke nodded, then jerked his thumb at the reporters. 'Brendan, get rid of them lot.'

Brendan stalked over to the huddle of raincoated men without a word, or at least without one that Luke could hear.

Sophie Kessler smiled pleasantly at Eileen. 'Don't worry about me, my love. I just wanted to be here today. You know, to see you out safely. You'll be wanting to be with your family just now. I'll go and find myself a cab.'

'We wouldn't hear of it, would we, Luke?' said Eileen.

Luke held open the back door of the car, gulping back the tears that were threatening to spill down his face, as he listened to the soft Irish voice of his mother. The voice still barely tinged with the cockney tones of her children. The voice he hadn't heard for eleven long years.

'You won't get a cab in this weather, Mrs Kessler,' he said, pulling himself together. 'Please, get in out of the rain. It'll be my pleasure to give you a lift.'

Luke made sure that Eileen and Sophie Kessler were settled in the back seat of the Daimler, before closing the door and turning to check on his brother.

Luke was surprised to find Brendan standing right behind him. He was holding a smashed camera, and the journalists were slouching away, muttering threats.

Before Luke could speak, Brendan was jabbing a finger in his brother's chest. '*It'll be my pleasure*?' His face contorted in disgust. '*Mrs Kessler*? Luke, what the fuck d'you think you're doing even talking to that woman?'

'Forget all that for now, Brendan. There's more important things to worry about. It's Barry Ellis. He got a tug. Early hours of this morning. His Sandy phoned me. She heard someone banging on the front door – guessed it had to be the law at that time – but she couldn't wake Barry up.' Luke rubbed his chin nervously. 'He'd had too much to drink, see. So she shot out the back and over the fence. I picked her up from a phone box and took her to one of my places over in Stratford.'

Brendan was *not* about to show any gratitude. 'You're being helpful for a change.'

'Don't have a go at me cos you've got the hump about Mum. I just thought you should know, that's all.' Luke took another step away from the car, moving closer to his brother. 'Cos let's face it, Brendan, it'd be a shame if anything happened to bring the law to the house today, and to upset Mum, wouldn't it? And anyway, even if Barry didn't work

31

for us, we've been mates with Sandy since we were kids. We owe her that much.'

Brendan took out his cigarettes and lit one, unable to say thank you, or well done, or even to argue. 'Was there any gear in the house?'

'Sandy reckons no, but I'm not so sure. Not now.' Luke paused. 'I made a few enquiries. They reckon, when they eventually woke him up, Barry lost it and gave one of the coppers a right whacking.'

'You're kidding?'

'No.'

'Why'd the silly fucker have to go and do that?' Brendan raked his fingers through his thick, black, collar-length hair, realising for the first time since he'd left the others in the lay-by that he was wet through. 'So even if there was nothing dodgy in the house then, there's sure to be plenty in there now?'

Luke shrugged. 'Reckon that's about the size of it.'

'I'll get into the office and make some calls.' Brendan tapped on the car window. 'See you later, Mum.'

Eileen looked straight ahead.

Luke got in behind the wheel. 'Right then, we'll take you home first, shall we, Mrs Kessler?'

'Thank you, dear, but just drop me in Oxford Street, if you don't mind. There's a few bits I need to pick up from Selfridges. Harold thinks I'm up here on a shopping trip. Though why he thought I came out so early!' It was typical Sophie, chatty and friendly as ever. She took off her chocolate-brown leather gloves and put them in her matching handbag, then unfastened the buttons of her camel cashmere coat and eased it away from her neck. 'You know, I've never seen it rain so hard.'

Eileen said nothing, nor did she do anything to try to make her damp, old-fashioned two-piece any more comfortable as it clung limply to her body. She just stared out of the window, watching the world flash by, a world that had somehow become so busy, fast and crowded. She felt stunned by the clatter, and colour, and rush of it all, the details coming at her like a kaleidoscope.

'You wait till you get home, Eileen,' Sophie was saying. 'You won't know the place. The East End's changed so much. The world's changed. There's this ridiculous new decimal nonsense – I still convert back to the proper, old money, or they have you over in the shops if you don't watch them. And then there are all these young girls, they think nothing of living off the welfare nowadays. No man involved, a lot of the time. Just girls by themselves with babies. Shocking.'

As she carried on her commentary on the changing world, Sophie didn't seem to notice that Eileen continued to gaze out of the rain-streaked window, sitting there as if she were alone, cocooned in her own place, where no one could reach her.

'And everyone goes abroad for their holidays now. Did you know that? Everybody. Never used to hear of that in our day, did you? Not unless you had a good business and were well off. And they've all got phones and cars – all of them – and central heating. They expect it, even on the estates. You should see the tower blocks that have shot up all over the place. And the kids running wild while their mothers sit about smoking and drinking coffee all day. Not like we used to live, eh, Eileen?'

Even Sophie was beginning to realise that she was prattling on, but what else could she do – sit there in silence?

'Me and Harold, we got fed up with the way things were going, so we moved out. We're in Essex now – Abridge. Nice place. Classy. My Harold thinks he's lord of the manor, the silly old sod. You should see him in his wellington boots when he takes the dogs out. Green they are, like the ones he's seen the neighbours wearing. An East End Jew in green wellies! I daren't laugh at him though, he's so touchy about things like that. He's still in charge of the businesses, of course, but the boys do most of the day-to-day stuff. Tell you what, you'll have to come over and see us sometime. Have a bit of dinner with us. Catch up on old times. And who knows, once you see the fields and trees, you might even want to buy a little bungalow for yourself out there. I'd like that, you being nearby. What d'you think, Luke, d'you think your mum'd like the countryside out our way?'

'Dunno, Mrs Kessler,' he said, smiling politely into the rear-view mirror. 'Not really thought about it.'

Sophie returned his smile with a weak effort of her own, relieved that at least one member of the O'Donnell family was acknowledging her. 'Hark at me, chatting on. I'm so excited to see your mum, I'm forgetting myself. So tell me, Eileen, tell me how you are.'

Eileen considered for a moment, and then at last the words came spilling out.

'I told the Review Committee that I'm a Catholic and I'm very sorry that someone died. It's not right that a man should have lost his life. But what I didn't say was that it might have been a sin, and a crime, but I'm glad I did it. Being in there was terrible, but I'd go through it all over again if I could have my Catherine back for just one day.'

Sophie could think of nothing to say so she patted Eileen's hand.

Eileen pulled away as if she'd been attacked. 'I'm sorry,' she said, her voice so small that Sophie and Luke could barely make out what she was saying. 'It's a long time since anyone's touched me without meaning me harm.'

In the O'Donnells' minicab office on the Bethnal Green Road, Pete Mac sat on the corner of the desk tapping the end of a pencil up and down like a drumstick.

Paula, the cab controller, pressed her headset closer to her ears. 'Sorry, love,' she said into the little hands-free speaker, 'you'll have to repeat that.' She flashed a look at Pete Mac. 'Only it's a bit noisy in here.'

Kevin Marsh screwed up his eyes as if in pain and grabbed the pencil from Pete's hand. 'Who are you? Keith Moon's ugly uncle?'

The door opened and Kevin swung round, knocking cold, sugary tea all over the bookings log. Paula said nothing, she just pulled a box of tissues from the desk drawer and began mopping up.

'Out the back,' said a grim-faced Brendan, walking straight past them.

'Brendan,' Kevin called after him as he followed him through into the private office. 'About Barry –'

'Yeah, I know, Kev. He didn't turn up this morning cos he got collared.'

'On my life, Brendan, I only just found out. Sandy called my Gina and she called me here. I swear I didn't know.'

Pete Mac pulled a face to show he doubted that very much indeed.

Brendan dropped down into a tan leather armchair that stood beside the big black ash desk in the back office. 'What I've heard is that they pulled a fucking drugs raid on him – the bastards. As if I don't pay them enough to leave us alone, they have to go and fit up poor old Barry for dealing.'

Kevin felt as if his breakfast was about to make a reappearance. 'I think it's a bit worse than that, Brendan. He went off his head and gave one of the coppers a good hiding.'

Brendan forced the heels of his thumbs into his eyes. 'So I heard.'

Pete Mac puffed out his already chubby cheeks. 'I bet they got the right needle with him over that.'

'No?'

For once, Brendan's sarcasm silenced Pete immediately, but it didn't stop Kevin. He wanted to make it very clear that he hadn't known what had happened to Barry. 'Yeah. And they've fitted him up for some other nonsense as well, over Haggerston way. A post-office job. They're saying he smashed the clerk's head in with a pickaxe handle in front of a queue of punters waiting for their fucking pensions or something. But everyone knows he ain't got the bottle for nothing like that since he found Stevie Shea.'

Pete Mac rolled his eyes – here we go again, more excuses for that bloody moron.

Kevin glared at him. 'And my Gina wanted to go over and see if Sandy was all right, Brendan, but she said she had to keep her head down for a few days. Keep out of the limelight.'

'Yeah, don't worry yourself about Sandy. Luke's got her sorted out.' Brendan dragged the nails of both hands through the dark shadow of stubble on his chin. 'But all I can do for Barry right now is to get a brief over to see him. And anyway, we've got other things to worry about.' He stood up. 'I've got to get home for a bit, get changed and shaved, and I want you two to get yourselves back over to Bow Common and move Kessler's gear into one of the new lock-ups. And tell Anthony to give the place a good clean-up. We've got no idea who might be nosing around later. Or what might have been said.'

Despite it being against his habit or inclination to ever question Brendan, Kevin felt compelled to speak up for his old friend. 'Barry would never grass anyone up, Brendan.' But then he paused and added quietly, 'Not if he's in his right mind, he wouldn't.'

'In his right mind?' Pete Mac threw up his hands. 'You said it, Kev. The bloke's a bloody nut job.'

Chapter 3

Brendan took the stairs two at a time down into the big basement kitchen of the house on the Mile End Road where he had lived for all of his thirty-five years.

He was a fit man, apparently at ease with himself, and in control of everything that surrounded him. But those few who knew him well would have noticed the bottom lip drawn back between his teeth and the slightly narrowed eyes, and would have realised that, in reality, he was desperately trying to control his temper as he figured out why things weren't going the way he wanted them to.

He checked out the room. Eileen was sitting stiffly upright in an easy chair next to the now redundant kitchener that had become little more than a shelf for displaying an arrangement of dried flowers and wheat ears. Then there was Luke sitting at the perfect pine table that Brendan had bought to replace the one that had been in the kitchen since Eileen and Gabriel had first moved into the house all those years ago. Caty, his twelve-year-old niece, was sitting across from her Uncle Luke staring morosely through drooping curtains of glossy, chestnut-brown hair, while her mother, Patricia, was busying herself filling the kettle at the shiny stainless-steel sink. High above her, the narrow window, set up in the wall at street level, let in little of the grey mid-morning light, streaked as it was with the rain that was still coming down in sheets.

'D'you like the way I had the place done up for you, Mum?' Brendan asked, tossing his keys down on the table. 'The old place don't look too bad, does it, eh?'

Eileen didn't reply.

Patricia looked over her shoulder at the elder of her two brothers. 'Tea, Brendan?'

'Thanks.' He straddled a chair, facing his mother, and tried again. 'I suppose you've heard about these petrol shortages and all this electricity blackout shit – sorry, Mum, I forgot myself – all this blackout business that's going on. Well, none of it's going to worry you. I'll see to that. You won't want for anything. And what do you think of your new cooker? It's got what they call a griddle and everything. You'll be able to cook a turkey in that thing as big as our Luke's head come Christmas.'

Still no response.

Caty stared down at the table, her eyes as blue as Brendan's had been at her age – before he'd taken to the drink almost as enthusiastically as his father had done before him. She was absorbing every awkward moment.

Brendan wouldn't let it go. 'Why didn't you let us come and see you, Mum?'

'In that place?'

He sat up straight. At least she'd answered him. 'We were all so worried about you. You should have let us visit. It wasn't right keeping us away.'

Patricia set down the tea things next to Brendan, deliberately making them clatter against the tray. 'Luke's doing well for himself, aren't you, Luke? Tell Mum about your business, go on.'

Brendan was about to light a cigarette, but instead he pulled it from his mouth, flicked off his lighter and cut off his brother before he could say a single, boastful word. 'Yeah, Luke's doing really well, Mum. But you know him, he's far too modest to say so himself. He's got properties all over the place. Even some right over in Stratford, Plaistow and Forest Gate. He's bought up all these houses and turned them into flats. Just like old man Kessler used to over in Notting Hill. Mind you, Luke's the first one to get in round that way, so there's no real competition, no threat from any nasty Rachman types for him to worry about. Not like Harold Kessler had. And now he's the regular king of the slum landlords round there, aren't you, mate? Gets them old tenants out no trouble. And now – this is a bit of a new venture – a few of his places have some very attractive young ladies living in them and all.'

41

Luke jumped to his feet. 'What's got into you, Brendan? Today of all days.'

'What, my business is always *dirty*, is it, but anything you set up is somehow clean? Don't get it myself, Luke. Maybe Mum understands.'

Eileen, recognising how close she was to weeping, dropped her chin until it almost touched her chest, and put her fingertips to her mouth – so much bad feeling between her children. Bad blood some would say. And maybe they were right.

Caty held the glass of milk that Patricia had given her, eyeing Brendan, the uncle she rarely saw, and Eileen, the grandmother she didn't know at all, over the rim. She was fed up being treated like a child. Everyone kept everything from her. But these people were her family, and, creepy as they were, she was entitled to know what was going on with them. It was bad enough being sent to the rotten church school in Wanstead now she was in the seniors. The girls there all thought she was dead common, living in Stepney, and all the girls in Stepney thought she was a snob because of the disgusting uniform she had to wear. It was as if she didn't fit in anywhere, even in her own family. It was all so unfair.

Patricia slapped her hands on the table. 'Right, Caty,' she said, trying, but failing to sound cheerful. 'We'd better be going, love.'

'Mum!' She dragged the word out to three whining syllables. 'I've not finished my milk yet.'

'And I thought you were always saying you hated the stuff. Now come on.'

'Sit down, Pat.' Brendan kneaded his temples with his thumbs. 'Let's just forget it, all right?' He sighed loudly and then turned on a smile. 'You can have a bath later on, Mum. I've had the boxroom converted into a bathroom, and a top-of-the-range suite put in for you. Dark claret it is. With gold taps shaped like dolphins. It's got a shower cubicle and everything. Looks like a posh hotel up there. And wait till you see the cream shag pile I've had put through the house.'

Eileen raised her head and looked at her daughter. 'I think I'll be going up for a rest.'

Brendan felt panic rising from his stomach to his chest. He had to take control. 'I gave Pat the money to get you a load of nice clobber and all, Mum. It's up in your new wardrobes. I had them fitted by this firm from down the Roman. White they are, with brass handles. Really smart. One of them's got a mirror that covers the whole door.'

Patricia picked up her handbag. 'Brendan, just leave it for now, eh? Mum needs a bit of time. She's tired. Come on, Caty, don't let me tell you again, Nanny wants a bit of peace.'

'I'll get one of the lads to drive you.'

'It's okay, Brendan, I've got the car.'

'What – I can't do anything for anyone no more? So what's wrong with my help all of a sudden?'

'Pat's right, Brendan,' said Luke, ruffling Caty's

hair. 'We should let Mum rest. Come and get your coat, Caty, and I'll see you out.'

As Caty reluctantly followed her uncle over to the stairs that led up to the ground-floor hallway, Eileen rose to her feet.

'Wait.' She reached out to her daughter and hugged her, holding her close. Then she walked hesitantly over to her grandchild.

Doing her best to smile, Eileen brushed her lips against the top of Caty's head, breathing in the scent of her hair. 'You're a beautiful, beautiful girl, Caty. And I'm so proud of you. You're just how I've imagined you all these years.' She stepped back to look at her, holding her at arm's length. 'And that gorgeous auburn hair. It made a great mix, your mum being a brunette and your dad being a redhead. You probably won't believe this, but you're the girl of my dreams. I used to fall asleep at night and see you. And you're exactly like I hoped you'd be. All I could ever wish for. Your mum's done a grand job with you.'

Eileen closed her eyes, her chest rising and falling as she felt the air filling her lungs – air that hadn't been breathed in and out by all those other women. Then she turned and took her daughter's hand. 'So, Patricia, how is he then?' Another hesitation. 'Pete Mac.'

'You know him, Mum, same as ever. We're all fine.'

Eileen nodded as if she were no longer listening.

'I'll be off now.' With that, she climbed unsteadily up the stairs and left them standing in the kitchen staring after her.

Patricia blew her nose. 'She looks so old.'

Brendan was stunned. After all he'd done for her – not a word for him. Not a single, bloody word. Having a kid, was that really all it took to get her to be proud of you? How fucking hard could that be? He'd settle down with Carol and have a bloody houseful of kids if that's what she wanted. And it'd be something her precious Luke wasn't ever likely to beat him at, not unless some sort of miracle happened that changed him overnight into a real man.

Luke took Patricia and Caty out to their car and then came back down to the kitchen. He was concentrating on buttoning up his long, black leather coat, anything to avoid looking his brother in the eye. The last thing he wanted was another row, but he couldn't leave without saying something.

'Nice one, Brendan. You managed to upset everyone in one single pop. That takes some doing that does, even by your standards.'

'Not staying, Luke?' Brendan opened one of the new oak kitchen units and took out a bottle of brandy. 'Better things to do up Soho, have you? Got some nice feller waiting for you?'

'If I had, do you really think I'd tell you? Wait for you to laugh at me? Call me filthy names?'

45

'You bring it on yourself.'

'Look, Brendan, this ain't to do with me. It's Mum I'm thinking of.'

'Blessed St Luke of fucking Stepney.'

'Just listen to yourself, will you? This is all too much too soon for Mum. Go easy on her at least till she settles back in.'

Luke started back up the stairs, but then turned and looked at his brother. 'Before I go, I just want to say one more thing. While you were mouthing off about me and my properties, Brendan, I didn't hear you complaining about that gaff of mine over Bow Common I lent you to stow your hookey gear. Or about the place I came up with for Sandy to stay in.'

'Just piss off, will you, Luke? And leave me alone.'

Brendan sat by himself at the table with the still-full bottle in one hand and an unused glass in the other. He had been there for almost an hour, fighting his craving to drink the stuff until he was insensible, so he could just wipe away all his resentment at Luke, the resentment at him being their mother's favourite that had come flooding back – just as if she'd never been away. But, as always, he was also battling with his terror of turning into his father.

He couldn't stand it any longer. He got up and emptied the alcohol down the sink.

He threw the bottle in the bin and filled the kettle

46

instead. Perhaps he really should think about settling down. Why not marry Carol and have kids? He'd have to do it one day. Why not sooner rather than later? And why not with her? He was sick of being treated like he didn't matter in his own poxy home. Let his mother try and ignore him when he had a whole tribe of little chavvies running around the place.

He spooned coffee into a mug and glanced up at the wall clock. Ellie should be well on the way to the ferry by now.

Christ, his mother was going to be shocked – no, not shocked, she'd have fucking kittens – once she realised just how far her husband's bastard had ingratiated herself with the family, especially with Eileen's beloved Luke. And all while she'd been rotting away in prison . . .

But she still wasn't going to be half as shocked as Brendan had been that morning, when that Kessler woman had turned up and had got into Luke's car just like she had every right.

That whole fucking family made him sick to his stomach. They had more front than bastard Brighton.

Chapter 4

brendan twenty. twenty-five to prin . . . . nd set of
something, because she to many, making the d
going to an opium den, but your aesthetic hadn't felt
an American back-bencher to life. The rest of home
he back in the bad fresh you'd have ever could have
became subtle. It was under smell. I by been white

He might have been standing in a drab, cement-floor
lock-up, behind a row of grubby terraced houses in
Leyton, with the only light coming from a single,
bare swinging bulb, but Brendan was no longer the
sour-faced man who had left his mother to her rest
just a few hours earlier. In fact, his mood had
improved no end, and he was looking very pleased
indeed.

'Bloody hell, we've had a right touch here. Look at
this little lot.' He ran his hand over the stacks of
plastic-wrapped packets that half filled the runs of
wooden shelving standing against the far wall. 'I
knew there was a lot, but when you see it in the light,
all set out like this . . .'

'I don't know about you, Brendan,' said Anthony,
who usually looked after the O'Donnells' working
girls, but who, because of his enormous size, was also
brought in on other jobs when a bit of extra muscle
might be called for, jobs such as collecting money
owed, frightening people who stepped out of line – or
minding valuable merchandise – 'but I reckon that's
speed.'

'Well, it definitely ain't the packets of Golden

Virginia we was expecting.' This wasn't just one of his sometimes terrifying mood swings, Brendan was genuinely happy. Okay, his mum wasn't acting as if she was exactly pleased to see him, but he was going to work on that, and anyway, he knew he had to cut her some slack. It was understandable her being a bit confused after what she'd been through. But why shouldn't he be happy? He had all that lovely dough to look forward to from the arms run. And now, to cap it all, here was this very nice, and unexpected, little bonus.

As far as Brendan knew, speed hadn't been a part of the Kesslers' trade – not until now. His information was that they had decided a few years ago to stick to importing what they knew – hash, rolling tobacco and porn films. It was where they had the contacts, and they'd made good, regular money. Life had been easy, and they had been content. But they'd obviously changed their markets, realised that it was speed that was getting to be the real earner.

It made Brendan laugh. If you read the papers or listened to people talking, you'd think there was no money about, that the whole bloody country was in trouble. But he'd heard the dealers who supplied the clubs and pubs saying how they couldn't get enough of the stuff. It was what all the kids wanted now. And not only the kids. The older lot didn't mind a bit of it, if it came in pill form.

He was looking at a very tidy little sum on those shelves.

But best of all, what made Brendan the happiest, what made his grin so wide, was that it had once *all belonged to the Kesslers*. Every last grain of it.

Sweet.

Kevin puffed out his cheeks. 'They must be well in with customs if this is the kind of load they're bringing in.'

'Too true, Kev.' Brendan did another mental count of the packages; it was like bloody Christmas come early. 'Anthony, what's that kid's name?' he asked over his shoulder. 'You know, the one who hangs around in Arty Burns's snooker hall. Always goes in there alone. Obviously doing a bit of trade.'

'The freaky-looking one with the big-soled boots and all that blond curly hair?'

'That's him.' Brendan's hand went unconsciously to his immaculately tied silk tie – stylishly wide but nothing lairy, that wasn't his way. 'Dresses like a clown.'

'That's Milo,' said Anthony. 'Timmy Flanagan's youngest.'

'Yeah, old Timmy's boy – God rest his soul. Go and get him and bring him round the cab office. I might have a job for the young chap.'

Brendan took a final look at the shelves, and then walked over to the narrow access door that had been set into the up-and-over shutter. He stepped outside, checking that no one was hanging around in the alley.

'By the way,' he said, poking his head back inside the lock-up. 'Either of you got any idea where that prick Pete Mac's got to?'

Kevin's and Anthony's embarrassed shrugs told Brendan everything he needed to know. His brother-in-law was hanging around with some tart somewhere.

Christ, he really was a waste of space. If he hadn't have been married to Patricia, he'd have been long gone, Brendan would have seen to that. Still, at least when he was screwing around he wasn't causing anyone any trouble.

Pete Mac smiled contentedly. He had met the two Liverpudlian sisters in a club a couple of weeks ago. They'd had a few laughs about the three of them being redheads. The girls had given them his number and he hadn't thought much more of it. That's what birds did when you bought them drinks. But then, and he still couldn't believe his luck, he'd been going through his jacket pockets, checking for handker-chiefs with lipstick on them, odd earrings, that kind of thing – otherwise there'd be more nagging when Patricia took his suit to the dry-cleaner's – when he'd come across the cigarette packet with their number scribbled on it.

Why not? he'd thought.

Now, not only was he lying here in a big double

bed in a hotel – well, a B & B – in Paddington, having had a big smile brought to his face by the two very cute red-haired sisters – three redheads in a bed, there must be a word for it, yeah: bliss! – but the girls reckoned that back home everyone knew they were two of the best hoisters in the business. And now they were talking about settling in London for a while, and – this was the tasty bit – lifting to order for him. Fur coats, jewellery, and all that fancy gear that posh birds, and tarts with old men who had a few quid, couldn't get enough of. And all he had to do was get them a flat.

Would he be interested?

Now, let's think about it. He was thirty-eight years of age. His wife took no notice of him. His kid had more time for Luke, her fruit of an uncle, than she did for him. Brendan treated him like he had shit for brains and had no right to do anything – even though he'd been part of the bloody family since he was a teenager – and he still paid him wages like he was a fucking employee.

So, would he be interested . . .

Not many, Benny!

Pete Mac might as well have died and gone to heaven.

As Anthony walked through the door, a few people looked up. But most of the men, and they were all men, carried on smoking, chalking cues, and taking apparently languid, but actually totally focused shots at the coloured balls on the dozen tables that filled the twilight world of Arty Burns's personal fiefdom – a snooker club over a row of shops on the Barking Road in Plaistow.

The only person really to take notice of his entrance was Arty himself, who, compared to Anthony's mountain-like build, was more like a small molehill.

'Anthony! Surprised to see you here today. How are you? Let me get you a beer. Something stronger? You do remember you picked up Mr O'Donnell's share two days ago, don't you? We've not got anything like full cash boxes again, not yet. You can look for yourself. Would you prefer a cuppa tea? Cheese roll or something? Nice and fresh they are. The old girl in the baker's made them up for me this morning.'

As Anthony put one of his huge hands on the man's shoulder, he felt the little man's skinny frame become rigid with fear. 'You're all right, Arty. I'm here looking for someone.' He stretched out his arm and beckoned with a saveloy finger to a relaxed-looking man in his twenties, who was leaning against the door jamb of the lavatory, hands in his pockets and a self-contented smile on his face. 'And he's standing right over there.'

The young man raised his eyebrows, pointed to himself and mouthed, 'Me?'

Despite his misgivings, Anthony nodded. He was

sure that Brendan knew what he was doing – he couldn't have run all his businesses so successfully if he didn't – but this bloke made Anthony feel very uncomfortable. Anthony himself had made one or two concessions to changing fashion: his shirt had a longish collar, his jacket had a bit of a waist and his lapels were wide. He even had a droopy moustache – although that wasn't really from choice, he thought it looked daft with his shaven head, but his wife had insisted he grow it, so that had been that.

But this bloke was something else.

Big, blond, permed afro hair; flared, dark red, velvet trousers, pink shirt – pink, for Christ's sake! – a paisley kipper tie, rainbow-striped tank top, and blue platform-soled boots.

Brendan was definitely right about one thing: he could have stepped straight out of the circus.

Deep breath. 'You're Milo Flanagan.'

Milo nodded cheerfully. 'That's me.' His accent was pure East End. At least there was something normal about him.

'Brendan O'Donnell wants to see you.'

'I'll get me coat.'

Anthony might have known to expect the fur-trimmed, floor-length embroidered afghan.

Milo winked at Paula as Anthony hurriedly steered him through the minicab office and into the doorway of the private room at the back.

54

Brendan was waiting for them.

He was about to invite them in, but he didn't have the chance. Before Anthony could stop him, Milo was across the room with his hand extended in enthusiastic greeting, like a hyperactive candidate canvassing votes before a general election.

'Hello, Mr O'Donnell.'

'You've heard of me.'

'Course I have. Everyone's heard of the O'Donnells. My old feller was always saying how he knew the family.' He turned to Anthony to reinforce his point with a friendly grin, and then back to Brendan. 'Your dad made you lot famous.'

'Yeah, the old man was a legend.' Brendan pointed Milo towards one of the leather chairs. 'But me, I'm different. Gabriel wanted to know everyone – and wanted everyone to know him. He loved it, being seen with all the faces in the pubs and clubs, and hanging around with all the celebrities and stars. But me, I like keeping what they call a low profile. I value my private life, see, because I'm a businessman, and being private's a sensible thing to be. That's why I employ people for their skills. They do their job, and, other than that, I don't wanna know. So long as they keep their noses clean, and don't draw attention, they lead their own lives.'

'Cool with me, Mr O'Donnell.' Milo made himself comfortable, folding his arms and resting a booted ankle on his knee. 'Now, I'm guessing that if you wanna talk to me it'll be about drugs.'

'You're a straightforward bastard, I'll give you that.'

Milo shrugged, his afghan moving up from his narrow shoulders like a living creature. 'No point in beating about the bush, you being a businessman and everything. And I know that you know my business is drugs. Just another commodity to be bought and sold. And I'm good at that – buying and selling.'

Milo was clearly warming to his topic. 'You see, it's simple, Mr O'Donnell. At the bottom of the heap, there's the pushers. They're the ones who get the kids interested. Hang around the school gates and that. They let 'em have the gear for a good price – good quality and all – get 'em hooked and reel 'em in. Now the pushers, they buy their bits and pieces from local dealers, and they in turn buy from the bigger dealers, the ones who supply on a more serious level. And them dealers – they buy from the importers. And the importers do their business with the producers.' He rubbed his hands together. 'Importing. Very nice game. I'm gonna have some of that one day.'

Anthony winced. He was talking to Brendan as if he was an amateur. He might have heard of the family, but did this little herbert really have the first idea who he was talking to?

'But until then, what can I do for you, Mr O'Donnell?'

Brendan looked at Anthony and exploded with laughter. 'Cheeky little fucker, i'n he?'

Harold Kessler was sitting in what his wife called his den, a large room overlooking the grounds at the back of their Essex mansion. Hidden behind high walls and electronic gates, the recently built house looked as if it might belong to a pop star or a footballer. But Harold was neither of those, he was the head of the Kessler family, and the one with ultimate responsibility for the family businesses – businesses which might be described as being slightly less conventional than either sport or music. Although it could, in all honesty, be said that he was also in the entertainment industry. Then there was the haulage company, a very useful sideline and cover for their other activities, and, very importantly, a convenient explanation for the family's wealth.

Harold Kessler's sons Daniel and Sammy sat on the large, deep-buttoned plum velvet sofa that ran along one expensively – if flashily – flock-papered wall, while his nephew, Maurice, lolled in a wing-backed chair, his leg slung over one of the arms. A not unusual scene in the Kessler household, because although the 'boys' were now in their thirties and had places – and a succession of casual relationships – of their own, when they weren't working or playing, the three of them spent most of their time at Harold and Sophie's place in Abridge. And it had to be said that

57

Daniel's supposed live-in girlfriend Babs didn't object to the arrangements. She and their three children – David, Michelle and Paul – lived in a nice detached house in Gidea Park, handy for her mum and dad's place on the estate at Harold Hill, and near the market, park and schools. Everything that Babs had ever wanted, in fact.

What was unusual on this dull, November afternoon was the presence of two police officers, each balancing Sophie Kessler's second-best china on their knees as if they were having tea with the vicar – or perhaps the rabbi.

'So, the way we see it, at the moment, the best bets are, from the look of it,' one of the officers continued, tiptoeing carefully through the minefield of suggestions, 'is that your driver had been having it away with the bird, and her husband's found out and he's had them. And burnt out the truck in temper.' Pause. 'Unless she was just a hitchhiker who came unstuck with her choice of lift. But that wouldn't explain the fire, of course.' Another, longer, more awkward pause. 'But you know what vandals are like nowadays.' He took a mouthful of the now cold tea, then added a bit feebly: 'They'll put a match to anything.'

Luck was with the officer. Harold Kessler had no interest in making him squirm. Not today.

'Thank you, gentlemen,' Kessler said, with an apparently obsequious dip of his shiny bald head. 'You've been a real help over this terrible business.

Two deaths, such a waste.' He tutted sadly. 'I'll contact my insurance company. Tell them what you said. Doesn't seem as though anything need be too difficult about the claim. Now . . .' He opened the desk drawer and took out a thick padded envelope. 'My son, Danny, will see you out.' He handed the packet to the officer who had done all the talking. 'A little thank-you for your kindness, gentlemen. For the widows' and orphans' fund, of course.'

'Of course, thank you, Mr Kessler. Very generous.'

Daniel, solemn as an undertaker, showed the men out to their car. When he returned, his expression was rather different. He dropped down on the sofa next to his brother.

'Top-quality fucking speed that was, Dad. Good enough to cut to at least double the quantity. Maybe more. And it had to be this time we lost it. The time I risked bringing in enough of the fucking stuff to spot for all the gaffs I had lined up for the massage parlours. Twelve properties, and all at just the right sodding price, and in the perfect bloody area. Good as in my hands they were. I was gonna start having all the East End trade right out of that queen Luke O'Donnell's hands. And what happens? This. So what am I gonna do now? Ask the Baxters if I can have the places on fucking HP? I'm gonna look a right bleed'n mug.'

Sammy reached over and patted his brother's leg.

'Sorry, Dan. I know how long you've been planning this.'

Daniel held his head in his hands, flattening the springy blond, Pre-Raphaelite curls that had, at last, come into fashion. But style was the last thing on Daniel's mind.

'I'd bet my last fiver it was them O'Donnells who did this. It's got their fucking name written all over it. That dirty-eyed bastard of a driver must have found out what he was carrying and gone and told them.' He gripped his hands into tight, angry fists. 'The fucker's just lucky he burnt to death before I got hold of him. Cos I tell you what, the O'Donnells are gonna be sorry they ever did this to me.'

Harold raised his shoulders and spread his arms in an extravagant shrug. 'So it's happened the once, son, and it's very upsetting. But do we really want to start all that business again with the O'Donnells? We're not doing too badly, are we, boys? The Soho shops are making us a nice living with the films and magazines. And the betting always shows a good profit.' He took a cigar from the humidor on the inlaid rosewood desk. 'And, thank God, at least they left no evidence in the truck.'

'It gets to me, Dad, that's all. That lot come out on top every bloody time, while we scratch around, having to be grateful for whatever business the bastards *allow* us to get on with.'

Maurice put down his cup and saucer on the onyx

and brass side table, swung himself around off his chair and strolled across the room to the window behind Harold's desk. He looked out at the mist gathering over the river that ran along the bottom of the garden.

'Do you know,' he said, his Manchester accent still as broad as on the day he had first been sent by his parents to stay 'for a bit' with his Uncle Harold's family in London, 'I love the life I've got down here, and, like Danny, I hate the thought of them Irish bastards messing with it. So, if you're interested, like, I know how to get hold of a bit of scratch in a hurry. In fact,' he turned to face them, his face cracking into a nasty grin, 'I've got the perfect plan.'

Perfect plan?

They should have realised there and then that there was going to be a problem.

'The way we get the stake for your property, Danny, is with a bank job. A big one. I've been working on it for a while now. And you and Sammy are more than welcome to be part of it, cos it's gonna take a team. Not a big one, just the three of us.' He smiled politely at his uncle. 'No offence, Harold, but this is a young man's game.'

Harold didn't look offended, he looked sceptical. As did his two sons. Very sceptical.

Maurice sat himself down and waited for their reaction.

Daniel was the first to speak. 'Look, Maury, I know you're family – so I'm really sorry to have to say this – but, first thing that comes to my mind is, why didn't you tell us about it before – if you really have been planning it for so long?'

Maurice was about to interrupt, but Daniel ploughed on. 'And second, we all know how you get. Let's face it, you're not a calm bloke, are you? And I really don't know if I wanna take the risk of you getting all twitchy, and doing something that I might think's a bit daft. Like you getting bored and pissing off and leaving us there roasting on the pavement.'

Maurice grinned happily, more than pleased with himself. 'That's what you don't understand, feller. We won't be going across the pavement. We are going to pay Mr Bank Manager a private visit at his lovely home in Surrey.'

Sammy looked imploringly at his father. 'Dad, you tell him.'

Harold Kessler shrugged. 'Maybe you should think about it boys. Sounds less risky than going in team-handed into the local high-street branch and putting the wind up the tellers. All these bloody have-a-go heroes crawling out of the woodwork, wanting their pictures in the papers, they're making it dangerous out there.'

'All right then, Maury, sell it to us. Prove you've thought it through.' Daniel Kessler sounded about as convinced as his brother looked, but he wanted those properties and, to do the deal, he needed a proper stake.

When Maurice had finished outlining the bare bones of his plan, he sat back in his chair, speech over, ready for questions.

And Daniel had plenty of those. He and his family had seen and done some pretty unpleasant things in their time – it was part of the tough and violent world in which they had chosen to live – but his cousin Maurice was a one-off and could shock even him. So he wanted to be very clear about what exactly this job would involve.

'You absolutely, stone-bonking guarantee we're not taking any guns, and that there's no strangers involved? Just you, me and Sammy. We're all the team that's needed?'

'Positive, feller. Two of us hold the wife in the house – big, scary, bad men, like – while the manager takes the other one of us to the bank. Then he opens the vault, gives us the cash, and before you know it we're back home. You've got the money you need for your properties, we've got a nice cut for ourselves – and a divvy for Uncle Harold, of course – and the fleet's lit up, feller. Simple as that.'

'We're gonna have to think about this.'

'Think all you like, Dan, but I'm gonna go in there in two weeks' time with two blokes willing to help me. I'll leave it up to you whether you're one of them or not.'

Harold broke the ensuing silence. 'I know you've all got a lot on your minds, boys, but come on, this won't buy the baby a new bonnet.' He pulled back his sleeve, exposing a sparkling, diamond-encrusted watch. 'Time you three shifted your arses up to Soho to check they've all got plenty of stock in, and while you're at it, you can pay a visit round the betting shops to make sure no one's having a weed. Expensive time, Christmas, and I don't want any of them bastards thinking he can treat his old woman to a mink stole on the strength of my earnings.'

When Sophie poked her head round the door of the den, Harold was lounging back in his chair, luxuriating in the ritual of lighting a cigar.

'They all gone?' she asked, collecting the dirty teacups and saucers on to a tray. 'The boys and the law?'

'All gone,' puffed Harold through a veil of lavender-blue smoke, and then added absently, 'So how was Eileen?'

Sophie perched on the edge of the sofa, facing her husband's desk and set the tray down on the floor. 'It's so sad, Harold. I think she's going to have a right time of it, adjusting to life outside again. I tried my best to get through to her, but I don't think she heard a word I said. It was like talking to a brick wall.'

She shook her head sadly. 'I just hope her daughter, or her boy, can help her.'

Harold frowned. 'Her boy? What, Brendan?'

'No, I mean Luke.'

'Him?'

'I know he's as bent as a nine-bob note, Harold. God help him. But he's a kind boy. Thoughtful. He gave me a lift, you know. Wanted to bring me all the way home. But I said that wasn't a good idea, that I'd told you I'd gone shopping.'

'Yeah?' said Harold, looking down his nose to study the red-hot tip of his Cohiba as he puffed away, drawing in the smoke.

'I didn't want Luke telling that brother of his that you knew I'd gone to meet Eileen. You know, Harold, that Brendan really is a nasty bit of work. There was his poor mother, bewildered by everything, upset, standing there in the pouring rain. And him? He wanted a row.'

She stood up. 'And there were all these newspaper people there, shouting questions and taking pictures of her.' She bent down to pick up the tray. 'I don't suppose they had a clue who I was, do you?'

Chapter 5

Brendan was whistling cheerily to himself as he turned the key to the street door of Carol Mercer's house. It was a three-bedroom end-of-terrace on a new estate in Hackney that Brendan had 'arranged' for her to move into through a friend of his – a friend who was something to do with the council. It wasn't a place he'd have chosen – Stepney and Spain did for Brendan – but she loved it, treating it more like a doll's house than a home, forever rearranging the furniture, getting new curtains and cushions, polishing and cleaning . . . And that was all just fine by Brendan. In his experience, if you kept a bird happy, then you saved yourself a lot of grief. And Brendan was going to make her a very happy bird indeed – he was going to marry her. And Christ knows, she'd been nagging him about settling down for long enough. And it would certainly get his mother approving of him for once.

'Carol, you ready, girl?' he called down the hall, staying outside on the step so he could keep an eye on the Morris Marina he'd borrowed from a driver at the cab office. If she was going to keep him hanging around, he'd have to treat one of the little chavvies playing football in the street to mind the car. It was hardly like leaving his Merc out there, but he'd appreciated the loan, and didn't want the bloke's motor getting damaged.

'Course I am, lover.' Carol came out of the back bedroom and wiggled her way along the passage towards him. She was wearing brown, knee-length suede boots, a mid-calf orange dress that was slashed almost to the crotch, and which dipped into a low V at the neck. The outfit seemed to be held together by nothing more than the metal-studded, brown suede belt she had slung low on her hips. She put her hands behind her head, puffing up her already big blonde hair. Standing as she was against the geometrically patterned silver wallpaper that dazzled visitors as they entered the place, she made quite a sight.

'So, what do you think?'

Brendan eyed her admiringly. 'Beautiful as ever, darling. And if we weren't going out . . .'

She lowered her chin and peered up at him through heavily mascaraed lashes. 'Seeing as you're in such a good mood, we could always go out later.'

'Tempted as I am, babe, I've gotta shoot round to see Sandy Ellis first. Make sure she's all right, and that there's no . . .' He hesitated, weighing up how much he could trust a bird like Carol. 'Problems.'

Carol's hands dropped from her hair. 'Aw, Brendan,' she whined. 'When you phoned you said you were taking me out. You never said nothing

about going round to see Barry Ellis's old woman.'
She flapped about a bit, not knowing how to vent her
anger, then, deciding to sulk, she hopped on to one
leg and struggled to undo the zip of her boot. 'So I got
all dressed up for nothing, did I? Thank you very
much.'

'No you didn't, Cal. Now get that boot done up
again. You've gotta come with me.'

'What, to see Sandy Ellis? You having a laugh?'

Brendan's jaw clenched. Marry this cheeky bitch?
Not in this fucking lifetime. He stabbed his finger at
her face. 'Don't you *dare* question me, or I really will
have a laugh – after I give you a good slapping. Now
get out to that car.'

As he shoved her towards the doorway, Carol
caught her shoulder on the jamb, making her flinch
with pain, but she knew better than to cry out.

Brendan drove through the rush-hour traffic along
Cambridge Heath Road, and Carol sat silently, still
sulking, beside him. She was fed up and her shoulder
stung from where the bastard had pushed her. As
usual, the rotten sod had just had to get his own way.

When Brendan whistled it wasn't just dogs that he
expected to come running. It made her so angry.

The trouble was, she liked being his girlfriend. He
was generous – very – with his money, and he was
really good-looking – a big plus considering some of
the animals she'd been with – and Carol liked it when

other girls couldn't keep their eyes off him. That and the fact that he was one of the most powerful men – if not *the* most powerful man – in the East End.

And she *loved* it when people were scared of him. That really turned Carol on.

But she liked it a whole lot less when she was the one he was scaring.

She glanced at him sideways, taking in the strong profile, the dark brown, almost black hair that curled into soft gypsy curls as it skimmed his collar. Then there were his eyes.

So blue.

All right, she'd give him one more chance.

But this time she really meant it.

Brendan steered the car off the Romford Road and pulled into a side turning, slowing down and ducking his head to check the door numbers of the neat little Victorian terrace.

Carol sat up straight. 'Why are we stopping in Stratford, Brendan? What are we doing here?'

'Sandy needs to keep her head down till this trouble with Barry's been sorted out.' A worrying thought popped into his mind. 'And this has to be a secret, right, Carol? No one's to know that she's staying here. Or that we've been over here to see her.'

Carol wrinkled her nose. He was taking the piss, wasn't he? Who on earth would she want to tell that she'd been visiting someone round here? These houses were awful – really old. And this one they'd stopped outside was worse than the rest. The little front yard was piled high with rubbish, and the curtains looked like they'd been hanging there since the place had been bloody built. It was disgusting.

'Don't worry, Brendan, I won't be telling anyone. I can promise you that.'

'Good.' He turned off the ignition. 'Now you ready?'

Carol didn't answer; she just stared at the house. At least it explained why he'd come out in such a dodgy-looking motor. He wanted it all kept quiet that he'd been here, and driving this crappy car'd do that all right. Who the hell would expect to see Brendan O'Donnell in this piece of shit?

'I said: you ready?'

'Look, Brendan, I don't wanna be difficult or nothing, but d'you mind if I wait for you out here?' She saw the look on his face. 'I'm not feeling that good.' And she'd feel even worse if she had to go in there with him, she could just imagine the stink.

Brendan threw open the driver's door, furious he'd even thought that the stupid little mare would know how to behave when you went to visit a bird while her old man was banged up. 'Please yourself.'

Brendan had to knock twice before he heard Sandy's wary voice asking who was there.

When she opened the door, he was shocked. Sandy

was almost as old as he was, and a good fifteen years or so older than Carol, but she'd always taken good care of herself and had never really looked her age. But, today, she showed every one of her thirty-four years. Her eyes were hollow; her usually glossy, shaggy lion-cut hair was unbrushed; and as for what she was wearing – it looked like one of Barry's old shirts, and as if she'd slept in it.

He acknowledged her with a nod and stepped inside, straight through the street door and into the sitting room of the little two-up two-down.

When he turned to look at her, Sandy's lips were pressed together in apology. 'The old girl only moved out recently, and Luke's not had a chance to clear out the furniture or anything. But you don't notice the smell after a while.'

She looked exhausted, defeated. 'Sorry.' She pulled the shirt collar up to her throat. 'I had to get out on the quick. And this was the nearest thing I could lay my hands on before I legged it.'

'You don't have to apologise to me, San.' He looked about him, deciding which of the threadbare chairs would do least damage to his suit. He settled for the manky-looking sofa by the side of the gas fire.

Sandy waited for him to sit down, visibly squirming as he put the flat, stained scatter cushion down on to the floor. 'Can I make you some tea? No, sorry . . .' She thought for a moment, gnawing at her thumbnail. 'Sorry, Brendan, I wasn't thinking. I'm not sure if there is any. The cupboards're not exactly full, and what there is, well, it looks a bit iffy. You know, old . . .'

'But you've been here since first thing yesterday morning. How've you been managing?'

'It's all right, the water's still on. And so's the gas, thank goodness, or I'd have frozen to death in this weather. And at least no one knows I'm here.'

Despite the strange circumstances, as Sandy dropped down on to the armchair facing him, Brendan couldn't help but notice her legs. They were long, and sort of polished-looking. Very nice.

He caught himself staring at her and immediately pulled himself together with a straightening of his shoulders and an unconvincing cough. 'Carol Mercer's outside. You know her?'

'Let me guess, young blonde girl?'

Sandy's attempt to lighten what was obviously not an easy situation for either of them passed Brendan by. 'That's the one,' he said. 'Like I said, she's waiting for me outside, so there's nothing funny about me being round here with you.'

'Course not. I never thought there was.'

'Don't think she fancied coming in.'

Sandy shrugged. 'She's only a kid.'

Brendan winced, and then – at last – treated her to a grin. 'Don't rub it in, San. I know I'm a few years older than her, but I'm not drawing me pension just yet, girl.'

'You can't fool me, mate. I know exactly how old you are. You were the year above me – remember? Well, you were when you did the teachers a favour by coming in for the odd day now and again.' She tried another smile. 'I fancied you something rotten back then. All the girls did.'

Brendan frowned. 'I never knew that.'

'Liar. You knew all the girls were after you.' Her smile faded as she reached out for one of the packs of cigarettes piled on the old-fashioned tiled mantelpiece. 'And Luke knows me, eh, Brendan? Knew I'd be climbing up the wall if I didn't have plenty of fags.'

'At least he got something right.' Brendan shook his head in wonder. 'I can't believe he brought you here.'

'Don't be like that. The poor sod didn't have much choice, did he? It was bloody four o'clock in the morning when I called him. Pitch dark and pissing down with rain. I must have sounded hysterical, not knowing what was going on, standing in a phone box, freezing cold and wearing nothing but Barry's shirt. Not even a pair of slippers on me feet. What else could he do?'

'Maybe.'

She offered Brendan a cigarette and they smoked in silence for a while. 'Luke said Eileen's back home. How's she doing?'

'Your old man's being held in police custody, you

73

don't look like you've had any sleep – which don't surprise me, the state of this dump – and you're asking me about Mum?' For want of something better to do, Brendan loosened his tie. 'I appreciate you asking, Sandy. She's fine.'

He spent a bit more time on his tie, tightening it again and then smoothing it down. 'So, how are you, if it's not a stupid question? Which it definitely is.'

What was up with him? He sounded like a sodding teenager.

'Brendan.' She leaned forward, resting her elbows on her knees, her hands clasped in front of her. 'I'm gonna tell you something. It's about Barry. I think you've got a right to know, seeing as how good you've been to him – and me – over the years. It might explain a few things.' She tapped her thumb nervously against her teeth. 'But you've got to promise me you won't hold it against him.'

'Go on.'

'He's got into drugs.'

'Don't be daft, San.' Brendan sounded relieved. 'We all like a bit of a smoke. If anything, he's got more sense than me. I worry I'm getting too much into the booze. Like the old man did.' *Why was he telling her this? It was like he was in the sodding confessional or something*. 'A bit of puff's the least of his worries.'

'No, Brendan, you don't understand. It's more than that. A lot more.' She took a long, deep drag on

74

her cigarette. 'It started after he got ill. You know, after finding Stephen Shea. At first it was tranqs, on prescription. But then that wasn't enough. And lately, well, let's just say it's got worse. A lot worse. He's been spending so much money. So much more than he's been bringing in. That's why that post-office thing they're blaming on him . . .' She looked away, unable to meet his gaze. 'I think he probably did it.'

'Bloody hell, Sandy. You are kidding me, right?'

'I only wish I was. I've been working in a launderette on the Commercial Road just to pay the rent. But Barry don't know that, Brendan. And promise me you won't tell him.' She laughed mirthlessly. 'It was the only bloody place I could think of that he wouldn't go in. But I even had to leave there, when one of the customers told me he'd been in dealing of a night.'

Brendan smacked the side of his fist on the arm of the sofa, and Sandy's head snapped up. She'd said too much.

'Brendan, I –'

'It's all right, San. It ain't your fault, girl.'

'It was heartbreaking seeing how he got. Everything he earned went up his nose, or in his arm, or down his throat.'

'If it was that serious, why didn't you say something?'

'You'll never know the number of times I nearly phoned you. But I could only think about how you'd

75

all react if you knew he'd been using like that. I suppose I was surprised you never noticed.'

Brendan ground out the stub of his cigarette. 'We all just put everything down to his nerves. You know, after what happened. And that he'd sort of –'

'Gone off his head?'

'Yeah.'

'He might as well have done. In the end I didn't know which way to turn. I'm sure he must have been borrowing money, cos he'd sold everything indoors that wasn't bolted down months ago. Then I got a letter last week, threatening to cut off the electric, so I borrowed a few quid off Gina, you know, Kev's wife. Pretended I was buying Barry a surprise for Christmas.'

'Jesus, Sandy. I had no idea, girl. Look, you mustn't worry. When all this is straightened out – and it will be – I'll find you something to do. A nice little number in the minicab office during the day shift.'

'But you've got Paula in there already. And she's got kids to keep.'

'I don't believe you, San. Always looking out for other people.' He took a roll of notes from his inside pocket, took a small wad for himself, and held the rest out to her. 'You take this for now. No one knows you round here. You can go out safe enough.'

'Thanks, but I don't need it. I mean, I'm not exactly dressed for shooting round the supermarket, now am I?'

'Take it anyway. Go on. Just in case. And in the meantime I'll send someone round with a bit of shopping for you. Just let me know if you need anything special.'

'I wouldn't mind some clothes.' She looked around the grimy little room. Another smile. 'And a few bits of cleaning stuff wouldn't go amiss either.'

Brendan stood up. 'I've, you know, enjoyed this.'

She looked puzzled. 'Eh?'

'Talking. To you.'

'Good. I'm glad.'

He surprised them both by kissing her gently on the forehead. 'I'll be in touch, all right?'

For some reason, that simple gesture was too much for Sandy; she dropped her chin as her eyes began to well up, the tears spilling down on to her cheeks.

'Sandy, look at me.'

She peered up at him through a watery blur.

'You mustn't worry yourself, okay? We'll get him straightened out. Get him off everything. The lot. Christ, I can get his supplies cut off –' he snapped his fingers '– as easy as that.'

Brendan got back in the car and slammed the door angrily.

Carol ignored him; she was too busy checking her make-up in the rear-view mirror that she had twisted round to bother herself with him and his moods.

He steered the car away from the kerb, but before

77

they'd even reached the end of the street, he stamped on the brake, shooting her forward, and leaving her with a smear of Damson Shine lipstick streaked across her jaw. He snapped off the courtesy light, leaving them in the dark save for the rain-diluted orange glow of the street lamps.

'Brendan! What is wrong with you? How am I meant to see what I'm doing?'

'*What?*'

'Well, you drag me over here and then you –'

The force of the back of Brendan's hand smacking her across her face had Carol reeling back in her seat.

He reached inside his jacket, pulled out what was left of the roll of notes and, using just one hand, guided the car back into the kerb, ignoring the angry driver of the car behind him, who was hooting and gesturing as he was forced to swerve to avoid him.

He peeled off a few fivers for himself and threw the rest in her lap. 'Here, get a cab. I've got things to do.'

'But it's pissing down out there.'

He reached across and opened the passenger door. 'Out.'

He jerked the mirror back into position, and drove on into the early-evening traffic, heading west, back towards Stepney.

He didn't even look at her as he sped away, didn't even bother to check in the mirror to see if she was all right. He had other things on his mind. Important things.

Like why the hell was the thought of Sandy being stuck alone in that shithole getting to him so much?

And what the fuck was he going to do about Barry Ellis?

Chapter 6

By the time Brendan pulled up outside the phone box opposite the Little Driver pub in Bow Road, he had calmed down and his mind had cleared.

First he made a couple of calls to reliable contacts, men who could ensure that regular deliveries would get through to Brixton with no questions asked except how much they would be getting paid. Then he searched in his wallet for the direct, personal line of DI Hammond, a police officer who'd recently transferred down to London from Birmingham. A man Brendan had been introduced to at a charity boxing evening in Bethnal Green. A man who had put a very interesting proposition to him.

Brendan shot his cuffs, straightened and tightened his tie, smoothed back his hair – a man in control – and dialled the number.

'Mr Hammond?'

'Speaking.' The Brummy accent identified him immediately.

'It's Brendan O'Donnell here. Remember? We had that little chat at the boxing do the other night.'

'Of course, I remember. It was a most enjoyable evening.'

'And d'you remember how you said you might be able to get me into that place you was talking about?'

'Certainly, I do.'

'Well, I'm at a bit of a loose end tonight, and I was wondering if now would be a convenient time.'

'I don't see why not.'

'Good, cos there'll be a drink in it for you, Mr Hammond. A right nice one.'

'I shall look forward to that.'

As Brendan drove into the red-brick garden square that sat on the vague borders of the City and the West End, where residential and corporate properties became almost indistinguishable from one another, he could just make out DI Hammond, through the swishing swoop of the windscreen wipers, waiting for him on the far corner.

Save for the concession of a cheap, chain-store raincoat, the police officer was apparently oblivious to the rain. He was a mild-looking man, in his late forties, and a bit old-fashioned. If you were being honest, dull would probably be how you'd describe him – undeniably more civil servant than dashing crime fighter.

And that suited Brendan just fine.

He let the car cruise to an easy halt and pushed the passenger door open wide.

'Mr Hammond, good to see you. Please, get in.'

*

81

'So I really won't need you with me?' Brendan was studying the very ordinary piece of card that was, apparently, his pass down into the Aladdin's cave that lay hidden beneath the police station close to Holborn. 'I must admit, it seems a bit unlikely, Mr Hammond. Say they recognise me? Like I told you, I was a bit of a rascal in me youth.'

'You'll be fine, Mr O'Donnell. Any friend of mine is as good as family down there.'

Brendan nodded, taking it all in. 'So, how's the real family then, Mr Hammond? Well are they?'

'Actually, since you're asking, Mr O'Donnell, I have to say: no. Mrs Hammond hasn't been too well at all. It's a shame, but she's taking a bit longer to settle herself down here in London than either of us had expected. But then the leafy suburbs of Birmingham are a very different kettle of fish to this place. She's seen the doctor, of course, but all he could suggest was that she could do with a break, a rest away from it all. But you know what policemen's wages are like, Mr O'Donnell. Public scandal in my humble opinion. Still, that's the price of being a public servant in today's world. Shame, it would have been nice to give her a little treat.'

Brendan clapped his hand on the steering wheel. 'Don't say another word, it's as good as done, Mr Hammond. You can take her down to my . . . to my *friend's* gaff in Estepona. Lovely part of Spain, that is. And let's face it, if every bleeder on the old jam roll's having two weeks away every year, then I'm sure a hard-working man like yourself and his wife deserve getting a fortnight's worth of sun on their backs.'

'That's very generous of . . . of your *friend*, Mr O'Donnell. And I'd really like to do that for my Betty. Be sure to thank him for me, won't you?'

'It'll be my pleasure to do that, Mr Hammond. Go over there for Christmas if you like. Or wait till the weather warms up a bit. Whatever you fancy. Just let me know and I'll make sure you get the keys. There's a local couple keeps it all in order over there – English they are, so no problems with the old lingo or nothing. And, while we're at it, how about calling me Brendan?'

'Thank you, I will – Brendan.'

'You know, Mr Hammond, I like to be sure of the strength of a man before I do business with him, know how he'd react at the death, and from what I can see, I think we're gonna get on just fine together.' He held out his hand to seal the deal. 'There's gonna be money in that hand next week, Mr Hammond. Gonna be a nice little drink for you to treat yourself, while you're down in Spain.'

Mr Hammond's smile could have lit up the gloomiest of November evenings. 'Thank you, Brendan, I'm touched. And please, I'm Bert to my family and friends.'

*

It was ten o'clock. Brendan had left DI Hammond a couple of hours ago and, being eager to try out the apparently magic pass he had been given, he had gone directly to the police store in the basement in Holborn, and – to his surprise – he had actually been let straight in. Just like Hammond had said.

Now Brendan was standing in the entrance to the Bellavista, a club and barely disguised knocking shop, in a cul-de-sac in Shoreditch. Despite the decor being a bit dated, the place was buzzing.

The red velvet and gilt had once been state of the art, when the O'Donnells had taken it over back in the early sixties, and had had it refurbished as the first of their new-look East End clubs. It was still a place that had the power to make Brendan feel tingles of nostalgia for the 'old days'.

He scoped the room and laughed quietly to himself. As always, it was full of punters wanting to drink and meet willing women. The old man had been right, that would never go out of fashion. As he'd got older, Brendan had come to realise that Gabriel, when he wasn't pissed, hadn't been quite the fool that his son had sometimes thought he was. But it was hard respecting your father, when you were a flash, hot-headed kid with more going on in your trousers than in your brain. Shame he'd never had the opportunity to tell his dad that. And a shame his dad couldn't see what a success his eldest son had made of his life.

He spotted Kevin up at the bar.

'All right, Kev?' He settled himself on one of the high stools and accepted the glass of whiskey from the barman without a word.

'Yeah, all right.' He sounded fed up. 'I was just, you know, thinking about Barry. The poor fucker.'

'Yeah.' Brendan scratched at his chin. 'You're right there, mate. He is a poor fucker.'

Brendan had thought a lot about Barry tonight: when he'd been looking into Sandy's eyes, and after he'd chucked Carol out of the motor. And that was why he'd made the decision to phone his contacts, to make sure that Barry had plenty of gear while he was stuck inside on remand. Brixton was a real rathole, a place where it wouldn't take a lot to break someone as unbalanced as Barry Ellis. So, from Brendan's point of view, and despite what he'd told Sandy, keeping the bloke nicely topped up was a very sensible thing to do.

The fact that he was going to keep Barry supplied didn't make Brendan feel guilty. He wasn't going to waste his sympathy on a tosser like him, even if he had known him all his life. All Brendan cared about was that the bloke kept his trap shut. And, thank Christ, Sandy had inadvertently shown him a way to make sure that that's exactly what he would do. No cravings equalled no need to get upset. That was why Barry would have everything his little heart desired.

'You know, Kev, I had a meet with that copper,' Brendan said, in between sipping his drink, and calculating how many of the girls were sitting idle and how many were upstairs with punters. 'He gave me this pass thing.' He leaned in close to Kevin. 'Gets you into this massive basement place, right under this nick up the City. You should see it. Like a fucking cash and carry, it is. Magazines, films, photos, the lot. All the really hard stuff they pull in during the raids. Some stuff even Anthony would close his eyes at. And more than I'd ever bloody hoped for. But they want some serious cash.'

'How much?'

'Let's just say we're gonna have enough from that gear we chored off the Kesslers to make a start, but we're gonna need another bit of bunce every bit as big, to show them we're not fly-by-nights. That we intend to take this business seriously. Then we can have what we like.' He raised his glass. 'There's some very valuable merchandise down there, Kev.' He snorted with laughter, unable to believe it. 'They'll even copy the bastard films for us. You should see all the confiscated equipment they've got.'

He leaned back and folded his arms. 'You know, I think we're gonna need a meet with the Kesslers in the very near future – explain how they'll be taking our supplies for their shops from now on. And at our own very special prices.'

Kevin raised his eyebrows. 'Blimey, meeting up with that lot? Now that does sound serious.'

Brendan was finding it hard to wipe the grin off his face. 'Very serious. And, aw yeah, before I forget. Take a ton out of the till before you leave tonight. I want your Gina to get some things for Sandy Ellis. Clothes, a bit of grub and that. The poor cow's in a right state in that pisshole Luke's stuck her in. And make sure you give Gina a few quid to say thank you to her. From me.'

'Sure, course I will. Gina'll know what to get her. But you don't have to treat her or nothing. She'll be more than happy to do it.'

'No, I'd like to. She's a good girl, your Gina.' Brendan spoke as he moved towards the door.

'Thanks, Brendan, she'll appreciate that.'

'And another thing,' said Brendan, stopping and turning around. 'Tell Gina that Sandy needs some tea bags, will you? She ain't got none, poor cow.'

Kevin didn't laugh. He honestly wasn't sure if Brendan was having a joke or not.

Just a couple of miles up the road, on the other side of the now metaphorical, but still very real boundary of what had once been the solid divide of the old City wall, DI Hammond sat with his colleague, DC Medway, in an ornately tiled pub. It was actually an old gin palace, one of the few remaining examples of the Victorian art of dispensing hard liquor to the masses. And Bert Hammond, with his own interest in control, particularly of the lower orders, found the place very much to his taste. It showed how such things could be done. And that was also why he wasn't drinking alcohol: he didn't like to lose control of himself either. So he was sipping at a glass of soda water with the merest hint of bitters to colour and cloud the liquid.

But it didn't mean he wasn't enjoying himself. He was enjoying himself a great deal.

'Not a bad evening's work, eh, Medway?' Hammond winked – a gesture that didn't look entirely right coming from the very proper DI. 'And next time there's going to be a *nice little drink in it*, as that slimy Irish git might put it.'

He took a small taste from his glass and brushed his finger across his unfashionably clipped tooth-brush moustache. 'Plus we get the O'Donnells and the Kesslers back at each other's throats, of course.'

'Just like in his father's day,' said Medway, remembering it all too well. They were memories he didn't really care for.

'So I understand from studying the files.' Hammond rubbed his hands together. 'Divide and rule, eh, Medway? Divide and rule. A good lesson for us all.'

'Yeah, great, another turf war, just what we want.'

'I do hope that's not an example of your patronising London sarcasm, Medway.'

Medway put down his pint and shook his head. 'Course not, sir. Course not.'

Chapter 7

Carol had to grab hold of the edge of the seat as the taxi driver swerved through the afternoon traffic, but she was too lost in her thoughts to complain. It was a whole week since Brendan had dumped her in the street in Stratford, and just three weeks until Christmas, yet she still hadn't heard a single word from the rotten, conniving git.

She looked at the bags stacked by her feet on the floor of the cab. Christ, she was pissed off. She'd just been shopping in the West End and she'd had to choose – choose, if you don't mind – between two pairs of shoes. She'd caught the superior look on the stuck-up mare of a saleswoman's face. It was humiliating, that's what it was.

And another thing, how exactly was she meant to buy Christmas presents if Brendan wasn't giving her any money? She already knew what she wanted to get him: something really expensive.

How, exactly, was she supposed to do that?

There was the money she had stashed away, of course – having carefully put two-thirds of everything Brendan had ever given her into a special account. But that was emergency money, not bloody shopping-for-rotten-Christmas-presents money.

'Here. Stop here,' she ordered, tapping on the glass partition.

The taxi driver hadn't been surprised when she'd given him the address on the dodgy estate. The floor-length silver fox might have cost a few quid, but it was obvious that a kid like her didn't get that sort of clobber by spending her days in a typing pool.

She counted out the exact fare, and swung the cab door shut with an angry slam, making the driver call after her, but she didn't give a bugger. Carol Mercer had other things on her mind. Like getting Brendan back exactly where she wanted him.

Carol was about to put the key in the front door, when she pulled back, a perplexed frown on her face.

The front-room curtains were closed.

She'd never have left them like that when she went out this morning. It looked horrible, like she had a coffin in there or something.

She put her bags carefully to one side of the step. Took off her fur coat, folded it up and put it on top of the pile, then slipped off her high heels. She hadn't been looking after herself since she was fifteen for nothing.

Making as little noise as possible, she let herself in, ready to scratch the eyes out of anybody who'd been stupid enough to dare to touch any of her lovely things.

She was momentarily fazed to see Anthony standing there, blocking her way into the hall.

But even Anthony – who despite her best efforts to keep quiet had heard Carol coming in the door – was no match for her.

'Take one step towards me, you fat bastard,' she said, her sparkly blue fingernail jabbing him in the chest, 'and I'll tell Brendan you tried to touch me up. Now get out of my way.'

'All right, calm down.' Anthony backed away from her, until his way was blocked by the firmly closed door of the front room.

'You can't come in here, Carol. Sorry, love.'

'Aw can't I?' Carol aimed a swift kick at his shins. It didn't hurt – she wasn't even wearing shoes – but Anthony was so shocked that someone so little had so much front, that it gave her the benefit of surprise. She was under his arm and through the door before his brain had had a chance to crank into gear.

'What's going on?' She was stunned, riveted to the spot.

There was this bright light. It was weird, really intense, throwing shadows that made the room – *her lovely front room* – look totally different. Unfamiliar. And there were men. Strange men. Standing around smoking. *In her house*. She'd never have allowed that.

So what the hell was going on?

She shaded her eyes with her hand as if she were

looking out to sea. This was her room – her own beautiful room – but everything was wrong. It was as if she'd never seen the place before. Well, not like this she hadn't.

It took her a moment to make out what she was seeing. And even then it didn't make any sense.

Brendan was there. And so were what looked like a film crew – four men she'd never seen before, complete with camera and a microphone. And along the far wall on her sofa, under the front window, were two completely naked women – one black and one white – and they were touching each other. *On her brand new, bloody sofa.*

'What the fuck do you think you're doing?' She launched herself across the room at them, but Anthony wasn't about to be caught out again. He grabbed her round the waist as if she were no more than a toddler and hoisted her off her feet.

Up until then, the men in the room – Brendan included – had been too engrossed in the action between the two women to notice Carol's entrance, but now, all eyes were on Anthony and his wriggling, kicking, cursing captive.

'Bloody hell, Carol,' said Brendan, with a little snort of laughter. 'What's up with you, girl? You look like your drawers are on fire.'

The two women started giggling.

'Letting brasses fucking *do it* on my sofa? You bastard, Brendan.'

Being told off by a little trollop? Brendan didn't like that. He didn't like that at all. 'There's no need to get excited. We're only testing out a bit of recording equipment.'

'Look at them. Look at what they're doing. On my bloody new sofa.'

Anthony was finding it increasingly difficult to keep hold of her. 'Can I put her down?'

Brendan wasn't interested in Anthony's problems. 'No need to pull that face, Carol. You wasn't exactly a ballet dancer when I met you, now was you?'

'Stripping's one thing, but that,' She pointed angrily at the two women, her legs still flailing around. 'That's filth.'

Brendan turned to the man who had been operating the camera. 'Hark at her,' he said, with a salacious smirk. 'She was dressed up like a cowboy who'd forgot to put on his shirt and strides, when I met her. Hat, boots and a gun holster, that's what she was wearing. Very classy.'

Everyone in the room except Carol started laughing.

'Don't you dare talk about me like that.'

Brendan didn't bother looking at her. 'Go to bed, Carol.'

Her objections were growing quieter, her thrashing around less wild. 'It's three o'clock in the afternoon.'

This time he did turn to face her. 'Do us all a favour and just piss off out of it.'

They didn't even wait for her to close the door.

'Who's that?' It was one of the men.

'No one, just some little scrubber. Now, you two, get back down to it, or you can piss off an' all.'

Carol leaned against the wall in the passageway, flinching as someone slammed the door shut behind her.

She could hear the men talking and laughing.

This was all that Sandy's fault. Until Brendan had gone to see that horrible slapper, he'd been all over her, couldn't get enough of her. Now she might as well have been something he'd trodden in, something that had spoilt his fancy, handmade shoes.

The men had stopped laughing. Carol moved closer to the door.

'So you definitely reckon the Kesslers don't make their own films.' It was Brendan speaking.

'From what I've heard and seen –' it sounded like the man with the camera '– it's all French and Dutch merchandise they stock. Everything imported. Comes in off the boats, then they distribute it in their lorries.'

Carol leaned closer.

The Kesslers. Brendan was always going on about them. Always saying how much he hated them.

She listened a bit more.

'Well, that's all gonna change.' It was Brendan again. 'Because, I tell you now, they ain't gonna be able to resist taking our stuff for their shops. Not only have I got personal access to the sort of gear that'd make your hair stand on end – if you had any –' more laughter '– but a good friend of mine has offered to make as many top-quality copies as I want him to of our own private productions. And all in a nice safe place where no one can touch us.'

She heard a round of approving chuckles.

'And the artistic efforts we're offering are going to be something a bit special.' This time it was only Brendan laughing. 'I mean, some of these birds coming into the country are so desperate they'll do bleed'n anything. I've already had this pair. Like *Last* fucking *Tango in Paris* it was. With me playing Marlon sodding Brando. But I had to use marge, didn't I? I mean, couldn't afford best butter, now could I?'

The other men joined in with his laughter, and one of them said: 'You dirty bastard, Brendan.'

'Yeah, good, innit? They're so fucking strung out, they'll do anything for their next fix.'

Carol made the mistake of slapping her hand against the door in temper.

Brendan was out to her before she had even realised what she'd done.

'I told you to get in that bedroom. Now, before I get wild, I suggest you get out of here. Right now.'

'But this is my place.'

'*Your* place? Don't be stupid, Carol, and don't go getting me any more wound up than I already am, or I might just lose me temper with you. In fact, I'll tell

96

you what, you've done me a favour. You've made me realise I've had enough of you. So go on, get out, and don't let me see you hanging around here again. All right?'

Carol narrowed her eyes. She wasn't going to have this. 'What a big man,' she hissed at him. 'Throwing your own unborn baby out on to the street.'

'My what?'

'I'm nearly seven weeks late, Brendan. *Seven weeks*. I was gonna tell you, but I didn't know how you'd –'

'Do you think I'm a complete idiot?'

She stepped back, the wind completely taken out of her sails. 'How d'you mean?'

'You're no more pregnant than I am.'

'Yes, I am.'

'Bollocks, you are.'

'I am!'

'Here you are then.' He grabbed her hand, pulled some money from his pocket and slapped it into her palm. 'There's more than enough there to get rid of it. If you really are carrying. And I'm sure you know plenty of old witches who can help you out. Now get out of my sight, we're trying to work here.'

'But what about all my things?'

'Give me fucking strength.' Brendan rapped his knuckles on his teeth. 'Look, you can come back in the morning. I'll give you till midday to get your stuff together. Then, and I mean this, Carol, I don't wanna see you anywhere near here again. Right?'

It was just before nine the next morning. Luke let himself into the O'Donnell family house on the Mile End Road and crept quietly along the hallway in case his mother was still sleeping.

As he started down the basement stairs to the kitchen, he was taken aback to see Brendan sitting at the table, nursing a mug of tea.

'You're up early.'

'Blimey, you're sharp, got new blades, have you?'

Luke sat down opposite his brother. 'It was you I was hoping to see as it happens, Brendan. Wanted to know about Sandy, if she still needs to stay over there in –'

'What, got tenants queuing up to move into that stinking gaff, have you? Can't let her have it for just a few more days?'

Luke threw up his hands. 'Here we go. Why do you always have to think the worst of everyone? We're not all as bloody awkward as you, you know. I was just wondering if she needed to be moved somewhere else. *Somewhere a bit nicer.* Now we haven't got the law on our heels, and we've got time to think about –'

Brendan jumped to his feet. 'And why do you think I give a fuck about what happens to Sandy?'

Luke held up his hands in surrender. 'Bloody hell,

Brendan, keep you hair on, mate. What the hell's got into you?'

Brendan sat down again and poured himself more tea, then – begrudgingly – held up the pot by way of offering some to his brother.

Luke nodded, and Brendan got up again to fetch him a mug.

'It's that bloody Carol Mercer. She's got me all agitated,' he said, opening the cupboard over the sink. 'I chucked her out yesterday, and what does the rotten cow do? She goes and announces she's bleed'n pregnant.'

'And you still chucked her out?'

'Course I did. I mean, how do I know whose kid it is? She ain't exactly the fucking Virgin Mary, now is she? So I gave her some dough to get rid of it. But for all I care she can keep the money and use a bloody knitting needle and a bottle of gin.'

'*You watch your filthy, blasphemous mouth.*'

Brendan twisted round to see his mother, in her ancient candlewick dressing gown, gripping the back of Luke's chair to steady herself.

The mug slipped from Brendan's hands and smashed into pieces in the stainless-steel sink.

'Mum, you don't understand.'

Eileen turned on her heel and hauled herself back up the stairs, clinging to the banister as if it were a mountaineer's rope. 'Don't you dare speak to me.'

'But even if she is telling the truth, d'you really

want me to be like Dad, and have a bastard hanging round me neck for the rest of me life?'

Eileen stopped at the top of the stairway. 'No matter how much I despised what your father did,' she said, without turning to face her son, 'I'd never have wanted the child's life to be taken before it was even born.'

It was now a few minutes to ten that same morning, less than an hour since Brendan had walked out, leaving Luke to deal with their mother. He had driven from Stepney to Stratford in far less time than it should have taken him, having driven with an anger-fuelled recklessness that made even his usual aggressiveness behind the wheel seem mild in comparison. But as soon as he spotted Sandy in Maxine's All Day Café on the Romford Road he relaxed. A smile came to his face, and he swaggered through the doorway as if he were entering the grand dining room of a distinguished restaurant rather than a greasy spoon in east London.

Sandy was sitting at one of the only three occupied tables, Brendan having guessed rightly that the full-English breakfasters had long since left for work, and the tea-break rush was yet to begin.

'Been waiting long?' he asked, pulling out one of the ill-matched, vinyl-covered chairs.

Sandy shook her head. Her hair, now clean and glossy, fell about her face in soft, fair wisps, and, he couldn't help noticing, the red roll-neck sweater she wore tucked into her plain black maxi-skirt emphasised the womanly curves of her body in just the right way. Sort of feminine, not showy or tarty like Carol would have looked.

'No, not long. And anyway,' she lifted her chin to the window, indicating the second-hand car lot across the street, 'I've been busy guessing which of the passers-by would stop to admire the "car of the week".'

'What, that Capri?' His tone was dismissive.

'You might not like it, but I do. Barry always used to say he'd get me one. You know, one day. A purple Capri, with real leather seats. Aubergine, did you know that's what they call that colour?'

'No, I didn't.'

She offered Brendan one of her cheap cigarettes – she'd long since run out of the stack Luke had left her, and wasn't about to blow the money Brendan had given her on expensive brands.

She lit one for herself. 'Not gonna happen now though, is it? I'll never have my dream car.'

'What I don't get is why you protected him for so long.' This was just as much of a mystery to Brendan as the relationship between his mum and Luke.

'I'm loyal,' Sandy said, with a resigned shrug. 'And he needed me. So . . .'

'D'you love him then?'

That threw her. 'That's my business.' She swirled

101

the burning end of her cigarette around in the debris in the ashtray, unwilling to meet Brendan's gaze, then said quietly. 'Truthfully, Brendan, he wasn't the Barry I knew any more. Not once that stuff got hold of him. But how could I just leave him to it? We've been together such a long time. So I just did what I had to do – the best I could – to look after him. Still, it's out of my hands now, innit?' She raised her eyes to meet his. 'Do you reckon he'll get sent down for very long?'

'If it's my turn to be truthful, San – yeah, I do.'

Her head slumped forward. 'Shit.'

'I know. But if you're still interested, at least I've got a job for you.' He leaned back in his chair – casual, not bothered. 'The pay's good. Regular.'

Her head jerked up, she was almost smiling. 'Really?'

'Yeah. And it's got a nice little place to live in and all.'

'Brendan, you don't know how much this means to me. I could start as soon as you like.' She leaned forward, excited to be seeing a way out of at least part of the crap she was in. 'Is it all right for me to be back in circulation then? I'm not being ungrateful or nothing, but I can't wait to get out of that place.'

'I've spoken to some people and, so long as Barry keeps schtum about you being in the flat with him at the time of the raid, there's no need for you to be involved in any of this. And from what I've heard, he ain't saying nothing to no one. And . . .' He hesitated, considering his words. 'Look, Sandy, I don't even know if you wanna hear this, but I've had some gear sent in to him. Nothing too serious,' he lied. 'Just something to ease the pain a bit. I didn't like the idea of him suffering in there.'

'Thanks, Brendan.' Sandy's eyes brimmed with tears. 'Mad, innit, I'm grateful that he's got the stuff that got him and me in all this trouble in the first place.'

'It took some doing, San, believe me. He really did give that copper a good hiding.' Brendan reached out and took her hand. She was shaking. 'Now, about this job. I'm setting up one of these new agencies. For escorts. And I want you to run it.'

She pulled her hand away and patted herself hard on the chest as she almost choked on the smoke she had just inhaled. 'Escorts? You're kidding, right?'

'Don't go getting the wrong idea, this ain't gonna be nothing nasty.'

'No? So what is it gonna be then? A dating agency for young ladies?'

'I don't take that sort of lip from no one, Sandy.'

'And I ain't running a bloody knocking shop. I've done some things in my time – plenty I ain't very proud of – but running toms ain't one of them.'

'If you'll just listen to me. I've gone right into it, and I guarantee your part will all be above board. Not a lot of difference from what Paula does in the cab

103

office. You take the bookings, and we charge the punters a basic fourteen quid a night. And we'll have nice girls – clean and that.'

'So there's no "extras" involved then?'

He flinched at her sarcasm, but didn't comment on it. 'That's up to the girls. If they want to charge for anything else, fine. And we trust them to pass on to us whatever percentage we've agreed beforehand. And we'll know they're not cheating on us, because every now and again we'll slip in a ringer to see if they're doing it by the book. And because it'll be run properly, by you – if you fancy it, of course – they'll never know if it's a plant working for us, or a genuine customer they're dealing with.'

'How much will they bring in for you then, each of the escorts, after these percentages have been worked out?'

'Three, three and half a week.'

'*Three hundred and fifty quid?* Bloody hell, Brendan.'

'Exactly. A lot of money. And that's why I need someone I can trust to run the books. You've got a brain, and you're classy, and that's why I'm asking you to do it.'

'What, needs someone classy to run toms, does it?'

'There's no need for that sort of talk, Sandy. Like I said, they don't have to do anything they don't want to.'

'So they'd be happy to work the whole night for a

bit of dinner and a few gin and tonics, would they?'

His handsome face creased into a broad grin. 'You've got me there, girl. I said you had brains. But come on, you've gotta at least give it a try. And I know that if you're sorted out, Barry'd feel a lot better.'

She couldn't argue with that. 'Say I didn't like it?'

He shrugged. 'Fine. No bad feelings, you just walk away.' He took a moment to stub out his cigarette. 'And I'm sure we could come up with some sort of arrangement so's you could stay on in the accommodation. Till you found somewhere else to live, of course.'

Chapter 8

While Brendan tried to convince Sandy that she had a great future working for him, Carol was standing in the front room of what she had stupidly believed was her home, staring down at the two pathetic suitcases full of clothes and make-up – the sum total of her life.

At least the bastard had coughed up the cash for an abortion. The thought brought a thin smile to her lips; not only was the money an unexpected bonus, but she'd actually conned big man O'Donnell into thinking she was pregnant. She'd well and truly treated him like a mug. And that was more than a bonus – that was a real pleasure.

But Carol had little else to smile about. She picked up the cases with a sigh, carried them outside and set them down by the doorstep before locking the door as the note on the coffee table had instructed her. She was about to post the key back through the letter box, but decided against it and slipped it into her pocket. She'd drop it down the first drain hole she came to. Let him sort that one out. Then she snatched up the bags again and tottered unsteadily down the path, balancing on her high, platform shoes, with her silver-fox coat flapping around her legs in the stiff wind that threatened yet more rain. She glared straight ahead, just daring her neighbours to even twitch at their curtains.

She paused at the gate. What now? What exactly was she supposed to do?

As a last resort there was always the tiny flat over the bookie's in King's Cross, the one she used to share with two of the girls from the Cactus Parlour. But they were a thieving pair of bitches, and Carol wouldn't be able to close her eyes once they got back from the club, in case they turned her over.

Or there was always that pillock, Peter MacRiordan . . .

He couldn't keep his eyeballs in their sockets whenever she was around, and she knew there was no love lost between him and Brendan. And if what everyone said was true, Pete Mac wasn't averse to setting up little love nests to keep his bits of stray well out of sight of his Patricia. In fact, she guessed that he'd take great pleasure in thinking he was having one over on his condescending bully of a brother-in-law.

He was so stupid she could probably even get him to tell her all sorts of things. She'd learned from a very young age that having information about people was never a bad thing, and knowing something that might somehow cause Brendan aggravation was very appealing. Because, whatever else happened, she wasn't going to let him get away with treating her like this.

She checked her watch. Quarter past ten. Brendan had given her till dinner time. She had plenty of time to go back inside and call him.

As she unhooked the telephone receiver from its holder on the kitchen wall, Carol Mercer looked around the immaculately clean and tidy room for what she knew would be the very last time. She could have cried with the injustice of it all.

'O'Donnells' Cabs, how can I help you?'

'Paula!' she said, putting a happy smile in her voice. 'Is that you, babes? This is Carol.'

''Lo, Carol. Wanna make a booking, do you?' Paula knew Carol would prefer to roll in wet tar and then walk over broken glass rather than get in one of the O'Donnells' scruffy minicabs, but it amused her to aggravate the toffee-nosed little trollop. 'You'll have to hang on, I'm afraid. Not sure what I've got available at the moment.'

'Er, no, you're all right, thanks, Paula. I'm fine. I just wanted to speak to Peter MacRiordan. Is he there?'

Why would Carol Mercer want to talk to Mr Potato Head? 'Er, Pete Mac, you say?'

Carol noted the pause. 'I've got a message for him. From Brendan.'

Paula nodded to herself – that explained it. 'He's in the back office. I'll let him know.'

'Can't you just give me the number?' Carol's smile was fading fast. 'I'll call him direct.'

'Sorry, sweetheart, Brendan's express orders. I don't give that number to no one.' Paula was more than up to Carol Mercer.

'But this is urgent.'

Oh, yeah? Why was that then? Perhaps this wasn't as straightforward as Carol tart-features Mercer was pretending.

'Tell you what,' said Paula, all helpful suggestions, 'you give me *your* number and I'll get him to call you back.'

When the telephone finally rang – nearly ten minutes later – Carol was just about ready to pick up her bags and go round to that bollocking cab office and stick Paula's mike right up her fat arse. She could imagine the ugly, soapy mare taking her time, finishing her coffee, writing down bookings, and then – how kind – shifting her lazy, rotten carcass from her chair and walking through to the back office to give Pete Mac the message.

Carol was getting pissed off being treated like muck by everyone who had anything to do with the O'Donnells. But there was something she wanted from Pete Mac so, as far as he was concerned, she was going to be sunshine its fucking self.

'Hello, Peter,' she purred.

'Yeah? Who's this?'

Bloody hell, he was dim. 'Peter. It's me, sweetheart, Carol Mercer.'

That bucked him up. 'Hello, darling. What can I do you for?'

Keep smiling. Keep it going. Stick out your tits to get the mood right. 'I'm sorry, but I had to tell you, Peter. It's been driving me mad.' Pause for effect. 'Peter, I can't help myself. It's just that I'm really attracted to you.'

'Fucking hell, girl.'

Now she definitely had his attention.

'Brendan'd go fucking potty if he knew.'

'I know. That's why I've had to keep it hidden from everyone. You know how he gets.'

No answer. What was wrong with the man? She was offering it up on a bloody plate.

'Peter, can we meet up? Today maybe? I know Brendan's busy, and I can jump in a cab. Right now if you like. He'd never find out.'

Like a dinosaur slowly coming to the realisation that it was standing on a sharp stone, Pete Mac's brain gradually and painfully whirred into action.

Shit. He was already on a promise from the red-headed sisters, and he didn't want to upset them. They were all set to go hoisting for him, which would definitely help with all the expenses he was mounting up. But he couldn't turn this down.

110

'I can't tell you how sad it makes me to have to say this, Carol, but I can't. How about tomorrow?'

Sod it, she'd have to go to a hotel. But she was buggered if she'd pay out for more than one night. Or even one night for that matter.

She bit her tongue to stop herself from telling him to go fuck himself, and did a quick run-through of the places she'd be prepared to stay for a few days. Not too expensive – she didn't want to frighten him off before she'd even started working on him to get her something more permanent. And somewhere she wouldn't be familiar to some cow of a receptionist from the old days – when she'd still been charging by the hour.

Got it.

She breathed down the phone at him: 'I can't say I'm not disappointed, Peter, because I am. Very. It's taken a lot of courage to make this phone call. But I can wait. In fact, I'll be ready and waiting for you tomorrow.' She added, pointedly: 'First thing in the morning, okay? At the Winchester Hotel in Bloomsbury. Do you know it?'

Pete Mac was sniggering like a twelve-year-old. 'Don't worry, Carol, I'll find it.'

'You've made me so happy.' She treated him to a tinkly little giggle. 'You won't keep me waiting, will you, Peter? Promise me you'll be there by ten at the very latest, or I'll think you've changed your mind, won't I? And that'll make me ever so sad.'

111

'I'll be there, darling, you can bank on it.'

Gotcha! He'd be there before checkout time. She wouldn't have to pay the night's bill. 'I can't wait, sweetheart. See you in the morning.'

As he put down the phone, Pete Mac was grinning like a panting hound. The red-headed sisters, and now Carol Mercer . . .

He'd always known his day would come.

The following morning, Carol Mercer, dressed only in a bath towel, opened the door to find Pete Mac standing outside in the hotel corridor, just as she had expected. What she hadn't expected was the bunch of tired-looking carnations that he was pointing at her like some parody of a Victorian suitor coming to call on his young lady.

She just about managed to stop herself from bursting out laughing.

'Peter,' she cooed. 'How sweet.' She took the flowers, puckered her lips and kissed the air about a foot away from his mouth. 'Come in, please.'

As he swaggered into the room, he took in the chintzy, English-country interior, and Carol took in his expensive dark blue suit, his slightly tatty brown suede shoes, his thinning red hair, jowly face and his heavy, wobbly belly.

'Still raining,' he said.

'Oh, Peter, I'm so glad you're here. I've decided that this isn't a temporary thing, I've walked out on

Brendan for good.' Carol threw out her arms to him, and the loosely fastened towel fell to the floor.

Pete Mac's jaw dropped open, and, as he ripped his shirt in the zip of his fly in his hurry to pull down his trousers, Carol Mercer knew that not only did she not have to worry about her hotel bill, but, from the look on his face, getting a more permanent roof over her head wasn't going to be too much of a problem either.

To Carol's further relief, Pete Mac's performance was mercifully brief and unadventurous. He went through the motions and was propped up on the pillows, and halfway through a cigarette, all in ten minutes flat.

Carol snuggled into his chest.

'Peter, you do know the reason I walked out on Brendan, don't you? I couldn't get you out of my mind.' She tried an experimental sniffle – would he crumple when she cried, or run a mile?

He fannied about finding an ashtray on the bedside table, then ground out his cigarette and wrapped his arms around her. 'Poor kid. Why didn't you say something before?'

'I wanted to, but I didn't know what you'd say.' Sniff. 'You being married to Patricia and everything. And Brendan being your brother-in-law.'

'Pat don't mean nothing to me, Carol, I just feel sorry for her, that's all. That's why I've stuck by her and the kid for all these years. How could I leave the poor mare, when she thinks the bloody world of me?

And as for Brendan – not got no time for the bloke. No time whatsoever. Never have, never did.'

'He scares me.' She let a tear drip on to his arm. 'What am I going to do, Peter? I've got no money, but I can't go back home. He'd kill me if he knew what I felt about you. So where can I go?'

Pete Mac considered this puzzle. He had a flat, but he'd got the red-headed sisters holed up in there. And he didn't want them upset. They weren't only up for anything, but they'd soon be bringing him in a good few bob with their hoisting. He'd just have to find somewhere else for her.

'Don't worry, darling, I'll give you some money and you can stay here for a few days, while we get you a place sorted out somewhere.'

'You are so sweet.' She ran a finger through his sparse wiry chest hair. 'And I'm really glad you don't like Brendan. That makes me feel a lot less guilty.'

Pete Mac cupped her breast in his hand and leaned over her, licking at her nipple. 'But I hope it don't make you feel a lot less naughty.'

'Course it doesn't,' giggled Carol, ready to gag at the stench of him. 'And we know who else doesn't like Brendan. And we know he *hates* them.'

'Who's that then?'

'The Kessler family. So why's that then, do you think, Peter?'

*

'What's this all about, O'Donnell?' Having refused to sit down, Daniel Kessler was standing in front of Brendan's desk in the private office at the back of the cab firm. He was flanked by his brother Sammy and his cousin Maurice. They were all dressed in long dark overcoats, which they had no intention of taking off.

This definitely wasn't a social visit.

Daniel sunk his hands deep into his pockets. 'We get this call out of the blue demanding a ridiculous amount of money to be paid over. For what exactly?'

'Aw blimey, did I forget to explain?' Brendan slapped a hand against his forehead. 'My memory.' He leaned forward and flicked through some papers, as if too busy to be having this conversation. 'We've got some merchandise for you. For the shops. Films, magazines. Proper hardcore. Expensive stuff. Good earners.'

'Say we don't want it?'

'You ain't got no choice, pal.' Brendan stacked the papers into a neat pile and weighted them down with a heavy stone ashtray. 'Remember, you're only working in the East End because we tolerate you. Or do you want to start rowing again?' He scratched distractedly at his head. 'Me, I'm more than ready to take you on, Kessler. More than ready.'

For want of something to say – and to save himself from landing Brendan fucking O'Donnell a square one right on the chin – Daniel sucked at his teeth. He just knew it was him who'd had the speed out of that lorry.

Brendan leaned back in his chair. 'Good, we understand one another. Now, I think you need to start thinking fast, because now we're in business, I'm gonna give you one week – seven whole days, mind – and you are gonna have that money for me. Or I am going to be very cross with you, Kessler. And, who knows, I might just find myself having to get someone in who can run the shops properly. The way I want them run.'

Brendan stood up and walked over to the door. He pulled it open and said over his shoulder, 'Turn the light off when you leave, lads.'

With that he walked out, leaving them standing there.

'Fuck you!' Daniel Kessler spat out the words as if they were poison. 'The money that bastard's talking about, even if we stripped every betting shop, and then managed to get enough together to fund another consignment from Spain, we'd never do it in time.'

Maurice sat himself down in Brendan's chair, and clasped his hands behind his head. 'Now I know we're all agreed that we ain't ready for a full-scale battle with the bastards.' He lifted up his legs and plonked his feet down on the desk, the heels of his shoes leaving greasy black polish marks in disrespectful tramlines across its shiny glass surface. 'So, my bank-job idea suddenly seem attractive to you then, does it, fellers?'

Chapter 9

Luke finally reached out for the phone that stood on his black acrylic bedside table. It was the fourth time it had rung – or rather trilled its irritating trill – in the last ten minutes. Whoever it was was certainly persistent.

'Yeah?'

'Luke, it's me, Ellie.'

It sounded urgent.

'Ellie? What's wrong?'

'You! You haven't called to let me know the arrangements for coming over to London, and I am so fed up with waiting. It's driving me demented over here. I'm telling you, if I don't get away from Aunt Mary and this bloody farm, they'll be taking me away in handcuffs.'

Luke hoisted himself up to a sitting position. 'That's not funny, Ellie. Now take a deep breath, and calm down. You're sounding just like a whiny kid wanting another sweetie.'

'I don't mean to, Luke. Honestly. But it's Friday night, ten days before bloody Christmas and there is absolutely nothing to do over here. Nothing. Not a single, solitary party.' There was a slight hesitation.

'Well, except for deadly family things. And I'm twenty-two years old, for Christ's sake. Twenty-two. Not fourteen. And I want a bloody life.'

Luke reached out for his cigarettes and lighter. 'D'you think you might be exaggerating a bit, Ellie? Overreacting?' He frowned as he drew in the first lungful of smoke. 'And making a big mistake. Because I'm telling you, things ain't exactly easy over here at the minute either. Brendan and Mum are at each other's throats, and I'm stuck in the middle of the pair of them.' He put his hand over the mouthpiece. 'Ssshh, Nicky. In a minute.'

'Ignore me then.' Nicky rolled over, tugging the bedcovers away from Luke.

'And if she ever finds out that Brendan got you involved in doing that delivery over to Ireland for him, that would just about put the tin lid on it.'

'I don't need you starting on me as well, Luke.'

'I know, I'm sorry, love.' He smiled to himself, imagining her standing there pouting at the phone.

'It's not as though I don't deserve a bit of fun. I work like a slave with those horses. You should see me. I'm practically running the place. Luke, please, let me come and stay in London with you. Please.'

'I told you –'

'Only for a while. I won't get in the way. I promise. I've really thought about it. I was going to ask Brendan, but I already guessed what Eileen would have to say.' Ellie sighed dramatically. 'You probably don't want to hear this, Luke, but you should hear the things Aunt Mary has to say about Eileen. Honestly, she is such a cow. And while I don't understand the half of it, your mam's still her sister-in-law, when all's said and done.'

'Ellie, like you said, you don't know the half of it.'

'But I know what it's like living over here in Kildare. It's like living with a witch. You should see the schedule she's got mapped out for me over Christmas. If I'm not mucking out, I'm expected to be in the house smiling at the bloody priest and the old bags from the village, while they down tumblers of sweet bloody sherry after Mass. Then I'll be expected to help with the mountains of sodding food she'll insist we all swallow. And that's without the washing-up. Oh, Luke, *please*. I'm truly going to lose my mind if you don't let me come over and live in London.'

Luke ground out his cigarette. 'Finished?'

'I suppose so, but you have to –'

'Ellie, I'll see what I can do.'

'Promise?'

'I promise. I'll try and sort something out, and I'll call you back tomorrow or Sunday. Okay?'

'Oh, Luke –'

'Bye, Ellie. Aw, and you might start watching that tongue of yours. I don't like to hear women swearing.'

Luke put the phone down and ran his hand over

Nicky's strong, muscular back, just the touch making him smile with pleasure and longing. 'If you want to go to that club, we'd better think about getting up.'

Nicky turned over and smiled back up at him. 'I'd much rather stay here in bed with you,' he said, pulling Luke down on top of him.

He touched his lips gently against Luke's. 'You know, I like it, the way you're nice to your little sister. You really care about her, don't you?'

'Nearly as much as I care about you.' Luke looked down into Nicky's eyes and wondered at how his life could have changed so much in just six months. How being with Nicky had made him happier than he could ever have imagined.

Carol Mercer paid the cab driver. She'd have liked to have told him to wait for her, but she couldn't afford to waste any more money. This was the third club she'd been to in search of Sammy Kessler, and the few pounds she'd allowed herself for the evening were running out fast. She'd now got plenty of information about him and the other Kesslers from Pete Mac, and even more about the O'Donnells. And it was about time she started making use of it. She could hardly credit some of the things Pete Mac had told her. It was bordering on the ridiculous – he was such a big mouth, and worse, he was dumb with it. A very dangerous combination that had made her

121

realise pretty quickly that she'd have to be careful about every single word she said to him.

Unfortunately, there was one thing the lard ball hadn't been able to blab about – well, not with any certainty, anyhow – and that was where Sammy Kessler spent his Friday nights. So Carol had had no choice, she'd had to jump in and out of cabs, visiting all the places Pete Mac had so much as mentioned.

She'd had to go by cab as she could hardly walk through the streets or jump on a bus – not the way she'd got herself done up. But then again, if she hadn't made the effort to glam herself up, she needn't have even bothered looking for him in the first place. If there was one thing she'd learned from her time with Brendan O'Donnell – *that bastard* – it was that faces like him and Sammy Kessler had girls throwing themselves at them from every direction. So she had to be sure of standing out from the crowd to even hope of getting his attention.

She looked up at the sign above the door – here goes, another punt – unbuttoned her coat – sod the cold – and tottered up to the biggest of the three bouncers.

Please, let this be the place.

'Hiya,' she said, running a lavender-painted nail lightly across his chest. 'I'm meeting Sammy Kessler. He here yet?'

'Yeah,' the man said to her breasts. 'I'll take you through, darling.'

122

As they went inside, Carol saw him standing alone at the bar. She knew it was Sammy Kessler from the grainy photographs she'd seen in the evening papers, but he still wasn't really what she'd expected. Jewish blokes were meant to be all dark and handsome. Well, he was handsome, in a rough sort of way, and much more of a bloke than a chap – the type she liked, actually – but he had long curly hair, touching the collar of his jacket, and it was much fairer than she'd imagined it would be. He'd probably been a right little snowball as a kid. In fact, if he'd been wearing a long white frock instead of a black three-piece suit, he'd have looked exactly like the pictures of the angels they'd had on the walls of the hostel where she'd stayed when her mum had first chucked her out.

'The young lady you're expecting,' said the bouncer, handing her over like a package before heading straight back to his door duties. He was experienced enough to know that you only stood with the Kesslers if you'd been invited.

'Hope you didn't mind my little fib,' said Carol, swinging her shoulders in a parody of a shy schoolgirl. 'But I've heard so much about you, and I so wanted to meet you.'

'Aw yeah?' Sammy looked about him as if seeking out someone – anyone – more interesting.

This was going to be tougher than she'd thought. She moved closer. Still no bloody eye contact. What did she have to do, get her tits out or something?

'You're famous, you are.'

'Right.'

'I'm Carol Mercer. I used to be Brendan O'Donnell's girlfriend.'

There. Now the bugger was interested.

'But I walked out on him. Got bored.'

Why wasn't he offering her a drink?

'But I still keep in touch with Pete Mac.' Much too close in touch, unfortunately, the vile, greasy pig. 'He's told me a lot about you. Like you going out with Brendan's little sister, Catherine. And how terrible it was when she got shot dead by mistake, because of her dad and all that. That was so sad. Really horrible.'

A different look had come over him. Distaste? No, something stronger than that. It was real, deep-down hatred. She'd have to be careful what else she said.

Sammy put his glass down on the bar. 'Pete Mac? Why would I wanna hear anything that gobshite's been saying?'

'I suppose he is a bit thick.'

'Tell me something I don't know.'

She looked up into his eyes. 'At least he's only married to an O'Donnell. And I don't think he reckons them much, not when it comes down to it.'

'Look, darling, if you don't mind, I've got to –'

She took a gamble and stepped sideways, blocking his way as he attempted to leave. 'Don't be like that, Sammy. I only want to keep you company. And maybe there's stuff I could, you know, tell you about. Things about Brendan.'

He looked her up and down. She had some bottle, give her that. But she wasn't his type, not by a long chalk – too young and too cheap-looking for his taste. Although it might be entertaining to string her along for a while, if only to wind up O'Donnell. And who knows, maybe she might have picked up some interesting stuff. She seemed bright enough for a bird.

'I'll take you out for a drink. Next week.'

'Not tonight?'

'No. I'm busy tonight. Business.'

'Even for little me?'

'It's family business,' Sammy said, putting an end to it. He checked his watch, and started towards the door. 'See you here. Eight o'clock. Tuesday.'

Sod it. Now she'd have to spend the whole weekend in that miserable rotten hole that Pete Mac had got her over the tobacconist's shop in Bow. What was it with this lot and their families? They were hard as nails with everyone else, violent thugs who didn't give a shit, but have their mums snap their fingers, or their brothers phone them, and they jumped to and did as they were told like meek little bloody lambs. She was glad she didn't have a family to tell her what to do.

Really glad.

All she wanted was her little house back.

God, she missed it: all nice and clean and

everything in order. Mind you, if she played up the Brendan thing with Sammy, got him in a state where he was trying to outdo him, maybe she'd get something even better.

Chapter 10

It was just over an hour since Sammy Kessler had left Carol standing in the bar. Despite the biting frostiness of the night air, sweat was glistening on his top lip.

He and Daniel were standing behind their cousin Maurice outside the front door of a solidly middle-class, detached house in Surrey. A warm yellow glow was coming from the downstairs windows.

Maurice rang the bell.

Sammy swallowed hard, his mouth as dry as if it had been wiped out with a dishcloth. He pulled up his scarf, leaving only his eyes on show.

Daniel did likewise, covering most of his face with navy cashmere, and then flexed his fingers, ready to use the cosh in his pocket.

The door was opened by a man in his early forties. He was dressed casually – corduroy trousers, Aran sweater and Viyella shirt, yet his manner was as formal as if he'd been standing there in white tie and tails.

'Maurice,' he said, the slight quaver in his otherwise authoritatively clipped intonation betraying his apprehension. 'Tried to call you.'

'Did you, Charles?' replied Maurice, leaning up against the jamb.

Sammy and Daniel exchanged puzzled looks. These two *knew* each other?

'Sorry, old chap.' Charles let out a long, slow, sighing breath, as if deeply disappointed. 'Been a bit of a hitch, I'm afraid.'

'A hitch, eh, feller?' said Maurice, shoving the man to one side. 'I think we'd better come in and discuss it then, don't you?'

Maurice now had Charles pressed up against the sink in the kitchen at the back of the house.

'What d'you mean, feller?' Maurice's face was almost touching his. 'We can't get in there till tomorrow fucking morning?'

Charles gulped, lifting his chin to avoid Maurice's breath. 'Please, keep your voice down. Daphne's through in the dining room.'

Maurice leaned even closer to him, his chest pressing against him. 'Maybe it's time we joined her.'

Charles opened the dining-room door as if trying not to disturb a sleeping child. 'Daphne. A surprise. We have guests.'

A slightly faded woman, sitting at a bulbous-legged oak table, looked up. She was writing in a leather-bound book with a fountain pen. Standing behind her, in the bay window, was a long-haired, teenaged girl, wearing a smocked peasant blouse and flared, hipster jeans; she was decorating a luxuriant, ceiling-high Christmas tree.

Daphne smiled sportingly. 'How lovely. Can I make anyone a drink?'

Maurice plonked himself down on the table, right next to where she was sitting, making her start. He picked up the book and flicked through it before letting it fall from his fingers. 'What's this then?'

'A note I keep. Of people who've been for dinner.' Daphne glanced over at the girl, who was staring at the three strange men in their wide-lapelled, flared-trousered suits, a blue-and-silver glass bauble dangling from her hand on a gold thread. They were men of a type that Daphne and her daughter rarely came across, and especially not in their own home. 'And what they ate when they came,' she finished, distractedly.

'That's right,' said Charles. 'And that's why you're checking it now, isn't it, Daphne? Because we've got people coming tonight. In about an hour. Pre-Christmas drinks, then supper.'

'Don't give me that, feller.' Maurice snorted derisively. 'If you were having people round tonight, why isn't she all dolled up?' He grasped Daphne's chin, pinching her flesh, and turning her head towards her husband. 'Look at the state of her.'

'Charles? What's happening?'

'Mum!'

'It's all right, Fiona,' Charles said. 'Everything will be fine.'

'And it's already nearly nine o'clock. Everyone knows your sort are tucked up in bed with a cup of cocoa by ten. So don't fanny around with me, mate. Now, are you coming to the bank with me or what?'

'I promise you. This new time lock won't let me open the vault until six o'clock tomorrow morning.'

'Charles?' Daphne was now very close to tears. 'What's going on?'

Maurice levered himself off the table. He pointed to the girl. 'You, sit down here by your mother. And keep schtum.'

'Do as he says, Fiona,' said Charles. 'Sit down and be quiet.'

'Good advice, feller. I'd hate to have to hurt a pretty young girl like her.'

Daphne swiped her eyes with the back of her hand. 'Oh, my God, Charles, I've realised who they are. You must do as they ask. They're those people they were talking about on the news. The IRA kidnapping gang.'

Maurice, who had just walked out into the hall, burst out laughing. 'We're not the Irish, love,' he called over his shoulder, 'we're the frigging Jews.'

Sammy went out after him. 'What're you up to, Maury?'

'Blimey, feller, get a grip. I'm just going out to the car. I brought some ropes and gags along just in case.

Good job too if he's telling the truth and we've really got to keep them three quiet all night.'

'You never said there'd be a kid involved.'

'You never asked.'

'We never had a tree when I lived up in Manchester. Except over the park, like. But they didn't have balls.' Maurice laughed, amused at his own wit, as he stroked a finger down the girl's cheek.

'Leave her alone,' hissed Charles, straining against the rope that was binding his wrists behind his back.

'I'm all right, Dad.' Fiona shivered, despite the warmth of the room.

'Will you leave off?' snapped Sammy. He was looking down at the floor, and could have been speaking to any of them. He knew he shouldn't have got involved in this. It was Daniel who wanted the money for the property deal with the Baxters, not him. Now here he was holding three hostages, all trussed up like bloody oven-ready chickens ready for roasting, in a posh house somewhere in the middle of fucking Surrey. And if that wasn't enough, the woman looked as if she was about to wet her pants, the kid might well start screaming her head off at any minute, and the sodding bank manager looked the type to suddenly come over all like Batman and try to protect his family and his firm's dough. And they could all identify Maurice, because for some stupid fucking reason he wasn't even wearing a bloody mask. How had he been so totally brainless as to go along with Maurice and his foolproof fucking plan? Why hadn't he just taken the night off, and gone out with that bird of O'Donnell's? It couldn't have been much worse than this.

Maurice patted the girl's face, hard enough to sting. 'Now you behave, Fiona.' He said her name as if recounting a nasty smell. 'And nothing's going to happen to you. But you start getting difficult, like, and I can't guarantee you won't get hurt. All right?'

Daphne dropped her chin. 'I need to use the lavatory.'

Maurice nodded. 'Sure, I'll come with you. But you do just want a piss, don't you? I don't think I fancy watching you doing the other thing, love.'

Charles launched himself to his feet. 'Please, don't do this. How would you feel if it was your wife? Your child.'

Maurice turned down his mouth and shook his head. 'Haven't got a wife actually, feller.' He was grinning. 'But I reckon I've got plenty of kids knocking about the place.'

Sammy was beginning to panic. This was supposed to be straightforward, easy, now look at it. This was the sort of situation that could so easily get out of hand, especially with someone like his cousin around. 'Maurice, let her go to the lav, mate. I'll stand outside the door – make sure she don't try and run away or get out of the window or nothing.'

'I'll have to think about that one.'

'Maurice, please,' begged Charles. 'It's not her fault they installed that new timing device. I tried my best to let you know, but I couldn't get hold of you.'

Daphne turned to her husband. 'You *knew* about this, Charles?'

'Blimey, she's got a sour-looking gob on her, ain't she, eh, feller? No wonder you come up with this plan. Get you enough money to get away from her bloody moaning, eh? Got yourself a bird tucked away somewhere, have you? Some little sort who works at the bank?'

'This was meant to be just between the two of us. You gave me your word.'

'What, like I'm your best pal or something? Your mucker from down the golf club? Sorry, feller, you've got the wrong idea. This is the real world. But tell you what, I'll be fair and make you a deal. You stand up, I'll untie your hands, and you take your trousers off. Then I'll let her go and have a piss.'

Charles looked away. 'No.'

Maurice shoved him backwards knocking him to the floor. 'Don't be silly, Charlie boy.'

Sammy stepped forward to intervene, but Daniel stopped him, grabbing him angrily by the arm. Daniel wasn't happy about the way things were going either, but Sammy had to keep control of himself. Showing disunity looked weak. And that could be as dangerous as Maurice going off on one.

133

He watched, grim-faced, as Maurice loosened the knots and waited for Charles to slip his hands out of the loops of rope.

'Sensible feller,' he said, when Charles, his head hanging low, eventually freed his hands. 'Now, off with your kecks.'

As Charles stepped out of his trousers, Maurice shook his head and tutted loudly. He was pointing at Charles, but speaking to his wife and daughter. 'Humiliating that, don't you reckon? See, you'd have to rip my head off before I'd do something like that. And in front of your wife and kid . . .'

'I'll get you for this, Kessler.'

Maurice shook his head and slowly turned to face him. 'Don't be daft, Charlie. You're in no position to get anyone. Because if you so much as try it, I'll have to tell your bosses all about that raid we did back in '71.' Maurice grinned at his cousins. 'Cleared the bank right out an hour before the staff got to work. Single-handed, I was. Mind you, according to the story this feller gave to the law and his bosses, there were six of us did it. And every one of us was armed with a sawn-off shotgun. Like a bloody gangster movie.'

Now Maurice was staring at Daphne and Fiona, as he jerked his thumb over his shoulder at Charles. 'Bank gave you a reward for that, didn't they, Charlie? You lying fucking hypocrite. For you being so brave, like. Your old woman and kid here, they

134

were away on holiday at the time, if you remember. It was only because they were gonna be here tonight that you said I'd need two people to help me. To make it look authentic, like. By holding the poor cows hostage. Then you could go boohooing to your bosses. Say how you had no choice in the matter – *they were holding my family, threatening to rape me wife and daughter, do all sorts of nasty things to them if I didn't do as I was told*. That's why I never bothered with a mask.' He giggled happily. 'I mean, he's hardly gonna risk grassing on us, now is he? He'd be out of the bank and into the nick quicker than a street-corner tart dropping her drawers. It's a shame really – it's his plan, but we get to keep all the dough.'

Charles lunged at Maurice, but Maurice batted him away as if he were nothing more than a bothersome fly at a Sunday-afternoon picnic.

'Now you really are being daft, feller.'

As Maurice began punching and kicking her father, Fiona vomited over the table, and Daphne began to cry softly into her chest.

Chapter 11

Pete Mac shut the door of the flat behind him and took a deep lungful of chilly, early-morning air. Like a sumo wrestler about to face his opponent, Pete Mac was preparing himself.

He was going home to see Patricia.

He'd been away for three nights now, staying at the flat with the red-haired sisters and nipping round for a quick visit to Carol Mercer in between, but, seeing as it was the day before Christmas Eve, Pat would be bound to expect him to at least put his head round the door. So he was going to do the right thing and show his face for a half-hour or so before going to the cab office to find out what was happening with Brendan.

Or should he say to get Brendan's orders for the day . . .

He had no choice on either point. If he didn't go home there'd be murders, and the last thing he wanted was another rucking from Pat. And if he didn't drop into work, Brendan would start leading off as well. And he was already feeling more than a bit pissed off.

It was the Liverpool girls. They were getting to him.

He liked the redheads all right, they were a right laugh, game for anything – he had no complaints there – but he was beginning to suspect that maybe they hadn't been entirely honest about their hoisting skills. Either that or they were having him over. They'd been in the flat for over three weeks now and there hadn't been a sniff of any of the gear they reckoned they were going to lift for him, which meant that they were getting to be an expensive hobby. Especially now he had Carol Mercer on the firm as well, even though the rooms he'd got her over in Bow were as cheap as piss. Perhaps he should give the pair of them the bum's rush, and concentrate on young Carol for a while. That'd be funny, that would, turning up at clubs and that with her. It'd get right up Brendan's nose. If he had the bottle to do anything that mad, and didn't mind having his head ripped off.

Maybe he'd just keep all three of them going for a while. Why shouldn't he treat himself? Not many fellers could say that they had three bits on the side at once. But then he wasn't any ordinary feller, was he? He was Pete Mac.

Even knowing that he would probably soon be facing one of Pat's famous silent treatments, and Caty's sneering dismissal of anything he had to say, he didn't actually mind that much any more. Because as he drove towards his house in Jubilee Street, Pete Mac was feeling rather content with the way the world was treating him.

He was a one-off, and he knew it.

*

Luke was sitting drinking coffee in the corner of the office that Sandy had set up in one of the bedrooms of her new home on Old Ford Road. He watched her as she copied notes from a rough pad into a formal ledger. He thought she looked happy. And he was right – she was, or rather as happy as she could be, knowing that Barry was banged up on remand in Brixton. But moving into the house had certainly done a lot to cheer her up.

From the moment Brendan had shown her the place – could it really be only a couple of weeks ago? – Sandy had loved it. She could still hardly dare believe that the high-ceilinged, three-storey Victorian house complete with a basement 'airy' on the Old Ford Road was hers. And that wasn't all. At the front it faced on to Victoria Park, with its big graceful trees covered in frost in the early mornings and dripping with rain in the afternoons. Then there was the canal with its swans and ducks and even the occasional barge, right there at the back. She could actually walk down to the water from the kitchen door.

It was all too beautiful for words.

And after the nightmare years of looking after Barry – cleaning up after he'd vomited or soiled himself yet again, and having to witness the last few things she owned disappearing as his cravings drove him to sell even their clothes – Sandy couldn't believe her luck. Now it was more like living in some wonderful dream.

She even liked the work. Admittedly, she hadn't been sure about it at first. Running an escort agency had seemed so sleazy, even after the horrors she'd been through with Barry, but she'd been surprised at how quickly she'd come to accept it. And it wasn't as if she had much contact with the girls. She interviewed them, and phoned them with appointments, and made the arrangements for Anthony to collect their money – having a constant string of girls coming to the house would have looked suspicious even in an area where, it went without saying, people didn't ask questions. But if she had been forced to have more direct, personal exchanges with the escorts, it would have been a small price to pay for the stability she was now enjoying and the comfort in which she was living. It was an odd feeling, but it seemed as if the past few years had happened to someone else, a sadder, more wary, probably more frightened person. A person she would never want to be. Not again.

She owed Brendan a lot.

The telephone rang. Sandy cleared her throat, and, in a fair imitation of a Home Counties accent, made an appointment for a Mr Lawrence to have a companion for tomorrow evening – no doubt a special Christmas Eve treat for himself. She flicked over her page of notes, put down her pen, and leaned back in her chair.

'All right, Luke, lovely as it is to see you here –

again – you do know how busy I'm going to be today, don't you?'

'You're getting that phone voice down to a fine art, San.' He swirled the dregs of coffee round in his cup, watching the thick sediment form into a muddy spiral. 'You know what I'm doing; I'm keeping an eye on you. I don't like you being involved with Brendan like this. And it's not as if there's any need. You can come and work for me. Start tomorrow. Today if you like.'

'What is it with you O'Donnells? Can't you get staff or something? Am I the only worker left in sodding London?' She paused. 'You're all beginning to make me feel like a bloody charity case.'

'Don't be daft, Sandy. We've been friends long enough for you to know that's not true. And for you to know I don't like what Brendan does. He tries to make out that I'm as bad as him, but we all know that's not true. I've never liked the life him and Dad thought was normal, and I've always done my best to steer away from it as much as I can. I'd hate to see you getting dragged down to his level.'

'What, you reckon I'm not capable of looking after myself, do you? That I can't make my own decisions? Thanks very much.'

'Don't be like that.' He was still studying his cup.

'If you must know, Luke, Brendan makes me laugh. Makes me feel like a woman again. Like I'm alive. And it's a nice thing, having my life back.' She picked up her pen and flipped open her book as if to start work again. 'It ain't easy living with a junkie, you know.'

He slowly raised his head and looked at her. 'Does Barry know about you seeing Brendan? Cos remand in that place can do a bloke's head in. Especially when he knows he's up for a right handful.'

She gave up the pretence of working, stood up and went over to the window. 'Do you want the truth, Luke? I really don't know. Because he won't see me. Won't see anyone. Almost Christmas, and he won't even let me visit him.'

'Mum was like that.'

'Yeah, so I heard. I suppose that's where the poor, daft sod got the idea from. But he even sends me letters back. Don't even open them.'

'I'm sorry.'

'I know. Now go on, piss off home and see Nicky, I've got work to do before Brendan gets here.'

He stood up with a sigh. 'So, what you doing for Christmas?'

She turned to face him. 'If the wish on my lucky star comes true, I'll be slobbing about in bed in my nightie: drinking tea, eating toast and Marmite, and laughing my head off at Morecambe and Wise. Why? Wanna join me?'

Brendan winced as he spotted Milo leaning against the wall in his usual place in the snooker club. Not that it was very difficult to spot him; he was, after all, the only one there with big, blond Afro hair and wearing a plum-coloured, crushed-velvet suit draped over his scrawny frame. But while he wasn't exactly hard to miss, looking as he did like a gift-wrapped, yellow lollipop, it wasn't his fashion advice that Brendan was after. He'd turned out all right, a good little worker, even if he did look a ponce.

'Oi, Flanagan,' Brendan called to him, jerking his thumb towards the bar.

'All right, Mr O?' Milo stood with his back to the bar, his elbows propped on the counter.

'You've done well shifting all that merchandise, Flanagan. You're a good lad. Discreet and fast.'

'I do me best.'

'Can't ask more than that of someone,' said Brendan, brushing away Milo's mimed offer of a drink. 'And I've decided this could be a useful little sideline, so we'll be getting another consignment for you to handle in the new year. In the meantime, here's a little Christmas bonus for you.' He winked as he handed over a wad of notes. 'I believe in showing appreciation where's it's due.'

Milo watched Brendan as he bowled out of the club, whistling a slightly off-key rendition of the Slade Christmas song that seemed to be playing everywhere you went. Milo knew he was watching a man who understood that all eyes were trained on him

– and who didn't give a flying fuck. This was his world. He owned it.

'What's up with him?' asked a short, pale-faced, middle-aged man standing behind the bar, his roll-up bobbing up and down from his bottom lip as he spoke. 'He usually comes in, growls, checks if Anthony's collected the week's takings, and then finishes off by threatening one or two of us with a bit of light GBH.'

'Must have had a bash over the head,' suggested a squinty-eyed youth chalking the tip of a very expensive custom-made cue.

'No, it's a lot worse than that,' said Milo. 'From the whispers I've heard, it seems like the hard man's gone and fallen in love.'

Brendan was still whistling the Christmas song when Luke, breathing heavily, caught up with him just as he was putting his key in the street door of the O'Donnell family home on the Mile End Road.

'Hang on, Brendan,' puffed Luke. 'Before you go indoors, I need to ask you something.'

'You wanna get yourself fit, mate. Look at you, wheezing like some old pensioner.'

Luke lifted his chin. 'I had to park right up there, and then I saw you at the street door, and I wanted to catch you to have a talk.'

'Well, come inside then, it's bloody perishing out here.'

He shook his head. 'No, I don't want Mum to hear what I've got to say. And before you say anything, nothing's wrong. Well, not really.'

'Come on, Luke, spit it out, or I'm going indoors and leaving you out here.'

'It's Ellie. You know she's camping out at mine. I was wondering if Mum would wear it, d'you think, if I asked if she could come over and have a bit of dinner with us all? I'd hate to think of her alone on Christmas Day.'

Luke considered for a moment, deciding whether he should go for broke and say what he really wanted to. What did he have to lose except for an increasingly annoying lodger? A lodger who – much as he loved the little mare – thought it was fine to drape her dripping underwear all over his bathroom, to leave her dirty plates all over the kitchen, and not to give him and Nicky a moment alone together.

And those moments with Nicky were becoming more important all the time; he knew he was going to really miss him when he went back to see his mum for Christmas – even though it was just for the one day.

He found himself smiling; he was bang in love with the bloke.

Here goes.

'And ask if she could stay for a night or two. Maybe three. What d'you reckon?'

'Cramping your style, is it, having our little sister

144

around?' Brendan grinned and punched Luke on the arm.

'No.'

'All right, I'm only mucking about. And who knows, Mum might even *ask* her to stay here, once I tell her my news.'

'What news?'

'Come in and listen for yourself.'

'Mum, I want you to hear me out before you go mad. I thought you should know that Ellie's over from Kildare. She's been staying at Luke's for the past couple of days, and I want you to let her come here for Christmas dinner. Maybe stay a night or two.'

Eileen, who was sitting in her now usual place in the easy chair by the old, disused kitchener, looked up from the knitting that had become almost obsessive – a way of keeping the world away because she was 'busy'. Her expression was calm, but her voice was anything but. 'You want me to have your father's bastard in my home?'

Brendan flashed his eyebrows at his brother. 'Least she's speaking to me, eh, Luke?' Then he turned back to Eileen. 'Mum, Ellie's an O'Donnell. She dropped the Palmer from her name a long time ago. And Aunt Mary's raised her right. She's an O'Donnell through and through. A decent Catholic girl.'

'Decent?'

'Look, Mum, this is important to me. I am loyal to no one but my family, you know that. And that's why I've brought this up now. I know you're gonna be chuffed about this.' He winked at Luke, then turned back to his mother. 'I'm thinking about settling down, getting married and having chavvies and that. Some time in the new year. I'm gonna bring her round for Christmas dinner, and I want you, and Patricia and Ellie – my sisters – to meet her and welcome her.'

Eileen stood up. 'You do as you think fit. You always do. So why change now? Bring whoever you like.'

Luke waited for his mother to climb the basement stairs and leave them alone in the kitchen. 'Married? You? Does Sandy know about this?'

'Course not.' He went over to the wall cabinet and took out a bottle of Jameson's and two glasses. 'I ain't asked her yet.'

'You're gonna ask *Sandy* to marry you?'

'Bloody hell, give the man a fucking coconut. You didn't think I meant Carol, did you?'

'What, got Sandy pregnant, have you?'

Brendan ignored the sarcasm, and poured them both a drink. 'I'm going round there soon as I get washed and changed. She's expecting me.'

'But I bet she ain't expecting this,' Luke muttered.

'What's that?'

'Nothing, Brendan. Nothing at all.'

*

146

Brendan was in the sitting room of Sandy's new house, his big, muscular body almost spilling over the sage-green Draylon armchair.

Sandy sat facing him, on the very edge of her seat. She was looking at him as if he were speaking in some obscure language she'd never heard before.

'You've done this out lovely, San. You've hardly spent any money, but I can't believe how good it looks. I reckon Luke was right about this place, it's gonna be a good little investment. They won't knock these gaffs down, not like them on Grove Road. He's a clever little bleeder, give him that. Knows his property all right. Maybe I'll have to listen to him more often, eh?'

He paused to light two cigarettes, handing one of them to Sandy. 'He's even started talking about doing up old warehouses down the docks. Although fuck knows who'd wanna live in one of them. But they might be worth having a butcher's – see what the SP is, eh?'

'Brendan, will you stop going on about property? You've just dropped a right bloody bombshell in my lap, and now you're talking about flaming warehouses.'

He reached out and took her hand in a tender gesture that surprised them both. 'How many times have you said yourself that you've just been looking after Barry, like he was your brother or something? I

147

can give you more than that, San, I can give you a good life. A really good life.'

'You're serious, aren't you?'

'Never been more so.'

'But your family, what would they think?'

'That I'm a lucky bastard, and you must be mad. I know I've had birds that'd make grown men weep, but I want something more than that now. And, let's face it, neither of us is getting any younger.'

'Jesus, Brendan, you certainly know how to turn a girl's head, don't you?'

'Well?'

'I dunno. I suppose I'll have to think about it.'

'Course you will. And by the way, Pat's doing Christmas dinner round mine and Mum's, and you're invited. Now get your coat, we're going up West to celebrate.'

The possibility that he and Sandy might not have anything to celebrate, because she might turn him down, hadn't occurred to Brendan, and he'd already booked a table in a restaurant in Greek Street complete with a bottle of chilled Dom Perignon.

Just half a mile away from where Brendan and Sandy were now sipping the champagne, Sammy Kessler was in bed with Carol Mercer, Brendan's very recent ex.

The hotel he had taken her to wouldn't have been Carol's first choice, but it was a damned sight better than that grotty dump Pete Mac had come up with. And sex with Sammy – boring as it might be – was a far more pleasant experience than it was with Pete. Sex didn't mean much to her anyway, other than as a means to an end. But if she didn't want to be stuck by herself above the tobacconist's, with only a visit from Pete Mac to look forward to over Christmas, she'd have to do something fast.

'What're you doing over the holidays, Sam?' As she spoke she ran her fingertips up and down the inside of his thigh. 'Or don't you take no notice? You being Jewish and that.'

'You are kidding, right?' Sammy chuckled, making his eyes crinkle. 'You'd think Mum'd had been taught by bloody nuns and blessed at birth by the Pope himself to see the way she goes to town. We have the lot. Paper hats, a tree, presents, decorations. It's a right schemozzle. And the food, she even does roast pork and crackling to go with the turkey. Lays the lot on for the family, she does. Same every year. And if all of us weren't there, she'd kill us.'

That sounded promising. 'What, *all* of us?' She moved her hand closer to his groin. 'Is that an invite?'

'Don't be silly, Carol,' he said, throwing back the covers. 'Now get yourself up and out of here.

Danny's coming to pick me up in half an hour and I wanna have a bath.'

Close to tears – of fury and frustration, mingled with a good dollop of desperation – Carol got up and stood naked beside the bed. She'd worked so hard to get herself a decent place to live, and now everything was slipping away from her again. Why did blokes treat her like this? It was so unfair. Other women got what they wanted, and it wasn't as if she was asking for much. A bit of love, being part of a proper family, knowing that she belonged somewhere, and that someone cared about her – really cared.

She'd have to sort something out soon or she'd wind up back in some rathole like that stinking hostel she'd stayed in, exhausted from walking the streets all day, but terrified to fall asleep because of what the other girls might do to her if she let her guard slip for a single moment.

She pasted on a smile, leaned on the bed and thrust her breasts towards him. 'So where's my present?' she asked, her voice husky and low, convinced he wouldn't be able to resist her.

'What? Aw yeah.' Sammy lifted his jacket off the dressing-table stool and took out his wallet without looking at her. He counted out eight five-pound notes and threw them on the crumpled bedclothes. 'You get yourself something nice. Now hurry up, will you, or Danny's gonna be here.'

'But when am I gonna see you?'

'I thought I told you to hurry up,' he said, striding over to the bathroom without so much as a backward glance.

He might just as well have slapped her face.

Chapter 12

Patricia, with Ellie's and Caty's goggle-eyed help, carried on serving the meal as if Brendan arriving with Sandy, and then announcing to them and to the rest of the family – Eileen, Luke and Pete Mac – that Sandy – whose hand he was clutching, like a school-boy with a crush – had agreed to marry him in the summer, was perfectly normal behaviour. And the fact that the O'Donnells' talk would more usually have been about the various family 'businesses' – even if it was Christmas Day and they were in the formal upstairs dining room – rather than about wedding dates and bridesmaids, and whether top hats and tails would be worn, was not so much as mentioned.

Even Pete Mac didn't make any smart-mouthed comments, although one about whether Barry was going to be invited to the do was bubbling along nicely on the tip of his tongue. But Brendan appeared not to notice the atmosphere and carried on speaking nineteen to the dozen, directing most of his comments to Eileen.

'You know, Mum, I'm so glad you're home, it wouldn't have been the same if you weren't gonna be there. And I've decided we'll have the full works, a church and that, cos I know you'd like me to do it right. It won't be Catholic though, cos Sandy's C of E, ain't you, San? But it'll still be religious and that.'

Eileen's only response was to pick at the mound of food on her plate, more food than she'd seen in years, and beautifully cooked by her daughter. But how could she eat when everything around her had gone mad? There was this girl, *her husband's bastard*, actually living under her roof as if it was normal, moral, nothing wrong with it. And her son was talking about marrying Sandy, the woman who had lived with Barry Ellis for fifteen years without being married – a man who had worked for Brendan doing God alone knew what for even more years. And all this was being done and discussed in front of Caty, her beautiful, innocent little granddaughter.

The world was no longer a place that Eileen either understood or liked very much. In fact, life in prison had made more sense than all this. At least there had been rules that had to be followed.

'Tell you what, Luke, I am gonna put on such a do. We'll find somewhere right swanky, and we'll invite everyone. Everyone. They'll never have seen anything like it.'

Pete Mac considered his question about Barry's possible invite, but thought better of it, and just contented himself with stuffing as much food and lager as he could manage into his face.

'Tell you what, San, I've been to some dos in my time, but I'm gonna surprise even meself. I can't wait to see the look on the Kesslers' faces, when they see how much I've spent.'

Pete Mac had to react to that one. 'The Kesslers?'

'Yeah, course. How could I resist? Mum gets on well with old Sophie, don't you, Mum?' No response, so he squeezed Sandy's hand and looked at her instead. 'And we've gotta show Danny, Sammy and Maurice how it's done, eh, girl?'

Sandy just smiled.

He turned back to Eileen. 'You know that Danny Kessler's got three kids, don't you, Mum, and he ain't even married to the bird.' Another squeeze of Sandy's hand. 'That wouldn't do us, would it, babe? Living together over the brush.'

If Brendan noticed Sandy's embarrassed discomfort, he didn't show it.

Eileen could have wept with relief. The meal was over. The food – some of it at least – had been eaten, drinks had been drunk, and crackers had been pulled, and she could escape at last. Get away from the noise and the sight of her husband's whore's child. Desperate as it had been to sit through it all, Eileen had forced herself, doing her best to look as if she were enjoying it, knowing that Patricia and Caty had made so much effort to make it nice for her. A special day to share with her family – God help her.

Eileen pushed back her chair. 'Patricia, that was a wonderful spread. Thank you. You and Caty worked so hard.' She stood up. 'I'll just clear the table then go and have a rest.'

Patricia nudged Caty to her feet. 'Don't be silly, Mum. Me and Caty can do that. You go and have your lie-down.'

'That was the best meal I've had in ages, Mrs O'Donnell,' Sandy said, smiling at Eileen, doing her best to join in without being pushy. 'And the least I can do is help wash up.'

'No, I won't hear of it.' This time it was Ellie, palms out to show she'd brook no argument. 'You stay up here, have a drink with the lads, and talk about wedding plans with your –' she paused '– *new fiancé*.' She wrinkled her nose at Brendan. 'And it'll give me a chance to get to know my little niece, now won't it?'

Only Luke and Patricia noted the look of horror on Eileen's face as Ellie took young Caty's hand and led her away to the kitchen.

Sandy looked at each of the three men as they sat there swallowing booze, and talking about deals she didn't understand and people she didn't know – all in the shorthand that had grown up between them over the years.

Brendan was looking pleased with himself, Pete Mac was beginning to look a bit pissed, and Luke just kept looking at his watch.

Sandy smiled at him. 'I can see you keep sneaking a look at the time, Luke. You missing Nicky, are you?'

Pete Mac and Brendan both swivelled round to stare at him.

'Blimey, Luke,' said Brendan, shaking his head and now grinning as ecstatically as if he'd just been given tickets to the Cup Final, with West Ham the guaranteed winners. 'I was right. That *is* why you wanted Ellie out of the way. You've got yourself a bloody girlfriend.' He turned to Sandy. 'Might even have a double wedding eh, San? What d'you think, girl?'

'Girlfriend? Him?' Pete Mac spluttered into his lager. 'Stop pissing about.'

Luke shot a look at Sandy, who turned away, her cheeks burning. 'Sorry, Luke, I didn't think.'

Brendan frowned then slapped his hand on the arm of his chair. 'Aw, fucking hell, Luke. It's a *bloke* kind of Nicky, innit? I should have known it was too good to be true.'

Sandy smiled feebly at Luke. 'You'll have to bring him to the wedding.'

Pete Mac's explosion of laughter could be heard all the way down in the basement kitchen.

There was no laughter – even of the sarcastic kind – in the large house set in its lovely gardens in Surrey. Charles, now an ex-bank manager, was alone, Daphne

156

and their daughter Fiona having left as soon as Maurice had phoned through to say that the vault had been cleared and that Sammy and Daniel could be on their way. Charles was sitting at the dining table, facing the half-decorated Christmas tree. He had an almost empty bottle of vintage port in front of him and an empty pill bottle in his hand.

Having come to the conclusion that he had nothing left to live for, Charles had done something about it.

Out in rural Essex, Sophie Kessler was in her element. Despite her misgivings about Danny's 'girlfriend' Babs being the mother of her eldest boy's children without being his wife, she had to admit that it was wonderful having the little ones in the house, and seeing their faces as they unwrapped the mountains of presents that Father Christmas had left for them under the tree. Maybe next year they'd celebrate Hanukkah as well. She wasn't a bad girl. And the kids were like angels. Who knows, maybe Danny would even marry Babs one day. She'd like that. But for now, things were pretty good the way they were.

Sophie couldn't help thinking back to when her own boys were little more than babies, and how they'd be so excited and get up so early on Christmas morning that it was still dark.

Sophie Kessler was a happy woman. Blessed.

And her boys were also feeling pretty blessed –

there'd been a lot more in that bank vault than even Maurice had expected.

Carol poured yet another bottle of bleach down the lavatory she was forced to share with the other lodgers in the rooms in Bow. She didn't get it, the way people lived, like animals. But at least with them all disappearing – obviously having places to go to celebrate Christmas – she had the opportunity to clean the place up a bit, make it decent.

As the tears trickled down the sides of her nose and plopped down into the pan, Carol resolutely broke into a wobbly, gulping rendition of 'Silent Night'.

Chapter 13

It was half past eleven on a cold but bright January morning. It being a Saturday, and with no pressing business – but with definite signs of a hangover making themselves felt – Brendan had only just got up. He came down the stairs into the kitchen, tying his bathrobe and yawning, mouth wide open, and making no attempt to cover his mouth.

He stopped dead on the bottom step. 'Where the fuck did you get that?'

Eileen, who was standing at the sink, looked over her shoulder at him then returned to her washing-up.

Ellie, who was over by the table, glanced up at him even more briefly. She was bent double trying to fix a lead to the collar of a boisterous Dobermann puppy that was bouncing uncooperatively around her feet.

'That's a nice way to say good morning, isn't it?' she chirped at the dog.

'Don't play me for a mug, Ellie. I asked where it came from.'

'If you'll stop shouting at me for one minute, Brendan, I'll answer you. If you must know, Luke brought him round last night, after you'd gone out. He's for Eileen. Her Christmas present. Two weeks late, of course, but that's Luke for you. Kind as anything but so distracted with his property deals and whatnot all the time . . .'

Eileen closed her eyes as she heard the affection in Ellie's voice as she spoke about Luke. She didn't quite know how, but the girl had managed to settle herself into the house, and into Luke's affections, as if she'd always lived there. As if it was the most natural thing in the world. If only she knew that Eileen tolerated her because every time she set eyes on the girl, God help her, it tore Eileen's heart to see how much like her darling Catherine she was – perhaps then she wouldn't feel quite so cosy.

Ellie pulled the puppy towards her and kissed his velvety head. 'But he is so *cute*, aren't you, Bowie? That's what I called him, when Eileen couldn't decide. And now I'm taking him out for a walk for her.'

'Fuck the poxy dog. I'm talking about that.'

'Brendan!' Ellie let the lead drop to the floor as he strode towards her. 'Don't talk to me like –'

'*The fucking coat.*' He flicked the back of his hand across the mink-lined, brick-red, suede trench coat that she had draped around her shoulders. 'Where did you get it?'

He stepped back, clipping the edge of the puppy's paw, making it dive under the table, yelping pathetically.

Eileen gripped the side of the sink.

Brendan now had Ellie by the shoulders. 'No show, don't you realise, you silly little tart? No flashy show.'

'It's only a coat.' Ellie sounded a lot braver than she was feeling.

'Yeah, the sort that someone with plenty of money can afford to wear when they're taking the fucking dog out.'

Ellie tried to shrug, but his fingers were digging into her. 'Or the sort that a dodgy chequebook can buy,' she said, her attitude an uneasy mix of wariness and cheek.

Eileen spun round.

'*What did you say?*' Brendan was shaking Ellie so hard she thought her head was going to fly off. '*Are you telling me you've been kiting?*'

'It was Milo.' Ellie started sobbing. She was terrified, no one had ever treated her like this, and now even Eileen was shouting. 'He took me to Knightsbridge. And we bought some clothes. So?'

'You stupid little idiot, you're taking a dog out, and you're wearing that?'

'I don't get it,' Ellie gulped between her sobs. 'You had me drive that horsebox, but I –'

'*But you weren't wearing a fucking hookey mink.*'

'Oh, Ellie, what have you done?' Eileen sighed, as she walked over to them, drying her hands on her apron. 'Brendan, leave the child alone. Right now. And, Ellie, you sit down and I'll make you some tea.

161

Brendan, you phone Luke and tell him to bring this Milo round here, whoever he is, and deal with him.'

The shock of hearing Eileen addressing them both directly had them obeying her more quickly than if she'd held a gun to their heads.

By the time Luke arrived with a chipper-looking Milo Flanagan, it was nearly one o'clock. Brendan was dressed in a pair of dark trousers, a black roll-neck sweater and heavy black shoes. And Ellie was no longer wearing the coat. It had been thrown across the table and was lying there like a carcass on a butcher's block.

Luke kissed Eileen on the cheek. 'Everything all right?' he said in friendly greeting.

'Luke,' she said, stroking the puppy that was now curled up asleep on her lap, 'I'm sure Brendan explained on the phone. So if you'll just take Ellie out for an hour, and have a chat with her about things, Brendan will deal with this . . .' she didn't raise her eyes from the dog '. . . young man.'

The 'young man' was now looking far more worried than cheerful.

'Sure,' Luke said calmly, despite his genuine surprise at hearing his mother not only saying more in one go than he'd heard her say in the whole two months since she'd been out, but that she had apparently started addressing both Ellie and Brendan by name.

He kissed her again then turned to his half-sister. 'Come on, Ellie, let's get going.'

Eileen waited until she heard the sound of the front door closing. 'Not here, Brendan,' she said, still without looking up.

Brendan snatched the suede coat off the table with one hand and grabbed Milo's arm with the other. His mother had asked him to do something. Something she knew Luke couldn't do.

And he felt the happiest he'd done in years.

Milo was sensible enough to listen without speaking as Brendan drove them through Stepney in the direction of the City. He just sat there and waited for the bollocking to start. And here it came.

'You never, ever get any of my family involved in any of your shit ever again. Got it?' Brendan began. 'And you never, ever go anywhere near Ellie unless I'm there or Luke's there. You never, ever do any kiting while you're working for me – *if* you wanna *stay* working for me. And now,' he drove down Cannon Street Road and pulled on to the Highway, 'I'm gonna teach you a lesson, Flanagan. And if you listen, and learn, I'm gonna let you carry on selling the gear for me. And if not, I'm gonna kill you. And I think you know my reputation to understand that I mean what I say.'

Milo wasn't sure what was going on, but he was glad he hadn't had anything to eat or he would now be sitting surrounded by a very undignified puddle of spew.

Brendan parked his car in sight of the Tower, in the shadow of the high, blind walls that surrounded the St Katherine Docks. Despite the cold of the bright winter's day, he didn't bother with a coat, but he did pull on a pair of leather gloves. 'Right, you, follow me.'

Having palmed a fiver to the watchman on the gate, Brendan led Milo into the once bustling docks that were now part smart new development and part building site. Being a Saturday afternoon, the building site was deserted, and that's where Brendan was heading.

Milo was so shocked by the first punch, that when Brendan swung round and whacked him in the guts for the second time, he still didn't try to protect himself. The blows from Brendan's leather-covered fists came one after another until Milo collapsed on the ground, bloody and semi-conscious.

If he'd been a bit less dazed, he might have been able to save his face from the worst of the kicking by curling himself into a ball. But violence wasn't usually part of young Milo's world – he'd always left that to others.

Little did Brendan realise that he was doing something that Milo Flanagan would find very hard to forgive.

*

While Milo was being taught his 'lesson', Ellie was sitting in the passenger seat of Luke's car, about to get a lesson of her own.

'I wouldn't mind but wasn't it Brendan who bloody introduced me to Milo in the first place, at that pub we went to for New Year. You should have seen him, Luke. He was like a madman. I really thought he was going to hurt me.'

'Being violent to get his own way – that's just part of the game for Brendan. Believe it or not, he don't mean anything by it. Well, not anything personal.'

'But I'm his sister.'

'I don't think he sees things that way. Not exactly. Family's important to him and nothing would ever change that, but in the end Brendan's a simple sort of bloke – people either do what he wants or they don't. And he treats them accordingly.'

He glanced in the rear-view mirror as he signalled to turn right. 'Now me, I do care about what happens to you, Ellie. I care a lot. So whatever else you do, you've gotta promise me you won't do anything daft like this again.'

'Why is it daft? I didn't get caught.'

'But you might have done. And just take it from me, it's daft to be doing two-bob stuff. Because you always risk getting caught and then people get nosy and that mucks up the big stuff. The stuff that's Brendan's life.'

She tried sulking for a bit, but couldn't carry it on for long. 'Where are we going?'

'Kilburn. A little flat I thought you might wanna see.'

'Kilburn? Isn't that where all the poor Irish live before they can afford something better?'

'You are such a snob, Ellie. I'm surprised you even talk to rough cockneys like me.'

'You're my brother, aren't you? Family.' She glanced sideways and was pleased to see she'd made him smile.

'All right, don't start getting clever. This is serious. Now you're living over here with us, it's important that you listen to me. That you understand how things work. When you're part of the world that Brendan's involved in –'

'And that you're involved in.'

'Okay, I put me hands up to that one, but it's not gonna be for much longer, Ellie. That's the difference between me and Brendan, he don't want anything else, never has. But me, I've spent most of my life working towards getting out of it.'

'But I still don't understand why he went raving mad about a bloody coat. It was okay for me to smuggle bloody guns for him. And if it was such a big problem, he could have just said.'

'The thing is, Ellie, that wouldn't have stopped you doing it again, would it? It's complicated. It's not just that you could have got caught, and given the law a reason to come sticking their noses in. It's that Brendan's got this thing, that it's a bad idea to be too showy about having a few quid, when you're out and about mixing with the mug punters. The ones who ain't part of our world. And he's right, I suppose. That's why he likes everything to be kept low-key. You act lairy, spend too much, and them people, they start asking questions. Where's that come from? How'd he get that? That sort of thing. Then people get jealous. It's the flashy ones, the idiots you see all over the papers, mixing with Lord and Lady this and that, in nightclubs and posh parties, they're the ones that get nicked. They're too visible, see. Showy.'

She raised her eyebrows only slightly as she did a quick price survey of Luke's superbly cut suit, his handmade shoes and his chunky gold cufflinks, not to mention the Daimler he was driving.

'Brendan even still buys a bit of gear on the book.'

'Sorry? Whatever you just said, made no sense at all to a little Irish girl like me – like most of everything else you say.'

'On the book. Hire purchase. Buy a telly – have it on the book, pay by instalments, just like all the neighbours.' He stopped the car on the corner of a nondescript side street off the High Road. 'There it is, halfway down the street. The one with the lamp-post outside. And before you ask, no I am not driving up to the street door in this thing.'

*

'You said it's important not to have anything "flash" or "showy", Luke, but this place is a bloody joke. It looks as if nothing's been touched since the 1950s. And I'm talking about 1950s back home, not in London. It's bloody awful. Who the hell lives here? Not one of your friends, I bet.'

'Dad liked it like this.'

'*Dad*?'

'Yeah. This was his and Rosie Palmer's place.'

'My mother lived here?' She ran a finger through the dust on the sideboard. 'So this was the place Aunt Mary used to bring me to, to see her and Dad before he . . .'

'Before he died. Yeah.'

Ellie looked about her, trying to remember.

'Do you miss your mum?'

She shook her head. 'It's sad really, I never knew her that well. I don't even know if she's still alive. Aunt Mary would never let me talk about her. But I wish I had known her. And Dad.'

'He was my dad too, remember. I can tell you about him.'

'It's all so weird, Luke. For years I thought I was an only child and now I've got you and Brendan and Patricia.'

'And Catherine. You'd have liked her.' He reached out and touched her hair. 'You look so much like her.'

'You all really loved her, didn't you?'

His chin dropped. 'Yeah.'

'And you really love Nicky too.'

He looked up and smiled ruefully. 'Unfortunately, I do.'

Ellie frowned. 'Why unfortunately?'

'Listen to you. You'd never think you were an innocent little Catholic girl from Ireland.'

'I think we're all agreed I'm not that any more.'

He stroked her cheek. 'Even if Nicky is the best thing that's ever happened to me it's not exactly easy having a boyfriend.'

'No, I suppose not.' She looked around again, trying to get a sense of what it had been like when she'd been a little girl. 'Why do you still keep the place?'

'Sentimental reasons,' he said flatly.

It didn't seem right to tell her that it was actually one of their slaughters, the places they kept to divide up and store any proceeds of jobs they did. A place to stash any money they needed to keep well away from their other businesses before it went over to Kildare to be laundered through the stud farm. The farm that had been Ellie's home for as long as she could remember. And nor did it seem right to tell Ellie that her mother, Rosie Palmer, had only been allowed to live in the flat because of Gabriel O'Donnell's 'generosity' and that she had been thrown out the very day after Eileen had killed him.

Ellie went to the window and stared out at the

grubby, down-at-heel street. 'Just think, I could have been raised here if Mum had wanted me.'

Luke put his arm round her shoulders, constructing the lies as he spoke. 'You never knew, Ellie – I don't know why we never told you – but your mum wasn't well for a long time. She wanted to care for you, but she couldn't. Soon as Aunt Mary found out how sick she was, she came over here to collect you like a shot. Her baby niece needed her.'

When she turned to face Luke, tears were streaming down her face. 'You've all been so good to me. And I've never shown any of you how grateful I am. I've acted like a bloody fool, and I am so sorry. And I am so sorry I upset Brendan. I didn't mean it. I've been just like a stupid spoilt kid.'

'Don't cry, Ellie. Here.' He gave her his handkerchief, and she blew her nose noisily.

'Do you think Brendan will let me stay here in London? And still be bridesmaid at the wedding?'

He hugged her to him, kissing the top of her head. 'Course he will, sweetheart. You're family.'

He could so easily have added – *God help you* – but didn't think it would be of much help, not in the circumstances. What he said instead was: 'And do you mind watching your *bloody* language? Cos it ain't very ladylike.'

Chapter 14

Butchy Lee, the middle son of a travelling family, who used to spend their winters in Canning Town, had earned himself a fair bit of money from some very simple schemes. Keep it simple was, in fact, his motto – provided by his wife – and probably a good thing too, as he wasn't the brightest of men. But he could perhaps be counted as being among the luckiest. Not only was Butchy's wife very beautiful, she was also very smart. When Butchy won just over £142,000 on Littlewood's pools, she persuaded him it was time to settle permanently, and to use twenty-nine and a half grand of his prize on buying a beautiful home in Hertfordshire, complete with a sizeable tract of land. The purchase meant they had a big imposing house in which to bring up their kids, and plenty of space for Mrs Lee's horses – she too came from Gypsy stock and loved the creatures. Then there were the outbuildings that they turned into guest cottages, a gym, an indoor pool, garages, and a suite of offices from which Butchy's accountant and his eldest daughter ran his businesses. One of the most 'interesting' of which was the illicit night-time sulky racing – another of Mrs Lee's winning ideas.

This activity involved the illegal blocking-off of a stretch of the nearby A10, on which single-seater, horse-drawn, two-wheeled vehicles were raced against each other at great speed. Large amounts of money, alcohol and pride were involved in these very popular events, and tempers were often frayed to such an extent that side bets were usually to be had on the outcome of the resulting bare-knuckle fist fights.

But to prevent excessive violence breaking out, Butchy's daughter – a young woman who took after her mother in both the looks and the brains departments – came up with an impressive addition to the proceedings. Holding a cine camera, and steadying herself with her elbows, she would kneel up on the back seat of an open-topped car driven by Butchy, filming the horses speeding towards her. Thus, in one go, she provided both a definitive answer to any disputes as to who had won, and a nice souvenir of the races for all concerned.

It was obvious to Brendan, when he'd enjoyed the odd evening attending such meetings, and had gone back to the house for a few drinks and a bit of supper, that Mrs Lee had been responsible for her husband investing that part of his winnings very wisely indeed. The attraction of the fine-looking house, and the proximity of the charming little Norman church in the meadow next door to Butchy's land – complete with a vicar willing to turn a blind eye to the fact that the happy couple didn't actually live within the parish, but who were prepared to donate handsomely to 'church funds' – had Brendan convinced that this was exactly the right place for him to make Sandy the new Mrs O'Donnell. It was perfect. Somewhere he could put on a show for his family, friends and assorted faces from the East End, all while avoiding the prying eyes and subsequent questions of the outside world.

The two hundred guests were welcomed into a marquee, in the field next to the church, by a solo saxophonist and by uniformed staff who had been hired in for the day – leaving several fancy hotels in the West End short-staffed due to a sudden epidemic of 'gastric problems'. The staff were, to say the least, a bit surprised by the sort of people they were greeting. But a pattern soon began to emerge – cauliflower ears, bent noses and gold teeth for the men, and bleached hair, plunging necklines and a surfeit of diamonds for their partners.

These definitely weren't the sort of people they were usually employed to wait on, but having been offered five times the rate they were accustomed to receiving per shift, who were they to argue? Even if they were told that if they didn't *keep schtum* about everything and anything that happened during the day, they would very definitely regret it. And from the look of the guests they had no reason to doubt the warning.

*

173

While the guests who were staying the night were being shown to their rooms and cottages, and the others sipped champagne or light ale and generally turned up their noses at the unfamiliar ingredients in the canapés, Sandy was getting ready upstairs in the master bedroom of the main house.

Mrs Lee had done Sandy proud. Fine Gypsy lace had been draped over the bed, early-summer flowers filled the vases that stood on either side of the dressing table, and white ribbons had been wound around the mahogany frame of the cheval glass, which had been set up to face the tall Georgian windows so Sandy could see herself in her wedding gown in the best possible light.

Mrs Lee was not in the room with her as she dressed, she'd left that special moment to the family – or rather to members of Sandy's family-to-be: Patricia, Ellie and little Caty. Mrs Lee had thought it a real shame when she'd heard that Sandy had no family there of her own, and that they'd turned their backs on her years ago when she'd moved in with Barry Ellis. She wondered at how times had changed. No one turned a hair about such things nowadays. Still, Sandy had the O'Donnells now; they were her family.

As she fussed around the bride, Patricia was doing her best to also keep an eye on Caty and Ellie, making sure that they didn't get anything on their bridesmaid dresses. If she had anything to do with it, today was going to be perfect. Not like her own farce of a wedding, when she'd been sick as a dog with morning sickness, and had still stood before the priest in a virginal veil and a dress that was too tight round the middle.

Sandy's dress was beautiful. Needing little persuasion from Patricia and Ellie, she had chosen a white Juliet-style gown, with a deep-scooped neck, dotted all over with tiny pink and pale green satin rosebuds. She'd drawn the line at the headdress and veil they'd wanted her to wear – after all, she wasn't sixteen years old any more – but had compromised by agreeing to wear a single string of pearls woven into her hair like a delicate tiara.

After giving the bride and her attendants a final once-over, Patricia was satisfied that there was nothing more for her to do.

'Right then, I'll get myself downstairs to Mum. Can't leave her alone for too long, can I? Not with all them people around.'

Sandy, dry-mouthed at what she was about to do, nodded. 'Thanks, Pat, you've been a real help. And, I don't know how to say this, but I think it's lovely of your mum coming today. With it not being a Catholic do and that.'

'Don't be daft. She wouldn't have missed it for the world.' Patricia kissed her on the cheek. 'You look beautiful, San, really beautiful.' She pressed her hand to her mouth and sniffed. 'I'll see you three in church,' she said through her fingers.

Her mother had barely left the room, when Caty stomped over to the looking glass and glared into it. 'I can't believe you made me wear this get-up. Look at me. Pink satin! I look like a flipping Sindy doll. I never wanted to be a bloody bridesmaid in the first place, but then Nan promised to buy me a new record player, and I thought I was at least going to have a bloody choice about what I'd wear. I mean, just look at me!'

Caty was just about to pull the garland of flowers from her hair when Sandy came up behind her and grabbed her by the upper arms.

'Ouch! You're hurting me!'

'Good. You might be able to get away with all this shit with that lot, you saucy little cow, but not with me, all right? And as for you –' She let Caty go and jabbed a finger at Ellie. 'You can get pissed and have it away with who you like, and whenever you like, you little scrubber, but not at my wedding. Got it?'

'I don't know what you're talking about.'

'Don't you? I was watching you. Down there.' Sandy pointed to the sash window at the far end of the room. 'Look for yourself. Go on. Down there.'

Ellie gingerly swished across the room and peered down. Bugger. She wasn't lying. You could look right down into the stable yard. She must have seen her with Milo.

'I saw you down there, when you said you had to go and speak to Luke. You were letting that hippie-looking freak practically rub himself off against you, your dirty little mare. And I can smell the gin on your breath from here.' She narrowed her eyes. 'You know, I don't get it. You two have been given so many chances in life, been brought up to be so nice, been to good, expensive schools, and had everything your greedy little grabbing hands ever wanted, and what do you do with all them chances? You act like sodding brats. But you've come unstuck with me, girls, because no one's gonna spoil this day for me. No one. I've bloody earned it after what I've put up with over the years.'

Caty's face was set in an expression of pure contempt as she stared back at Sandy's stony face, while Ellie had taken a sudden interest in her white satin pumps.

Earned, that's what Sandy had just said. Ellie realised that she'd have to watch herself with this one. She'd thought Sandy was a right 'yes woman', but here she was dictating the odds like she was her mother or something – or worse, like she was Aunt Mary. And she wasn't even an O'Donnell.

Sandy glared at them. She wasn't about to break the silence. Let the pair of them suffer.

They didn't have to suffer long.

There was a knock on the bedroom door and Luke's voice – unusually nervy, asked. 'You all right in there? The vicar's called the guests through to the church, and he's ready as soon as you are.'

'Thanks, Luke,' Sandy said, to the door, her voice now light and happy. 'We'll be one minute, okay?'

'Don't make it any longer, San, if I've gotta lead you down that aisle, you'd better do it quick before I bottle out and make a run for it.'

'You silly sod,' she said affectionately, then, spinning round, she pointed at each of the two young women in turn. 'Now, smile, the bloody pair of you,' she hissed under her breath. 'Or you'll have me to reckon with.'

Sandy rotated her shoulders as if she were about to go into the ring to do fifteen rounds with John Conteh, then, pasting on a bright smile, she said joyfully: 'Why don't you come in, Luke? We're all ready.' Then threw over her shoulder: 'Aren't we, girls?'

Chapter 15

With most of the guests thanking their lucky stars that it was a brief Church of England service rather than the full Mass they'd been dreading, they were all back in the marquee within the hour – primed and ready to eat and drink, and, of course, to pass judgement on the O'Donnells and all the other families present.

As they sorted out which of the large round tables they had been assigned to, the band, standing on a dais to the side of the long top table, struck up a syncopated version of 'I'm Forever Blowing Bubbles'.

'Do you know who's paying for all this?' said Daniel Kessler, as he examined a slice of smoked salmon that he'd speared on the end of his fork. 'We are, that's who.' He held it out in turn to each member of his family sitting at the table. 'Us lot. With the profits from all that gear they keep pushing on to us for the shops.'

Maurice, who was eating his salmon rather than waving it about, lifted his head briefly from his plate. 'You've got to admit though, feller, it's very high-quality merchandise they produce.'

He turned to Sophie Kessler. 'And 'scuse me, and all that, Aunt Soph, but they come up with films and magazines that surprise even me. I mean, I've not blushed since I was a nipper and I pissed me pants on me first day at school, but the films they've been getting hold of . . .'

Sophie ignored him. 'Harold,' she said, 'I see Eileen's got up, probably going to the Ladies. Think I'll join her. Go and have a word. Make sure she's okay. And,' she leaned in close to her husband, 'make sure that fool nephew of yours remembers there are children present.'

Harold shrugged – 'Sure' – then turned his attention back to his boys. 'Maury's right, and we're earning well out of the arrangement.'

'No,' said Daniel, 'we're earning what the O'Donnells say we earn out of it. And no matter what they say, I *know* it was them who had that Spanish load off of us. And do you know what, I've had enough of them fuckers. It's right back to how it was in old man O'Donnell's day. Us doing what that arsehole Gabriel told us to do.' He threw down his fork, making the three children sitting at the table – his three children – sit up straight and stare warily at him. 'And having to be grateful for the crumbs off their poxy table.'

'I wouldn't mind having a taste of that particular O'Donnell's crumbs,' said Maurice nodding towards Ellie, who was sitting alongside Luke at the top table.

'I can't believe how much she's like Catherine.' It was Sammy. He had hardly been able to take his eyes off her since he'd first seen her in the church. It was as if he was a boy again, sitting in his brother's car wondering how he was ever going to tell his family that he was in love with Gabriel O'Donnell's youngest daughter.

'Come on, feller,' said Maurice, 'cheer up. She's been dead for bloody years now, and anyway, I thought you were all cosied up with that Carol sort of Brendan's.'

'You kidding?' said Sammy absently, still staring at Ellie. 'I had enough of her weeks ago. She did her nut when I mentioned O'Donnell was getting married. Said it should have been her walking up the aisle. Well, he's welcome to her if he can be bothered to have her back.'

'I thought this do was gonna be a laugh,' said Maurice rolling his eyes. 'Come on, Sammy, at least we got all that dough from the bank, surely that makes you smile, feller.'

'I don't like it, you know.' Sophie linked her arm through Eileen's as they walked across the grass towards the house, in the warm afternoon sun. 'All these unmarried girls with babies. It's not right. My Danny's – what does he call her? *Girlfriend*. Girlfriend! She's got three babies with him.' She sighed. 'What must everyone think of us? They're

181

registered in his name, of course, so – officially – they're Kesslers, but as for any thought about their religion . . . Nothing. Not that I've ever asked her, but I bet the girl's never so much as set a foot in a *shul*.'

'*Shul*?'

'Sorry, a synagogue. It's so sad, Eileen, the old traditions all going.'

'I suppose it's like you said, Sophie, on that day you met me outside the prison. Times have changed. And the new ways are passing us older ones by. Believe me, the only reason I came here today was to see my little granddaughter. She was so excited about being a bridesmaid. But why they couldn't have had a proper Catholic service . . .' She snapped open her handbag and took out her handkerchief. 'It's all such a farce, I had to get out of there for a bit of air.'

Sophie stopped suddenly, pulling Eileen to a halt beside her. 'At last you're talking to me. This is more like it. Sometimes when I call you, I feel like I'm chatting away to myself, you're so quiet.'

She took Eileen's hands in hers, a gesture that had Eileen's eyes brimming with tears, reminding her how much she'd missed such human contact.

'It's important to talk about things, Eileen, to get things off your chest.'

Eileen pressed her lips together, her eyes fixed on their entwined fingers.

'I can't imagine what it was like in that place for you. With all those terrible women.'

'I'm no better than them, Sophie.'

'Yes you are, Eileen. You acted out of love for your children.'

'Maybe I should have loved them more, and my own beliefs a little bit less. I had a lot of time to think while I was in there. And I can't tell you how many times I wondered what would have happened if I hadn't forced Patricia to marry Pete Mac just because she was expecting. And then her losing the baby and everything. I went over and over how things might have turned out differently if I hadn't been so sure I was right.' She shook her head despondently. 'I just don't know what to think. It's like Sandy. She was never married to Barry Ellis. She just lived with him for all those years. And now she's married to my . . .' Eileen hesitated. 'My son. Brendan. And I can guarantee that getting married will make no difference to the way he carries on.'

Sophie took out her cigarettes and handed one to Eileen. 'Perhaps some people, and things, never change.' She sparked her lighter. 'Now, how about we have these, then have a wash and brush-up, and get back to the do?'

They continued their walk towards the house in thoughtful silence, until they got to the graceful sweep of steps that led up to the big front door.

'Young Ellie,' said Sophie, as if experimenting with the sound of the name. 'She's a very pretty girl.'

'She's Gabriel's daughter.'

'I thought she might be.'

Eileen blew a plume of lavender smoke high into the air, watching it rise. 'And she's the living image of my Catherine.'

'I thought that too.'

Eileen frowned in confusion. 'You met Catherine? When?'

'No, I never met her. But a few years ago, a long time after it all happened – years after – I went downstairs to the kitchen one night, for a drink of water, and I found Sammy sitting by himself at the table. He was looking through a stack of black-and-white photographs. It was the first time I'd seen him cry since he was a little boy. They were pictures of him and Catherine. Taken when they'd been out to the coast for the day. Larking around and grinning at the camera.'

Eileen nodded. 'I know the ones. She had her copies kept hidden in her bedroom. I found them there. After the funeral.'

'It must be so hard for you.'

'And for your Sammy. Luke said they really loved each other.' Eileen turned her head away. 'It doesn't seem possible, but she'd have been thirty last New Year.'

'Is Ellie's . . . Ellie's mother still on the scene?'

Eileen's head jerked round, and she looked into Sophie's eyes with a hardness Sophie had never seen before. 'Gabriel's whore, you mean? No. His sister

Mary saw to that. Chased her away good and proper.'

'Mary. Is she the, how can I put it politely, the very stern-looking woman on the top table?'

'That's her.'

'So she has some use other than frightening burglars then.'

The meal was over, and the guests were now mingling, looking considerably more relaxed as jackets and hats were thrown off, sleeves rolled up, and high-heeled shoes kicked under the tables.

Pete Mac was sitting astride a chair next to Brendan. 'Look at the state of him.' Pete gestured with his pint towards Milo Flanagan, a vision of glam-rock perfection – except for a jagged scar through his left eyebrow, a permanent reminder of the beating Brendan had given him.

'Typical of you, Pete,' tutted Brendan. 'You are looking at one of our brightest boys there. Very bright indeed. Needs to be kept in line, but he's quick to learn.'

Milo caught them watching him and raised his glass in salute.

'Aw yeah?'

'Yeah, he knows his own game, understands all the wrinkles and how to sort 'em out.'

'What, like Butchy Lee's stupid little brother Reuben did? He's doing a ten stretch for dealing.'

Brendan didn't bother to mention Pete Mac's own

particular, spectacular brand of stupidity, this was his wedding day after all, and he was in a good mood, for Christ's sake.

'That's cos he was old school, Pete,' he said, patting his brother-in-law on the back. 'Like the old man was. Didn't understand the future, modern ways and how they work.'

'That's easy to say, but –'

'Listen, and you'll learn something. I'll tell you how that silly bastard Reuben Lee got done, shall I? He bought a nice little load off the Moroccan police – straight from the donkey's mouth, so to speak. Handed over a right big bundle for it and all. Then what happens? The silly fucker's a sitting duck, i'n he? The law arrest him at the border, nick back the gear, take a massive backhander off him to let him go, give him a bit of the merchandise back as a gift – very kind, thank you very much – and then customs are waiting there ready to feel his collar when he crosses back through Spain. Moroccan fuckers have grassed him up for a bigger divvy of the gear with the mob in Spain. Fucking amateur.'

'So why bother with it if the law's got it all tied up?'

'Jesus, you really do sound like the old man, Pete.' Brendan leaned forward and tapped Pete Mac's forehead with his finger. 'Because, genius, it's the way forward, the way for the modern businessman. We ain't gas-meter bandits. And we don't want none of that fannying about going across the pavement, doing silly little smash-and-fucking-grabs and hiring petermen. No, *this* is the way forward. And the Kesslers are our route into all them lovely supplies of speed, and young Milo is its very weird, if pretty, public face.' He winked happily. 'Now, if you'll excuse me, Pete, I have guests to meet.'

As Brendan walked away, Pete Mac's eyes met Milo's, and for all his stupidity, Pete Mac recognised something in the boy's expression that Brendan had completely failed to see – pure burning hatred.

The only lesson that Brendan had taught Milo Flanagan was to despise the one who had taught him.

The first guest to get Brendan's attention was DI Bert Hammond, who was sitting with his wife, drinking a pint of weak lemonade shandy. Hammond was tapping his toes, and wagging his head cautiously to the band's version of 'In the Summertime'.

'Bert,' said Brendan, shaking his hand, 'thanks for coming and helping us celebrate our special day.' He turned to Mrs Hammond – as broad-beamed and rosy as her husband was slight and pale. 'And this must be your lovely lady.' He inclined his head politely. 'Welcome.'

Mrs Hammond blushed even redder. 'We really appreciated the invite to the wedding, Mr O'Donnell,' she said, her Birmingham twang as marked as her husband's. 'And we did enjoy our stay in Spain over Easter, we really did, didn't we, Bert?'

'We did indeed, my dear.'

'Good, good, I'm glad to hear it. You'll have to go over there again, Mrs Hammond. I'll fix it up for you. Me and Sandy are flying over for our honeymoon, but then it's all yours. Any time you like.' He treated her to a smile, and then pointed at DI Hammond. 'But not until after the first Thursday of next month, Bert, cos I'm inviting you to join me and the boys at a boxing do on Park Lane. I know you're partial to the fight game, so make sure you put it in your diary. Sixth of June. It'll be a good evening's entertainment.'

Brendan flashed his teeth once more and walked away.

DI Hammond took another sip of shandy. 'I'm partial to a fight all right, O'Donnell.'

'What was that, Bert love?'

'Nothing, Betty, just thinking aloud, my dear.'

Brendan did a bit more glad-handing, pausing every now and again to check on Sandy who was on the dance floor with a circle of blonde wives and girl-friends, bopping away to the band. Finally, content that he'd had a few personal words with everyone he needed to, he went back to the head table, and called the room to order by taking off his shoe and banging its heel on the table.

'Right, now I know I promised there'd be no

188

speeches,' Brendan hollered, slipping his foot back into his shoe, 'but I do just want to say a few words.'

There were slightly drunken cheers and catcalls from all parts of the tent.

'First of all, thanks to Sandy for being daft enough to have me, and to the bridesmaids for looking like a pair of angels.' He raised his glass to more cheers and whistles. 'And to Luke for being not only my brother, but the best man, and for standing in as father of the bride.'

Brendan beckoned him over. 'We got him cheap, as a job lot,' he said, patting him on the cheek to loud applause.

'To Mum and Patricia for looking so beautiful.' All eyes turned to Eileen, as a chorus of 'Hear, hear's rippled round the crowd. 'And thanks to all them people who have been so loyal to me over the years. As you all know, I don't take kindly to people who disrespect me or my family.' There was a ripple of nervous laughter. 'But I do like it when we are able to do such profitable business with another family – the Kesslers.' He stared for a long, challenging moment at the Kesslers' table. 'And what a pleasure it is supplying them with all the merchandise for their specialist shops.'

Daniel half rose to his feet, but his father stopped him.

'Leave it, boy,' said Harold Kessler, grinding down on his cigar. 'Not the time or place.'

'So, I'll raise my glass to a full and happy future for us all.' Brendan swallowed his drink in one go and raised the empty glass. 'Now get dancing. The band's costing me a bloody fortune!'

As the singer launched into a Tamla Motown medley, Milo walked past Brendan on his way to join the dancers, but Brendan hooked him round the neck and drew him backwards.

He put an arm each around Luke and Milo's shoulders. 'I'm a very happy man, lads,' he said, the slight slurring of his words showing the first signs of all the drink he'd taken. 'And I'm gonna be even happier. Because what them Kessler fuckers don't know is that I'm gonna take over all their import trade. Every last bit of it.'

He sighed contentedly. 'Not straight away, mind, because I'm gonna wait till the time's right. Gonna surprise 'em when they're least expecting it. We don't wanna have to bother with none of that fighting lark no more, we ain't fucking cowboys and Indians, not like in the old days.'

Brendan pinched into Milo's shoulder and shook him. 'You've done good work for me, Flanagan, been a good servant. But it's time we expanded. And the money'll come in just right for some plans I've got to do a few more deals with the chaps over in Ireland.'

Good fucking servant? Milo Flanagan swallowed his desire to kick Brendan O'Donnell right in the balls, because there were other ways for a bright young bloke to get the better of a loud-mouthed pisspot like him. And Milo was nothing if not young and bright.

And screwing O'Donnell's spoilt little mare of a sister, Ellie, hadn't been a bad place to start.

Patricia was sitting with Eileen at one of the tables.

Ellie waved to them from the dance floor, but they didn't seem to notice, so she made her apologies to her partner – a flat-nosed thuggish-looking man who might have been surprisingly light on his feet but gave Ellie the creeps – and went to join them.

'Isn't it about time you had a dance, Pat?' she said, dropping down on a chair next to her. 'I don't know why you're sitting here like you're waiting for a bus.'

She followed Pat's gaze, and saw that she was watching Pete Mac talking and laughing with two young blondes. 'Oh, you're keeping an eye on that husband of yours, are you?'

Eileen took a gulp of her drink. Why had she come here today? She could have just waited and seen the photographs of young Caty.

'No, Ellie,' said Pat flatly, 'I'm not keeping an eye on him, I'm just being disgusted by him. And by those two. Look at them. Acting as if they don't care who sees them, touching and pawing another woman's husband. Christ knows where their own blokes are.'

'Drunk somewhere, I suppose,' said Ellie, looking

191

around at the increasing number of men slumped back in their chairs.

The two young women hanging around Pete Mac were well aware that Patricia was watching them, and were playing up to the fact. Everyone knew that Peter MacRiordan lived by his own marital rules and that he responded well to a bit of flattery.

'That wife of your'n performing again, is she, Pete?' said one of them in a breathy little voice. 'Poor you. Don't let you out of her sight, by the look of it. And everyone knows how good you are to her.'

That you're an overgenerous idiot, ripe and ready to be conned, was what they really knew, she thought.

The girls glanced at one another. 'And I've heard all about them two sisters you set up in that right nice flat an' all. They're having you over, did you know that?'

Pete Mac's dumb grin faded. 'How d'you mean?'

'It's obvious, innit? There's all that dosh they should be earning for you going out hoisting, but what are they doing? They're sitting around all day on their lazy arses doing bugger all, while you're keeping them.'

'You sure that's a definite?' Pete Mac had been having trouble making sense of what the redheads were playing at. They reckoned they were top shoplifters, but so far he hadn't seen much evidence of it – in fact, he'd seen bugger all. 'They really are hoisters then?'

'Take my word for it. Best in the north of England, that pair. And they're taking advantage of you, Pete. I don't get it, I really don't. Good bloke like you being taken for a ride by them scheming scouse tarts.'

'And you know what else,' said the blonde lookalike standing next to her. 'I reckon that Carol Mercer's taking you for a mug an' all. She's the sort who wouldn't think twice about having it away with someone else behind your back. And all while you're picking up the bills.' She put a hand flat on his chest. 'You know why, don't you? You're too good to 'em. You are. I'm telling you, Pete, if you had someone like us two in that flat them sisters are in, we'd make sure we looked after you. Really well.'

Pete Mac's grin returned. 'Yeah?'

'Yeah.' She licked her finger and ran it across his lips. 'Come outside and we'll show you.'

As she watched her husband leave the tent with his arms wrapped round the blondes who were walking on either side of him, Patricia rose to her feet. She was shaking. 'Look at him. The bastard. That's it. I've had enough. There are going to be some changes made, or he can sling his bloody hook.'

Eileen closed her eyes, unable to bear her daughter's pain.

Ellie's attitude was far more sanguine. She folded her arms across her chest and leaned back in her chair. 'Good for you, girl. We'll have you burning your bra next.'

As the band struck up the opening chords of 'Tie a Yellow Ribbon', Ellie took hold of Pat's hand. 'Come on, let's have a dance.'

Pat stood up and Ellie winked at Eileen. 'They can't keep us O'Donnell women down for long, can they, Eileen?'

Brendan had also been watching Pete Mac. Even though he'd promised himself that nothing would go wrong today, and that he would keep control of his temper come what may, he couldn't let this one go. Couldn't let his moron of a brother-in-law get away with treating Patricia like that. Not in public, he couldn't. It reflected too badly on him. Made the family a laughing stock. And whoever had brought the birds along weren't gonna be exactly thrilled when they sobered up either.

He stormed outside after the three of them.

It didn't take Brendan long to find them. Pete Mac was leaning back against a tree with his trousers bunched around his ankles. One of the blondes was on her knees with his penis in her mouth, while the other one was standing over her with her top off, leaning forward so that Pete Mac could fondle her breasts, while she kissed him full on the mouth.

Brendan grabbed hold of the standing blonde's hair, and yanked her backwards. Her yells causing the

194

kneeling one to stop her ministrations to Pete Mac, and to look up to see what was going on.

Mistake.

Brendan struck her – whack! – across the face with the back of his hand.

Then he started on Pete Mac. He used one hand to pin him by the throat to the tree and balled the other into a fist that he pulled back ready for action. But, much to Pete Mac's relief, he hesitated.

'You are this close to getting a good hiding, you stupid, fat fucker. And the only reason I'm not gonna beat your brains to a pulp is that you're family. And fighting in the family is a sign of weakness. And I ain't gonna make even more of a show with all these people around. But you just remember that I can have you any time I feel like it.'

'Brendan, you've got me wrong, mate, I love Pat.'

The girls were scrabbling around to tidy themselves up and to back away before Brendan noticed.

'Yeah, course you do. And so long as she puts up with you, you're all right, you ponce.' Brendan spun round and faced the girls. He jabbed a finger at them as he spat out his words. 'I don't for one minute suppose I'd ever recognise either of you manky pair again, but if you've got any sense whatsoever, don't you ever make yourselves known in my company again. Now piss off before I get really upset.'

With that he turned back to Pete Mac, shaking his head contemptuously. 'Put your fucking prick away, and get back in there to your wife. You wanna fuck about, at least be a bit fucking subtle about it, you wanker.'

Neither Brendan nor Pete Mac noticed DI Hammond standing behind the flapping entrance to the tent, watching and listening to their every word.

A few moments later DI Hammond was sitting with his wife back in the marquee, tapping his toes to the band's thumping rendition of 'Signed Sealed Delivered'.

'You know the old saying, don't you, Betty, my dear,' he said, his eyes fixed on Sandy who was still enjoying herself on the dance floor along with most of the other women. 'Marry in May –'

'– and rue the day,' Mrs Hammond finished for him with a pleased and happy smile.

'Exactly. Well, I think it won't be long at all before this particular new bride is going to rue this day very much indeed.' He sighed contentedly. 'And I must say, I am looking forward to witnessing the repercussions.'

Chapter 16

Brendan and Sandy were driving back from Gatwick airport to the Mile End Road. They had spent their honeymoon at Brendan's villa in the hills high above Estepona on the Costa del Sol, and were looking tanned, healthy and prosperous – a handsome couple in every sense. The contrast between hot, sunny Spain and the miserable, overcast skies and grey, grimy streets of east London couldn't have been more pronounced.

Sandy sighed loudly as they pulled up outside the house, but Brendan didn't notice the shabbiness. All he saw was his family home – the place where Eileen now lived, not with him any longer, not since the wedding, but, by some unspoken agreement, with his half-sister Ellie.

Brendan used the key that he still kept on his chain to let them in, and Sandy followed him down the stairs to the kitchen.

Eileen was sitting in her usual chair, Ellie and Patricia were sitting at the table, and Caty was kneeling on the floor playing ball with Bowie – no longer a pot-bellied puppy, but a fit, sleek young dog.

Sandy put on a smile and handed Eileen a flat, red

leather box. 'It's a little present, Eileen. From Brendan and me.'

Eileen took it with a nod, opened the lid and took out a row of pearls. 'They're lovely,' she said quietly.

'Let me see, Eileen,' said Ellie. 'Oh, they are so beautiful. Here, let me fasten them round your neck for you.'

Sandy forced another smile. She'd never had much to do with Eileen O'Donnell in the days when Gabriel had still been around, but on the odd occasion when they had met up, Eileen had always been kind to Sandy, and she'd appreciated it. But in the run-up to the wedding she'd made it very clear that she disapproved of Sandy and Brendan getting married.

It was strange, being disapproved of by a woman who had actually killed her husband. But it was as though, regardless of what she had done, Eileen was like most other women of her generation. She knew her place, and thought that others should know theirs too.

And Sandy's place, according to Eileen, should have been supporting 'poor old Barry' as he had come to be known over the years.

If only Eileen knew the truth about his drug taking and all the associated madness, perhaps then she'd have understood why Sandy had married Brendan; why she had been prepared – no, more than that, *keen* – to do something that would give her a good life after everything she'd been through. And perhaps then she'd be more sympathetic than critical, and it wouldn't be like talking to a brick wall whenever Sandy tried to speak to her. But then ten years inside could do strange things to a big, tough man, let alone to a frail-looking, middle-aged woman, who'd done little more in life than raise her children and look after her man – before her moment of madness had turned her entire world upside down.

Sandy was only glad that Brendan had agreed to move into the house on Old Ford Road. No matter how she tried to sympathise with Eileen, she really couldn't have stood living under the same roof with a woman who she felt was continually judging her.

Especially when that someone was a murderess.

'Did you get anything for me, Auntie Sandy?' It was Caty, the voice and face of an angel in her neat little convent uniform – and the mind and cunning of a she-devil. 'And for Ellie?'

'Course we did, sweetheart.' Sandy found another smile. 'And for your mum.'

'Really?' said Patricia. 'For me? I didn't expect anything.' She went over to the sink to fill the kettle. Brendan followed her.

'You look really happy,' she said to him.

'I am, Pat. I only wish you were an' all.' He stood back so she didn't splash his pale cream, linen flares. 'You don't have to stay with him, you know,' he said, lowering his voice.

'I'm beginning to realise that.' She half turned to

face him. 'Must be Ellie's influence, with all her women's-lib talk.'

Brendan frowned, clearly not impressed. 'He still going to the boxing tomorrow night?'

'Boxing?' She looked blank.

'I got the tickets before me and Sandy went away. Charity do, up the West End. And make sure he remembers it's dinner suits. And, sorry, Pat, it's lads only.'

Patricia raised an eyebrow. 'Of course.'

He looked over at Sandy, who was showing Ellie the fringed lace shawl she had brought back for her.

'Sandy's persuaded me to let Luke bring some mates with him,' he said, scratching his stubbly chin.

'Right.' Patricia said the word slowly, with a lift of her chin. 'Mates. That'll be nice for him.' Then she burst out laughing.

'What?'

'You. It is 1974, you know, Brendan.'

Brendan might not have liked what she was laughing about – or her women's-lib nonsense, for that matter – but at least it made a nice change to see her without the usual downtrodden scowl on her face.

The next morning, as Pete Mac scoffed down his bacon, beans, eggs and fried slice, Patricia reminded him about the boxing do, but there was no need. He was looking forward to it.

He just hoped he could get all the things he had to sort out done and dusted before it was time to get ready.

Number one on Pete Mac's list was the sisters from Liverpool, and that was why he was now standing in the bedroom of their flat, looking at the half-dozen handbags that could have come straight off a cut-price stall in the market. The sisters were standing on either side of him, heads bowed as if they were being scolded by the headmaster for running in the corridor.

'Is this it?' he said, picking up one of the bags and tossing it straight back on the bed. 'I told you after that fucking wedding that if you didn't stop trying to con me, you'd be out on your pretty little arses. Now I wanna see some top-quality gear in this flat, or that's it. And while you're at it, you can get me a watch. From Bond Street. One of them new digital jobs, or whatever they call 'em.'

After a further ten minutes of admonishment, Pete Mac left them to think about what he'd said.

Waiting until he closed the front door behind him, one of the sisters said to the other: 'S'pose we'd better stop flogging all the stuff off to that Milo one. Cos we don't wanna lose the flat, now do we?'

'No,' said the other girl, 'not till we've got enough cash together to get somewhere nice.'

*

Feeling he was on a roll in this laying down the law business, Pete Mac's next stop was Bow and a visit to Carol Mercer.

She opened the door in a tiny baby-doll nightie, her big blonde hair gently tousled, and wearing full make-up. She'd been expecting something like this for the past few days, and had made sure she was ready.

His eyes widened, but he was here on business, not for a quick tumble. But then again . . .

'I'm a fair man, Carol,' he said, walking through to the bedroom. 'I told you after the wedding – you had two weeks to find yourself somewhere else. No argument. Done deal.'

'Don't be like that, Peter.' She came up behind him, leaned her head on his back, and put her arms round him. They didn't meet because his belly was in the way. 'You don't know how hard it is for a young girl like me. Men take advantage. I go and look at a horrible room somewhere, and the landlord thinks that I'll –'

'Cut the crap, Carol,' he said turning round to face her. 'You know what I like. Just show a bit of appreciation and I'll see what I can do.'

Carol was down on her knees with his trousers unzipped before the dozy-arsed lard bucket had a chance to change his mind.

When she had finished the job, Carol hurried through

to the shared bathroom on the landing and spat into the sink.

Christ, she despised him. Almost as much as she hated Brendan. And as for his going on and on about the poxy wedding. Why the hell did Pete Mac think she had any interest in how 'beautiful' and 'lovely' that rotten cow Sandy looked, and that he liked women to look 'feminine' like that? Why should she care that Brendan O'Donnell was married?

And the way Sammy Kessler treated her wasn't a lot better.

How had it come to this? She'd have to get her life back in order soon or she'd go off her head.

She lifted her chin and looked in the mirror. Pete Mac was standing behind her – stark naked. His face ruddy and slicked with a film of sweat.

Oh God, surely not again?

He confused her by tossing her his car keys. 'I'm gonna have a wash. Run down to me car and get me dinner suit out of the boot. And don't be long, Cal, I'm in a hurry.'

Milo stood in front of the full-length mirror in the bedroom of his flat in the tenement block in Poplar, checking out his profile.

'What d'you think, babe?'

'Gorgeous,' Ellie breathed into his ear. She was standing behind him, completely naked, having watched him, fascinated by his easy, self-confident beauty, as he'd bathed and dressed, making himself ready for his boys' night out at the boxing do.

'You'll have to get going soon, Ellie,' he said, looking straight ahead at her reflection. 'I'm being picked up and I don't think it's time to tell Brendan about us yet.'

Ellie grabbed his wrist and stared at his watch. 'Bloody hell, Milo, I had no idea it was that late.'

She ran around the room picking up her scattered clothes, pulling on her underwear and swearing softly to herself.

'Time goes so quickly when I'm with you,' she said, pulling up the zip of her boot. 'One last kiss then I'm off.'

Milo pulled her to him and almost crushed her in his arms. He could hear her breath coming faster as the excitement flooded through her.

'Come on, Ellie, give me a break, or I'll never get out tonight.'

'Would that be so bad?' she whispered into his ear.

'Yes. Brendan's expecting me.'

He took her by the hand, picked up her bag and led her through the hallway to the front door. 'I'll call you tomorrow.'

'Promise?'

'Promise. Now go!'

Milo listened for the metallic clang of the lift door then went back to the bedroom and picked up the phone.

204

'Good evening,' a snooty-sounding woman answered, '*Sunday World.*'

'Dave Seymour, please.'

'*David* Seymour?'

'Yeah, that's the bloke.'

He listened to a series of clicks and crackles, then heard: 'In-Depth team, David Seymour speaking.'

'Hello, Dave, it's me, Milo.'

'Problems?'

'No, I'm just checking you've done the legwork getting yourself well in with that little fruit, Nicky Wright, and that everything's in place for this evening.'

He smiled very happily at David's reply.

The inside of the flat above the Moulin Bleu in Frith Street always surprised new visitors. And that pleased Luke O'Donnell. In contrast to the streets and clubs below, it was light, airy, clean and contemporary, with a few large abstract paintings spotlit on plain white walls. He liked living in Soho, it was a place where you could be yourself and no one bothered you. Even if you were 'different'.

Luke was in the bedroom getting ready for the boxing evening, fiddling around unsuccessfully with his bow tie, while Nicky was in the bathroom, gurgling along to the Rubettes on the radio as he brushed his teeth. He was far more relaxed than Luke.

'So, who's this friend you're bringing tonight?' Luke called through to him.

'Not jealous, are you, sweetie?'

'Don't you dare pull any of that camp crap tonight, Nicky.'

'Would I let my lovely boy down?'

Luke ripped the tie from round his neck. 'Do this bloody thing for me.'

'Temper.' Nicky padded through from the bathroom. He was wearing trousers, but his smooth and tanned chest, and his immaculately pedicured feet, were bare. He took the tie, looped it back over Luke's head, and then moved round behind him. Then he put his arms over Luke's shoulders and began tying it into a bow.

'I am going to behave beautifully. You told me I should bring someone, so I'm bringing along a very nice boy called David. And, before you ask, he's not queer, he's just a friend. A customer at the record shop. Very grown up, only buys jazz, knows how to conduct himself. And nice and butch to impress your Brendan. Like you said, as far as anyone needs know, we're all just blokes out together, eh, Lukey?' Slowly he ran his knee up the back of Luke's leg.

Luke gulped, looked at his watch, and undid the tie again.

'We've got twenty minutes,' he said, pushing Nicky on to the bed.

As Luke kissed Nicky, his mind whirled with what

206

had happened to him during the past year since they had met in the poky little record store where Nicky worked in Old Compton Street. Luke had known almost right away, had never been surer of anything in fact, that his future was going to be with Nicky – that whatever else happened, he was going to spend the rest of his life with him.

Chapter 17

Sitting with Brendan at the table for eight in the plush hotel on Park Lane were Pete Mac, Luke, Luke's boyfriend Nicky Wright, Nicky's new friend David Seymour, DI Bert Hammond, DC Jim Medway and Milo Flanagan.

At the centre of the massive, chandelier-lit room was a raised boxing ring, around which all the tables had been arranged, with just enough space left between them for the waiters. These evenings were always popular with those who wished to be seen doing their bit for charity – regardless of what the cause might be – and to have the opportunity to treat their guests to a night out, a way of either saying thanks for services rendered, or to oil the wheels of future deals.

And tonight Brendan was doing both.

He ordered four bottles of champagne, and three each of whiskey and vodka, then took off his jacket and set about making sure everyone was introduced.

DI Hammond raised an eyebrow as Nicky was pointed out to him. 'So, you're Mr Right, eh?' he said. In other circumstances, his Birmingham accent would have been enough to have earned him a punch on the nose, never mind what he'd have got for the sarcasm. But not tonight.

Brendan turned to DC Medway, hurriedly changing the subject. 'Remember our gaff down in Limehouse, Jim?'

'Do I? We had some nights down there, all right,' said Medway, the alcohol he'd already consumed in the upstairs bar at Brendan's expense making him forget the presence of his boss. 'Bare-knuckle fights, plenty of booze, and birds with big thrup'nies taking the bets. What more could you ask from a night's entertainment?'

'You're right there, Jim,' said Brendan, then added pointedly, 'Shame you missed it, Bert.'

Luke leaned back while the waiter set down a prawn cocktail in a leaf-shaped glass dish in front of him. 'It'll be unrecognisable round there soon.'

'There he goes again.' Brendan waved his spoon at his brother, mentally totalling the number of vodkas that Luke had already swallowed. Still, who could blame him? He was probably finding the situation as uncomfortable as Brendan – sitting there with his *friend* in a public place. And Christ alone knew what part the other bloke – *David* – played in it. Jesus, he didn't want to even think about it.

'Property,' he went on. 'That's all you hear out of him. Reckons that the docks are gonna be a gold mine one day. But who'd wanna live and work round that shithole unless they had to, I don't know.'

Pete Mac scraped the last of the pink sauce from his dish, shoving the shredded lettuce to one side. 'Unless they had access to the bonded warehouses, eh, lads?' He licked his spoon clean. 'Gear we used to have out of there, eh.'

'How do you mean?' asked David, speaking for the first time since he'd said hello to everyone.

Brendan's forehead creased almost imperceptibly. 'Ignore him, mate. Here, have another drink and eat up. They're already bringing in the main courses.'

David noted Brendan's discomfort. He took a small mouthful, thinking as he chewed, and then put down his spoon. 'And what do you do, Milo? You look like you should be in a pop group. Playing in the clubs.'

'Funny you should say that, David, it's not a bad guess. I do spend a lot of me time in clubs, as it happens.'

'Really? What sort of line are you in?'

Brendan leaned across the table and tapped his butter knife on the side of Milo's glass. 'Now that'd be telling the man, wouldn't it?'

Milo tossed down his spoon and leaned back in his chair. He didn't like being shut up. He'd thought it might be a laugh coming along tonight, seeing David pumping them for information. But he was beginning to wish he hadn't bothered. There had to be easier ways to have the O'Donnells.

Luke was also beginning to wish he hadn't come.

He felt sick. Maybe he should try and eat something.

The waiters came round and placed a great slab of bloody steak, adorned with little sprigs of watercress and a grilled Vandyked tomato in front of each of them.

Luke tasted the bile rising in his throat. ''Scuse me, chaps,' he said, standing up. 'Gotta go to the Gents.'

'You're mad,' Pete Mac called after him. 'Look.' He jabbed his knife towards the boxing ring. 'The comedian's coming on. He's brilliant this feller. Remember, we saw him at that stag do we went to with Kevin and Anthony?'

'Yeah, all right, Pete,' said Brendan, smiling reassuringly at DI Hammond and flashing a warning glare at Nicky to stay put. 'Think Luke's feeling a bit rough. I'll go and see to him.'

With the audience roaring at the comedian's joke about a virgin, a Welshman and a pound of ripe peaches, Brendan wove his way through the crowded room, acknowledging people's greetings. As he came to the table where the Kesslers were sitting with their guests, he paused briefly.

'All right, Sammy,' Brendan said, studiously keeping his eye on where Luke was heading. 'I hear you're scraping up them crumbs from my table again.' He shook his head in mock sorrow. 'Schtupping Carol Mercer, eh? Still, I don't mind someone having my leftovers. Wouldn't do for me, of course, but I ain't like you, now am I?'

Milo, who had been watching Brendan, waited for him to move on, then he too rose to his feet.

'Think I'd better go before the fights start and all,' he said, before he threaded his way across the room.

He too stopped at the Kesslers' table, taking just a moment to drop a piece of folded paper in front of Danny before carrying on towards the Gents at the far end.

'Now what's *that* all about?' asked Sammy, still clearly rattled by Brendan.

Danny squinted at the paper. 'It's a note,' he said. Then a smile spread slowly across his face. 'That weirdo's got the right arsehole with the O'Donnells. Reckons he's ready to have one over on 'em.'

He carefully refolded the paper and put it in his top pocket. 'Interesting.'

Luke and Brendan finished up in a quiet lavatory way up on the third floor next to a small bar area. After the ordeal of sitting among all those men with Nicky, knowing that Brendan didn't approve, and only being able to imagine what ninety-nine per cent of the rest of them there tonight would have to say about his and Nicky's relationship, Luke really didn't feel like having to be pleasant to strangers.

'You know, I don't get you, Brendan,' Luke said, throwing cold water over his face. 'You carry on alarming about not drawing attention to yourself, and then you go inviting all those people to your wedding,

212

spending all that money. Now you've got us all here tonight, spending even more money and, according to the programme, O'Donnells' Cabs are even sponsoring one of the bloody rounds.'

'That, Luke,' said Brendan, positioning himself in front of the urinal, 'is because we're among our own. Or I thought we were meant to be. That David bloke's asking enough questions.'

Luke leaned forward, pressing his forehead against the cold glass of the mirror. 'He don't understand. He knows Nicky from the fucking record shop, for Christ's sake, not from Borstal or the nick.'

'Well, perhaps you'd better explain to him that it's not right for someone to be so fucking nosy.' Brendan zipped his fly and went to the run of sinks to wash his hands. 'If you're sober enough.'

He threw his used towel into the basket and draped his arm round Luke's shoulders. 'Just be careful, eh, Luke. Just be careful, mate.'

With the tables cleared of any evidence of dinner, cigars lit, glasses charged, and with both the comedian and the final item in the charity auction over – only fifty quid for a pair of Ali's signed gloves! Brendan doubled it – the fights, all amateur bouts, and all billed as being fought in strict accordance with ABA rules, were under way.

The place erupted into yells, whistles, cheers and jeers. Bets were laid, wads of money changed hands, more drinks were drunk, and blood and sweat sprayed over those 'lucky' enough to be sitting close to the ring.

Come eleven thirty, the final bout was over. Very few jackets were being worn, and not many of the audience could lay claim to any degree of sobriety.

Brendan showed out to a waiter. 'Another three bottles of Remy,' he said, before pulling the man down by the shoulder and whispering something in his ear.

The waiter looked at the money that Brendan had pressed into his hand. 'Of course, sir,' he said with a bob of his head.

A few moments later, the curvy teenaged girl, who had held up the cards announcing the rounds, came over to the table, still dressed in the silver bikini she'd been wearing as she strutted around the ring.

'Right, chaps,' grinned Brendan, wrapping his jacket around the girl's shoulders. 'I'm off. So, anything else you want, just tell the waiter. Luke'll see to the bill.'

David, one of the few men in the room who had carefully paced his drinking, watched Brendan steer the girl towards the big sweeping staircase that led up to the main reception area. 'Didn't I hear Brendan say he'd arrived home from his honeymoon yesterday?'

'That's right,' said Pete Mac, belching loudly.

'Surely that's not Mrs O'Donnell?' said David innocently.

Luke, now very drunk, looked at him as if he were thick. 'Course it's not. Sandy's a lovely woman. Wouldn't see her acting like a trollop.'

David glanced at Nicky. 'Sorry, I don't understand.'

Luke stretched across the table for the last of the vodka, knocking over a line of empty tonic bottles. 'Brendan might be totally in love with Sandy, but he don't live by the same rules as other people.' He drained the liquor into his glass. 'He can go with who he likes, and, to him, he's doing no wrong. He's not betraying Sandy, cos she don't know what he's getting up to.' Luke considered for a hazy moment. 'This is his private life. Nothing to do with her.'

Pleased with his explanation, Luke leaned in close to Nicky.

DC Medway and DI Hammond both muttered something about finding the lavatories, and excused themselves.

Luke paid them no attention. 'You'd never do that to me, would you, Nicky?' he slurred. 'Cos it's only me you want, innit?'

Nicky slipped his hand under the table, and cupped it over Luke's crotch, making him smile with pleasure. 'Get us a room upstairs, Lukey, and I'll show you who I want.'

David, flicking through the souvenir programme – three pounds for thirty-two glossy, black-and-white, sponsored pages – was wondering, not for the first

215

time in his career, about the powers of alcohol to loosen tongues, banish inhibitions and to destroy supposedly strong men's will.

God bless it.

He was also wondering when he would get to talk to Milo again. They'd had their meetings and phone calls, of course, setting the whole thing up – David getting in with Nicky had taken time and care – but now, after seeing them all together tonight, he was really intrigued by how someone like Milo fitted into the O'Donnells' set-up.

Milo's own thoughts weren't a lot different. He himself was wondering how he fitted in with these bullying pissheads. Since Brendan had shut him up, he hadn't said anything other than answering the odd question as briefly as possible, but he had been taking in every little thing that had gone on. And they all confirmed why he didn't like the O'Donnells. Why he didn't like them one little bit.

And that most of all he didn't like Brendan – the cocky, big-mouthed whoreson, who had made him look a fool in front of everyone by interrupting him and as good as telling him to be quiet.

The time had come for Brendan O'Donnell to be taught a lesson for once.

If only he knew what Milo had in store for him.

Chapter 18

The sky was the colour of the lead nicked off a church roof; it was humid as a swamp, and Carol Mercer could feel the sweat trickling down her back. She was standing in a baking hot telephone box just along the street from her miserable rooms. She now hated those rooms almost as much as she had hated the childhood home she had shared with her mother until she'd been thrown out on to the street.

She was in the phone box because she couldn't stomach using the filthy phone she was supposed to share with the other tenants. As with the rest of the place, its dirtiness disgusted her. But at least she'd had a temporary reprieve as far as money was concerned: Pete Mac had stumped up for another month's rent after the 'favour' she'd done him last night.

The thought of what she'd had to do for that money made Carol shudder. She still had the taste of him in her mouth, and if it hadn't been unladylike, she'd have spat on the floor. Although looking down at her feet, it seemed that plenty of people had far fewer qualms about such behaviour.

Carol puffed out her cheeks in a weary sigh and rang yet another number.

''Lo?'

At last, a result. Sammy Kessler had answered in person.

Okay, Carol, she urged herself. Concentrate, girl. Be bright and cheerful. There's a lot riding on this. This could be the way to get somewhere decent to live, and to get shot of that animal Pete Mac.

'Sammy! How are you?'

'What? Who is this?' Sammy Kessler was straining to hear her over the babble of excited male voices echoing behind him. The chorus of shouts erupted into excited whooping as the men urged on the favourite as it moved closer to the winning post.

'It's Carol, of course. Who'd you think it was?'

'Look, darling, I'm busy right now.' Sammy snorted air down his nostrils as a vision of Brendan's smirking face came unbidden into his thoughts. 'Really busy.'

She bit back what she wanted to say, deciding it would be wiser to carry on with the little-girl act. 'But you're always busy, Sammy. And you know what they say about all work and no play –'

'I don't give a fuck about what anyone says, d'you hear me? But since I've got you on the line, I might as well tell you now, I'm gonna be a whole lot busier. So don't bother phoning me again, all right? Phone O'Donnell if you want a fucking night out.'

Carol heard the click of him cutting her off.

She let the phone drop from her hand, leaving it to swing wildly from its cord.

Someone tapped on the glass. 'It's gonna pelt down out here in a minute,' yelled an elderly woman, pointing at her shopping trolley as if it were somehow a deciding factor in her argument. 'You finished yet?'

'No, but he fucking will be,' snarled Carol as she barged out of the booth past the now open-mouthed woman. 'They all fucking will be once I start talking.'

'Bowie'll be just fine, Eileen,' said Ellie. 'I left him some extra Bonio by his basket, and a fresh bowl of water.'

Eileen nodded absently. She was sitting in the passenger seat, while Ellie drove them through the West End traffic in her new pride and joy – the bright yellow Hillman Imp that Luke had bought her. 'Thanks.'

Eileen hadn't wanted the puppy at first, had baulked at having responsibility for a dog after so many years of having all her decisions made for her. And she'd been more than happy when Ellie had taken over caring for the creature, but she'd soon realised that he could provide a useful alibi, a reason for refusing to go out, and for not doing things that scared or worried her.

She stared out of the window at the packed pavements and the lines of crawling traffic. If she valued being left alone so much, what did she think she was doing going out shopping? And with Ellie of all people.

And yet here she was, with Ellie chattering away to her as if this were the most normal thing in the world. But for Eileen it was anything but. Not only was the world so strange and so busy, so full of noise and bustle and bright colours, and crammed with people rushing everywhere, there was also the unexpected problem of having to see Ellie every single day.

When looking at her was just like looking at Catherine.

She wasn't like her in her ways, of course. Not at all. Her temperament was far more like Brendan's. No fear or shame, bold as brass and twice as determined. But when Eileen looked at that lovely face of hers, it was as if she'd been blessed with having a second chance with her beloved daughter.

The frightening thing was, as time passed by, the differences between their two faces – Ellie's and Catherine's – were blurring, becoming hazy, as they gradually merged into one. It was unnerving. As though she was losing Catherine all over again, but getting her back at the same time. Even when she dreamed about her, her face became Ellie's.

It had been the unsettling similarity between the two that had been the key to Luke persuading Eileen to let her to stay in the house in the first place. If she'd shown her the door it would have been just like turning Catherine out on to the street.

And it was also the reason why Eileen had finally given in and agreed to come out shopping with Ellie.

Life and everything about it was so confusing.

Ellie flicked the indicator stalk, and turned off Oxford Street, easing the Hillman into the short queue of cars waiting to go down into the underground car park below the big, leafy square.

'Thanks for coming with me today, Eileen,' she said, pulling forward on to the ramp. 'You know, I was saying to Patricia, I feel like a country bumpkin walking around in the clothes I brought over with me from Ireland. Don't get me wrong, they're fine for Kildare, but once I saw myself in the outfit that Patricia helped me pick out for the evening do after the wedding, well, I knew I had to do some proper shopping or go around looking like a fool.'

Eileen couldn't let that one go. 'So why ask me to come with you? Sure, I've no more idea about fashion than the dog. Why not ask Patricia? Especially when you two seem to be getting along so well together.'

Ellie smiled, her cheeks folding into the dimples that made her look even more like Catherine, and that made Eileen's senses almost leave her. 'All right, Eileen, you've seen through me. I'll be honest with you.'

Her smile faded as she turned to look Eileen directly in the eye. 'Patricia was busy today. Because of me. I persuaded her to go and get something done with her hair. Get some layers put through it. Buck it

221

up a bit. She's a good-looking woman, and it'll take ten years off her. Give her a bit of style and some new confidence in herself, so she can show that eejit Pete Mac that she's still got it, and what he risks losing if he doesn't stop playing his stupid games.'

Eileen's eyebrows lifted slightly. Good girl, she thought. But then came the blow, the one that deep down she had been expecting ever since Ellie had first set foot in the house.

'And I wanted her out of the way because I wanted it to be just the two of us today, Eileen. I wanted you to myself, with no chance of anyone interrupting us. Because I want you to tell me something. The truth. About why you killed my father. I've asked the others but they tell me everything except what I really want to know. Skirting round things, claiming they're not sure about this and about that. So it's down to you, you're the only one who can tell me why you did it. And I think you will, because you understand that I've got a right to know. And because now I know you better, I'm positive you had a reason to do what you did. And that it's got to be something more than him having an affair with my mother.'

'Quite a speech,' said Eileen, displaying no emotion.

'Quite a situation,' said Ellie.

The car behind them started honking, but neither of them showed any sign of hearing it.

'I guessed this was going to happen,' Eileen said to

222

her lap. 'That if you stayed in London, the time would come.' She considered for a moment before turning to Ellie and saying: 'If you're sure you want to know, then, all right, I will. I'll tell you.'

'Jesus, Eileen, you really are one for surprises. I never thought it'd be this easy. I thought I'd at least have to get you a bit pissed.' She slapped the steering wheel. 'What the hell. Let's get this thing parked and go and have a drink anyway.'

Ellie pulled forward at speed, bouncing the car forward in a series of amateurish leaps, watched with knowing disdain by the driver of the car behind them.

'There used to be an Italian place in James Street,' said Eileen, steadying herself with a hand on the dashboard. 'Not far from here. I used to have lunch there with Sophie Kessler, years ago, after we'd been shopping. It had little booths that made it cosy – and private. It might still be there.'

They emerged from the car park, just as fat summer raindrops the size of two-pence pieces started splattering down on to the hot pavement.

'You up to running?' asked Ellie, taking Eileen by the arm.

Eileen nodded and Ellie hurried her across the parched grass to the cover of an overhanging canopy at the back entrance of a big department store.

'You'll be all right here for a couple of minutes,' said Ellie, noting how Eileen nervously distanced herself from the huddle of shoppers doing their best to protect themselves and their bags from the worst of the cloudburst. She obviously preferred to risk getting wet than stand close to them. 'I won't leave you for long, I'll just nip back and fetch my umbrella from the boot.'

With that she sprinted back to the car park, holding her handbag over her head in a futile attempt to keep her hair dry from the now teeming rain.

Ellie was just about to slip the car key into the lock, when a rough hand clapped over her mouth. 'Give us your bag, bitch.'

In a single fluid move, Ellie spun round as she ripped the hand away from her face and twisted it up the back of its owner – a scruffy-looking teenager – making him yelp with pain. In her other hand Ellie had her car key, which she touched to the side of his neck. 'You picked the wrong fecking one with me, you cheeky little bastard. You dare move and I'll rip your bloody throat out for you.'

The boy held his head as still as he could, not knowing that all she was holding to his flesh was a key. 'Listen, darling, I –'

'No, if you've got any sense *you'll* listen. I come from a very scary family, a family who would really hate it if anything nasty happened to me. But today must be your lucky day, because I'm the nice one. So I'm going to let you go. But first I'm going to give you a warning. You never, ever come down here again, or you might just be unlucky, make a mistake, and pick on me again. And next time perhaps I'll forget my manners and have you on your back with my heel in your face before you know what's hit you. Or maybe worse, I'll get one of my big brothers to do it for me. Do you understand me?'

He risked the briefest of nods.

'Okay.' She took a breath and let him go.

Let him go? Was that the stupidest thing she had ever done?

Ellie could have wept with relief as the youth zig-zagged off towards the shadows of the stairwell. She dropped her head and closed her eyes, concentrating on nothing but being still, the way she did when she fell from a horse and had to calm herself before getting back in the saddle.

'Ellie?' It was Eileen. She was standing by the lifts, her hair glistening with raindrops in the dull glow of the fly-dirt-encrusted strip lighting.

Eileen started running towards her. 'What's wrong? Are you all right? Is everything okay?'

'Sure, everything's grand. But look at you, you're all wet.'

'I couldn't stand there with all those people any more, I . . .'

Her words trailed away. 'But never mind that. That scruff you were talking to, was he bothering you?'

'No! The eejit thought I'd *lend* him some money,' she said, rolling her eyes as if nothing of any account had happened. 'Can you believe it?'

'This isn't Ireland, you know, Ellie.' There was now something that looked almost like motherly concern on Eileen's face. 'People in London can be very dangerous.'

Ellie, her mouth open and her brow lowered, turned away from Eileen on the pretext of opening the boot to search out the umbrella.

London can be dangerous?

Was the woman being sarcastic? It was genuinely hard to tell. But, whichever way you looked at it, it was a bit rich coming from a woman who had killed her own husband. Still, she'd have to swallow those feelings if she was to have any hope of finding out the truth about her father's death.

This was going to be some drink.

While Ellie and Eileen were joining the early-lunch crowd in the trattoria in James Street, Patricia was standing in the doorway of a very expensive hair stylist's in a square at the back of Regent Street. She was looking up at the sky. The rain was still pouring down and the clouds were low, dark and heavy, threatening a long, wet, muggy afternoon.

From the corner of her eye, she caught the image of a well-dressed man, hurrying along the street, holding a copy of the *Daily Telegraph* over his head as a makeshift umbrella.

'I'd go back inside for a while, if I were you,' he smiled at her over his shoulder as he trotted past.

'Don't want to spoil that hair of yours, young lady. Very pretty.'

Patricia looked at him as if he'd lost his mind.

Pretty? No one had called her that in years. She turned and considered her reflection in the plate-glass window of the salon.

Maybe she didn't look too bad after all. And maybe Ellie was right – perhaps Pete Mac had better watch out if he didn't want to lose her.

Eileen broke a bread stick in two, was about to eat a piece of it, but changed her mind and placed the bits side by side on the pink tablecloth.

'When I went in that place, you know, the prison, I was so cocky.'

'You, Eileen? Cocky? I can hardly believe that.'

'What I mean is, I thought all the women and the girls in there were ignorant. Beneath me. Despite what I'd done – killing my own husband – I felt superior to them. But the thing I hadn't worked out, not back then, was that you can cure ignorance. You can learn, find out how to change things. Make them better. But what you can't change is stupidity. No, that's another thing entirely. If you're stupid you're stuck with it. And that wasn't only a problem for a lot of those women in there, I soon realised it was my problem too. I understand that I'm as stupid as hell. I chose to do what I did because I honestly thought it would be best for my children. That it was the way to make it all stop.'

Ellie leaned forward, her expression and body language challenging whatever Eileen had to say. 'I know my father wasn't exactly a saint – I remember, Aunt Mary always used to make the joke: my brother Gabriel, he was no angel – but I don't understand what was so bad about him for you to kill him.'

'Now you're showing your ignorance, Ellie. Well, I hope it's ignorance, and not stupidity.'

'What do you mean?'

'Too many women stay with men, bad men, because they think they have no choice. They put up with them, and suffer at their hands just because they're married to them, when what they should be doing is protecting themselves and their children by getting them as far away from them as they can.'

'So why didn't you leave?'

'Because women like me don't do that.'

'That makes no sense.'

'I know.' Eileen looked around as if seeking help. 'Look, there was this woman, she came to the prison to give us a talk one day. She was an "expert" on wife battering – if you can believe such a thing exists. She came in to help us poor souls by giving us the benefit of her wisdom. She was a small-minded do-gooder in lots of ways, talked down to us, acted much the same way as I'd acted towards the other women when I'd first gone in there, I suppose. But she did tell us one incredible thing.'

She sipped at her drink, wanting time rather than

the taste of the wine. 'Every single week, two women die at the hands of their own men. Can you believe it?'

Ellie shrank back in her seat. 'Are you saying my father used to beat you?'

Eileen lifted her chin and stared up at the ceiling. 'No. But I am saying he was a violent bully. And it was his fault that Catherine died.'

'No, that can't be right.'

'Believe me, it can. There was trouble with the Kesslers. He told the boys to sort it out, made them take a shotgun to frighten them. But what none of us knew – apart from Luke – was that Sammy Kessler was seeing Catherine. She was in the car with Sammy when the gun went off. It hit her in the neck. She stood no chance.'

'No!'

'Yes. If Gabriel hadn't made the boys take the gun, my baby, your sister, would still be alive today. I couldn't take any more. When Catherine died, I knew I had to stop him. Stop him from destroying the rest of my children.'

'And you want me to believe that's why you killed him?'

'It's the truth.'

'But I don't understand. Luke and Brendan both told me that Catherine died in a car crash.'

'That's what they wanted everyone to believe.' Eileen unfolded and refolded her napkin. 'But it wasn't true. The truth is, it was Gabriel's fault. Simple as that. Trouble is, I know now – too late – that my killing him was all a stupid waste. Regardless of anything I did – or can do – the boys are going exactly the same way as their father.'

'As *my* father.'

Eileen didn't comment on the correction. 'Even Luke. No matter how he tries to convince me – and himself – otherwise, I know he's not the innocent he pretends to be.' Eileen pressed her fingers to her lips. 'And look at yourself, Ellie, caught up with Brendan. Impressed by his madness – and don't try to pretend otherwise. Because I know how it is. Their world is a mad, bad place, and they're spiralling down into its vile and rotten depths. Luke as well as Brendan. And you have to think about whether you want to go with them.'

'Aren't you being a bit –'

Eileen ploughed on as if Ellie hadn't spoken. 'Maybe if I'd not done it, if I'd not killed him, but had just stayed at home, maybe then I might at least have been able to have some influence over Luke.'

Eileen moved the pieces of the bread stick around, placing them back together as if it was a single whole again. 'I don't know. I don't know anything any more.'

Ellie took a big gulp of her Chianti. 'Sure, you're not alone there, Eileen.'

Chapter 19

Less than a mile away from the restaurant where, a couple of days ago, Ellie had sat listening to Eileen, and even closer to the hair salon where Patricia had begun to realise that she might actually have some value as a woman, the Kesslers were in the back room of one of what they referred to as their dirty bookshops. Though books were only a part of the merchandise they had on offer.

In the front of the shop, Bug Eye, the peeping Tom who worked the public counter, was eavesdropping rather than spying for a change. Ignoring his smattering of Monday-morning customers, he was lurking by the door to the back room, curious to know why the young man with the blond Afro and the extravagant dress sense was in there talking to Danny, Sammy and Maurice.

'Like I say, I don't know anything about any of your past arguments with the O'Donnells, that was all before my time,' Milo was saying, leaning in his usual casual way against a wall full of shelves stacked with Super 8 cine films. 'Except what I've heard from that trappy git, Pete Mac, of course. But I'm just here to let you know what I do know – that Brendan

O'Donnell is intending to have all your trade off you. Every bit of speed you bring in, he's planning to have it.'

He offered round his cigarettes. Only Maurice took one.

'And how do you know that then, feller?'

'He wants me to handle it all for him.'

'*You what?*' Danny lunged forward, but Maurice stopped him before he could actually grab hold of Milo.

'And,' Milo went on, apparently not fazed at all, 'before you think you can just go round there team-handed and stop him with a bit of well-placed violence, you ought to know that he's well in with the Irish.'

'Do us a favour.' It was Sammy, he looked knowingly at Daniel. 'Now we know you're talking a load of bollocks. Course O'Donnell's in with the Irish. He *is* fucking Irish. Just like your family are – *Flanagan.*'

'I mean the grown-up Irish.' Milo took a moment to light his and Maurice's cigarettes, letting his words sink in. 'The very bad, political boys. The ones with the fucking bombs and that. Which means that not only have you got to be careful, but I have too. Because I intend to do up Mr O'Donnell like an 'alf-rotten kipper, and I definitely don't want that lot on me back.'

'Aw yeah?' Sammy still sounded sceptical. 'Why would you do that then?'

'Because that bloke has got right up my nose lately, and I ain't having it. And that's why I came here today – with the information about the speed – because I thought that might make you feel the same way about him as I do.'

'We already do, thanks, feller,' said Maurice. 'We take all the risks selling the merchandise in the shops and he takes the majority cut. We might as well be running a fucking supermarket for him.'

'You finished talking about our private business, have you, Maury?' Daniel said flatly. He sat down on the corner of a packing case and folded his arms. 'Look, Flanagan, much as I'd like to think I could trust you, I don't know the strength of you, do I, mate? First of all, you shove that bloody note under me nose at the boxing, like a kid in the fucking playground, then you come bowling in here like you was our best friend or something. But how do I know this ain't a set-up? That you ain't doing this for the O'Donnells. Sticking your snotty Irish nose in our business.'

'I won't take offence, Danny, cos I understand your concerns. But I'm gonna prove myself. I guarantee it. See, I've got a way to have them bastards. Then you, and me – all of us – we'll all be laughing.'

'At least listen to him, feller,' said Maurice, pointing to Milo with his cigarette. 'I know that I for one would very much like to keep all this fucking gelt

233

we're earning. You've seen the figures on that calculator thing of your dad's, Daniel, seen them with your own bloody eyes. The tills are overflowing, fivers bursting out of the bastards. And what happens, we have to clear them out to pay them fuckers for their sodding *merchandise*.'

'Maury.' Danny's voice was warning his cousin, but he paid no heed.

'How about you, Sam?'

Sammy shrugged. 'You know Danny's always made these decisions.'

'Okay, Danny,' said Milo, totally businesslike, not a sign of the cheeky cockney always up for a laugh. 'Like I said, I'm gonna have the O'Donnells, so hear me out and just say if you're interested.'

'You've got five minutes.'

'Fine.' Milo grinned. 'Now, d'you happen to know anyone in Brixton who owes your family a favour?'

'Why?'

'Because we are gonna send a message to Barry Ellis.'

Ellie and Patricia were in the communal changing room of one of the many fashionable boutiques on Kensington High Street. Patricia was looking around self-consciously. Despite the fact that it was a Monday morning, and that she and Ellie were the only two women in there, Patricia still felt horribly awkward.

It was the first time she'd ever been expected to take off her clothes in such a public space before – face it, she just wasn't the sort of person who did that kind of thing. These days, she wasn't even used to taking them off in front of Pete Mac.

'Are you okay, Pat?' Ellie asked, clearly amused by her half-sister's discomfort.

'Yeah, course I am. And I'm really glad you persuaded me to come today. Especially when I see your'n and Sandy's clothes. I mean, I'm not exactly a fashion plate these days, am I? Not that you knew me when I was younger of course,' she babbled nervously.

'I wish I had known you,' said Ellie, suddenly serious.

Patricia was too caught up with trying to keep herself decent to notice. 'This is nice,' she gasped, struggling to pull up the straps of the halter-neck dress from somewhere deep down in the neckline of the brown-and-cream patterned blouse that Ellie had insisted Patricia should borrow from her. 'I'd never have chosen this on my own. It was bad enough going to that hairdresser's by myself, but I just know I wouldn't have had the courage to come into a place like this without you.'

'Good thing too,' laughed Ellie. 'Carrying on like that by yourself, they'd have called security. You look like you've been let out for the day.'

Ellie stepped forward and, with a few uncere-monious tugs and jerks, hoiked the blouse right over

Patricia's head, leaving her in just her bra and the unfastened dress.

'Ellie!'

'What? Sure, you've still got your undies on.' She looked at it critically. 'And doesn't that look like it was made before the war? Even Aunt Mary wears less scaffolding under her bosoms than that thing you've got on there.'

'It's comfortable,' Patricia said, straining to pull up the dress and secure the straps behind her neck without exposing too much flesh. 'And anyway, what does it matter? Who cares about the state of my underwear?'

'You should care, that's who,' said Ellie firmly.

'There.' Patricia turned to look at her reflection in the mirrored walls. 'What do you think?'

'Hang on.' Without comment, Ellie unhooked the fastening of Patricia's now exposed bra. 'Let's get this thing off you and have a proper look.'

Patricia checked guiltily about her, as if she'd just been caught trying to stuff a stolen frock down her knickers, and then eased the bra straps down over her arms.

'So, tell me, have you ever thought about having your tits made bigger, Patricia?'

'*What did you say?*'

'I saw an article about it in a magazine. *Cosmo*, or *Nova*, I think it was. They can do it, you know. Lift 'em high and blow 'em up like balloons. It's a grand idea. Especially for a woman of your age. Sure, it'd give you a new lease of life.'

'You cheeky mare, I'm only thirty-seven.'

'First mistake, Patricia. Never admit to being more than twenty-nine.'

Ellie turned sideways on to the mirror and studied her own reflection as she cupped her breasts in her hands.

'Milo reckons mine are perfect.'

'Milo?'

In reply, Ellie flashed her eyebrows and her breasts – lifting her cheesecloth shirt up over her face – making Patricia snort out loud.

'You are so rude, Ellie.'

'No I'm not. I'm just my own woman. Like you're going to be when I finish with you.'

'I don't know about that.'

'Well, I do. Because no one treats my sister the way that that Peter MacRiordan treats you.'

Patricia avoided Ellie's gaze, busying herself searching through the mound of garments that Ellie had insisted they take into the changing room.

'What was Dad like, Pat? Did he treat Eileen the way Pete Mac treats you? Is that why you put up with it? Because it was what you got used to when you were a kid?'

Patricia clutched the embroidered velvet pinafore dress she had selected from the pile to her chest. 'This is a bit out of the blue.' She sounded flustered.

'Not for me, it's not. I think about it all the time. What he was like, why Eileen did what she did. Even about Aunt Mary putting up with Uncle Sean. He's an eejit, that one. He'd drive a saint to murder, let alone a bitch like Mary. But there's your mam, quiet, respectable even, and she goes and does something like that. I'm telling you, Pat, I've heard her version of it, but it's still all a bloody mystery to me. And getting to the bottom of anything in this family's worse than breaking in a bad-tempered colt – you never know when you're going to get a kick up the arse.'

'Mum hasn't been herself since . . . Aw, you know.'

'I understand that. But Eileen's told me stuff about my dad, and Catherine, and how she died. But it's nothing like Luke and Brendan have told me. I'm sure Luke knows more than he's letting on. But will he say anything? Will he feck. And as for Brendan, there's no point even considering asking that one. It's like they're all talking in code, hiding things, protecting one another. But I'm bloody family, for God's sake.'

Patricia dropped her hands from her chest, letting the dress fall to the floor. 'If I tell you the truth, Ellie – the truth that I know anyway – about Dad's drinking, and his temper, and his womanising, and . . .' Her throat flushed red, as her words staggered to a painful halt.

'I promise I won't tell anyone. You don't have any

worries there, Pat. And, to make it fair, you're not to tell anyone about me and Milo.'

'By anyone, I presume you mean Brendan.'

'Of course I mean Brendan. Finding your way with that one is like dealing with Aunt Mary in a bloody three-piece suit.'

Chapter 20

Despite it being only eleven o'clock, DI Bert Hammond was drinking whiskey with Brendan in the O'Donnells' Bella Vista club in Shoreditch. Or rather he was holding a full glass of the stuff, which he hadn't so much as sniffed at, let alone tasted. He left the heavy boozing to Brendan, who was making a good job of finishing his second refill, only just drawing the line at knocking it back in one go.

DI Hammond looked about him, as if checking for eavesdroppers – even though there wasn't a single customer in the whole place, and the barman had, very sensibly, put himself far away enough from them so as not to be accused of the punishable offence of sticking his oar in where it wasn't welcome.

Hammond leaned towards Brendan and said in low, confidential tones: 'I'm glad you could meet me this morning, Brendan. You see I've had a troubling weekend. Very troubling. The good lady and I were meant to be going home on a little trip to Birmingham to see her mother, but I was – unfortunately – otherwise engaged, having to have meetings with some very objectionable people.'

He made another, slightly more dramatic check

around the still-punterless room. 'Thing is,' he went on, rubbing his stubbly, salt-and-pepper moustache with the knuckle of his index finger, 'there are a lot of very unpleasant rumours flying around.'

'Aw yes, Bert?' said Brendan, only half listening, his real concern being that the barman should fill the now empty glass he had just set down on the counter. 'And what sort of rumours would they be then?'

'I'm afraid to say they're about your brother Luke.'

Brendan was immediately on the alert. He didn't like people talking about his family, and he especially didn't like it when people had things to say about his brother, but most of all he didn't like it when people said smart-arsed things about his brother being 'different'.

'Aw yeah, Bert. What sort of things would they be then?'

'That he's started running knocking shops.'

Brendan snorted with aggressive, dismissive laughter.

'Oh dear, Brendan, I don't think that's the right attitude to take at all. I know I wouldn't find it funny, if I were you, because that's not the half of what they're saying.' That stopped the flash, cockney git in his tracks. 'In fact,' Hammond went on, noting with pleasure every tiny twitch on Brendan's face that showed the policeman had hit the target, 'there are so many rumours flying around about all manner of things to do with your family – and the Kesslers, as it happens – that it would have me rather worried if I were in your position. Silly little things, admittedly, in some cases, but from people who, although they don't know that much, know enough to start some very nasty aggravation if they feel like it.'

Brendan *really* didn't like this. The Brummy wanker was acting as if he was the one calling all the fucking shots. He knew plenty of senior coppers who played the potentially dangerous game of socialising with the very people they were supposed to be nicking. And, usually, it suited them all: wheels were oiled and everyone got on with their business, and enjoyed the backhanders, thank you very much all round. But there was something about this bloke that was starting to get on Brendan's nerves.

He slammed down his glass. 'Who? Just tell me the bastards' names, and I'll show 'em fucking rumours. I'll shut this crap down right now.'

'Don't go getting yourself all agitated, Brendan. It's no one who needs matter. Not for now, anyway.' Hammond was really enjoying himself, stirring things up with his invented stories that could – oh so easily – be true. Carry on at this rate, and he'd not only have all the evidence his superiors wanted about corruption in the force, but he'd have a very tasty bonus, the East End jackpot – plenty of solid gold dirt on the O'Donnells and the Kesslers.

He looked at his watch. 'But I'll make sure I keep

you informed if there are any further developments. That's all I have to say for now, as I'd better be on my way.'

But Brendan had plenty more to say, and he wanted Hammond to hear every word of it. 'No, hang on a minute. About Luke. On my life, Bert, he's a fucking landlord, nothing more. We all know how things have changed round here. And he's taken advantage of it and he's gone legit. I swear he has. He's got all these respectable building contracts, and . . .'

Brendan was casting about wildly, he couldn't let Luke get pulled in over something like this – over anything – he wasn't strong like Brendan. He'd crack like cheaply laid tarmac if they got hold of him.

'I'm telling you. Contracts with local authorities and everything.'

'What, like that Mr Paulson we've all been reading about in the newspapers? He's been a very naughty boy according to those reports. Bribes, dodgy contacts, and who knows what else he's been up to. And I know it's getting him into a whole lot of trouble, having dealings with local authorities. You don't mean to tell me your brother's involved in that sort of business, do you, Brendan?'

'I told you, on my life, Bert, he –'

'Listen to me, Brendan, I'm getting in very deep here, letting you know the score on all this, but I'm warning you: there are people who don't like outsiders running toms round there. You . . . People should know that and take note. All right? Now, I really do have to be on my way.'

The moment Brendan saw Hammond steer his car out on to Folgate Street, he rushed back into the club, reached across the bar and snatched his car keys from the hook under the counter.

'If any of the boys want me, I'm shooting round Luke's. And I'll be back at the cab office early afternoon.'

Brendan drove to Frith Street in less than fifteen minutes, ignoring the abuse from other drivers as he cut them up, jumping red lights, and narrowly missing those pedestrians who were daring enough to use zebra crossings in front of him. And when he slammed to a halt and parked outside the Moulin Bleu, he didn't even bother to look for someone to mind his car. He just locked it up and left it to the mercies of Soho.

After leaning on the bell for a good thirty seconds, Brendan was about to leave and try somewhere else, when the door opened and Luke stood there in front of him, wet-haired, barefoot, and wearing only a pair of faded, flared jeans.

'Sorry, Brendan,' he said, 'you caught me in the shower.'

'You're gonna be even sorrier when I've finished with you, you prat. Now get upstairs.'

Brendan followed his brother up to the top of the nondescript stairway, and then into the narrow lobby and through the door into Luke's large, bright living room.

'Hammond's tipped me the wink,' Brendan said, pacing up and down like an expectant father in a hospital waiting room. 'He knows what's going on in your properties.'

He spun round and jabbed a furious finger in Luke's face. 'This could blow everything, you stupid, fucking hypocrite. Once they start nosing around your so-called respectable stuff, we'll all be dropped right in it. The clubs, the escorts, the drugs, the films, even the fucking minicabs. There'll be no excuse to keep them out. And they'll just keep digging. And digging. And you don't even wanna know what the Irishmen'd do if the law start sniffing around over them guns.'

'No, this Hammond, he's got it all wrong, Brendan.' Luke's face was screwed up as if having to explain things to his brother was causing him great pain. 'I don't have anything to do with the girls.'

'So why have them there in the first fucking place? It's not even our sodding patch. People – them bastard Kesslers for a start – are gonna get the hump with you, with us, operating out that far east. You know we gave them our word that they could have that territory if they wanted it. And it's us who's meant to have the fucking hump with them, not the other way round, you moron. This could make us look stupid, Luke. *Stupid.*' Flecks of saliva were bubbling in the corners of Brendan's mouth.

'We did them a favour, acted like big men, let them have that area – the scraps off our table – and now we're creeping back there like two-bob merchants nicking it back. And I don't fucking like it.'

'Don't go getting narky with me, Brendan.' Luke had his chin in the air, a man wronged by his brother's accusations. 'It's not like I'm pimping for 'em or nothing. All them girls work for themselves. They just pay me for the rooms, that's all. I get a good day rate off 'em. And cos they don't care what state the places are in, it's an ideal set-up. As soon as I get enough money to buy up a few more places, I'll be able to invest in the first of them warehouses down the docks.'

'For fuck's sake, Luke.' Brendan threw up his arms, totally exasperated, then pulled off his jacket and threw it over one of the low-slung leather and chrome armchairs. 'I think we'd better have a proper talk about this, with you explaining exactly what you think you're up to, mate. Come on, let's sit down and have a drink. No, hang on.' He swiped the back of his hand across his mouth. 'I've already had a fucking skinful. Let's have a cuppa tea instead.'

Brendan started walking towards the kitchen door at the far end of the room.

'No, Brendan, please, sit down. I'll make you a cup and bring it through.'

But Brendan was already walking through the kitchen door.

As he stepped inside Brendan did a double take that wouldn't have shamed the Keystone Kops. 'What the fuck is he doing here?'

Nicky Wright, sitting at the breakfast counter wearing just a T-shirt and a pair of underpants, shrugged. 'Having a bit of a late breakfast.'

Brendan turned round and banged straight into Luke.

He smacked him flat up against the kitchen wall. 'I don't believe this, Luke. I've been through there saying all sorts of fucking private things about the business, and this little prick's been sitting here listening. Why didn't you fucking tell me he was here?'

Brendan didn't wait for Luke to reply. He shoved his brother to one side and pushed past him back into the living room. He snatched his jacket off the chair and headed for the door. 'You are beginning to seriously fucking annoy me, mate,' he said without looking round.

He paused in the doorway, still staring straight ahead, unable to look his brother in the eye. 'I just hope, Luke – really, genuinely, seriously, fucking hope – that that little slag back in there ain't more important to you than your family.'

'Brendan, he won't say anything, I –'

That was as far as Luke got before Brendan slammed the door on him and raced down the stairs out into the streets of Soho.

Chapter 21

'Brendan shouldn't be long now, Luke,' said Sandy, her neck stretched out as she peered wide-eyed at her reflection in the mirror stuck inside the lid of her make-up bag. She was stroking a crescent of plum-coloured shadow on to her eyelids, getting herself ready for an evening out on the town.

She lowered the silver quilted bag a few inches and looked over it at Luke, who was sitting across from her at the new farmhouse-kitchen table that she'd had delivered just the week before. The table that made *her* kitchen, overlooking *her* garden look even more beautiful than it already did, if that were possible. It was hard to take it all in at times – that this was really where she was living, that this was really all hers. That this was how her life was now.

'But you know what Brendan's like,' she added lightly. 'He said we were going out for something to eat at half eight, and it's already, what?' She glanced up at the wall clock. 'Nearly ten past already. Looks like something's come up, and if it has, he could be hours.'

She put the little brush back in its case. 'You sure there's nothing I can help you with?'

'No, you're all right, San. Long as I'm not in your way.'

'You're fine,' she said, but from the tension in his face, and the way he was fiddling with his car keys, she couldn't help feeling that Luke wasn't fine at all.

And she was right. Since Brendan had stormed out of Luke's flat yesterday lunchtime, warning him that he should put his family first, and that his loyalty was to them and not to Nicky, Luke hadn't been able to think about very much else. He'd wound up getting himself in such a state over it that he'd rowed with Nicky about whether they were going to spend the evening watching *Kojak* or listening to Nicky's latest Elton John album. It had got that ridiculous.

As a result of Luke's shouting and hollering, Nicky had stomped out of the flat saying he never wanted to see Luke again. And he hadn't come back all night, although Luke was sure he'd be home soon. They loved each other too much to let something as stupid as a row over whether or not they were going to watch the telly separate them.

Nicky was the one he wanted to spend the rest of his life with, and Nicky knew it. Luke only wished he had the courage to admit it to Brendan. But if he could unravel this mess with his brother, then he would at least have started moving in the right direction. He couldn't let things stay messed up, not when he was so close to getting his life the way he wanted. He was going to run a strong, legitimate

250

business that had nothing to do with the family. And that was why he'd come to talk to Brendan. Luke was going to explain that he'd thought about what Brendan had said, and he'd decided to give all the girls six months' notice. That would let him rack up a nice chunk of rent, which, added to the profit he'd make when he sold the houses, would leave him laughing. He'd have a good lump of that stake he needed to buy his first warehouse. It would be the beginnings of his property empire, and of his and Nicky's new life together.

'Talk of the devil,' said Sandy, getting to her feet, as the doorbell chimed. 'That'll be him now. Probably got his arms full of goodies and can't manage the key, the silly bugger. Honestly, you should see the things he brings home for me, Luke.'

She was talking to him over her shoulder as she walked out to the hall. 'He's so generous. Been that way ever since the wedding. Treats me like I'm some kind of a princess or something. I'm telling you, it takes some getting used to after what I've had to cope with over the past few years.'

But it wasn't Brendan.

When Sandy opened the door she was confronted by Anthony, who almost blocked out the light with his massive bulk, and – as far as Sandy could make out – Amber, as she called herself, one of the escort girls. Because, despite the warmth of the summer evening, Anthony was wearing a voluminous black mac, and he had the girl tucked away in its folds under his arm, shielding her from view.

Sandy didn't say a word, she just leaned back against the wall and let them pass her into the hallway.

For Anthony to turn up unannounced or uninvited with one of the escorts there had to be something very wrong.

'Go through to the kitchen, Anthony,' she said, then added hurriedly before he went in: 'Luke's in there.' She didn't want anyone saying anything out of turn because they thought they were speaking in private. That could start all sorts of trouble. And she didn't want that – not in her newly decorated kitchen, she didn't.

Anthony raised his head towards Luke in silent greeting and, surprisingly gently for such a big man, unwrapped his billowing coat from around Amber's shoulders.

Luke drew in his breath so loudly that Sandy turned to look at him rather than at her unexpected guests.

'Bloody hell,' murmured Luke, rising to his feet in almost cartoonish slow motion. 'What the fuck's happened to her?'

Sandy followed Luke's gaze to where Amber was standing, or rather bending over the table. She was gripping it for support, her chest heaving as she tried to surf across the pain. Almost the entire front of her body-hugging, ivory satin catsuit was stained with blood, her hair was soaking wet, and the side of her face that had been hidden by Anthony's coat looked as if it had been repeatedly smashed in with a house brick.

'Sorry for bringing her round here, San, but I didn't know what else to do. Couldn't take her to the hospital in this state, could I?'

Anthony pulled out a chair and eased Anber slowly down on to it. 'She didn't want to do what the punter wanted,' he said, his big face creased into a deep, angry frown. 'So he decided to *punish* her, the fucker. Doing that to a woman.'

He turned to Sandy. 'Sorry for the language, San, only it gets to me, how a so-called man could do something like that to a woman. He smacked the hell out of her, then he pissed over her – can you believe that? You should smell the poor cow's hair. Then he cleared off and left her in the hotel room. If you really think she does need the hospital, I could run her down there.'

Sandy very calmly walked over to him and put a hand gently on his massive forearm. 'No, not the hospital, you were right in the first place. That wouldn't be a very good idea. Too many questions. I'll see to things here now, Anthony. Amber did the right thing calling you. Just like she'd been told if there was ever any trouble, cos you're a good bloke and you handle these things well. Now you go and get yourself a drink. The cabinet's in the living room. Up on the first floor. Luke'll show you where.'

Glad of any excuse to get away from the upsetting – bewildering – sight of a battered woman, Anthony and Luke shot up the stairs in pursuit of the numbing effects of a large glass of anything containing alcohol.

'I couldn't believe it,' mumbled Amber through her torn and puffy lips. 'The things he wanted to do to me, Mrs O'Donnell. Wanted to put these things inside me. Said he'd read about it in these magazines. He had them with him. In his briefcase. Sharp things. Big things. Said he wanted me to look at them with him. Then do it. He seemed so decent at first. Nicely spoken and everything. And the hotel was lovely.' She started crying. 'I think he broke some of my teeth. It was horrible, really horrible. I thought he was going to kill me. It was only when I started screaming that he ran away and left me.'

Sandy put a cork place mat on the table then fetched a Pyrex bowl full of warm salt water and a clean tea towel from one of the drawers. She dampened the cloth and wiped it across Amber's cheek. Amber moaned pitifully. 'That really hurts, Mrs O'Donnell. Please, be careful.'

Sandy straightened up and took a deep breath. 'Stop whining, darling,' she said, dabbing again at the girl's bloody face. 'It's how we earn our living, giving blokes what they want. And do us a favour and stop wriggling about, will you, you're getting blood on my new table.'

On the other side of the kitchen door, Luke – holding a glass in each of his hands for Sandy and Amber, and a fresh bottle of whiskey under his arm – was listening with a baffled frown on his face. *How we earn our living*? He'd never heard Sandy talk like that before.

He waited long enough for her not to think that he might have overheard her, and then knocked quietly.

'Okay to come in?' he called.

'Sure, and tell Anthony to come down as well, while you're at it. These cuts are not half as bad as they look. He can get her off home once he's finished his drink.'

Much as he would have liked to have got out of there – although preferably without a beaten and bruised woman in tow, who, if anyone saw them, would no doubt raise eyebrows as well as questions about whether he was the culprit – Anthony didn't get the chance, because at a quarter to nine, and without a word of explanation for his lateness to Sandy, Brendan arrived home.

He ruffled Sandy's hair – messing up the carefully tousled look she'd created especially for their evening out – and threw his car keys on the new table, making her cringe. Then he turned to Luke and Anthony. 'Glad you two are here.'

He reached for the bottle of whiskey and poured himself a large measure into one of the glasses, apparently not caring that someone had already been drinking from it.

'Get her out of the way, San,' he said, acknowledging Amber's presence for the first time. 'Stick her in a minicab or something. I wanna talk to the boys in private.'

Sandy didn't have to ask if she too was being dismissed.

Brendan drained his glass and refilled it, while he waited for Sandy to remove Amber and herself from his presence, then he began.

'I've been contacted by the Irishmen. Been asked to get another consignment ready for shipping over there. A big one. We've got to fund it from our end, but then they're gonna as good as double our money soon as we deliver.'

'How's the delivery being done?' Luke didn't really need to ask.

'Same as before. Ellie driving the horsebox. That worked well.'

'Brendan, you can't get her involved again. Once was bad enough, but –'

'*Don't even think about questioning me, Luke.*' The sound of Brendan cracking his glass down on the table was drowned out by the volume of his voice. 'Because after that fucking *surprise* you sprung on me in your flat yesterday – with that little tosspot sitting there looking at me like he had every right – I don't think you're in any position, do you?'

Anthony kept his gaze fixed firmly on the glass in front of him. He was beginning to think that taking Amber home hadn't been such a bad proposition after all. Brendan in this sort of a mood wasn't a pretty sight.

Brendan topped up all their glasses to the brim. 'This is a great opportunity,' he said, as if he hadn't just been shouting like a maniac. 'Good as printing money, plus the Irishmen are the right people to have on our side. And while we're at it we're gonna take over the Kesslers' speed business and all, set ourselves up as sole distributors and importers. Cos that sort of money's gonna come in handy to fund these Irish deals.'

Anthony and Luke watched him drain his glass and pour himself yet another drink.

'And I've been thinking about what Hammond said to me the other day about your property, Luke, and, d'you know what I realised? We've been too generous with them Kessler bastards. For far too fucking long. We've been so soft with 'em, they've started taking our kindness for fucking silliness.'

He stretched an arm around Luke's shoulders. 'I dunno about you, brother, but I feel just about ready for a fight with them cunts.'

Chapter 22

It was Sunday lunchtime, and the Rose and Punchbowl pub in Stepney was packed with regulars enjoying a drink as they tucked into the roast potatoes, prawns and cockles set out on the tables and the bar by the landlord's wife.

The snacks were always regarded as a treat, a generous gesture, with nobody minding that they were also there to encourage a healthy thirst among the customers. It wasn't as though they were the type of punters who needed to have their arms twisted up their backs to encourage them to sup a few more pints, anyway.

Brendan, Luke, Pete Mac, Anthony and Kevin Marsh were sitting at a table in a far corner, close to a door marked 'Private', which led to the upstairs living accommodation. It was a place where they presumed they wouldn't be disturbed.

Brendan was floating his scheme for the job that would supply the balance of the cash to fund the arms deal with the Irish, and that would pump-prime the rest of his plans – the plans that would increase the O'Donnells' trade in every existing sector, and in a few, very profitable, new ones. And if it all went the way he hoped it would, there would also be enough cash left over to make up the shortfall for the stake Luke needed to start his new property business over in the docks. If he really had to, and if he still thought it was a sensible idea.

But, best of all, it would put the Kesslers right back where they belonged, and where they deserved to be – at the bottom of the stinking heap, just like the snivelling two-bob merchants they'd been before the O'Donnells had been so generous to them.

Brendan's scheme was simple: they were going to take out a security van.

The others heard him out politely enough – they weren't stupid, this was Brendan O'Donnell – but when he'd finished they were all left feeling distinctly unconvinced.

As usual, it was Pete Mac who blundered in at the front of the queue.

'Nah, Brendan, that'll never work. It's no good, not nowadays. They've got all them radios and that, ain't they? We'd never get away with it.'

'And that, genius,' Brendan said, rapping his knuckles on Pete Mac's forehead, 'is why I've planned it and not you, you pudden.'

Pete Mac's lips turned down in a petulant snarl. He knew the rest of them agreed with him, it was a barmy idea, but, of course, it had been him who'd been brave enough to say so. And him who'd been made to look like the prize idiot. Again.

It gave him the right hump. Perhaps Brendan thought it made him look big, humiliating his own brother-in-law in front of other people.

The cunt.

He swallowed down his pint in two gulps, and held up the empty glass without even bothering to look towards the bar.

A smiling, late-middle-aged woman appeared beside him. 'Yes, Pete? Same again?'

He stared ahead of him. 'Yes *the same again*,' he said in a mocking imitation of her voice. 'But it's Mr MacRiordan to you, you saucy mare.'

'Right, sorry, course it is. Sorry.' The woman flushed a deep, embarrassed shade of red. 'Mr MacRiordan. And can I get you other gentlemen anything?'

'Yes, please, darling,' said Brendan. 'Same again all round and stick it on the tab.' He palmed the woman a fiver, and winked at her. 'And have one yourself, love.'

'Thanks very much, Mr O'Donnell,' she said carefully.

'What's all this Mr O'Donnell lark? ' Brendan asked with a pained frown. 'How long have we known each other, Ivy? Since I was a nipper with the arse hanging out of me trousers, that's how long. And if you can't call me Brendan, now who can?'

She smiled, just grateful to get away from the

table, and not giving a flying fart about what she was supposed to call the nasty bastards.

Brendan bent forward and jabbed an accusing finger in Pete Mac's face. 'Can't you get it into that thick nut of yours, *Mr fucking MacRiordan*, that you have to keep things nice? Not only is it ignorant treating an old girl like that, but you're drawing fucking attention to yourself. And to me. You dozy-eyed bastard.' He shook his head and reached across for one of the packets of cigarettes littering the table. 'Just keep things subtle, Pete, eh? Discreet. Try and remember, for fuck's sake. Or we might as well just put an advert on the fucking telly about what we're up to.'

With very inopportune timing another woman appeared at Pete Mac's side. And this one didn't need Pete Mac's rudeness to get anyone's attention. She was the sort who immediately had the eye of everyone in the bar trained right on her. And it wasn't because she was fetching drinks.

She was in her early twenties, with white, bleached-blonde hair piled up on top of her head, and curling down in tendrils around her neck and heavily made-up face. She was wearing a mid-calf, halter-neck cotton dress that, even if it hadn't been flapping open showing off her thighs, would have been just as revealing, as it was made as good as see-through by the brilliant, early-afternoon sunlight streaming in through the windows that had been flung open to let some air into the fug of alcohol and cigarette fumes. But perhaps the most striking thing about her – well, as far as the other customers were concerned – was that she'd come into the pub carrying a dinner plate full of Sunday roast, complete with sploshing gravy that had made its mark down her very ample front.

She smacked the plate down in front of Pete Mac, treating his shirt and tie to their very own share of the gravy.

'You like it here that much, do you, Pete? Well then, you stay here, you bastard!' Her voice came out as an alarming, croaky growl. It was very loud.

'One o'clock you said you was coming round mine for your dinner. One o-fucking-clock. Now it's ten past poxy two. And do you know how many boozers I've had to go to looking for you?' She turned about her, making sure she had the full attention of her audience. 'Cos he obviously wouldn't have been indoors with his old woman, now would he?'

With that she marched over to the door, accompanied by a chorus of appreciative cheers and whistles. But she hadn't finished yet. She stopped in the open doorway, jammed her fists into her waist and spun round to face Pete Mac.

'Aw yeah, I meant to say. You might as well stick with them two red-headed slags of your'n, you tosspot, cos me and Rhona don't wanna know about moving into your flat no more. In fact, you can stick your bleed'n flat right up your hairy arse.'

The effect of the now direct sunlight coming through the open door on her gauzy cotton dress had the whistles being drowned out by an enthusiastic round of applause.

Brendan puffed out his cheeks. 'So much for keeping things subtle, eh, Pete?' He closed his eyes and dragged his fingers down his face. 'Now, who the fuck was that?'

'Dunno her name,' said Pete Mac, picking up a slice of roast beef from the plate, tossing back his head and feeding it into his mouth. 'I met her and her mate at your'n and Sandy's wedding,' he went on, his mouth full of food. 'Nice girls. You slapped one of 'em, remember? I ain't sure, but I think she was the one what gave me the blow job.'

Brendan shook his head, clenching his fists under the table, just *this* short of punching him. 'You are so classy, Pete. D'you know that? Very classy indeed, mate.' He was barely able to spit out the words. 'You don't know how proud I am to call you my fucking brother-in-law.'

Pete Mac grinned, surprised to be the object of such praise.

There were strings of beef stuck in his teeth.

Carol Mercer was stretched out on the pristine white sheet she had bought from a stall down the Lane to cover the stained, lumpy mattress, which stank out the room in her stifling lodgings. She was flicking through an ancient copy of *Woman's Own* which she'd lifted from the family-planning clinic when she'd gone to renew her prescription for the pill. Not that she actually had any need to take the bloody thing. Sammy had made it more than clear that he had no intention of having anything more to do with her, and even Pete Mac had gone among the bloody missing.

And the sodding rent was due at the end of the rotten month.

She tossed the magazine to one side. She really had to get her head round what she was going to do about her situation or she would be left so deep in the shit that she'd never be able to claw her way out of it.

But what she wanted to do first, what she *needed* to do first for her own pride and satisfaction, was show the arseholes who'd pissed her off that they couldn't mess around with Carol Mercer and get away with it.

She might have looked, and even acted, like a sweet, dumb blonde, but she hadn't been forced to look after herself since she was just a little kid without learning a thing or two.

It was almost five o'clock on the following Friday morning, when the security-van driver changed lanes, and entered the northbound core of the Blackwall Tunnel.

'I love it these summer mornings,' he said, narrowing his eyes as he tried to accustom them to the suddenly dim lighting inside the tunnel. 'No traffic about, no rain or fog to stare at and give me a headache. And knowing I'm going to get all the deliveries done nice and early, then back home and out in the garden with a can of lager in my hand, and the paper on my knee till teatime. Then a little stroll down the boozer, and all knowing it'll still be light for hours. You can't whack it, can you?'

'No traffic? Well, how about them two cheeky buggers?' His mate nodded his head towards a family saloon and a post-office van that had cut in front of them and sped their way into the tunnel. 'They must be doing bloody seventy.'

'Ignore the idiots. Let them be the first ones in the cemetery.'

'I wouldn't have thought a mail van could go that fast.'

What happened next meant that neither of them noticed the third vehicle, a builder's truck pulling into the tunnel behind them. They were too busy trying to figure out what was going on ahead.

The first of the speeding vehicles, driven by Anthony, had skidded sideways, and come to a halt, blocking the exit to the north side. Anthony got out, opened the bonnet and started fiddling about with the engine as if he were dealing with some kind of fault.

The second vehicle – a mock-up of a Royal Mail van – driven by Brendan, and with Luke in the passenger seat, had stopped a third of the way into the tunnel. It was now parked diagonally across the lanes, forcing the security van to come to a stop – which it did twenty yards behind it.

The builder's truck had also stopped, and was now pointing sideways, blocking the entrance from the south. Kevin Marsh and Pete Mac had jumped out of it and were busily erecting the police signs they'd taken from the back of the vehicle, declaring the tunnel closed due to a serious accident.

'Get on the radio,' shouted the driver.

His mate grabbed the hand-held mike and started twiddling knobs on his side of the dashboard. 'Can't get nothing 'cept a load of crackling. There's no contact.' He fiddled a bit more. 'Aw fuck. It's being in the tunnel.'

'Keep calm,' said the driver. 'They can't get us while we're locked in here, and soon as other drivers realise what's going on, they'll get help for us.'

'Don't want to worry you, but look in your wing mirror.'

The driver looked.

'You might be able to tell me I'm wrong, but, far as I can see, there is no other traffic. They must have blocked the entrance somehow. But . . . Aw sweet Jesus.' The driver's mate pointed at the windscreen. 'What I *can* see are two great big blokes wearing overalls and masks coming straight towards us. And one of them's carrying a fucking shotgun.'

Brendan rapped on the driver's side window, and

gestured for him to lower it. 'Give us the keys,' he shouted through the glass.

The driver shook his head, his eyes fixed on the gun. 'They don't open the back,' he shouted.

'We ain't thick, moosh. We know that. We just don't want you getting any ideas about trying to drive off, or running us over, or doing anything else silly.' He raised the gun and pointed it directly at the driver's face. 'The bullets in this thing can cut through armour plate,' he lied. 'And you don't even wanna know what it would do to your head after it's shattered this window.'

'Give him the keys,' said the mate. 'I ain't gonna be a dead hero, not on the wages we get paid.'

The driver took the keys out of the ignition, wound the window down a crack and let them drop down into Brendan's outstretched hand. 'We don't want any trouble, all right?' he said, his stomach gurgling as threateningly as if he'd just followed a night in the pub with a double-strength vindaloo. 'We'll do as we're told, but just do us all a favour and put that thing away.'

'Carry on acting sensible and you'll have nothing to worry about,' said Brendan, putting the keys in his overall pocket.

Without lowering his gaze from the driver's face, he said to Luke. 'Tell 'em they can get started.'

Luke trotted off back down the tunnel to the builder's truck, and he, Kevin and Pete Mac started unloading the oxyacetylene cutting gear that they needed to get them through the skin of the van and into where the strongboxes were held.

'All them years working for your dad in the scrapyard finally paid off, eh?' said Kevin, carefully pushing back his protective visor without disturbing the mask concealing his face. He looked at his watch. 'Twelve minutes. Not bad.'

He stepped back, a man pleased with a job well done. 'There you are, lads. I'll get this gear stowed back in the truck, while you start unloading.'

With the strongboxes secure in the back of the mail van, Brendan told Luke to get the engine running, and for Kevin and Pete Mac to draw the truck round to the front of the security van ready to leave the tunnel.

While they did as they were told, Brendan tapped on the driver's window again. 'One last thing,' he said, opening the driver's door with the keys. 'Now don't panic and no one'll get hurt.'

He pulled two sets of handcuffs from his trouser pocket. 'You,' he lifted his chin towards the mate. 'Right arm.'

The mate did as he was told.

'And you,' Brendan said to the driver, 'left arm.'

He handcuffed them together with one set of cuffs then looped the other pair through them and fastened them to the steering wheel. Brendan then relocked the door and put the keys back in his pocket.

*

The car, the mail van and the builder's truck left the tunnel at a discreet distance from one another, and at a sedate thirty miles an hour. Three vehicles and their now unmasked drivers going quietly about their early-morning business. Meanwhile, the queue at the south end of the tunnel was beginning to lengthen as furious drivers honked their horns and tried to do U-turns to get away from the jam, while those at the front slapped their hands on their steering wheels and swore loudly as they stared at the police signs telling them of the closure.

Fifteen minutes later the three vehicles, all stolen the previous week and decked out with false plates, had been wiped clean and dumped on a parcel of scrubby wasteland behind the railway goods yard in Stratford.

Brendan, Luke, Pete Mac, Anthony and Kevin had transferred the cash boxes to two anonymous Ford saloons and were now heading – via different circuitous routes and two more changes of vehicle – to the slaughter, Rosie Palmer's old flat in Kilburn, where they were to meet up in a couple of hours' time to divvy up the takings.

Kevin lit a cigarette and handed it over from the back seat to Brendan who was driving. 'Amount of boxes we got, we could do the deal with the Irishmen and still have enough left over to buy a bleed'n mansion in the country somewhere.'

'You'd be surprised, Kev, them places ain't that

dear, you know,' said Luke. 'It could buy us a whole row of mansions.

'But why waste it on property, eh, Kev?' said Brendan, winking at Kevin's reflection in the rear-view mirror. 'When there's booze, women and motors out there?'

Chapter 23

While Brendan and the boys were busily breaking into the security boxes that they'd taken over to Ellie's mother's old home off the Kilburn High Road, Ellie herself was with Patricia in a swish West End restaurant in James Street.

The restaurant was a couple of doors along from the Italian place that Ellie had gone to with Eileen a few weeks previously. Ellie had noticed it at the time, and she'd thought how modern and sophisticated it looked, just the like ones she saw in her magazines. She'd also noticed all the expensive-looking cars lined up outside, and had been surprised that there'd been so many. According to the news, times were hard, and the country was struggling to find its way out of some sort of economic crisis. But there wasn't much sign of it on this particular street.

Maybe all the restaurant's customers were in the same sort of 'business' as her family, and didn't have to concern themselves with money the way that – in Brendan's words – ordinary mug punters had to.

Whatever the explanation, it had certainly made an impression on Ellie. And telling Patricia that she wanted to have a girly lunch with her – so that they could get to know each other properly, as real sisters should – had proved to be the perfect excuse to go there.

Ellie sighed appreciatively as she and Patricia walked through the beautifully furnished dining room, with nothing to disturb the sophisticated murmur of conversation except the sound of heavily expensive silverware on elegantly simple white china. Regardless of what Eileen had done – and, in truth, the woman gave Ellie the creeps – and the admitted strangeness of the rest of the O'Donnells – with the exception, of course, of her darling Luke – Ellie loved her new life in London. And she was determined to visit as many of the fancier parts of the city as she could.

Ellie had also decided that there was no real hurry to do so, as she had every intention of staying in London for good. Not with bloody Eileen, that was for sure, but in a nice little flat of her own – somewhere chic and expensive.

Despite her preconceptions, Ellie couldn't help but be impressed by Patricia's behaviour, as they were shown to their table. Contrary to what she had expected from someone who had practically had a fit when she had had to use a communal changing room – and who put up with so much crap from Pete Mac – Patricia's attitude to the two waiters who attended them was remarkable.

As the young men pulled out their chairs for them,

and expertly flicked napkins from their folds, draping them across Ellie's and Patricia's laps, Patricia acted as if it were all commonplace to her, as if she did this sort of thing every day.

It was like seeing a different woman.

'Don't you look like you own the place,' Ellie whispered, leaning across the table, once the waiters had left them to consider the menus.

Patricia shrugged. 'I've been to places that'd make this gaff look like Kelly's Eel and Pie House,' she said, looking around at the other diners. 'And night-clubs like you wouldn't believe.'

'Really?' Ellie was intrigued. Perhaps it really *would* be nice to get to know her sister better. 'You go out much, do you?'

'When I was a younger, I did. Not so much now, of course. But you should have seen me a few years ago. The clothes I had then. You wouldn't have recognised me.'

Ellie watched Patricia's face as she scanned the menu, while at the same time polishing the cutlery on the edge of the tablecloth, occasionally pausing to check that each item was clean enough for her.

Again, Ellie couldn't help but wonder: how could this be the same person who put up with that pig of a husband of hers? Who let herself be treated like dirt.

Ellie slapped her menu down on the table. 'Okay, Pat,' she said, all smiles and encouragement. 'Let's get the ordering done with, then we can have a proper chat.'

'So you only married Pete Mac because you were expecting?' Ellie was working her way through a plate of chocolate profiteroles, while Patricia toyed with a tiny cup of coffee.

'No, I never said that. I said I was *forced* to marry him because I was expecting.' Patricia caught the waiter's eye and pointed to the empty Chablis bottle with a nod and a smile before turning back to Ellie. 'But I lost the baby.'

'So it wasn't your Caty you were expecting?'

'No. It was a little boy.'

'I'm sorry.'

Patricia shrugged. 'What's that Frank Sinatra song that Brendan loves?' She thought for a moment, the alcohol slowing her thinking. '"That's Life", that's the one: you pick yourself up and get on with . . .' Another moment to think. 'It. The race.'

'I'm no Frank Sinatra expert, Pat, but are you really saying that you think you just have to put up with things? Make do? Accept second-best? Worse, bloody *third*-best with that pig.'

'No, you don't understand. I've got my life. It's what I've settled for. I don't have much of a choice any more, now do I?'

'Don't be stupid, Pat. Course you do. Look at you, you're gorgeous. And with your new clothes and your lovely hair . . .' She lifted her chin towards the table by the window. 'And look at him over there; sure, he can't keep his eyes off you.'

'Don't be daft.'

'I'm not being daft, I'm being angry. You're worth more than this. You ought to have a bloody affair. That'd show him.'

'Ellie, you don't know –'

'Yes I do, I know that your man's doing his bit for the contraceptive industry, so isn't it about time you had a go too? Show the bastard what you're made of.'

Patricia snorted rather than swallowed her mouthful of wine and started coughing uncontrollably. 'For goodness' sake, Ellie,' she spluttered.

'Aren't I only speaking the truth? Why not have some fun?'

'Because Brendan would go mad.'

'*Brendan* would go mad?' Ellie stopped with her spoon halfway to her mouth, intrigued by the idea. 'You aren't worried about what Pete Mac would have to say? But you wouldn't want to upset your brother?'

'Brendan has standards – for me, anyway. But Pete Mac? He wouldn't notice if I was stretched out stark naked on the carpet in front of him, doing the business with the bloody milkman.'

'So if you don't want to have an affair, and you can't stand the eejit, why don't you leave him?'

'Can I tell you something without you laughing at me?'

275

Ellie had trouble swallowing her last mouthful of pastry. 'I'm not mocking you, Pat. And if you think I am, I'm sorry.'

Patricia reached out and took her sister's hand, and smiled, a genuine, warm smile. 'Don't you dare. There's far worse than that to be sorry about in our family. And plenty to be ashamed of.'

Ellie returned her smile. 'I like you saying that – our family.' Although for the life of her, Ellie couldn't understand how Pat could say she was ashamed of them, when she seemed more than happy to stay with them and do what they told her. Probably more of that *we all share the same blood* stuff that Brendan was always going on about.

There was a lot she had to learn about being an O'Donnell.

'So, what was it you were going to tell me?'

Patricia looked shy, almost furtive. 'When I was a *lot* younger I was a good-looking girl, and –'

'You still are.'

'No, I mean really good-looking. I'm not bragging or anything, just stating the truth, like saying I've got dark hair. And I used to have this dream. About going into modelling. Not that Dad or Brendan would have let me, of course. But I used to read all the magazines and, like I say, dream that I'd do it one day.'

'That's so sad.'

Patricia shrugged. 'If I hadn't drunk all this wine I'd never be saying this, Ellie, but instead of getting yourself caught up with Brendan – and before you say anything, Luke told me about you driving the horse-box, because he's worried about you – why don't you consider it? Modelling?'

'This is me we're talking about. A bloody farm girl.'

'Come on, Ellie, I've seen you, you've always got your nose in *Nova* and *Cosmo*, and the way you dress now . . . Look at you. I know you're my sister, but I mean it, you're gorgeous. You could make a fortune for yourself. And be safely away from Brendan's *businesses*.'

Patricia was totally taken aback as Ellie burst into tears.

'Modelling?' she sniffed into the hankie that Patricia hurriedly stuffed into her hand. 'Me? I can't even keep a boyfriend. Even when I let him do what he bloody well likes with me.'

'What d'you mean?'

'Milo Flanagan. I wasn't meant to be seeing him. *Brendan forbade it*. But I was. And I was so happy, Pat. But then he just stopped calling me. That was it, no explanation.' She blew her nose loudly. 'Perhaps my time with him was good training. Let men do what they like with me. But in pictures rather than in real life.'

'I'm not talking about the grubby sort that you get in those blokes' magazines. I'm talking about fashion, and proper photographic work. But never mind all that. Tell me something, have you called him?'

'No.'

'Why not? Don't you want to be happy? Go on, go and call him now. Say you're sorry, even if you don't know what for.'

As Patricia watched Ellie walk between the tables to the telephone mounted on the wall by the cloak-room, she closed her eyes. Was she really the right person to be giving advice about men?

After several false starts, Ellie finally dialled Milo's number.

'Y'ello?'

'Milo, it's me, Ellie. I wondered why you haven't called me.'

'I'm bored with you, sweetheart, okay?'

He felt a small pang of regret as he put the phone down. He'd actually liked the bird. But for all her education, and her nice way of talking, and her stories about living in the country with her horses, she was no better than a brass. But then what should he have expected, she was an O'Donnell, wasn't she? And they were a whole family of alley cats. And she'd been the last tie to be cut. Now he'd have no regrets about what he was going to do.

Ellie sat back in her chair and shook her head in answer to Patricia's questioning smile.

278

Patricia felt her face drain of colour. Why had she interfered? 'Sod him, sod the lot of them.' She beckoned to a waiter. 'Two brandies please.'

'So,' she said to Ellie. 'You're definitely tall enough; you're slim, and you've got a cocky enough attitude to do it.' She sipped at her brandy. 'The way you walked back from that phone, even though you were upset, you were gliding like a princess. And as for looks, if that bloody Penelope Tree can be in *Vogue*, then I'm sure you can.'

'Thanks very much.' Ellie muttered the words into her chest.

Patricia reached out and took her sister's hand. 'Ellie, I've no idea what that fool just said to you, but believe me, you're much too good for him. And, if you want this you can have it. I'll make sure you can. I'll sort it all out.' She fumbled around lighting a cigarette, trying to think what was needed. 'We'll have to get you a portfolio. I know you have to have one of them. And I'll get you to see all the right people; protect you from the bad ones.'

Ellie's head was still bowed.

'I really mean this, Ellie. I've got the money, I know people – well, people I'd have to look up again, but people I know wouldn't refuse me. I can make this happen for you. You can live the life I had snatched away from me.'

'Hang on, Pat, are you doing this for you or me?'

Patricia pulled her hand away. 'I'm sorry, I'm being silly.'

'No, you're not.' Ellie looked up and grabbed her hand again. 'That just came out wrong. You're so used to people telling you what to do, and Pete Mac being mean to you, that you don't recognise when you're just being teased. Pat, believe me, I know I'm not acting like it, but I couldn't think of anything I'd like to do more. It'd be fantastic.'

She leaned forward and smiled through her tears. 'Tell you what, let's go and buy Caty something really trendy.' Ellie held up her hand. 'And before you say anything, nothing too grown up or tarty. And then we go home and spend the evening watching telly with her, painting our nails, and having slimy mud face packs.'

'You are so like Catherine. And I am so drunk. But I'd like that, Ellie. A lot. And modelling, babe, that's what you're gonna do. You are going to be the best there's ever been.'

It seemed that Ellie's fantasy of leading a glamorous life in London was going to be made real by the person she'd have least expected could do so. And she wasn't going back to Kildare now – that was for sure.

'Thanks, Pat, and doing it together, with you, it'll be fantastic.'

*

By the time the two of them had finished their second brandy, Ellie's career and her new cosmopolitan existence had been mapped out in front of her. And Patricia was going to make sure that not one man was involved, who might hurt or spoil things for either of them.

Well, not unless he had a camera in one hand and a modelling contract in the other . . .

Chapter 24

Brendan arched his body backwards, stretching his neck and kneading his fingers into his kidneys. His back ached and his shirt was sticking to him where he'd been sweating from the efforts of the afternoon. First, he and the others had worked at jemmying open the cash boxes that they'd 'liberated' from the security van; then they'd had to open up the void under the kitchen floorboards hidden beneath the fridge so they could stow the bundles of banknotes; finally, they'd had to restore the floorboards and drag the fridge back in place to cover their handiwork. After being up since before daybreak, Brendan was well and truly exhausted.

But he couldn't remember feeling so pleased with the world in a long time. Even taking the piss out of the Kesslers at the wedding hadn't been as good as this.

'That's more than a tidy few quid,' said Kevin, offering round his cigarettes.

Brendan took one, tossed it in the air and caught it in his mouth like a performing seal with a fish. 'And we'll have the bunce off the Kesslers for this month's consignment of films and magazines in a few days to add to the pot,' he said with a victor's grin, the cigarette bobbing up and down between his lips.

Anthony turned on the single cold tap that supplied the deep butler sink, stuck his shaven head under the water and let it run down his neck. He then angled round so he could drink from the cool, gushing flow.

'I don't get this,' said Pete Mac, leaning back against the draining board, watching Anthony as if he were barmy. 'After all that work, all we get is a bloody swig of water. Remember when your dad was alive, Brendan? Rosie Palmer used to lay on a proper spread for us after a job. She used to do sandwiches, Scotch eggs, pork pies, and plenty of booze. That was the right way to celebrate after working your nuts off. Not sticking your bleed'n head under a tap.'

Brendan ran his hand over his five o'clock shadow. 'I dunno about you, Pete, but after I've been home and had a bit of a kip, then a shower, a shit and a shave, I'm gonna get meself changed into some nice clean clothes and go out for the evening and celebrate more than properly.'

He bent forward and checked his reflection in the side of the stainless-steel kettle. 'There's a very nice little brunette started at the Bella Vista last week. Tits like coconuts, she's got. And no trap on her at all. Just what I need.'

Up until then, Luke had hidden his lack of enthusiasm for having had anything to with the job.

He had just got on with speaking when he was spoken to, smiled in the right places, and done what was expected of him. He had only been tempted in the first place as it was a quick way of getting the wedge he needed for the warehouse – a step forward to setting up his new life with Nicky, and getting away from the family business for good. But Brendan's attitude turned his stomach. He couldn't stand the thought of what his brother was about to do, and he knew he had to get out of there before a row started.

He had really hoped that Brendan would settle down now that he and Sandy were together. Or that Brendan might at least be a bit – what was it he was always telling Pete Mac he should be? *Discreet.* That was it. But he should have known there'd be no chance of that, not with Brendan. It was always the same – one rule for him and the rest of them did as they were told.

Maybe Sandy had come to realise early on that that was how Brendan operated, and that was why she'd said what she had to the escort who'd been beaten up – that there was a price to pay for having a nice life.

Maybe.

But whatever the explanation, Luke wasn't in the mood to care very much at the moment. It was a terrible thing to admit, but his own brother disgusted him, just as his father had done before him.

'I'll be getting off then. Back home.' Luke

couldn't hide the look of disapproval on his face as he left them standing in the kitchen.

'He right makes me laugh, he does,' Luke heard Pete Mac saying as he opened the door to let himself out on to the street. 'He can get stuck in like the rest of us, no trouble, do a man's job, and do it well, but he can't stand it when you talk about enjoying the company of a few birds. I just don't understand that geezer, Brendan. I don't understand him at all.'

Luke paused in the doorway, listening.

Kevin and Anthony exchanged glances. They knew how Brendan's temper could erupt if anyone even thought about mocking his brother.

'How are you celebrating then, Pete?' asked Kevin, slapping him harder than was friendly across the shoulder, and widening his eyes in warning.

'Oi! That fucking hurt,' said Pete Mac, rubbing his flabby, stinging flesh. He sniffed noisily. 'I might pop out for a bit.'

'A bit of what, I wonder?' muttered Luke, slamming the door behind him.

'What did he say?' asked Pete Mac, his face screwed up as he tried to figure out what Luke had said, and whether or not it was an insult. 'I thought he'd fucking gone.'

'I never heard nothing, Pete,' said Anthony, stubbing out his cigarette in the sink. 'Come on, it's been a long day. Why don't we all get going?'

Anthony and Kevin went through to the sitting room to collect their things.

Pete Mac was about to follow them, but Brendan barred his way.

'Do yourself and the rest of us a favour, Pete, and learn from what just happened there. Always make sure you know who can hear you before you open that big gob of yours. All right?'

'Wasn't my fault the nosy bastard was listening,' he said, and skulked off to the sitting room.

If only Pete Mac had realised that Brendan was reminding himself as much as Pete about the risks of people eavesdropping, he might have put up a bit more of an argument.

Sitting in the single greasy armchair, in her grotty rooms, Carol knew exactly what she was going to do: she was going to have the whole bloody lot of them. Every single one of the men who'd treated her so badly – as if she was nothing more than a thing to be used and thrown away. And she was going to start with Peter MacRiordan.

What did she have to lose? She couldn't stomach staying in this dump any longer anyway – even if Pete Mac did decide to be 'kind' enough to let her stay another week. No, she would use some of the money she had put away to get herself somewhere decent. It was okay, she'd worked it all out. Soon as she was back on her feet, she'd find someone who'd treat her the way she deserved to be treated for once. Like a lady.

She went out on the landing to the payphone, wiped the receiver with a disinfectant-soaked cloth, and then found the number for the local police station in the dog-eared telephone book hanging from a chain fixed to the wall.

'Hello,' she said, speaking more clearly and slowly than usual. 'I want to talk to someone.'

'Can I ask what it's about please, miss?'

'There are things I know about someone. Bad things. He's tied up with a very bad local family.'

'Yes, miss, of course. Thank you. I'll make sure your message is passed on.'

Carol stared at the receiver. *He'd put the bloody phone down on her.*

The young constable on desk duty shook his head with the wisdom of someone who had been in the force for almost a whole year.

'Another loony been reading the Sunday papers, Sarge. All of these stories about gangsters on every street corner in the East End bring 'em out like a rash. This one reckons she knew all about a very bad local family.'

The sergeant put down his mug of tea on the counter, and picked up a pen as if to write. 'Nothing about Al Capone?'

'Not that she mentioned, Sarge.'

He went back to his tea. 'She wants to be careful,'

he said, 'or she'll wind up holding up a flyover somewhere.'

'Don't, Sarge, you're scaring me.'

A full hour passed before Carol stomped into the police station in person. It had taken her about a minute to get over the shock of having the phone put down on her, and another to decide what she was going to do next.

For starters, she was going to target someone too stupid to move quickly enough to cover himself before the law were on to him. Then, when they had him, and he started blabbing – he wouldn't be able to help himself – she was going to stand back and watch it all unravel.

It then took her about another forty-five minutes to get ready. On the whole, no mean feat considering the temper she was now in. The rest of the hour was taken up walking, or rather half running, to the police station.

When she got there, her temper hadn't improved, but the treatment she was offered certainly had.

The sight of the gorgeous young blonde striding up to his counter had the immediate attention of the constable who had earlier dismissed her so abruptly.

'Yes, miss? How can I help you?'

'You wouldn't listen to me on the phone. So I've got something else for you. Here's the names and the address of a bloke and two birds. Go round there first thing, while the lazy tarts are still in bed, and you'll find the pair of them with enough nicked gear to open another branch of John fucking Lewis. Now don't tell me that ain't good enough to interest you.'

Sandy stepped out from behind the screen, head down, as she fastened the top button on her shirt. She felt so tired. She'd had to leave home before eight o'clock this morning to make sure she got here for her appointment, and on top of that Brendan had got in really late last night and his boozy snoring had kept her awake until the early hours.

And the surroundings didn't improve her temper.

The dark-panelled offices, with their gilt-framed paintings, thick, sink-in-up-to-your-ankle rugs, and parquet flooring weren't what she'd been used to when she went to see the doctor. But when she'd told Brendan that she hadn't been feeling too well, he'd insisted she'd gone up to Harley Street. She could only thank God that he'd been too busy to come with her. He could be so touchy if people said something he didn't like, and the last thing she wanted was a scene in front of people like these. Even the nurse spoke like she was a bloody duchess.

'Please, take a seat, Mrs O'Donnell,' said the doctor, gesturing to the wing-backed armchair on her side of his wide partners' desk.

Self-consciously smoothing her hair, and then her

skirt, Sandy sat down. It felt more like having an interview than being told you had to take the tablets three times a day until it was all cleared up – whatever *it* was.

'Well?' she asked, quietly.

'Well, indeed, Mrs O'Donnell. First things first. You do appear to have a slight infection.' The doctor looked knowingly at his nurse, who answered with no more than a slight, but equally knowing, lifting of a single eyebrow.

'What d'you mean? What sort of infection? Is it bad?' Sandy's reticence had been wiped away at the very mention of the word 'infection'. 'Is that why I've been feeling so rough?'

He paused. Then he began speaking very slowly to Sandy, making sure that he avoided any direct eye contact with her.

'There's really no need to worry, Mrs O'Donnell.' He had – for a very fleeting moment – thought about suggesting that she might want to speak to the nurse about making an appointment for her husband to come along for treatment. The correct procedure. But after thinking about his most recent meetings with Brendan O'Donnell, he had swiftly reconsidered his recommendations for arranging a visit. O'Donnell was, after all, a man whose previous appointments with the doctor had included a very late termination for a girl who was clearly not legally of age, and a man who had the larger part of a pint glass imbedded in his cheek – and an extremely angry disposition.

The doctor smiled down at his desk. 'Nothing to worry about at all. Tube of cream. Apply when required. Problem'll disappear before you know it. But,' he lifted his chin a little and gazed over his glasses at the tips of his steepled fingers, 'I do have something else I need to discuss with you.'

Sandy gripped the arms of her chair. The bloke had looked up her fanny, tested her wee, and had taken about two pints of her blood last week, and he'd done the first two all over again this week.

An infection was one thing – everyone got a bit of cystitis now and again – but what the hell was wrong now?

It was now half past nine and Carol Mercer was standing outside Eileen O'Donnell's house at the Stepney end of the Mile End Road. She'd got there early because she didn't want to risk running into Brendan – not while she was telling Eileen all the things she had to say about her son, and definitely not afterwards either.

All the time she'd been with Brendan, Carol had never known him get out of bed before ten. Well, not unless he was on business of some kind.

That was a point. She nibbled nervously at her bottom lip. Say he had been out working somewhere, and had thought he'd just pop round to see his mum on his way back home?

She checked along the street. Not a single motor that he would have been seen dead in.

Good, he wasn't there.

Probably.

But say he'd borrowed a car like he had before?

Aw shit . . .

But if she didn't do it now, she really didn't think she'd have the courage to go away and come back later. She was shaking like a leaf as it was. But she was also determined that it was about time the bastard got what was coming to him. Let the big man know what it was like to be on the receiving end for once.

Carol fiddled with the mousy-brown curly wig that, along with the frumpy pleated skirt, white nylon blouse and make-up-free face, made her look unrecognisable as the Carol Mercer that Brendan had thrown out on to the streets with nothing more than a bit of shopping and a red face. Then she took a deep breath, lifted her chin, and marched boldly up the front steps to the street door.

Carol was more than a little surprised when it was opened by a very pretty, dark-haired young woman in a housecoat. She'd heard Brendan had got married recently and had moved over to Old Ford somewhere. But surely even he wouldn't have the bollocks to move his bit on the side into his own mother's place.

Well, not so soon, he wouldn't.

'Can I help you?' asked Ellie, her cultured Irish voice another surprise for Carol.

Irish? She could be family.

No, she wasn't the sort of scrubber who'd be a relative of the O'Donnells.

She had to be his bird. But fancy having her staying with his mum. She knew he was a bastard, but this took some beating, this really did.

What a fucking family.

But maybe she was the new wife? She was certainly young and beautiful enough for Brendan.

Carol lowered her gaze. 'I'd like to see Mrs O'Donnell, please. Eileen O'Donnell,' she added hurriedly, and did a quick flip through her mental index box of all the things Pete Mac had moaned on about when he'd talked about his *murdering witch of a mother-in-law*.

Got it.

'It's about church business.'

Ellie might just as well have closed her eyes and started snoring, so pathetic was her effort to hide her boredom. No one was going to spoil her plans for this morning. She was starting her new beauty regime, getting herself all polished and primped and prepared for the photographer who was going to take her pictures next week for her portfolio.

'Sure. Come in.' She gestured for Carol to step inside. 'I hope you won't think I'm being rude, but I was just going up for a bath.'

Carol smiled, but it only reached her lips. *Going up for a bath*. Lucky bitch. She'd had a bathroom once. In her lovely little house. All new, and tiled, and full of matching fluffy towels and flannels. 'Of course I won't think you're rude,' she said pleasantly. 'You go up and enjoy a nice soak.'

'Right. You'll find her down in the kitchen. The stairs are at the end of the hall.' Ellie called over her shoulder as she started up the stairs: 'Eileen, you've got a visitor.'

Then she high-tailed it up to the bathroom before anyone tried to include her in any talk about priests or Mass or bloody flower-arranging rotas.

Carol found Eileen down in the basement kitchen standing by the sink. She was switching on the electric kettle. Old habits died hard, having a guest meant making a pot of tea. There was a Dobermann sitting expectantly at her heel.

Carol wasn't keen on dogs. She wasn't scared of them, it was just that they got hair over everything. Spoilt things, stopped them looking nice.

'Who are you?' asked Eileen with a more defensive than aggressive frown. It felt wrong, this stranger in her kitchen, especially a stranger who had the advantage of knowing who she was.

'I'm somebody who's going to tell you the truth,' said Carol, more boldly than she felt. 'Don't suppose that happens much in a family like this, does it, Mrs O'Donnell?'

'I don't know what you're talking about, and I really don't think I want you in my home. So if you don't mind –'

'But I do mind.' Carol walked across the room and stood right in front of her. She'd have to be quick in case that Irish trollop decided to come down after her bath. If Eileen got nasty, Carol was sure she could take her as easily as snuffing out a candle, but she really wasn't sure about the other one. She looked as fit as a bloke. And if she was tough enough to put up with being married to Brendan O'Donnell she probably had the guts to put up a good fight as well.

'I've come to tell you about your son. About Brendan.' She held her chin high in the air – defiant. 'How he makes filthy, disgusting films. And makes women do things that would have you –'

'No.' Eileen took a step towards her. 'I don't believe you. Why are you saying these things?'

'Because he's making films with women who are too scared, and too drugged up, not to do as they're told. He's a brute, a bully, and he lives off filth and violence, and you should be ashamed to call him your son.'

Eileen turned away, and fussed around with the kettle, checking if it had boiled. 'I won't listen to you.'

'Well, I think that's a pity, because if you don't stop him –' Carol moved closer '– then perhaps I'll have to tell the law. And I've got plenty to tell them all right. Things about your whole bloody witch's brood. Things that they're into right up to their poxy necks. And you're no better for letting them get away with it.'

She hadn't planned to say that bit about the police, it had just come out of her mouth. But it wasn't a bad idea. Why shouldn't she grass the bastard the same way as she'd done with Pete Mac? If she'd been left with nothing, why shouldn't he lose everything as well?

Eileen's chest was rising and falling as if she'd just run round the block carrying a sack of spuds in each hand. 'I'm warning you,' she breathed, staring at the bulbous reflections in the kettle. 'If you don't get out of my house – right now – it'll be me who calls the police.'

'An O'Donnell calling the law? I don't think so, do you, love? But I'm ready to leave anyway. This place stinks of that filthy bastard son of yours.'

Eileen gripped the edge of the sink, trying to control her breathing. She felt as torn, confused and worn out as she had all those years ago when she had tried to put a stop to things in her own, sinful way. But all that had turned out to be was a stupid, misguided waste of so many things that it haunted her every waking and sleeping moment – knowing that she could have done things differently, better.

She felt totally exhausted by it all.

Carol was now so close to her that Eileen could

feel the heat of the girl's body as surely as the heat from the kettle. It was as if they had both been fixed to the spot.

Then there was the spell-breaking sound of someone clomping down the stairs. They both turned round.

It was Ellie.

'Eileen, I wondered if you'd seen my nail-varnish remover. Oh, sorry to disturb you, I didn't realise you still had company.'

'Sorry?' Carol shook her head as if she didn't understand the words. 'Your kind are never sorry. It was me Brendan should have married, not you.'

'What did you say?' Ellie strode across the room towards them. 'Eileen, who is this?'

Eileen would spend the rest of her years wishing that she had had acted differently, but as Carol grabbed the kettle, yanking it from its socket, and throwing its boiling contents into Ellie's face, she just stood there, screaming in horror.

Chapter 25

Despite his late night, Brendan was still exhilarated from the security-van job, and had been up and out only minutes after Sandy had left for Harley Street. He had now popped home to see how she was after her doctor's appointment.

He pulled up outside the house and looked across at the park, as he always did, to make sure that no little toerags were playing football too close to the fence. He wasn't about to have his motor dented by some budding Georgie Best aiming a goal shot too high.

Satisfied that the only games he could see being played were way over the other side by the lido, he pocketed his keys and turned to the house.

As he did so, his forehead pleated into a deep frown and he began walking very quickly, breaking into a run. Sandy was standing waiting for him in the doorway.

She never did that. Never.

This had to be important. And not in a good way.

'What is it?' he said, seizing her by the shoulders. 'What did the doctor say?'

'Oh, Brendan, I can't believe it.' Sandy's mouth

was so dry, her tongue was sticking to her teeth. 'I don't know how it happened.'

'What, for Christ's sake? What happened?'

'You know I had to go back to the doctor's?'

'Yeah, that's why I'm here. What did he say?'

'I'm pregnant.'

Brendan's expression immediately transformed into one of disbelieving joy. He wrapped his arms around her and kissed her tenderly on the top of her head. 'You have made me the happiest man alive, Sandy O'Donnell.'

'You're pleased then?'

'Pleased?' He kissed her passionately, holding her to him as if he would never let her go. 'That answer your question?'

'Do you think we can go inside?' she asked, now grinning as broadly as Brendan. 'All the neighbours'll be watching.'

'Good.' Brendan ran down the steps to the pavement and shouted along the terrace. 'I'm gonna be a dad!'

It took Sandy some minutes to persuade Brendan to come indoors, but nothing could dampen his mood.

He made sure she was sitting down, and then he pulled the phone over to the table.

'I'm gonna phone Mum,' he said. 'Believe me, this is gonna blow her away. She loves kids, San. Really loves 'em. And then I'm gonna call the rest of the family. And everyone I know. Then we are gonna start planning the biggest fucking party anyone's ever seen. It's gonna make the wedding look like it was put on by bloody pikeys.'

'I thought your mates who did the wedding were pikeys,' she said, laughing.

'Yeah, well . . .'

He joined in her laughter. And then he put the phone down, walked over to her chair, and stood there in front of her. 'Do you know, I love you, Sandy O'Donnell.'

It was the first and last time he would ever say those words.

When Brendan eventually rang his mother, the ambulance had just arrived to take Ellie away.

When the police turned up at the address Carol Mercer had so thoughtfully written out for them, Pete Mac was in bed with one of the two redheads. The other one had got up to answer the door. And with little more than the hand towel she'd grabbed on the way, the police hadn't had much difficulty in persuading her to let them in – *it's that or out here in the street, miss* – and that they were just making enquiries.

The bedroom, in fact the whole flat, was stuffed to bursting with all the gear that the sisters had finally hoisted over the past three weeks. If Pete Mac hadn't been cursed with such a dangerous mix of always claiming he was too busy and actually being bone idle, he might have organised the fencing, and wouldn't now be completely surrounded by incriminating evidence.

The sight of the uniformed officers coming into the bedroom full of hookey gear had the other sister bawling her head off, and in all the confusion – what a touch of luck – no one had so much as mentioned anything about them producing a search warrant.

'Please, don't blame us,' wailed the one still in bed. 'He made us do it.'

Pete Mac's mouth fell open, and he threw back the covers to get up, making the female officer present wince and avert her eyes at the sight of his wobbling, boozer's belly. 'Now hold up a minute.'

'Let the lady finish, sir.'

'Don't pretend you didn't,' sobbed the other one, throwing pathetic little-girl-lost glances at the two male officers. 'We had no idea who he was, we're down from Liverpool, see. Just trying to make a living – getting jobs in London and that. It's so hard up there. And we met him and he was really nice. But then he turned nasty. We were really scared of him. Then we found out he's part of this really horrible family – the O'Donnells. It was terrible.'

'Are you saying this man held you here against your will?'

The girls looked at one another then nodded.

'Both of you?'

This time the nods weren't so assured.

'Perhaps we'd better discuss this down the station.'

Carol was sitting smoking nervously in an interview room at the police station. The door was ajar as she waited for the WPC to come back with a cup of tea for her. So far she had only told them about Pete Mac, but at least they were now interested in what she had to say.

Thank God. Now she'd thrown that kettle of water over Brendan's wife – *why the hell had she done that?* – she was going to have to make sure she told the law everything, so that they got the bastard off the streets as soon as possible. Before he got to her.

She'd spent last night in a bed and breakfast, too terrified to go back to the rooms where Brendan or one of his goons might find her, but how long could she hide from him?

Carol heard a noise in the corridor and looked up hopefully. She hadn't had anything to drink since she'd got up and was gagging for some tea. But it wasn't the WPC. It was Pete Mac being led past between two big burly coppers. Behind him, weeping and snivelling, were the two red-headed sisters.

Pete Mac spotted her and spat on the floor. 'You just wait, you bitch,' he snarled.

It was rapidly dawning on Carol that Brendan O'Donnell was probably going to kill her.

She snatched up her bag, leaving her burning cigarette in the ashtray, and slipped out into the corridor.

'Everything all right, miss?' asked the now very interested young constable at the desk.

She flashed him one of her best smiles – teeth, the lot. 'Fine, thank you. They've asked me to come back this afternoon. Hope to see you then, eh?'

With that she was out of the door, down the front steps and running through the traffic towards Mile End tube station, thanking her lucky stars that her money was in the bank and not under the bed back in her rooms. She had no intention of going back to that place ever again.

But perhaps she should just make one more phone call, before she jumped on a train and went off to start what she could only hope would be a new life.

'Pat, it's me, babe. Pete. I'm in trouble. You've got to help me, but I don't want Brendan to know.'

'What sort of trouble this time?' Pat's voice was flat, without emotion.

'I'm down at the nick. I need you to call a brief, but, please, don't use the usual bloke, I don't want him telling Brendan.'

'Would this have anything to do with the fact that you were caught with two red-headed sisters – red-handed, should I say?'

'What?'

'I know all about it, Pete. Another one of your whores just phoned me. And do you know, I'm not sure if I can be bothered calling a solicitor or not. I mean, *three* whores?'

'Pat –'

'I'll have to think about it.'

Patricia put down the phone and picked up the piece of paper on which she'd written the solicitor's number that she'd looked up immediately after Carol Mercer had made her anonymous call to her.

She thought for ten long minutes about what she should do. Then picked up the phone and instructed the solicitor as Pete Mac had asked.

But after she'd made the call she still wasn't sure, not in all honesty, why she'd bothered.

This was pushing your luck a bit far, even for Pete Mac.

When Brendan eventually found his mother and brother on the fourth floor of the hospital, Luke and Eileen were standing staring through the glass wall of an isolation ward. They were watching Ellie, who was stretched out on her back, her face, shoulders and chest swathed in bandages. She was attached to drips in both arms, and was surrounded by flashing machines and monitors.

'How is she?'

Luke just kept staring at his sister, the beautiful girl who had looked so much like Catherine, and who had

had a whole, wonderful new life mapped out in front of her. A life that had now been ruined.

'How is she?' Luke's voice was low, restrained. 'Her face is destroyed, Brendan, that's how she is. And it's all your fucking fault.'

'My fault?'

'You're just like Dad. You wreck everything and everyone you go near.'

Eileen turned round to face him; she wanted to look her son in the eye as she spoke to him.

'A woman came to the house,' she breathed. 'She said things about you, things about films you're making in her house, and about things you're doing to young girls. Then,' she gulped back the tears, 'she did that to Ellie.'

Eileen drew back her hand and slapped her son as hard as she could.

Brendan ran down the four flights of stairs, barrelled across the hospital reception and snatched the payphone out of the hand a woman who was in the middle of a call.

'Fuck off,' he growled, punching out the number of the cab office. 'This is private.'

The woman, horrified, hurried away.

'Paula, it's me,' he spat through gritted teeth. 'I want you to get a message to Anthony. Tell him I want Carol Mercer found, and then I want her gone. Got me?'

Chapter 26

It had taken very little effort on the Kesslers' part to set the wheels in motion for Milo Flanagan's plan for revenge on the O'Donnells in general, and Brendan O'Donnell in particular. It needed only a few promises, very little time, and even less effort. It seemed that there were more than enough people in HMP Brixton who would be only too pleased to do the Kesslers a favour, especially if it meant having one over on the O'Donnell family. Of course, there had to be a nice bung in it for them as well. That, plus a guarantee that Brendan would never find out who had helped them.

And today, the day after Ellie had been scalded, and Brendan's own mother had slapped him, was the day it all began to slot into place.

Barry Ellis, with his thin, scratchy towel draped around his neck, was shuffling along in his prison browns – no longer conscious of the sickly, musty smell they gave off, after the months he'd spent on remand – heading towards the recess to empty his pisspot.

It was a stiflingly hot morning, the sort of July

weather when even if you'd just stepped out of a luxuriously scented cool bath, and were wearing, a soft, fluffy bathrobe, you would still feel immediately sticky and unclean again. But, surprisingly, Barry wasn't feeling too bad. In fact, he was feeling calmer now than he had done in months – probably in years. The medication they'd put him on was helping, and, apart from smoking a bit of draw, he was clean, and proud of it. There were still a surprising number of opportunities for him to get hold of any kind of gear that he might have fancied – and an amazing number of people who seemed all too keen to supply him – but he'd decided he didn't want it any more. He'd had enough.

Barry Ellis had taken back control of his life.

And now he was enjoying a feeling of relief, a feeling that he was genuinely relishing, a feeling that he appreciated more than anything else.

It was all down to the simple fact that Barry knew he was never again going to do any more harm to the people he loved.

He'd cut himself out like a cancer. His mum, his sister, her kids – he'd never be in touch with them again, so he wouldn't be able to hurt them.

But most of all he wouldn't be able to hurt Sandy.

He'd had a lot of time to think about things during the hours he'd been banged up in his cell, and it had come to him like a flash of glorious inspiration, when he'd remembered how Eileen O'Donnell had managed to handle her time when she'd been away. And he'd decided, there and then, that that would be how he could pay Sandy back for everything she'd done for him during those terrible years. The years he'd lost since the day he'd seen the dogs ripping Stephen Shea's body apart in the O'Donnells' scrapyard.

And now he was proud of himself. More proud than he could ever remember.

Barry Ellis had set his loved ones free.

Too many blokes expected too much of their wives and families while they were inside. But not him. No. He'd done the right thing. And he knew it.

Another few steps forward, closer to the echoing chatter coming from the tiled recess.

It was then that Barry first saw the big black man loping along the corridor, making his way straight to the front of the queue.

No one said a word, because he was the man who ran the wing, the one who even gave orders to the POs.

Originally from over Notting Hill way, he'd worked for the Kesslers since he was a schoolkid. He was one of the mob of heavies they'd brought back with them when they'd returned to the East End, thinking they could muscle in on the O'Donnells' turf without so much as a discussion on the matter.

Barry dropped back in the queue, hoping to make himself invisible. All he wanted was a quiet life – that would do him. The most he'd got involved in since he'd been inside was trading for his bit of dope. Keeping his nose clean, that was his plan.

He was so lost in his thoughts about how he would avoid getting sucked in if anything kicked off, that when the short, wiry man in his fifties sidled up to him and tapped him on the shoulder, Barry jumped as if the man's hand had burned into his flesh.

'All right, Ellis, get a grip, mate.' The man cleared his throat with a nastily phlegmy hack. 'What's the matter, got a guilty conscience, have you?'

Barry said nothing, knowing that the most innocuous of replies – if wrongly taken – could earn you a stripe on the arse from a bit of sharpened tin can stolen from the kitchens. Or even worse if someone really took offence.

The man remained beside him until they reached the recess. Still Barry hadn't said a word.

'Don't be like that,' whispered the man as he tipped his foul-smelling, dark brown urine into the sluice. 'Just trying to be friendly, ain't I?'

It was now Barry's turn at the sink, but the man was still at his shoulder.

'Listen to me, Ellis. I know everyone's keeping it from you, mate, but, in my opinion, a man's entitled to know these things. Specially when it's already being talked about all over the fucking wing.'

Barry made as if to walk away, but the man grabbed him by the arm. 'Listen to me, Ellis. We all know it's bad enough that O'Donnell's gone and married your old lady. I mean, *everyone* thought that was well out of order. Even the blokes who don't like you, and who don't usually give a fuck about nothing.'

Barry stiffened. The man had to be off his head. *Sandy and Brendan married?* They wouldn't do that.

'Blimey, from the look on your face, Ellis, I reckon I've just put me number nine right in it. What can I say? I'm sorry, mate. I was sure you must have known at least that much about what was going on.'

Barry resisted the impulse to shake his head.

'Well, you might as well know the rest. Sorry to be the one to have to tell you, mate, but he's messing her around good and proper. Acting just like that prat of a brother-in-law of his – you know, that Peter MacRiordan. Poking any bit of stray he comes across. And I mean *any* bit of stray – some right old dogs. I wouldn't fancy your old woman's chances of keeping herself all nice and minty fresh if he's doing that with all them old slappers, would you? And that's all apart from the laughing stock the arsehole's making of her. See, the poor girl ain't got a clue what he's up to behind her back. Thinks she's still the blushing fucking bride.'

The man waited for Barry to respond, but he said nothing – so he carried on.

'But, all that apart, mate, fancy you not having a clue about them two getting married. That's bad, that is. That must hurt a man. Can't imagine what that'd feel like if a bloke found out that sort of thing's happened with his bird, while he's stuck in here, not able to do nothing about it cos he's on remand.'

He waited just long enough to make his point. 'And then to hear how the cunt's been treating her . . .'

Barry left his pot standing in the sink. Then, ignoring the complaints and abuse from his fellow inmates about him disturbing their morning routine, Barry stuck himself in front of the PO watching over the recess.

'I wanna see me brief,' he said.

Those were practically the only words – apart from 'No, sir' and 'Yes, sir' – that the officer had heard Barry Ellis utter in all the time he'd been inside.

Chapter 27

Sandy was sitting at her desk, in the escort service's
office, upstairs in her and Brendan's home on Old
Ford Road. She was supposedly interviewing a long
succession of escorts to find out if any of them would
be capable of taking over the day-to-day running of
the business, when her pregnancy became too
advanced for her to continue working. Which was
going to be in about a week's time if Brendan had
anything to do with it. It had been bad enough finding
one of the girls who was suitable to act like a nice
little housewife, and stay in Brendan's place that he'd
been using as the film studio over in Hackney. But
this was even worse. Especially now, after what had
happened to Ellie, Brendan was practically wrapping
her in cotton wool.

While Sandy was as devastated as everyone else
about what had happened to the poor girl – although
she still didn't really understand how such a bizarre
accident could have happened without the dog even
getting slightly scalded – Brendan really was driving
her mad being so overprotective.

And now she had been interrupted by a telephone
call that was nothing to do with the agency, but that

the caller had insisted was urgent and really couldn't wait. She'd kill that Paula for passing on the number.

'Okay,' she said, the exasperation obvious in her voice. 'Now what's so bloody important?'

'So?' asked Brendan as she put the phone down. 'What was it? Another one of the silly tarts can't remember the address? We're gonna have to rethink this. Get someone reliable.'

'It wasn't anything to do with the agency.'

'So how'd they get the number then?'

'They said Paula gave it to them.'

He narrowed his eyes. 'Paula, now there's an idea. P'raps I should get her over from the cab office to stand in for you. She's bright as anything. And it'd be good to know she was here in the house with you in case you need anything.'

'Brendan. Will you stop talking for a minute and listen to me? It was –'

'It wasn't the doctor, was it?'

'For goodness' sake, no. It was Barry's solicitor. He wants to see me.'

'Why'd's he wanna see you? They cleared you of everything ages ago.'

'No, not the solicitor. Barry. It's Barry who wants to see me.'

'Why?'

'I don't know, Brendan. It's been so long, I thought

he'd just given up on me. That he'd heard we'd got married somehow, and . . . Aw I don't know.'

Brendan stood up and moved round the desk to stand behind her, gently massaging her shoulders. 'Don't you go upsetting yourself over him, Sandy. You're carrying a precious load there, girl. And you don't have to do anything that that –' He bit back his words, weighing up what he was going to say. 'Listen to me; Barry can't expect you to go running after him. Not any more he can't.'

'I suppose not, but –'

'There's no suppose about it. I'm looking after you now, Sandy. You're *my* wife. And you're having *my* kid. And you do not have to do anything just cos someone says you do. You got that?'

'Yeah, course.' She didn't need all this. She felt knackered enough as it was, without having to fight with Brendan. 'I know all that. But because I'm having the baby maybe I should go and see him.'

'I don't think I'd be very happy about that.'

'I don't feel exactly happy about it meself, but I am sort of relieved he wants to see me at last.'

She reached up to her shoulder, clasped Brendan's hand, and let her head drop back so she could see him. 'And I think it'd be only right, don't you, telling him face to face?'

'No, I don't, as it happens.'

She rubbed her other hand over her stomach. 'Brendan, I don't even know if the poor sod's found

314

out we're married yet. Please, I wanna do this. It'll be like putting an end to the past before the baby comes along.'

'If you're really going, then I'll go with you.'

Sandy shook her head. 'I don't think that'd be a very good idea, do you?'

Brendan shrugged. 'If that's how you feel.'

'Don't be like that, Brendan, please. I'll be fine, and you've got more than enough to do as it is, running backwards and forwards to the hospital and that.'

'Well, you ain't driving. Kev can take you.'

As she waited in the clammy heat of the waiting area of HMP Brixton, with its depressingly institutional decor, Sandy felt physically sick. All around her, fractious children were irritating their already tense mothers, who sat smoking obsessively, tugging at their ill-fitting clothes and patting their over-lacquered hair.

The feeling of desperation was as palpable as the odour of stale sweat coming from the POs in their heavy uniforms.

It'll be over soon, Sandy kept repeating to herself, uncomfortably aware that she'd started taking for granted the charmed life that she was now leading with Brendan. A life so far removed from the last few years she had spent with Barry that she couldn't think how she could have endured staying with him through all those terrible, unhappy, frightening times. Times when she had probably acted and looked not much different from most of these women she was now pitying.

It was like they said: it's lovely when you stop bashing your head against the wall.

She sensed the other women flashing curious glances at her. Most of them seemed to know one another, or at least to be able to fall into easy conversation. But she knew they had her down as an outsider – and they were right.

She felt as though her floaty chiffon dress, her well-cut hair, and her diamond solitaire engagement ring were glowing like neon signs saying *I know I'm better off than you, you poor cows. I'm not a pathetic waste of space, with cheap catalogue clothes and nicotine-stained fingers, with an old man who's gonna spend most of his life in and out of the nick like he's dancing some soul- and life-destroying version of the hokey-cokey.*

She fiddled with her ring, turning the stone to the back so that just the platinum band showed, and kept her eyes on the worn lino between her brand-new shoes, wishing she'd put on an old shirt and a pair of jeans.

At last, the door opened and the most military-looking man among the POs led them through into a room the size of the school dining hall at Sandy's secondary modern in Stepney Green. But in this room there was no childish swinging of school bags at your mates' backs, no shoving and joshing, or high-pitched laughter. If anything it was more like the dining hall at exam time.

There were rows of Formica tables with chairs facing each other on either side, all set parallel to the far wall that was decorated with nothing more than a large, plain clock, already ticking off the seconds to the end of visiting time. The room had no windows, but was brightly lit with harsh fluorescent strips that made even the visitors with their faces tanned from the hot weather outside look pasty and unwell. At the far side of the room, opposite the double doors by which they'd entered, there was a serving counter set in the wall selling tea, sugary and salty snacks and chocolate bars with gaudy wrappers that stood out in the otherwise dreary room like precious jewels.

Sandy looked around her in bewilderment. This was a world she knew nothing about, and one she would never willingly enter again. But she was here now, and she knew what she had to do.

Barry was already at one of the tables. Right at the front. Sandy wove her way towards him, apologising and catching the whispers as she moved forward.

It was an odd sensation, but from the snatches of conversation she picked up it really sounded as if some of the people there – the other prisoners – had known she was coming today, that they were expecting her, and were now sharing the information with their visitors.

She tried to shake it off – this place was making her as paranoid as Barry when he'd done too much cocaine – and did her best to conjure up a happy, but concerned smile ready to greet him.

'Hello, Bal,' she said, leaning across the table to kiss him.

He closed his eyes as her lips touched his cheek, and left them closed as he took a deep breath, taking in her scent, trying to find the words to say to her.

'Hello, San,' he said eventually. 'You're looking good, babe. Beautiful.'

'Thanks,' she said, 'that's really nice. Just what a woman in her thirties needs to hear.'

She felt pleased. This was getting off to a lot better start than some of the scenes she'd been envisioning over the past few days. She'd imagined everything from embarrassing screaming matches to heart-breaking accusations and denials, and even her walking out without saying a word because she just couldn't face him.

'I'm feeling really good.' Her face crumpled the moment the words left her mouth. 'I am so sorry, Barry. I didn't mean that the way it came out. It sounded like I feel good about you being stuck in here or something. I don't mean that. You know I don't.'

'That's all right. This ain't easy for either of us, is it?'

'No. You can say that again.' She scrabbled around in her bag. 'Here. Have a ciggy.' He unwrapped the cellophane and offered her one.

'No thanks. I don't any more.'

'Blimey, you not smoking?' He actually smiled, looking almost relaxed, bringing back memories of the old Barry, the one she'd known and fallen in love with when they were just a pair of daft schoolkids. 'What's happened? Someone told you it interferes with your vodka-and-tonic intake?'

'I'm off that and all.' She handed him her lighter. 'You might as well have this. I won't need it any more, and it might bring back some good memories.'

He took it and weighed it in his hand. 'Bought you that after me and Kevin did our first week at Gabriel's scrapyard. Give it to you when we went to that pub on the river. Thought I was the right bollocks, I did. Money in me pocket, new whistle on me back, and the prettiest girl in the East End on me arm.'

He lit a cigarette. 'Feels like it was a lifetime ago, when Gabe give me that job.'

'Don't seem possible he's been dead nearly twelve years, does it?'

'There's a lot happened since then.'

Sandy couldn't look at him. 'Yeah,' she said quietly. 'Like me marrying Brendan.'

'So I heard.'

Her head snapped up. 'You know?'

He made a noise that sounded like a laugh. 'One of

my fellow *guests* here in Hotel Brixton told me. Really enjoyed it and all, he did. Rubbed it right in, like salt in a wound. Loved it, the cunt.'

'I should have told you myself but you wouldn't see me.'

'How hard did you try?'

'Don't be like that.' She looked away again. 'I tried, okay?'

'Don't worry about it. I'd have been glad for you, knowing you was happy. Only problem is, you're not, are you?'

Sandy frowned angrily and jabbed a perfectly manicured finger at him. 'How dare you say that? After all the shit you put me through? But if you must know, I am happy, thank you very much. In fact I've never been happier.'

'You sound like you're trying a bit too hard, San. Gotta convince yourself how great everything is, have you?'

She leaned back in her chair. 'No, I've not actually, Bal. I'm happy because I'm gonna have a baby. Gonna congratulate me, are you?'

'Tell me you just said that in temper.'

She picked up her bag and started to rise to her feet, but he grabbed her hand, stopping her. 'Don't, San, please. I've got something to tell you. And it's too important for you to run off without hearing it.'

'Barry, why can't you just be pleased for me?'

'Pleased for you? How could I be pleased?'

'After what you put me through . . . How dare you? Surely me being happy means something.'

He stuck his elbows on the table and held his head in his hands. 'You haven't got a clue, have you?' he said, staring down at the cigarette burns on the Formica top. 'The reason I got you here was to try and help you, to protect you. I wanted to speak to you because I want to make *something* right after how I've messed everything up.'

He dropped his hands and looked into her face. 'Sandy, that *husband* of yours is fucking you about. The arsehole has got untold birds on the go. Dirty whores. Tarts from the clubs. Brasses. I never messed you about, not in that way, I didn't. I always had too much respect for you.'

Sandy's face betrayed nothing, but her voice wavered as she spoke. 'You're lying, because you're jealous. And I'm sorry about that, Barry, but –'

'No, babe, I ain't lying. I just wish I wasn't in here so that I could do something about it. So I could put a stop to that bastard hurting you. But I am in here, so all I could do was let you know. I couldn't think of another way. Believe me, San, I never ever hurt you on purpose. On my life I didn't. I never have and never would.'

Barry stood up and turned to the prison officer who was standing behind him. 'Get me out of here.'

He was about to leave, but first he turned to her and said: 'And I'll tell you something else, San. I'm gonna fucking have O'Donnell for doing this to you. I swear I am. One way or another.'

He walked out leaving Sandy sitting there.

The PO began unlocking the door to lead him back to his cell. He smiled imperceptibly as Barry spoke, having expected something like this after hearing all the gossip that had been circulating on the wing since Ellis had first asked for the visiting order.

'I wanna see DC Medway. He knows who I am. Tell him I've got some things to tell him. A lot of things.'

'Blimey, Ellis,' said the PO, 'once you start opening that mouth of yours, there's no stopping you, is there?'

By the time the car was crossing London Bridge on the journey back to the East End, Sandy could feel her heart drumming against her chest as if she'd run all the way from Brixton. Over and over she heard the doctor's words – *You have an infection, Mrs O'Donnell. Nothing to worry about*.

'That bastard works for Brendan, so course he's gonna say there's *nothing to fucking worry about.*' She hadn't meant to say the words out loud.

'Sorry?' Kevin frowned into the rear-view mirror, convinced he'd misheard her. 'You all right, Sandy?'

'No, not really. But I'm gonna be.' She shuffled forward in her seat. 'Look, I forgot to say, there's something I've got to do, Kev. Instead of taking me back to Old Ford, could you drop me over at Whitechapel?'

As Sandy climbed the front steps leading up to the entrance of the London Hospital, she understood what Eileen O'Donnell had done to her husband as clearly as if someone had written it up for her in ten-foot-high letters on the hospital walls.

You protect your child no matter what.

Even if it means you have to destroy its father.

Chapter 28

When Brendan came in, Sandy was sitting at the table in their bright, airy kitchen. She had a cold mug of tea in front of her that she was cradling in her hands; she was frowning, staring down into it as if she was searching for something.

'Hello, San. You know, I'm glad I never went with you in the end. I had the chance to talk to Ellie's consultant. And I told him, I said – no matter what it costs, mate, I want her sorted out. He was a bit toffee-nosed, and didn't say that much, but they all reckon he's the top bloke.'

Brendan threw his jacket over the back of the chair next to Sandy's. 'So, how'd you get on then? Doing all right, is he?'

He bent to kiss her head, but Sandy pulled away before his lips could make contact with her hair. She stood up and went over to a cork pinboard next to the wall-mounted phone.

'What the fuck is that supposed to be?' she said, ripping a scrap of paper from the board without bothering to take out the drawing pin. She threw it on the table in front of him.

'What's what? What you talking about?'

'That.' She pointed at the bit of paper as if it disgusted her.

'Would you mind telling me what you're going on about?' He turned and looked about the room, his arms spread wide, as if appealing to a dithering jury. 'Because I don't take kindly to getting a coating. Never have done.' His voice grew very loud and he spat out the words through his teeth. 'And especially not in me own fucking house.'

'I asked you a question,' she said, sitting back down in her chair, refusing to be intimidated.

'How do I know?' He shrugged, turning down the corners of his mouth. Then sat opposite her, picked up the piece of paper and studied it. 'Phone number by the look of it.'

He rolled his eyes and smiled, the fury completely gone from his voice. 'I get it, Barry's had a go at you, 'n' he? Gone and got you all wound up. I said you shouldn't have gone.' He reached out to take her hand, but she wouldn't let him touch her.

'Yes, it's a phone number,' she said. 'And do you know what else, Brendan? I rang it. Her name's Priscilla – *Priscilla* – and apparently she's really missing you.'

His smile disappeared. 'Where did you get it?'

'Your leather jacket.'

He was back on his feet. 'You've been going through my stuff?'

She too stood up. 'You've been fucking whores?'

'Is that what all this is about? Me having a bit on the side with a tart?' His smile returned. 'It's you I want, darling. You know that.'

'Do I?'

'Course you do. Now come here.'

'Don't you even think about touching me. I am four months pregnant, *and I've got an infection*. The hospital says that they can only hope the baby won't be affected.'

She began weeping. 'You rotten, cheating, no-good bastard.'

'What hospital?'

'The one I went to because I didn't trust your stinking doctor, that's what hospital.' Tears were running down her face but she made no move to wipe them away. 'The one who's in your fucking pocket, too scared to do or say anything that might upset you.'

'No, San, you've got it all wrong.'

'I said, don't touch me.'

'Look, why don't we go out for a nice meal, and –'

'Because I don't want to, that's why.'

Brendan picked up his jacket and slung it over his shoulder. 'I've had enough of this. I'm going out for a drink. You'd just better be in a better mood when I get back.'

'Had I? What you gonna do to me if I'm not? Shoot me? Scald me? How about telling the truth for once? What really happened to Ellie?'

'Fuck off, Sandy.'

*

DI Hammond was sitting in the saloon bar of an old-fashioned pub – one that hadn't yet been reinvented as a wine bar – just over the border from the East End in the City of London. He was surrounded by men in suits enjoying early-evening drinks before getting their trains back to the suburbs. The noise level was deafening, but DI Hammond's laughter and the sentiment of his expression – despite his broad Midlands accent – still conveyed themselves very clearly to his London-born-and-bred colleague.

'That drop of poison someone had dripped in Barry Ellis's ear obviously worked a treat, Medway. And you handled the interview with him this afternoon very well. Couldn't have done a better job myself. And now,' he raised his glass, 'it appears we have our very own supergrass. Shame we can't get him to say a word against Luke O'Donnell as yet, but the rest of them are going to go down like bloody ninepins. And – joy oh joy – Medway, I hear on very good authority that there are gentlemen working in the Kesslers' dirty bookshops, who are getting a tad fed up with taking all the risks for none of the big money, and that they might well feel like doing some grassing of their own, if we pull a few raids and put the wind up them.' He sipped on his light-ale shandy, the enthusiasm glowing in his eyes. 'The time has come for me to show these cockney bastards who's in control. No offence intended, Medway, of course.'

'None taken,' said Medway, doing his best to hide his contempt for his superior. If Ellis's story hadn't been such dynamite, and that bloody brief hadn't been there, he might well have told him just to keep schtum and he'd see what he could do about getting him a few privileges. But now they'd all been landed right in it – right up to their bloody necks – and not only with the O'Donnells. Now the stupid Brummie bastard was talking about going after the Kesslers as well. The man didn't have the first idea about what the *cockney bastards* were capable of.

'Do you know, Medway, I'm going to make sure that you get a very generous "reward" for this.'

Medway brightened up a little. Having even a very small share of what the O'Donnells owned would be a little compensation for the mayhem that would break out if Hammond really did go after them. Perhaps the Brummy git wasn't entirely bad after all. 'Another drink, sir?'

'No thanks, Medway,' smiled Hammond, contentedly. 'I'm fine as I am. You know, I just love it when a plan comes together. Even if it is sometimes by accident.'

Nicky Wright unlocked the door of the flat, and walked straight into Luke who was in the hallway, obviously on his way out.

Luke gave him a hug. 'I know we've got plans, Nick, but Brendan just phoned me. He sounds like he's been on the piss for hours, but I can tell he's really worried. I'm not sure what's up, but I reckon it's gotta be about all these rumours that someone's got it in for him.'

'Add me to the list.'

'Don't be like that.' He stroked Nicky gently on the cheek. 'Sorry, but I reckon I'm gonna be a good couple of hours.'

'D'you want me to drive you?'

'No, it's all right, no point both of us having our evening spoilt. You listen to some music, have a drink, and I'll get back soon as I can. Let's see, he wants me to go over to his, and then I reckon I might have to shoot over to Kilburn –'

'Old Ford and then Kilburn, eh?' Nicky smiled at him. 'You get to go to all the best places. Now go on, get moving, and you'll be back all the sooner.'

Luke hugged him again, and touched his lips to the top of Nicky's head. 'Couple of hours tops. Okay?'

It had taken all of Pete Mac's solicitor's considerable skills and persuasiveness to achieve it – and even some references to Pete Mac that Pete had taken exception to, such as him hardly being a criminal mastermind – but he was now benefiting from those efforts, as he had been released on bail. It had also taken a lot of Patricia's money, as she had done as he asked and avoided letting anyone in the family know what was going on. It hadn't even occurred to Pete

Mac that he owed Patricia not only his freedom – however temporary – but also his good health, in that she had saved him from getting his head kicked in by Brendan.

He was now lounging on the sofa in the living room of their house on Jubilee Street, sniggering like a kid at an episode of *The Wombles*, while his daughter Caty glowered at him as if he were a moron.

The sitting-room door opened and Pete Mac and Caty both looked round to see Patricia standing there. She looked really good, with her stylish new haircut and her fashionable, well-fitting clothes, but she definitely didn't look very happy as she walked into the room.

Caty quickly decided that this was nothing to do with her and hopped it up to her bedroom.

Neither her mother nor father said anything as she left, acting as if they hadn't even noticed her.

Patricia stood in front of the sofa where Pete Mac was stretched out like a flabby ginger odalisque.

'Move out of the way, Pat, I can't see the telly.'

'Bugger the telly.'

'What did you say?'

'After everything you've done to me, I still sorted out the solicitor for you, got you bail, and you just walk back in here like you've got every right. Listen to yourself whining and moaning, while my little sister's stuck in that hospital. Her face burnt to hell, and her future ripped away from her.'

'I get it. That's what this is all about. You're upset cos of Ellie.'

'Upset? You don't know the meaning of the word. But you will do, believe me. Cos I've decided I don't want you here. And I don't want to help you any more either.'

'You what?'

'You nearly destroyed me once before, when Catherine got shot –'

'How many more fucking times? *That wasn't my fault.*'

'I want you out of here, Pete. Now. You're stuff's in there.'

She threw a holdall down on to the white curly rug. It was the first time he'd noticed it. This was no good. His brief had pulled the family-man card to get him his bail. If she went and chucked him out now, and they found out about it . . .

'Pat, darling, you can't do this. You've gotta help me.' He struggled to a sitting position then hauled himself to his feet.

'Maybe I'll see how you shape up after the trial, and think again. Maybe.'

'But you've gotta stick by me or they'll throw the book at me. You know what they think of anyone mixed up with the O'Donnells.'

'*Mixed up with the O'Donnells*?' Pat's voice was menacingly calm. 'You're more than mixed up with me, you bastard, I'm your fucking wife.'

331

He looked affronted. 'No need for that sort of language, Pat. You ain't a sodding docker, girl.'

'I really don't believe you.'

'There ain't nothing to believe. Just start acting like a sodding wife should act.' He paused, as he thought of how his mother-in-law had acted like a wife – she'd murdered her bloody husband. 'What I mean is, if you don't do your duty by me, I could wind up going inside.'

'Well, perhaps you should have thought of that before you got mixed up with all your tarts. Now get out, Pete, before I really lose my temper and call Brendan, and tell him about you getting nicked.'

'He still don't know yet?' This was the first bit of really good news that Pete Mac had heard in days.

'Not yet he don't, but don't tempt me.'

'Look, Pat, why don't we keep it like that? You know, just between ourselves. I mean, he ain't got no need to know now, has he?'

Patricia picked up the holdall and thrust it at him. 'I'll see how you behave before I decide what I'm gonna do. Now get out of my sight.'

She dropped down on to the sofa weeping – for Catherine, for Ellie and for herself – listening to her pig of a husband blundering his way down the hall to the street door.

Chapter 29

'I got here as soon as I could.' Luke followed Brendan along his hallway towards the kitchen, silently praying that all his brother wanted to see him for was to confirm the story that had started doing the rounds – that Barry Ellis was going to turn supergrass. Not that that wasn't bad enough in itself – it could mean the end of everything for all of them.

'So what d'you wanna do first, Brendan? Clear out the money from Kilburn? Or d'you want me to get Kevin to go and –'

'Fuck Kevin.' Brendan twisted round and leaned in so close to Luke that he could feel his breath burning on his face. 'And fuck Kilburn. I go out for a drink, I come back a couple of hours later, and she's gone. Left me a note saying I shouldn't try and find her. So, don't piss about with me, Luke, just tell me where she is.'

Shit. Luke swallowed hard. This was just what he'd dreaded. It was about Sandy. Brendan had guessed – rightly – that she'd turn to him for help. 'She's staying in one of my flats.'

'Give me the phone number.'

'Brendan, why don't we sit down and have a drink?'

'I've had a fucking drink. I've had a whole fucking bottleful of the stuff. Now give me that number.'

'Hadn't we better sort out Kilburn first? You know what they're saying about Barry talking, and there's all that dough –'

'Give me the number, Luke. No one walks out on me. No one.'

Luke stood at the kitchen window staring out at the canal. No wonder Sandy loved it here. It was a scene so peaceful that it didn't make sense that such madness was going on inside the house.

There was a very good chance that Barry – *poor old Barry* – was about to be the cause of their world blowing up around them, while his big brother was making a telephone call to a woman who could have made his life wonderful for him, but who he had treated like shit – just like he treated everyone else.

Sandy answered the phone. Brendan turned his back on Luke and lowered his voice. 'Sandy, it's me. I'm not having this. I'm gonna come round there and sort this out.'

'No, Brendan, I told you in the note, I don't want to see you.'

'Don't be an idiot, Sandy, you know you won't get away with this. I won't let you.'

'No, don't *you* be an idiot, you just listen to

someone for once, Brendan.' She sighed knowing that what she was about to say was completely stupid in one way – she'd be losing everything that Brendan had given her, everything that made her life easy – but in another way, it was all she could do, she had no choice.

'I really mean what I'm gonna say, so just hear me out. At first, I genuinely believed that we had a chance of having a life together. Despite feeling guilty about Barry, and all the things I knew you were involved in. But, and I'm being very honest here – I was prepared to be a hypocrite. I turned a blind eye so I could have that nice life. But I started noticing warning lights flashing, and bells ringing about what I was actually doing. And I started feeling bad about it all. That it just wasn't right. But then I found out about the baby, and it was all all right again. I was happy. Really happy. But then you gave me this infection, and I spoke to Barry, and I understood you, Brendan. Understood you better than you'll ever understand yourself. You infect everything you touch. Everything. Including me. And that's why you are never going to get anywhere near this baby. If it survives, that is, after what you've already done to it.'

Brendan's face had drained of colour, he wanted to do nothing more than find her and give her a good slapping. And he would have done if she hadn't been carrying his child. 'Is this all that women's-lib shit that Ellie's poisoned you with?'

'Only you would drag in that kid while she's lying in hospital. You are such an arsehole, Brendan. Don't you get it? I've just seen you for what you are, that's all. Try and be a man and accept it.'

'But them birds I had, they didn't mean nothing to me.'

'Well, more fool you for throwing away everything for something that meant so little.'

'I told you, I'm not gonna let you get away with this, Sandy. I'll make you see I'm right.'

'Brendan, please, try to listen to what someone else has to say, for once in your life. You don't solve your problems by shouting at people or threatening them, or by pretending they're not there. Your problems follow you around wherever you go. The trick is to turn round and face them. And that's what I'm doing. Facing up to the fact that you're no good. And try, just once you arrogant bastard, to see the world through someone else's eyes – not mine necessarily – anyone's. You're alive, you've got a choice. But poor old Barry, he's as good as dead.'

'What you on about now?'

'Luke told me what everyone's saying about him turning supergrass. So, it's obvious, innit? Soon as he gets out – you'll get to him and kill him. Or he'll go into hiding and be so terrified he'll get back on that shit, and so he might as well be dead. So you'll get him either way. You win as usual. Except with me. Because, whatever else you get away with, you are

336

not gonna get away with polluting my child.'

'Why the hell d'you think you can treat me like this? You knew all about me, knew I didn't live in a world like other people. My world's a place where everything's . . .' He raked his fingers through his hair. 'Aw, I dunno.'

'And whose fault is it that you live in that world? Not this baby's.'

'It's the only world I know.'

'You chose it, Brendan.'

'So did you. And it gives us a good life.'

'A good life? Yeah, I thought so an' all. It was like all them years I was with Barry, I learned to ignore the shit and the violence. Just saw it as the way you lot earned your living.' She let out a humourless puff of laughter. 'But cheating on your wife with whores? That I couldn't handle.'

'Sandy, please.'

'One final thing, Brendan. When I went to the hospital to see Ellie, Eileen was there. She told me what really happened. That the boiling water was meant for me. Because of you, and because I'm Brendan O'Donnell's wife. You're evil, Brendan, do you know that?'

There was the unmistakable sound of the receiver being put down in its cradle, but Brendan went on ranting as if she could still hear him. 'You won't get away with this, you cow. Do you hear me? That's my mother's grandchild you're carrying. My baby.'

He smashed the receiver against the wall, sending shards of plastic across the kitchen floor. 'Give me the address, Luke.'

'You know she'll be gone by the time you get there.'

'I said, give it to me.'

As soon as Brendan left the house, Luke went upstairs to the escort office, where there was a phone that hadn't been smashed to bits, and called his flat.

No reply. Nicky was probably in the shower. Perhaps something good had come out of this bloody mess. If he left now they could get to the restaurant and maybe on to a club. He'd call the maitre d' and get him to hold their table, then he'd shoot home and get showered and changed. He'd leave the phone numbers for the restaurant and the club, so Brendan could call him later if he decided he wanted him to do something about Kilburn and the shops.

As he scribbled a note, he took a deep breath and tried to figure out how this mess was going to finish up. Perhaps Brendan really had gone too far this time.

Luke, ripping his tie from his neck ready to jump under the shower, opened the door to his flat, and immediately froze. He could hear voices coming from the living room.

Fuck, surely it wasn't the law. They'd only started hearing the tales about Barry a few hours ago, and even then they hadn't sounded very likely. But who else could it be? Not pissing burglars, surely? He'd kill them if they spoilt his bloody flat. Or if they'd so much as touched a hair on Nicky's head.

He stayed out on the landing, and pulled the door almost shut in case anyone came out into the hall. Then he leaned as close as he could to the jamb, straining to hear what they were saying.

He could make out Nicky's voice. Shit, he wasn't gonna be chatting to burglars, was he? It must be the law.

Then there was another voice. Luke frowned. It sounded familiar somehow. He listened a bit more. *David Seymour*, that's who it was. That bloke who'd gone to the boxing do with them.

Luke smiled, relief washing over him. Nicky had asked a friend round for company. All this shit with Brendan was turning him into a bloody lunatic.

He was just about to go and join them, when the smile dropped from his lips. Nicky was shouting. Luke shook his head, not wanting to believe what he was hearing.

Then David was shouting over him.

'Just hear me out, Nicky. I know it was a bit underhand, the way I went about it, hanging around the record shop, pretending I was your new best mate and everything. But when I got the tip-off at the paper about you and O'Donnell, how could I resist it? This story's gonna be dynamite. Biggest I've ever

339

handled. Queers, cockney bad boys, murdered sisters and poisoned fathers. Jews. Irish. It's fantastic. Just talk to me, let me get your side of it, and it'll earn you thousands.'

'If you think –'

Nicky didn't finish. Luke burst into the sitting room, slamming the door behind him. 'You arsehole, Seymour.'

'Luke, thank Christ you're back.' Nicky ran to his side. 'I am so sorry. I had no idea.'

'It's all right, calm down, I'll handle this.'

Luke strode across the room to David, who was sitting on the edge of the sofa. 'Get up.'

David tried to object but Luke had him by the collar of his flowery shirt, hauling him to his feet.

'Now empty your pockets, and that bag, or I'll do it for you.'

David took his notebook from his jacket and handed it to Luke, then opened his briefcase and took out a tape recorder.

Luke snatched the machine from his hand and threw it the length of the room, smashing it to pieces against the far wall. Then he spun round to face David again. 'If you know what's good for you, you sit back down, and you keep that fucking trap of yours shut. Got it?'

It was over an hour later when the barman in the Bella Vista handed Brendan the telephone.

'Sandy? That you, darling?'

'No, Brendan, sorry, mate, it's me, Luke. Can you do us a favour and get over here? To the flat? Right now if you can. I think we might have a problem on our hands. D'you remember David Seymour, the bloke who came to the boxing with me and Nicky . . .'

Brendan's mood hadn't improved, and when he arrived at the flat, Luke seriously wondered if he'd done the wrong thing in calling him. He steamed straight into the living room, grabbed David by the hair and dragged him out to the kitchen.

Brendan and David were back in the living room in less than five minutes. David's left eye was already swollen shut and blood was pouring from his nose and his left ear.

Nicky gasped, 'What have you done to him?'

He moved as if to help him, but Brendan was too quick. He lashed out his arm, and struck Nicky across the face with the back of his hand, sending him crashing into the coffee table. 'Don't even think about it, you little prick.'

'Brendan, what the hell are you doing? Please, don't hurt him.'

'Save it, Luke, for someone who deserves it.' He pointed at Nicky who was flat on his back, his face grey apart from the red swelling across his cheekbone. 'That little fucker is nineteen years old. Fucking underage.'

'He's what?'

'You heard. And what with matey boy here – the bloke we entertained like he was family, treated him like he was something worth talking to – being a fucking journalist . . . Well, he's hit the fucking jackpot. Christ knows what he's already passed on to the papers. But I'm gonna enjoy meself finding out.'

'I swear –' David began, but Brendan just talked across him.

'This must have been what Hammond was going on about. All these rumours that're flying round about us. And we thought it was Barry Ellis we had to worry about. He might have fucked things up for Sandy and me, but I should have known he'd never grass on us.'

Luke was shaking his head as if none of it could be true. 'You told me you were twenty-three.'

'I'm really sorry, Luke.'

'Why did you lie to me?'

'You wouldn't have had anything to do with me.'

'I just don't believe all this is happening.'

Brendan put his hand on his brother's shoulder. 'Don't get yourself wound up, Luke. We've got things to do. I'll find out from that berk what he's said and who he's said it to.' He jerked a thumb at David. 'While you go and find Kevin and clear out Kilburn. Get the dough over to the lock-up.'

He tapped his thumbnail against his teeth. 'And I'll phone Pat to let her know what's happening, just in case the law decides to pay a visit.' He looked at his watch. 'Her and Mum should be back from the hospital by now. Then I'll meet you round hers later.'

'Brendan, if Seymour has been mouthing off, what do you think's gonna happen?'

'Just do it, Luke.'

'But how about Nicky?'

'What harm can come to him while I'm here? Now will you just get going? Go on, I'll see you round Pat's.'

As soon as Luke was safely out of the flat, Brendan picked up the phone.

'Sorry to disturb you in the evening, love, but can I have a quick word with Anthony?'

Brendan could hear Anthony's wife calling him, and the sound of children laughing in the background.

'Hello, mate,' said Brendan, 'watching telly with the family, was you? Send me apologies, but there's a couple of things. First of all, did you do that little job for me? Sorting out the trouble I had over that kettle?'

'Yeah, done and dusted, mate. That ain't gonna scald no one no more.'

'Right. Good. Now, I need you over here. At Luke's place. Soon as you can. I need a bit of help sorting out another little problem that's cropped up.'

Chapter 30

Brendan walked into Patricia's kitchen at just gone midnight. His hair was limp with sweat, and his clothes looked as if he'd worn them for a week.

He nodded to Luke as he sat down across the table from him. 'How was Ellie tonight, Pat?'

'You know.' Patricia fetched another cup and saucer from the cupboard over the draining board. 'I think she was glad that Mum went in again.'

'That's nice. Where's Pete Mac?'

'Him and Pat have had a bit of a falling-out,' said Luke, shooting a warning look at Patricia, who, from the expression on her face, really didn't need one. 'And he's cooling off in a hotel for a couple of nights. It's all right, Pat knows where he is if we need him.'

Brendan let out a long slow sigh. 'No thanks, Pat,' he said, as she set the cup down in front of him. 'Got any whiskey?'

'Course.'

While his sister went to fetch a bottle and some glasses from the sitting room, Luke leaned across the table and whispered urgently: 'What's happening back at the flat?'

'At least that's one thing I've managed to sort out,' said Brendan. 'Pity I can't sort out the rest of this fucking mess.'

'How do you mean?'

'Well, when I was phoning everyone, trying to find out what was going on – basically, what that bastard Seymour might have already blurted out – I had a bit of bad news. It seems these stories about Barry might well be true after all.'

'That he's turned grass? No. You sure?'

'Yeah. Can you believe it? *Poor old Barry*. First he sets me own wife against me, and now he's gonna stitch me up with the law.' Brendan shook his head in bewilderment. 'After how good I was to that man . . . Still, like I say, I've solved one of our problems. Them two won't be talking to no one.'

Patricia came back into the kitchen with the whiskey.

Her two brothers were staring at each other across the table with an intensity that made her stomach churn and her hands shake as she put down the glasses. She'd seen that look on the faces of men in her family too many times before. It was the sort of look that could turn trouble into anger, and then into violence, leaving women to weep and to pick up the pieces.

Luke grabbed his brother's hand. 'Brendan, you didn't hurt him, did you? Please, tell me you didn't.'

'What if I did?'

'I love him.'

'Don't talk shit.' Brendan's face was screwed up in repulsed contempt.

'*But it wasn't Nicky's fault.*'

'Aw no? So who let Seymour into our lives? Who conned you over how old he was?' Brendan filled his glass to the rim with whiskey. 'And anyway, by the time I'd finished with that other little toerag, he'd seen too much. But don't worry, I'm sure the lying little cunt didn't feel a thing.'

'Hang on, when you said you'd sorted it out . . .'

Brendan swallowed half the whiskey and immediately refilled his glass. 'I got shot of the pair of them.'

'*No!*' Luke was on his feet. '*You bastard, Brendan. You fucking bastard. You know I loved him.*'

Brendan sneered at his brother. 'That ain't love you feel, mate. That's your prick talking.'

'What would you know about anything? You're just like the old man. Everything you touch goes rotten. Catherine, Sandy, Ellie. And now Nicky.'

He moved towards the door, but Brendan got there before him and stood there, barring his way. 'You won't find 'em, Luke. They're gone for good. And they were lucky as it happens, cos they deserved a lot worse than what they got.'

Luke's chin was down on his chest and his arms were dangling loosely by his sides. 'He'd never have done anything to hurt me. Never. He would have kept quiet. Because no matter what filth you talk, I know he loved me.'

'Don't make me laugh. Why can't you just accept it? He had you over, Luke. Took you for a fucking mug.'

'*You bastard.*'

'Yeah, so you already said. But I don't get you, Luke. I only did it for you.'

'You've never done nothing for nobody. Nobody. It's always for you, no matter how you try to pretend otherwise. And you make me sick, do you know that? Sick to me stomach.' He slowly raised his head until they were facing one another. 'And I never want to set eyes on you again.'

'Please, don't do this, you two.' Patricia was still standing by the table, tears streaming down her cheeks. 'I can't take much more of this.'

Brendan stood away from the door to let him go. 'What, gonna go and stay with Sandy, are you? And don't look at me like that. I know you've gotta know where she is.'

Then he went over to the table and finished his drink, waiting until Luke had gone before he spoke. 'I'm going round Mum's. Dunno how long I'll be.'

He turned to look at her before he left. 'I ain't sure, Pat, but I think things are gonna go a bit wrong, girl.'

Brendan trudged down the steps into the familiar basement kitchen on the Mile End Road. Despite it being the early hours of the morning, he wasn't surprised to find his mother sitting there, knitting, with the dog at her feet. She never seemed to sleep much these days.

'All right, Mum? What you knitting?'

She actually smiled at him, making his heart lift with pleasure, as she held up an almost completed, white lacy baby's jacket. 'I started it at the hospital, while I was sitting with Ellie. I know it's difficult to say at a time like this, but we mustn't forget your good news, son.'

He knelt down on the floor beside her. 'Mum, I've gotta tell you something. Something important. There's something wrong.'

'You turn up here at this time of night. Why should it surprise me that something's wrong?'

'I've done something, Mum. I got rid of two people. And before you look at me like that, I only did it to protect Luke. He would have been sent to prison, Mum, and he could never have stood that.'

Eileen felt as if someone had forced concrete down her throat and into her chest, filling it up so only tiny gasps of air could get into her lungs. 'Is he safe now?'

'He'll be all right. I'll make sure of that.'

'I don't want him going away, Brendan. Please, take care of him.'

'Course I will, and I'd have looked after you an' all if you'd have let me. I'd even have done your time for you, Mum, you mean that much to me. The world.

You've gotta believe me, cos I really mean it.'

'I know you do, son, in your own way. Trouble is, you're too much like your father. You've never been able to love anyone as much as you love yourself.'

'What's wrong with me, can't I ever be good enough for any of you?' Brendan covered his face with his hands. 'Sandy's said she won't let me see the baby.'

'Oh, son . . .'

He dropped his hands and stared down at the floor. 'Yeah, I know. And that's all I want, Mum. To have Sandy and the baby. Hold 'em both in my arms.' He took out his handkerchief, wiped his face, and then stood up. 'I think I need a bit of air. I won't be long. Tell you what, I'll take the dog out for you, while I'm at it. Come on, Bowie, come on, boy.'

'Okay, son.' Eileen picked up her knitting automatically, but she looked at it and put it down again. More wasted time.

Not for the first time, or for the last, Eileen O'Donnell wondered at the madness of it all, the madness that could do such terrible things to a family.

Chapter 31

A soft trickle of sweat ran down his spine, as he moved slightly, adjusting his position to get the full benefit of the rays on his body. He'd wear the new linen suit tonight. Look the right business down in Puerto Banus. A month and a half in the sun had made him brown as a berry and twice as handsome.

When he'd got rid of the other place in Estepona, he really should have thought about buying a villa closer to the coast. There wasn't even a breeze up here in the hills. And, even with his eyes closed tightly shut, the sun still made patterns on his eyelids: blue and yellow shapes dancing around and aggravating him.

Fuck it, he loved it really.

He sucked in his gut. If he wasn't careful he was gonna go the way the old man had gone, flabby round the middle, old-looking. And he definitely didn't want that to happen. Not when there were birds like Anya around – tall, tits out to there, and a natural blonde. Very nice.

He fumbled around under the side table and found the suntan lotion, then rubbed the cream over his legs and face. He could do with Anya being here right now

– just to do his back for him, of course . . .

He grinned as he felt himself harden at the thought of her long, cool fingers running over his skin. Still, he could wait a couple of hours. In the meantime, he'd just have to make do with a nice cold beer.

He reached out for his drink.

Nothing.

He opened his eyes, squinting into the sun. Someone was standing over him. *Holding his fucking beer.*

'Bowie,' he shouted. '*Bowie!*'

'For Christ's sake, calm down, Brendan,' said the looming shadow that was still holding his glass. 'It's me.'

'Luke?' Brendan was up off the lounger, the sun cream mixing with the sweat on his forehead and dripping down into his eyes and making them sting. 'You daft cunt! No wonder the dog didn't fucking bark. Where the hell have you been all this time? Is Mum with you? How's Ellie and Pat? And what about Sandy? You heard from her?' He shook his head, grinning, and clapped his hand over his brother's shoulder.

'Why the fuck didn't you let me know you was coming over, dozy bollocks? I'd have sorted out a party for you.'

'I didn't want you to know.'

'Why not? Is something up?'

'I wouldn't know, Brendan. I've been staying over

at Aunt Mary's, keeping me head down, trying to think all this through. How to make sure the girls and Mum were all right. How to sort out this whole fucking mess. And do you know what, I thought about you every single day, and I realised exactly what I had to do. And that I was the only one who could do it.'

Brendan rubbed the back of his hand across his now streaming eyes, making the stinging and blurring even worse. 'Will you stop talking in fucking riddles, Luke?'

'I'm gonna put an end to it. All of it.'

With that, Luke dropped the beer, raised the sawn-off shotgun he was holding in his other hand, and shot Brendan full in the face, spraying shreds of his brain and fragments of skull all over the baking tiles of the poolside terrace.

Bowie ran off yelping and screaming into the scrub at the back of the villa.

Luke tried calling him back but the dog was too spooked to obey.

He took a breath, and stroked what had once been the top of his brother's arm. 'You destroyed every-thing I ever loved.'

Then he put the gun in his own mouth and squeezed the trigger.

July 1975

Chapter 32

Sandy sat in the old-fashioned offices of Tighe, Martin and O'Flaherty waiting for Mr Martin to read her the contents of the big brown envelope he had taken so much time to fetch from the clunking great safe set in the wall behind his chair.

She really was losing her patience. She had given up half a day's work – and pay – in the hotel where she worked in Brighton to come up to London, and that wasn't even taking into account the extra money she'd had to shell out for the baby minder to keep an eye on Lisa. And then there was the price of the train fare.

It was all right for the likes of Mr Martin, he had bloody money coming out of his ears, the money he charged people to give them advice. She could only hope it wasn't another attempt by Patricia for the bloody O'Donnells to get their hands on Lisa. She was just about sick of getting letters saying how much it would mean to bloody Eileen since she'd lost 'her boys' and since Pete Mac had been put away. They could beg and plead all they liked, they weren't getting their hands on her, Sandy wasn't going to let her child make the mistakes she'd made.

'Thank you for coming along today, Mrs O'Donnell.'

'It's Wilson. My maiden name. It's what I use now.'

'Oh dear, I see,' said Mr Martin, finally opening the envelope.

'I think it's my business what I choose to call myself, Mr Martin.' Sandy was very close to walking out, but . . . she was here now.

'Certainly, it's your business, Miss Wilson. But I'm afraid that it might present a problem.'

'Problem? How? What for?'

'Your inheritance. You see, Mr Brendan O'Donnell and Mr Luke O'Donnell have both left you considerable amounts of money and property in their wills, the stipulation being – and I might add that it was Mr Brendan O'Donnell who insisted on this – that you and your child should be known as O'Donnell, and that Mrs O'Donnell – senior, that is, Eileen – should know about it, and be able to send letters to your child, and be able to play some part in your child's life. Apart from that, this *very* considerable inheritance is yours to do with as you wish.'

Sandy flopped back in her chair, gripping the arms as though they were all that was keeping her from tipping over on to the floor.

'Can I have a minute? To think?'

Mr Martin nodded. 'Certainly, Miss Wilson.'

What she thought about was the tiny room that she shared with Lisa. The damp, the cold, and the scratching noises above the ceiling that kept her up most of the night. The long hours she worked, and how little she saw of her beautiful baby girl.

'Mr Martin, can I sell the property on?'

'It will be yours to do with as you choose, Miss Wilson.'

Sandy took a deep breath, and then pulled her chair up close to Mr Martin's desk.

'Sorry, Barry,' she said, making the lawyer frown in incomprehension. 'Where do I sign?'